For

Mom and Dad,

and

Anita and Mike

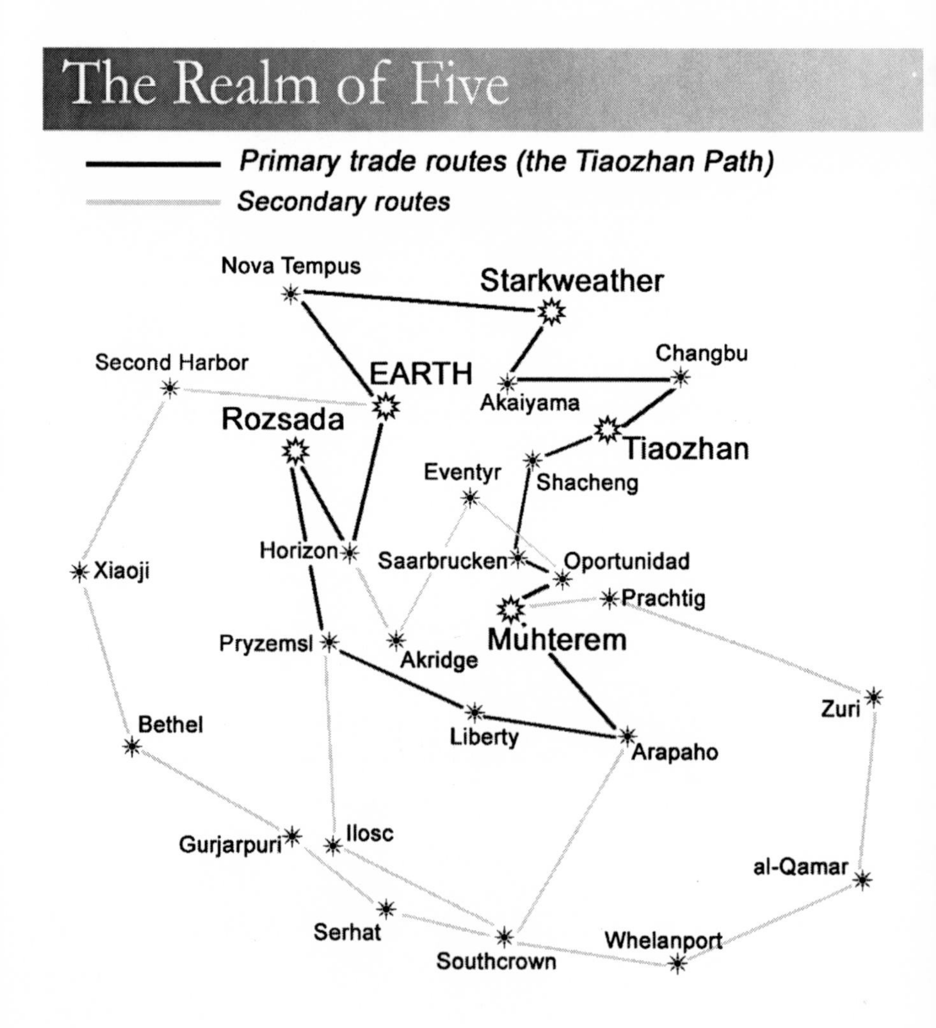
The Realm of Five
Primary trade routes (the Tiaozhan Path)
Secondary routes
Nova Tempus
Starkweather
Second Harbor
EARTH
Changbu
Akaiyama
Rozsada
Tiaozhan
Eventyr
Shacheng
Horizon
Saarbrucken
Oportunidad
Xiaoji
Prachtig
Muhterem
Pryzemsl
Akridge
Zuri
Bethel
Liberty
Arapaho
Gurjarpuri
Ilosc
al-Qamar
Serhat
Southcrown
Whelanport

STEVE RZASA
THE WORD UNLEASHED
Book 2
The Face of the Deep
WaterfordTwpLibrary
54478
DISCARD
The word unleased
SF RZA

THE WORD UNLEASHED by Steve Rzasa
Published by Marcher Lord Press
8345 Pepperridge Drive
Colorado Springs, CO 80920
www.marcherlordpress.com

Cover Designer: Jeff Gerke
Creative Team: Jeff Gerke, Dawn Shelton
Spaceships on cover designed by Kevin Monk, Astral Empires, www.scifirpg.com

Library of Congress Cataloging-in-Publication Data
An application to register this book for cataloging has been filed with the Library of Congress.
International Standard Book Number: 978-0-9825987-1-9

Printed in the United States of America

Then Jesus came and said to them, "All authority in heaven and on earth has been given to me. Go therefore and make disciples of all nations, baptizing them in the name of the Father and of the Son and the Holy Spirit, teaching them to observe all that I have commanded you. And behold, I am with you always, to the end of the age."

The Gospel According to Matthew 28:18–20

PRIMARY CAST

On the Six-Brace *Natalia Zoja*

◊ Baden Haczyk
◊ Captain Simon Haczyk, Baden's father
◊ Emi Akai
◊ Shen Renshu
◊ Owen "Ozzy" Zinssler
◊ Cyril
◊ Gail Salpare
◊ Jason

On Bethel

◊ Cadet Trainee Alec Verge
◊ Lt. Colonel James Verge, Alec's father; commander, 21st Lancers Expeditionary Brigade
◊ Commander Colleen Verge, James's sister; captain, *HMS Herald*
◊ Lieutenant Connor Verge, James's brother; commander, Coyote Squadron, Gold Beasts fighter wing
◊ Troop Master (brevet) Benjamin Sands, Troop One, Echo Company, 21st Lancers Expeditionary Brigade
◊ Major Branko Mazur, commander, Rozsade Ninth Fusilier Legion, "Berdysz" (Battle Axe)
◊ Assemblyman Bartholomew Heng, Bethel Colonial Freeholding

On Earth

- Professor Tara Douglas-Verge, Alec's mother; alternate representative, Congress of Worlds
- Julianna Verge, Alec's older sister
- Bridget Verge, Alec's younger sister
- King Andrew Justice Markham Douglas (Andrew II), Lord of the Realm of Five
- Najwa, Rozsade operative
- Representative Carina Sulis, Congress of Worlds—Expatriate Cooperative
- Commissioner E. H. Gironde, Koninklijke stabiliteitskracht (Royal Stability Force), KSK or Kesek
- Detective Inspector Konrad Toers, Kesek

On Navastel *Golden Orchid*

- Captain Charlotte Ruby Bell, pirate
- Dennis, first mate

On *HMS Interrogator*

- Detective Chief Inspector Nikolaas Ryke, Kesek
- Detective Inspector George Cotes, Kesek
- Captain Goro Sasaki

The adventure began in *The Word Reclaimed . . .*

Pirate Captain Charlotte Ruby Bell is given a sinister task—to destroy a ship carrying religious texts, any example of which are illegal. She does so, pleasing Detective Chief Inspector Nikolaas Ryke of the Kesek secret police. He offers her another assignment for a substantial fee.

Baden Haczyk and his father, Captain Simon Haczyk, are at odds over the death of Baden's mother years ago. En route to a cargo drop-off, their ship *Natalia Zoja* encounters pirates attacking another ship. Upon examining the wreckage of the destroyed vessel, Baden finds a Bible. Simon suggests selling it on the black market. Meanwhile, Ryke scolds Bell for her inability to destroy her target—the Bible.

At the Puerto Guijarro orbital habitat, Simon meets up with Hamid ibn Thaqib, head of a powerful shipbuilding company and a sponsor of Simon's business. Simon reveals that Christianity was in some way responsible for his wife's death. Baden shows the Bible to friend Gail Salpare. Ryke tries to apprehend him, but with the help of a mysterious man named Jason, Baden and the *Natalia Zoja* crew escape.

On Earth, Lancer Cadet Trainee Alec Verge completes a new stage in his instruction. His father, Lancer veteran Lieutenant Colonel James Verge, is sent to the distant planet Bethel to suppress an alleged rebellion, but James is wary, given Kesek Commissioner E. H. Gironde's influence over the king. Bidding farewell to his wife, royal cousin Professor Tara

Douglas-Verge, James joins the rest of his task force with Alec in tow, and finds his siblings—Commander Colleen Verge of *HMS Herald* and pilot Lieutenant Connor Verge—are also assigned. As the task force leaves for Bethel, a mysterious figure on Earth sets in motion a secret action.

On Earth, Tara attends the Congress of Worlds as an alternate for her planet, Starkweather. Congress allows a Martian pilgrimage to Mars, but Gironde's influence is apparent, prompting Tara to join a secret pact for a shadow Congress that aims to prevent the king's overthrow.

Baden and his friends learn of a secret location called Alexandria. The information was hidden in files kept on the wrecked ship containing the Bible. Just what Alexandria is, none of them know. They are soon tracked down by Bell and her pirates, but thanks to Jason's tricks, they evade capture once again.

The task force arrives at Bethel, where it is ambushed on the ground and in space by hidden Tiu Martian armored warriors as the Kesek men assigned to the force attempt to assassinate key officers. James and Colleen are able to rally their troops and defeat the Tiu, but not without the cost of hundreds of lives, including James' brother-in-law and second-in-command, Major Jonathan Douglas. *Natalia Zoja* arrives at Bethel in time to help rout the Tiu warships.

Baden and the *Natalia Zoja* crew meet with their contact. The people are stunned to find a Bible in their midst. It leaves Baden with a choice—will he give it to the Bethelites or take it to the Alexandria sanctuary as Jason recommends? His choice becomes more difficult when Jason reveals Baden's mother was involved with secreting Christian artifacts.

James interrogates one of the Kesek officers who failed to assassinate his sister and learns the Kesek commissioner was involved in the ambush. Before he can take action, however, his forces learn of an assault on Earth.

Tara watches Commissioner Gironde tell of a surprise Martian attack on Earth's fleet and the apparent kidnapping of the king. But then she receives a last-minute warning from a Congressman—Kesek is coming to arrest all the representatives.

And now . . . *The Word Unleashed.*

PROLOGUE

October 2602
Earth Star System

Andrew Justice Markham Douglas, King Andrew II of the Realm of Five, leaned forward from the padded leather seat of his plush space yacht and watched a pilgrimage in progress.

In the round viewport, he thought his face looked darker and more solemn than usual. He watched the Martian Hamarkhis pilgrim ships—eleven bulky, bulbous transport craft—drive silently through the diamond-studded space between Earth and Mars. He tried to imagine what it must be like for them. Long banished from the world they loved, the Hamarkhis returned every nine years to worship at sacred sites on the Red Planet's surface. He didn't think he would be able to bear such a separation from his homeworld.

The ships were on their way to Mars, and King Andrew's yacht was following roughly the same course en route to the Jovian moons for a holiday. The king leaned back into his seat and sighed. He needed the break from all the politics of the Congress of Worlds.

The king meticulously smoothed out a set of wrinkles in his black trousers and violet jacket. The rampant gold bear that was the symbol of his royal house glared up at him.

He swiveled in his seat to face the interior of his private cabin. There was a hatch at either end of the room. One led to the bridge, and the other led aft to cargo storage and the engines. Three more chairs identical to his were scattered about the cabin. A long, slender couch sat securely beneath another viewport opposite his. All were tasteful shades of brown and appointed with gold traceries. Even the tiled ceiling and deck of the cabin were polished to a glossy white and grey that glowed under soft yellow running lights spaced along the bulkheads.

The lights illuminated King Andrew's family where they sat with him in the cabin. His wife, Queen Maria, sat on the couch, holding a delver in her hand. She wore a slim, red jumpsuit that stood out against her soft brown face. She kept a diaphanous white scarf draped about her shoulders. King Andrew appreciated how the entire ensemble shimmered as she shifted.

She shifted because the two boys seated in her lap never ceased fidgeting. Phillip and Carter were twins, both bearing the features of their father. Handsome, if he said so himself.

Carter, the more serious-faced of the two, scowled across at Andrew. "Mother won't finish the story!"

"I believe she said she wouldn't finish if you two wouldn't hold still." Andrew smiled at him. "And you will listen to your mother, correct?"

"Yes." It was a glum answer. Carter settled back against his mother's arms. Phillip gave him a dirty look that made Andrew squelch the urge to laugh.

Maria waggled the delver in her hand. "Are you ready for me to continue?"

"Yes, Mother," Phillip said cheerily. "Please finish 'Marshal Jake.'"

Carter's scowl deepened.

"Then settle down." Maria pressed a button along the delver's edge. The screen lit up. She took up from where she'd stopped: "'Before Marshal Jake could move, he found himself surrounded by the evil Martian raiders. They outnumbered him greatly, and he knew he would have little chance to escape . . .'"

Andrew closed his eyes and let his imagination wander as Maria continued the story. He wondered fleetingly what it had been like, long ago, to read a story from a physical book. But that was centuries ago, before his ancestors banned printed materials in favor of maintaining an electronic information empire.

A chirp emanated from King Andrew's pants pocket. He reached down and drew out his own delver. The message light flashed: a commnote from the yacht's captain. White text dribbled across a black delver screen. *Come to the bridge, quickly.*

King Andrew's stomach churned. He eased out of his chair. "Dear, I must go see the captain for a moment."

Maria's eyes flicked up to meet his.

Andrew smiled back. Please don't ask. Nothing to be alarmed about.

He went out the hatch into the main corridor. He brushed his hand along the low ceiling as he walked past a trio of hatches on either side of the short, narrow walkway. Tiny blue lights cast a pale glow in the dim blue-green passageway. The hatch to the compact bridge was open. King Andrew had to hunch over a bit to step through.

The bridge had room for just three stations—the captain's seat at the center, a navigator's station filled with targeting and rangefinder screens to the left, and, to the right, a helmsman's post surrounded by holographic displays. Six curved viewports, each a meter across, offered a beautiful view of starry space and the Hamarkhis pilgrim ships. A wide monitor showing the same starfield split the viewports into two groups. The screens glowed bright.

Two young men sat tense at their consoles as the captain stood at stiff attention. All three wore the violet-trimmed black uniform of Earth Navy officers. Captain Dikembe, a burly man with skin several shades richer than King Andrew's, turned and offered a sharp salute. Perspiration beaded along his brow. "Your Highness! Robbins, close the hatch."

The helmsman did so.

Andrew wondered what could possibly make the man this nervous. "You called, Captain?"

"Your Majesty, our outbound course to the Jovian moons is taking us near the naval facilities at Trebizond Base. They send an emergency request for us to alter our course."

"Why?"

"Something is wrong with the Hamarkhis pilgrim ships. A few have deviated from their course." Dikembe turned to his navigator and snapped his fingers. "Give me the image!"

The navigator complied. A trio of his screens blinked. They showed a close image of the eleven Hamarkhis vessels, just as the king saw them out his own viewport, only in more detail and at greater magnification. Five appeared to be pulling away from the rest. Their antimatter drive engines blazed a furious white, apparently accelerating.

"They're pushing 25 gravities now, Skipper!" the navigator called.

"What are they doing?" Dikembe asked.

A map diagram flashed on a fourth screen next to the navigator. It showed five red dots following a slender red arc away from a longer green arc.

Dikembe stepped forward. He thrust a finger at the green arc. "Their original course." He pointed at the dots following the red arc. They approached a cluster of blue dots, likely Realm ships defending the shipyards. "The new course takes those five ships dead into Trebizond."

Andrew blinked. "Into the docking facilities?"

"No, Your Highness, into the shipyards themselves."

"But why would they . . . ?"

The king watched in horror as the five Hamarkhis transports had blazed into intercept range of the ships defending Trebizond.

"The defense pickets can't maneuver at that range," Dikembe said. He pointed again to the navigator's display at a line of blinking blue lights. "You can see—"

He cut himself off as tiny bright flashes appeared out the viewports. On the navigator's display, the five pilgrim vessels did the impossible: they launched weapons.

"I don't understand," Andrew said. "Those look like . . ."

Nearly one hundred missiles launched in the blink of an eye—from hidden single-fire tubes, perhaps—and raced toward the Realm pickets. An instant later, the patrol ships were obliterated.

"Uchafu!" Dikembe swore.

The king put his hand on the back of the captain's chair. His knees wobbled. "But . . . pilgrims . . . ?"

The navigator's screen showed a closer image of Trebizond Base. The quintuplet asteroids balanced at Langrage Point Four between Earth and the sun were covered with shipyards and repair bays. The king could see the slender hulls of Earth warships clustered at Trebizond One and Two—most of the Home Fleet was laid up there for refit and repair, including two of the monstrous men-of-war, the largest warships in existence. Normally the power in the sector. Helpless now.

The Hamarkhis ships dove at the bases, engines blazing.

"Captain," the navigator said, "they are on direct intercept with our fleet!"

"Stars," King Andrew said. "Isn't there anything we can do? Warn them, at least!"

"They already know. There is no way to miss those Hamarkhis ships." Dikembe's face was set in stone.

The Hamarkhis ships streaked into the midst of the laid-up fleet. Their images on the screen looked so small to King Andrew. But his mind filled in all the details of reality—the ships, the munitions, the power of the empire, plus thousands of tons of metal, composite materials, fuel, and explosives stored at Trebizond. And the men. The ships' personnel and the repair crews.

The sheer kinetic energy of all five Hamarkhis ships slamming into Trebizond in their suicidal run wiped the repair facilities from existence. Brilliant spheres of fire flickered across the screen and out the viewport—the Home Fleet meeting a violent and sudden end.

The helmsman bent from his console and retched.

King Andrew met Dikembe's horrified gaze. "Your Highness . . . the base . . . our fleet—"

King Andrew wanted to vomit too. "Captain, send a distress signal to any vessels nearby. Tell them . . ." He couldn't rid himself of the horror of what he'd just seen.

"Yes, Highness." Dikembe went to his console and sent the message himself. "I fear it will not come in time."

Andrew stared forward. "How could it?"

Dikembe turned to Andrew suddenly. "My king: Earth! Earth is undefended!"

Andrew had already come to the same realization. "This was the vilest betrayal."

"We've got to get you out of here!" Dikembe said, returning to his command chair. "Preserve the government in case—"

Keening alarms wailed from the navigator's station. "Bogey, Captain!" the navigator yelped, bending over his console. "Martian Hamarkhis design. Engine flare at bearing 180, mark 30! Coming in hot at 35 gees! Six light-seconds out."

The helmsman wiped his mouth and steadied himself on his workstation. "Going evasive, Skipper."

"Don't bother. We can't outrun them." Dikembe stabbed at the surface of his own console. "Approaching ship, this is Captain Dikembe of the Royal Yacht *Markham VII.* Identify yourself!"

The navigator's hands flew over his console. The image of a sleek, black saucer leapt onto one of his screens. King Andrew watched as a pair of projectiles shot out from its bow. "Missiles out!" the navigator said.

"Helm, move!" Dikembe said.

The helmsman wrenched the yacht to port and accelerated. King Andrew staggered backward as the ship's compensators struggled to keep up with the change in velocity.

Armor slammed down over the inside of the yacht's viewports as the approaching missiles unleashed electromagnetic pulses. Control panels flickered, lights flashed off and on before finally dying. All the monitors went dead.

King Andrew's throat closed at the silence. It meant the engines were down too. Orange emergency lights blinked on.

"They mean to board." Dikembe reached under his chair and drew a hefty grey Hunsaker Double-10 pistol. He offered it butt first to King Andrew. "Your Highness, I will alert the guards. Men, go with him!"

The king took the gun and waved the two officers, who drew their own sidearms, after him. They ran through the bridge hatch into the corridor. It too was bathed deep orange from the emergency lights. Their boots pounded on the decking.

King Andrew burst into the private cabin to find Maria holding the boys tightly to her. They looked at him with terrified faces as something loud clanged against the hull. Strange noises emanated from the aft portion of the yacht. The king felt helpless. What had been a comfortable living space minutes ago now felt like a tomb.

Four guards in black and gold armor burst into the opposite end of the room. Each bore a slim KM-88 assault rifle. "Sire! They've breached the hull! Get behind us!"

They turned and dropped into defensive formation. One guard sealed the rear hatch and backed away. The guards sighted their weapons on the hatch. The two navy officers took up posts behind them.

"Get the boys onto the bridge, Maria, and seal the hatch." King Andrew took her hand. He pulled her close and kissed her. "I love you."

"And I love you." She brushed a hand along his cheek. "Be careful."

Captain Dikembe stomped into the room and placed himself between the hatch and the king. "Take aim with care," he snapped. "Don't puncture our hull. Look for weak points in armor. Go for the heads if they don't have helmets."

Noises and angry voices echoed behind the hatch. It sounded to Andrew as if several people were hammering on it. His dread increased when the hammering stopped. What would they do to Maria and the boys?

The hatch began to glow a bright red. The troops in front of King Andrew tensed, their armor squeaking.

Captain Dikembe crouched near him and offered a tight smile. "I will guard you with my life, Your Highness."

"I will try to not disappoint your loyalty." King Andrew leveled his own gun.

The hatch dissolved in a flash of smoke and fire.

Shouts and gunfire erupted as armored assailants flooded through. His own men opened fire, felling the first three attackers instantly. But more surged behind.

Bright flashes flew past King Andrew's head. He realized the boarders were firing scramblers, stun weapons whose pulse shut off the body's voluntary nervous system, forcing the target's limbs to go limp while allowing his heartbeat and lungs to operate.

He caught brief glimpses of maroon and tan uniforms. They were oddly familiar, but out of place. They didn't look like Martian uniforms.

The guards shot more and more of the attackers. Five, ten, fifteen. But the scramblers kept coming—and finding their marks—and in another thirty seconds all of Andrew's men were disabled.

As if a door had swung open, the invaders swept into the cabin. They shoved the bodies of the king's men aside and turned their weapons on Andrew.

In that shocked moment he realized where he'd seen these uniforms before. His assailants were not Martians.

They were his own secret police.

Detective Inspector Konrad Toers sat hunched in the front passenger seat of a Kesek groundcar as it wound its way up a tree-lined hillside. He folded his arms crossly and glared into the misty evening. Rain dribbled down the outside of his window. The steely grey clouds swaddled the entire valley below. He closed the top button of his maroon coat in defense against the chill seeping through the tinted glass. "Faster, please."

The burly constable beside him grimaced. "Sorry, sir. This blasted rain's making that difficult."

Toers grumbled. He looked into a rearview mirror and was pleased to see the other four black and maroon groundcars keeping pace behind his. Toers returned his attention forward in time to see the sprawling five-story mansion rise behind the trees. He looked in faint envy at the stone and wood structure enclosed by low granite walls. In his groundcar's headlamps, it looked dark and foreboding—no lights on, internal or external. "No one to welcome us?"

The cars pulled up into a paved courtyard and parked before a wide stone staircase. It led up to a tall, wooden door carved with the ring and eight stars of the Starkweather seal. Still no lights came on. That irked Toers. This place was supposed to be under constant surveillance by Kesek assets. Had the estate been abandoned in secret?

Fifteen Kesek officers piled out of the groundcars. Most unholstered their standard issue KM3 pistols, but six carried scramblers to stun anyone on the estate.

Toers made sure he was the last one to exit. "Listen up." He wiped mist off his brow. "The household consists of five family members and eight staff, but we already know Colonel Verge and his son are not present. Arrest anyone you see. Bring them to me. Move!"

The officers split up into pairs. Six men went around the east side of the mansion, four went around the west side, and the remaining four went to the front door. The latter group included two technicians, who immediately hunkered over an access panel. Two officers stood facing the door, weapons leveled.

Toers joined them. He listened to the techs' murmurs, their tapping of delver keys, and the beeps from the access panel. A sudden clack shook the door. "Unlocked," one tech said.

Toers nodded to the two officers. One braced his shoulder against the door, hand resting on the knob. The other raised his gun.

They pushed inside.

Toers followed, sweeping his weapon around a very dark and empty vestibule. He pulled a hand beacon from his pocket and shone it about. The beam cast shadows behind a curving staircase leading to a second floor mezzanine. The light played off oil paintings of mountain landscapes and starry vistas hanging on the pale wood walls. It illuminated family portraits and images from what appeared to be camping trips that decorated the lower walls.

"Nice digs, eh, Inspector?" a sergeant said.

"Definitely wealthy, but not ostentatious—like the Verges themselves, as recorded in our files," Toers said. "It's always a pleasure to see that Kesek's information is accurate. Get the lights on."

One of the techs fiddled with the illumination controls by the front door. Toers winced as a brilliant light lit up the vestibule. It sparkled off the pale stone and brass fittings on the wooden cabinets. He squinted up at the shimmering chandelier. "Impressive."

His comm unit beeped at him. Toers dug it out of a jacket pocket. "What have you found?"

"Sir, Team One here. We've checked the entire west side of the house, and we're searching the outbuildings now, but there's no sign of anyone. Looks like they left in a hurry, though. Found some open closets and clothes tossed about. The main vehicle bay's doors are wide open, and there's no vehicles in sight."

"One of the other representatives must have warned Professor Douglas-Verge. Blast," Toers said. "I knew we should have rounded her up immediately. See what else you can find."

"Yes, sir."

Toers returned the comm unit to his pocket. His sergeant hustled up to him, boots clattering on the floor. He had a mottled green backpack in his hand. "What is it?" Toers asked.

"Detective Inspector, we found out what happened to our surveillance." The sergeant upended the bag. A clump of wires and fur landed with a soft whump.

Toers bent over it. He wrinkled his nose—something was burned. He drew his delver from a pocket and poked at the remains. "One of our robotic spies. Squirrel, by the coloration. Hmm."

"Someone used him for target practice, sir."

"No doubt shortly before they left." Toers locked eyes with the sergeant. "Why wasn't the surveillance failure reported?"

"Could've slipped by the techs. Maybe the Verges have friends inside Kesek. Or maybe—"

"Never mind. Put out a search for the Verges' delvers. If they try to access the Reach for news, we'll—"

"Uh, sir . . ."

"Now what?"

The sergeant wordlessly rustled into the backpack and then handed over three delvers.

Toers sighed. "Perfect."

"Guess we have to track them the old-fashioned way, huh, sir?"

Toers glared at him. "Look up all her known contacts. Disperse the teams to those locations. If you need more men, contact our New Denver office."

"Yes, sir."

Toers rubbed his face. This was not going well. All he had to do was track down Professor Tara Douglas-Verge, alternate from Starkweather to the Congress of Worlds, and her two daughters. Three women. Surely he could find three women.

But where had they gone?

Frustrated, he kicked at the remains of the robotic squirrel. He glared at the family images hanging on the wall. The smiling Verge family mocked him, especially Professor Douglas-Verge's dark face.

Then Toers looked more closely at their surroundings in the portraits—aspens and pine. They framed a cabin.

Toers smiled.

• • •

Tara Douglas-Verge held tight to the reins of her horse. The mare was an Appaloosa, brown with white splotches. Tara had ridden her many times over the past years, usually on warm summer outings.

But now she shivered. Her stomach knotted with worry. It was cold up here in the Big Horn Mountains more than two hundred kilometers east of the Verge estate in Jackson, Wyoming. A light snow drifted down through branches of leafless aspen and shaggy Douglas fir, glowing in the scattered moonlight. It cast the head of her horse in a pale aura. She looked about the long, wide ridge perched several dozen meters above a winding ice-covered stream. All was eerily quiet save for the gurgling of water beneath the ice and her horse's shuffling of its hooves.

Tara wore a long, mottled grey and white parka. The pseudo-fur lining tickled at her neck. The grey insulated trousers and white boots kept her toes from freezing. She patted the two brown packs secured behind her saddle. She pulled her white fleece cap snug over her ears and turned to her daughters.

Bridget and Julianna waited for her farther up the snow-covered ridge. They sat astride a pair of Appaloosa stallions and wore snowsuits identical to hers. Tara could see Bridget's dark face watching her in the moonlight, the anxiety visible even from such a distance. It was like looking at her younger self. Julianna's bold expression was equally recognizable. The moon was so bright tonight they didn't need to use their handheld beacons, which was a good thing.

It was that moonlight that kept Tara amongst the shadows of the pines, watching every dark corner as if it concealed a lurking danger.

Bridget's horse shuffled down through the snow. "Mother, we shouldn't wait any longer." Her voice sounded as loud as a groundcar engine in the solid silence of the mountain air.

Tara held up a gloved hand to hush her. She glanced at the sky.

"Like those rats could ever sniff us out up here." Julianna's voice carried easily across the distance. She jerked the reins to turn the stallion around. "How far is it?"

"About an hour." Tara tried smiling, mainly to reassure Bridget. Her younger daughter stayed close to her side. "It's been a long time since we went riding."

Bridget nodded. "Uncle Connor's ranch in Montana, three summers ago."

Julianna gestured to them. "C'mon, let's go." She urged her horse on, but seemed to have little luck pitting her impatience against the animal's stubbornness.

Tara gently urged her horse on to meet her. Bridget followed. When she reached Julianna, Tara reached over and ran a hand over the stallion's mane. "There now, be easy."

The stallion whinnied and pawed at the snow. But when Julianna tried a gentler restart, he stepped off without hesitation.

"Hard to believe this is how people used to travel all the time." Tara shook her head. "No cutters, shuttles, hovercraft, groundcars—"

"Mother?" Julianna's eyes were steely even though her voice had acquired a quiver.

"What is it?"

"Do you think . . ." Julianna chewed her lip. "Are Father and Alec okay?"

Tara sighed. She sidled her horse closer to Julianna as they crossed the ridge, following its slope down into a narrow valley.

Tara drew her older daughter into a brief hug. "Your father is the finest Lancer in the Realm, Julianna. He is strong and he will protect Alec. Don't forget, they aren't alone—your Uncle Jonathan, Uncle Connor, and Aunt Colleen are with them."

"They could all be in danger," Bridget whispered.

"I know." She did indeed know. Tara struggled now to hide the tears burning at the edge of her eyes as she thought of the last time she'd shared a laugh with her brother, Major Jonathan Douglas: their family gathering before he had shipped out to the Bethel system with Tara's husband, Lieutenant Colonel James Verge, and their son, Cadet Trainee Alec Verge. James's sister, Commander Colleen Verge of the *HMS Herald*, and his brother, fighter pilot Lieutenant Connor Verge, had gone with them.

If Kesek and the Martians were working together to attack Earth, then the mission that had led so many of her family away from Earth had probably been an ambush as well. What had become of them?

James. She missed him so much. A part of her always felt empty when he left Earth. But this time the ache was more profound—she knew quite well he could be in danger. Or already dead.

"They will be all right, girls," she said firmly. It was easy enough to reassure them. Now just convince yourself.

The Verge girls wound their way down a narrow path into a rough clearing hidden from the view of the old highway and nestled in the shadow of a mountain peak. Hooves crunched through the snow that had already accumulated on the fallen leaves, though many trees still bore their autumn decoration. A white, fluffy layer coated the top of the sagging cabin they now approached. Memories warmed Tara in spite of the cold.

They tied their horses to a nearby stand of aspens. "Let's get indoors, ladies." Tara pulled her two packs off her horse as the girls followed suit.

They trudged through the half-meter-deep snow toward the front door. Tara finally allowed herself to relax. She tried not to think about Representative Carina Sulis's panicked message that had, just seven hours ago, sent them on this flight. She tried not to think about the Kesek officers who might even now be swarming across the continent seeking members of the Congress of Worlds. Her king was lost and Earth was under attack, but Tara Douglas-Verge wanted desperately to shield her daughters from it all. At least for a while.

Tara unlocked the cabin's front door and pushed it open with a creak. Then she gasped and dropped both packs.

A young woman wearing a close-fitting white jumpsuit sat serenely in a chair next to the sole table. Golden light from a portable lamp on the wooden table flickered across the olive-skinned, aquiline profile of her face and her close-cut black hair. Her nearly black eyes shone keenly. "Professor Douglas-Verge. I am thankful you arrived safely."

Tara was stunned. Bridget pressed close to her. Julianna, though, tossed her packs aside and put her hands on her hips. "Who are you?"

"Your helper in time of need." The young woman rose. "My name is Najwa. *Insh'allah.*"

CHAPTER 1

October 2602
Bethel Star System
Bethel, New Grace

"Now faith is the assurance of things hoped for, the conviction of things not seen."

Baden Haczyk lowered the Bible that was nestled in his hands. He couldn't believe he was reading this stuff, out loud no less.

Even harder to believe were the four hundred Bethelites raptly listening to him read.

They crowded before him in the wide-open central square of New Grace. The formerly tranquil grassy knoll looked like a war zone. Mangled robots, Martian and Starkweather, were scattered everywhere. Most buildings lining the square were skeletal remains of their beautiful brick, stone, wood, and permacrete selves. Charred black was the color of the day.

But even as the stench of burnt everything assaulted Baden's nose, he wondered at the faith of the people standing under this cloud-speckled blue sky in awed silence. Everyone looked at Baden as a constant breeze rustled the leaves on the few scorched trees left standing.

He hoped they didn't see the same gangly, skinny youth with messy brown hair that he saw the last time he'd looked in a mirror. The steady wind gusted. Baden shivered and rolled down the sleeves of his favorite orange shirt.

The quiet crowd was an exception to the bustle all about. Emergency workers in blue jumpsuits crawled in and amongst the shattered buildings. Baden saw dozens of dog-sized robots leaping and burrowing as the humans directed them. Searching for survivors in the rubble.

Beyond the crowd, Starkweather Lancers in grey-green fatigues moved wrecked robots. Some picked over the remains of shattered Martian bots, looking for technical tidbits, perhaps. A shadow flashed over the crowd. Baden looked up in time to see a pair of Lynx fighters soar above the square. The shriek of their ramjets shook his insides a second later.

Baden looked down at the rest of the passage he was supposed to read. It was a litany of heroes. Abel. Noah. Sarah. Joseph. He couldn't bring himself to read aloud of their faith and suffering. He'd read enough for now.

"Thank you, Baden." Assemblyman Bartholomew Heng stepped up beside him. The kindly man with the Asian features had made it his business to act as a buffer between Baden and the other Bethelites. They all wanted that book so badly. They wanted to know every word.

Baden wished they'd just leave him be. Yet here he was. A reluctant preacher.

"You have done a fine job." Heng smiled broadly. He was shorter than Baden and wore a plain-cut blue coat over his rough workman's trousers. "It means so much to our people to hear the Word of God proclaimed."

"Yeah. Uh, you're welcome." Baden tried a smile. It felt weak. He gave a half-hearted wave to the crowd before him. They cheered. Sweet nova, they cheered. At him or at the Bible, either one. He felt queasy.

"Look, uh, I need to . . . go. You know, I need to go find the rest of the crew." Baden scuffed his boot in the green grass. Now there was a strange experience: grass. Life on a cargo six-brace, flitting from station to station, didn't give him much time to enjoy the surface of any hospitable planet.

"I understand." Heng gave his arm a sympathetic squeeze. He faced the crowd. "Thank you! Take these words that have fallen on your ears and pray over them. Meditate upon them! There is so much more we must hear!" He waved his hand at them.

The crowd waved back. Some applauded. Their faces were so open and happy. Baden had to shake his head to make himself stop seeing them. Sudden anger overpowered him. They were reacting to that blasted book. Because they were crazy.

"You think I'm going to be back for a repeat performance?" Baden stalked off without looking at Heng. He didn't want to see any disappointment on his face. He pressed between some of the smiling Bethelites—a pair of middle-aged women and their children.

"I had hoped you would." Heng kept up beside him, albeit with more steps. "They did take such great joy from it."

"Yeah, well . . ." Baden couldn't deny that.

The breeze blew a sudden smell of—what was that, salt? Sea salt. Sea spray, it was called. He'd looked it up on the Reach.

Baden stopped in mid-stride. Heng kept moving for a second. Baden knelt and freed a few blades of grass from his boot. He rubbed them between his fingers, marveling at the sensation. They found a new home in his sleeve pocket, next to a certain orange data disk.

Heng cleared his throat. "Would you please consider returning tomorrow?"

Baden sighed. "Maybe. I don't know."

"It would help alleviate their suffering. So many died in the attack . . ." Heng seemed to deflate. "But you have problems too, I know." He managed a small smile and walked away.

Yeah, problems. Baden grimaced. Like what he was going to do when Kesek eventually caught up with him and the rest of the crew of *Natalia Zoja* for possessing a text-in-violation.

The crew were waiting for him at the east edge of the square. His best friend, Owen Zinssler—"Ozzy" to Baden only—blond goatee, slim and pale-faced, nose buried in a delver that had its guts hanging out the back. Cyril, big and burly, ridiculous blond moustache, silent and just, well, Cyril. They stood by a stand of trees that were half-burned and stripped of leaves. Not far beyond a pair of six-legged Lancer robots—hexamblers, Baden had heard them called—went trundling by the square with power cells strapped on their backsides.

And there was his dad. Simon Haczyk. The captain, and the one face Baden didn't want to see right now. Simon's stern, pale green eyes stared right back at Baden. The square jaw twitched with—concern? Disapproval? Baden couldn't tell anymore. Both made him irate.

Dad jerked his head. The breeze rustled his dark brown hair. For the first time Baden realized just how much grey was in there. His heart almost went out to him. Then Dad spoke. "What happened with Heng? Is he going to buy it?"

It was the third time he'd asked. "No, Dad. I told you, I'm not selling it."

"That was kind of the point of us coming here." His dad waved his hand around the square.

Baden caught sight of some of the crowd setting up tents near the perimeter. So many had lost their homes in the battle.

His dad's words snapped him back to their conversation. "We give them their farming machinery, get paid, and you get rid of that book. Not get up and preach to the local yokels."

"Well, maybe I like reading to them," Baden said. It wasn't a total lie. He felt the power behind the words as he spoke them aloud, even if they had no meaning for him. Baden felt the yearning of the Bethelites and felt an inexplicable hunger to know what they knew. "Not like I'm gonna hand this thing over to them to read."

Dad sighed. He scratched the whiskers on his chin. "Look, Baden, I know you've gotten attached to this book, but just think about the trouble it's brought us."

"Hey, as far as I see, Kesek and its pirate goons are the ones bringing the trouble," Baden said. He jabbed a finger at his dad. "They were the ones who shot at us and hurt Ravenna. This book didn't do any of that."

"Yeah. Ravenna." Dad folded his arms. Going for his best father-in-charge look. "And how do you think her daughter feels about that, hmm? You think she wants any of us to get shot over that thing?"

Baden peered past his dad's shoulders. Gail Salpare stood some distance back from the crew, deep in conversation with a pair of young Bethelite women. Baden's frustration with Simon began to dissipate as he watched her freckled face crinkle with laughter. The wind jostled her short auburn hair and shifted the red work shirt she wore over tan pants. She'd urged Baden to keep the Bible. She felt there was some purpose beyond profit for it falling into his hands. Baden believed her.

"She's with me on this, Dad," he said firmly. "She knows this hasn't been my fault."

"Never said it was your fault. That book—"

"Cool your rockets, Dad! You think this book just hops up and smacks people in the face?" Baden yanked the Bible from his pocket and waved it under Simon's nose. His dad flinched. "It doesn't do anything! It's just a book! The problem is the people who read it. You get harmless nuts who want to kiss it—like these Bethelites—or you get the crazies who want to burn down anything to do with it—like Kesek!"

"That's why it's a danger!" Simon yelled back.

Baden saw pairs of eyes turn their way. Owen finally looked up from his delver, his face a muddle of confusion and concern. Cyril blinked nonchalantly, ignoring the sparrow pecking at a crab apple in his beefy palm. Even a pair of Bethelite workers installing a power transmitter on the edge of the square glanced at them.

"It's a magnet for trouble. And I don't want it on my ship!"

Baden shook his head. "Yeah, well, that's not my problem." He stalked off.

"Baden—"

"Later, Dad. Not now."

He got a short ways from his dad when Owen came running up. "Hack, you blow a thruster again? You got the Skipper all riled up. Remind me not to ride nav with him on the barge when we head back up."

"Good plan."

"So what's up?"

"You heard."

"Oh. The book." Owen licked his lips. "You could sell it."

"Not happening, Ozzy."

"C'mon, Hack. Paper's worth it! Plus it's an illegal book, right? Text-in-violation, according to our arrest warrants on the Reach."

"Your comm system down, Ozzy? I said no."

"Yeah, sure." Owen waggled the delver in his hand. "Check this. I got my own project. Grey delver."

Baden's jaw dropped. Just what they needed. More trouble. "Ozzy, that's illegal!"

Owen rolled his eyes. "Duh. So's your Bible."

"Oh. Point taken."

"Anyhoo, these Bethel folks got it in their heads that they can use a grey delver to store a full record of your Bible before we go traipsing off with it."

"And you're willing to oblige?"

"Of course." Owen spread his arms wide. "Ozzy will provide."

"For a good price, I bet."

"Hey, this ain't no charity gig, if that's what you mean. This is prime work." Owen batted a couple of gnats away from his face. "Ugh—lousy dirtball. Yeah, so, this delver can hook up to the Reach, but it's got a false memory. The grey module's where the real goods get stashed. Kesek can send an inquiry and they get jack, see?"

"Smooth." Baden tapped the delver's screen. "Unless Kesek figures things out and takes a peek under the lid. They'll nail these people and you too."

Owen's grin was supremely confident. "No sweat, Hack. I'm wanted already."

Baden shook his head. "So how are you gonna get the Bible on there? Text scanners ain't legal, either."

"Er—I thought they told you." Owen scratched the back of his neck. His bravado shifted abruptly to embarrassment.

"Tell me what?" This sounded suspicious.

"Well . . . weren't you gonna read it?"

"I've been reading it, a few chapters at a time." Baden's brow furrowed. "Wait. They want me to read it all?"

"That's the idea."

"The whole thing?"

"Yep."

"Out loud? For this?" he gestured at the delver.

"Why do you think that Heng guy's been on your case to preach so much?"

"I'm not preaching, Ozzy. You can only preach if you believe what you're saying. I don't."

"Not what it sounds like to me."

"Blast." Baden looked down at the Bible still clenched in his hand. He didn't believe it—at least, he didn't think he did. Not like the Bethelites. So why couldn't he just jettison it now?

Ask, and it will be given to you; seek, and you will find; knock, and it will be opened to you.

The words were like a hammer blow to Baden's mind, yet they were as soft as the breeze caressing his face. When his head cleared, he found himself hanging onto Owen's shoulder. Sweat trickled down his chest.

"Hack, you okay?" Owen asked. "You getting bad signals again?"

"Yeah." Baden was glad Owen didn't tease him about the words he heard in his head. Owen would tease about practically everything but that. "I'm all right."

Footsteps pounded across the grass. Baden looked up into Gail's worried but oh-so-beautiful face. She put a soft hand against his cheek. The touch was like a lightning strike. "Baden, did it happen again? Are you hurt?"

"I'm . . . I'm okay." He swallowed hard. Be cool. Be nonchalant. Stop staring! "What about you?" Oh, good one. Smooth line.

"You mean Mom?" Gail sighed. "Owen showed me where to look up the news from Puerto Guijarro in the Reach. She's resting in Hamid's clinic in the Baja Sur neighborhood."

Baden exhaled. "So she's safe. I was hoping Kesek hadn't gotten their paws on Ravenna."

"Don't worry, she's a big girl." Gail looked suddenly sheepish. "Some of the, uh, Bethelites offered to pray with me about it."

Baden looked across to the young women. "Is that what you guys were talking about?"

"I had some questions and those girls were kind enough to help," Gail said. "I wanted to know more about their lives on this planet."

"Lemme guess—they told you about the bugs." Owen angrily swatted at something over his head.

Gail poked Owen playfully in the arm. "You big baby. Don't you see how . . . I don't know . . . how *big* everything here is? There's no barrier between us and space, just a huge blanket of sky! It's not like Puerto Guijarro or school, with rock and metal around as a safety net. I can't get my mind around it." She looked at Baden. "I wanted to know about their faith too."

"Their religion sounds crazy." Baden straightened. He shoved the Bible back in his pocket.

"Well, there's a difference in those two words. Religion is what they do with what they believe. Faith . . ." Gail paused. "Faith is their walk with God. At least, that's what they said."

Walk with God. Baden felt like ever since he'd heard about the Bethelite's God, all he'd done was run. He looked over at a ruined building. A handful of rescue workers in blue coveralls dug through the debris. "How's that walk going for them?"

Gail's face took on a mischievous smile. "Much better, thanks to you."

That knocked Baden off target. "Me?"

"Your Bible reading helped them realize that they were putting all their effort into working for God's favor, when all they had to do was believe in Him and call on His name for forgiveness."

Baden opened his mouth to say something clever but got nothing.

Owen helped. "They sound like vac-heads," he said cheerfully. He clapped an arm around Gail's shoulder. "You should spend some more time with your man Ozzy instead of these dirt-siders."

Gail wriggled out of his grip. Baden caught the flash of annoyance on Owen's face. "They're no crazier than any of us," she said firmly. "Just 'cause you two can't understand them—"

"Hey, I understand." Baden winced as Gail and Owen gave him skeptical looks. "What?"

"You ain't exactly the president of their fan club, Hack."

"Well, I dunno." Baden kicked at a branch. He missed. "Most of the time it's all insanity, but every once in a while it seems like maybe . . ."

Gail reached out and touched his hand. "It sounds like you need to ask somebody else about this."

Baden met her eyes. "I wish I could talk to Mom about it."

Gail nodded. "I know. But since you can't . . ."

Baden sighed as he realized where she was going with this. "Right. Where is Jason?"

New Grace's main square was ten blocks from the shoreline. Baden enjoyed the quiet as he walked down a long, main avenue lined with squat rowhomes and shops. It would have been more relaxing if many of those buildings hadn't been burnt-out wrecks or if bomb craters and debris weren't blocking whole sections of road.

The main avenue dumped him out on the narrow dockfront street right by the ocean. A never-ending stretch of private fishing docks and mooring ramps jutted out from the permacrete seawall into the shallow bay. All manner of seagoing vessels—one-man dinghies, multiple-person skiffs, and full-crew fishing trawlers—were tied up. Men and women in dirty, wet clothes bellowed commands and laughed at jokes as they pulled on ropes and hefted boxes. Many more slips were empty. Baden saw a few specks way across the water that were probably fishing craft at work. He wondered what it was like to bob along on a seemingly bottomless bowl of water.

Baden spotted Jason standing at the end of one of the narrow docks. It was in need of repair and looked largely abandoned, save for a pair of cast-off fishing poles. The weatherworn boards creaked under Baden's boots as he walked toward him. The sea salt smell he'd caught at the main square was overwhelming now. Plus the smell of dead fish.

Baden stopped about a meter behind Jason. The other man wore a pair of tan shipboard pants and a light blue sweater with the sleeves rolled up, revealing pale forearms. He didn't turn. A trio of white seabirds wheeled overhead. Their inky striped wings flashed under the afternoon sun. Raucous shrieks reminded Baden of some of the more inebriated patrons of the Freighthound Tavern back on Puerto Guijarro.

And that, of course, reminded him of Gail. Lots of things did these days.

"Guessing games are not my favorite," Jason said. He didn't turn around.

Baden fought down his irritation. "Didn't see you at the show."

"Oh, I was there." Jason did look over his shoulder then. Baden shivered at the enigmatic smile on that calm, near-perfect face. He hated the way Jason's athletic body flexed beneath his shirt with every movement. Even his black hair was cut perfectly. "I wasn't readily visible, you might say."

"Practicing your skulking on the villagers?" Baden laced disdain through his words. "Some guest."

"Are you here to attempt to insult me or do you have a purpose?" Jason asked coolly.

Do I have a purpose? The question shook Baden unexpectedly. How many times had he asked himself that very thing over the past few weeks? "I— You need to tell me more about yourself. And about Mom. I mean, *can* you tell me more? Please."

Jason stared at him for a moment, then turned his head back to the sea. His fingers, clasped behind his back, wiggled up and down. "Very well. I believe I can trust you that far."

"Gee, thanks," Baden said.

Jason turned fully. "I told you Hannah Haczyk was one of the Seventy."

"What does that mean?"

"It means she was one of a select group of people scattered across the Realm who dedicated their lives to protecting the gospel of Christ—specifically, the documents that preach of His Good News."

Baden's stomach churned. Here it was. Something to explain the strange behavior and newfound beliefs his mother had acquired while he was away at school. Before she died. "What did Mom do?"

"She passed information to us, and we to her, about sightings of Christian documents. I understand from others that she was fearless in this regard. But she was smart too—she never used comms or delvers. She only delivered face-to-face."

Baden digested this. She must have done her work when she and Dad had docked *Natalia Zoja* at stations. Baden swallowed, his heart thudding. "Did . . . did my dad know?"

Jason shook his head. "No. She told few of her work and would not have jeopardized it by telling unbelievers."

That stung. "Not even her unbeliever kid?" Baden snapped.

"Baden—"

"Shut it! You're probably gonna tell me she snagged those papers and books just like you did!" He jutted his chin angrily. "That she was a thief just like you! Was that the cross she carried?"

Jason stiffened. "I won't defend my methods to you."

They went silent. Baden turned away, and they ignored each other for a few minutes. Baden spotted the three seabirds—they'd alighted on the corpse of a crustacean on the rocky beach and weren't sharing well. One pecked at the other, and received twice the same from the third.

A sudden bark pierced the air. A lean, russet-haired hound bounded into them. The seabirds shrieked as they leapt into the air. Their animosity was forgotten as the dog grabbed up their meal in its jaws.

Baden ran a hand through his hair. He was about ready to yank the stuff out. This was pointless. Kesek was going to space them both anyway. He'd better stop acting like a two-year-old. "Hey, Jason . . ."

Jason looked back at him.

"Look—I'm sorry. It's just . . ." Baden sighed. "This whole thing of Mom being some kind of secret agent is wild. I'm just sorry she didn't think she could tell me. Or Dad."

Jason took a step toward him, the boards creaking underfoot. "Baden, from all I heard, she was a good and faithful woman. She was cunning, but she was also warm-hearted. I'm sure she loved you both."

Tears stung the corners of Baden's eyes. "But she didn't tell me."

Jason put a hand on his shoulder.

"If I'd known—"

"What would you have done?" Jason's tone was kind. "Would you have repeated the words back to her, simply to please her, without truly believing? No, Baden, that is not faith. You and your father did not believe as she did. And you would not have fooled her."

Baden tried not to think of his mother sad. He focused instead on childhood memories—hide-and-seek in *Natalia Zoja*'s cavernous cargo bay, quiet story times before bed, the warmth of her arms and the melody of her voice.

Mom.

"She was well valued by the Seventy," Jason said. "We were all saddened when we heard she was killed."

Baden nodded glumly. "Pirates. That's what Dad said. There isn't much else to know beyond the police reports." He didn't really want to think about that, but he could sate his curiosity on another point. "Who are the Seventy?"

"I cannot tell you, because none of us know the names of all the adherents. I myself know only a half dozen. Of those, I only met with one face-to-face." Jason's voice barely carried over the gurgle of the tide around the dock pilings. "What I know is the Seventy's reputation. They saw the persecution that believers now face long before it crested to this level. A few men and women channeled their resources into . . . shall we say, protective measures. More than 180 years ago."

Baden ran the number in his head. "So around the same time the King banned all printed information."

"Precisely. It was not just the Bible the Seventy wanted kept safe, Baden, but all writings of the true faith." Jason lifted his gaze to the seabirds. They shrieked as they dove down to the dockside, apparently in competition for food. The rumbling hiss of the surging surf dulled the sounds. "They were thorough, clever in how and where to hide the documents. But Kesek was far too efficient in its destruction."

Baden looked at him carefully. "They needed somebody with an edge over Kesek. Is that when they found you?"

"They didn't find me, Baden. They made me. And my eleven brothers."

"Made you? Out of what, permacrete and titanium?"

"Close. How old would you say I am?"

"What is this, guess the coordinates?" Baden blew out a frustrated breath. "I dunno, 30? Maybe . . . 27?"

"You're a bit off." Jason's smile faded a bit. His features seemed to tighten. "Try 86."

Baden felt as if the dock had disappeared from under his boots. "Sure. Not possible."

"All things are possible. We were the solution to the Seventy's problem—twelve men, fearfully made and modified to be mankind's apex."

Fear crept along Baden's spine. It would certainly explain Jason's level of knowledge, his training, his overall strength and endurance. "That kind of gene-fiddling's banned."

"And with good reason. But the Seventy felt they had extenuating circumstances." Something like pride warmed Jason's face. "Kesek has no idea what—*who*—they're up against. They still think it may be just one or two of us. We did manage to slow the rate of destruction for a time. We won back some documents. And got better at hiding others. But when the Bible was lost, we thought our efforts might be in vain."

"Then somebody found it." Baden pressed a hand to his pocket and the Bible within. "One of your guys."

"Timothy." Jason said the name with such devotion that Baden felt true sympathy for the man. "He was more than a friend. He was a brother and a comrade in our cause."

A nav screen light went off in Baden's head. "He was on that ship. *Capernaum.* The wrecked one we found at Muhterem."

Jason nodded.

"So he had the Bible." Baden's mind whirled. That ship was included in the information on the data stick now resting in Baden's sleeve. He, Owen, and Gail had found it. Along with a map to—

"Alexandria. I believe you want to know more about it."

Baden wanted to grab him by the shoulders and tell him not to read his mind. Instead, he mustered up all the nonchalance he could and said, "Sure."

"It is a refuge, perhaps one of many, where the relics the Seventy . . . collected . . . have been placed." Jason squinted up into the sky at Bethel's golden afternoon sun. "I never knew where it was. Timothy was one of the few trusted to deliver items there. The map said it was at al-Qamar?"

"Something's at that system," Baden said. A mysterious set of coordinates from the data stick.

"You see now that I must continue his mission." Jason gazed at the sun. "The Seventy are devoted to this work, as am I. The Bible must be kept safe. And it is certainly not safe here. You wave it about as if it were a delver. Do you have any idea how precious it is?" He seemed to stop and collect himself. "But I will not take it from you. God's hand is upon you, Baden. So we will see what His plans are."

Baden had a nagging sensation as to how that statement translated. "So you want me to make the choice. Whether to take it to Alexandria or not."

Jason looked at him. "That would be optimal.

Perfect.

Thankfully, Baden's comm chirped. He dug it out of a pocket, angry that he had to make a decision like this when all he wanted to do was listen to a little Miles Davis and talk to Gail. "Yo."

"Where are you?" It was his dad.

"At the docks with Jason. Why?"

"Get back up to the square, now."

"Yeah, okay." Baden waved Jason over. "We're coming."

"Baden?"

"Yeah, Dad?"

"You need to hustle."

Right. When the suns go nova, maybe. "Aye, Skipper." Baden snapped off the comm and shoved it back into a pocket. He wished he could do the same to his dad. "C'mon, Jason, let's not keep the captain waiting."

The square was almost empty. Only a handful of families remained. One was having a picnic. Others played games. All of them cast wary glances at a quintet of armored Lancers that bounded through on patrol. Baden bet they were getting sick of seeing soldiers around their once peaceful town.

Along the north edge of the square a row of some eighty tents had sprouted from the ground like greenhouse plants in a time-lapse simulation Baden had watched once at school. Rescue workers moved among the tents offering supplies and gestures of encouragement. Lancers, along with Rozsade fusiliers in their black and red uniforms, still worked to dismantle the downed robots.

Baden spotted Simon, Owen, Cyril, and Gail in a cluster under a pair of skinny maple trees that seemed untouched by the fighting. His dad was talking to a tall, slender navy officer. Her blazing red hair, tamed by a tight ponytail, stood out against her tan uniform and white shirt. She was pretty. And it looked to Baden like his dad was nervous about whatever she was saying. Of course, he could be nervous because she was pretty.

She wasn't alone. A Lancer in brilliant green armor—Troop Master Somebody, Baden thought—stood protectively at her side. His helmet was split open to reveal a surly expression on his young Amerindian face. A long lance and heavy black rail-gun were secured to his massive back. Baden whistled in awe.

Simon spotted them. "Good, you're here."

"Didn't start the party without me?" Baden sidled up next to Gail. She smiled at him and held his hand. Baden thought his heart might just burst.

He heard Owen snicker. He aimed an elbow jab at his friend but missed.

Simon gestured at the female officer. "This is Commander Colleen Verge, captain of the Battle corvette *HMS Herald*," he said respectfully. "Captain, this is my son, Baden."

Commander Verge nodded. "Baden. A pleasure."

Baden gave a small wave. "Hey.

Her blue eyes perused him. Baden felt like he was under a scanner. He spotted the same silver-rayed black hole pin on her collar as his dad wore. Hard to believe both were captains—one spit-and-polish, the other five o'clock shadow-and-swagger.

"You probably remember Troop Master Benjamin Sands," Simon said. "Our tour guide."

Baden thought his dad awfully brave or very stupid to needle a guy who was three meters tall and wearing powered battle armor. He didn't look happy to be there. "So what's the prob?"

"Our pickets posted at Bethel's sundoor detected a ship earlier today," Commander Verge said. Her voice was quiet but firm. "It is not one of ours."

Uh oh.

"It is a Martian Tiu scout."

Baden exhaled in relief. At least it wasn't Kesek.

His dad shook his head. "They probably sent one to see why they didn't hear back from the force they sent after your ships, Captain."

Commander Verge smiled. "We would not have defeated the Tiu warships without your assistance, Captain Haczyk."

Dad blushed. Stars, his dad blushed! Baden wished he had an image recorder.

Baden looked between his dad and Commander Verge. "So . . . what?"

"So maybe you shut up, Expatriate, and let the commander speak," Troop Master Sands said with a voice so rough it sounded like a growl.

"He didn't ask you, rust-for-brains," Owen snapped.

Sands took a stomp forward. Owen yelped. Simon's hand went immediately for his gun holster, but Commander Verge held up both hands at chest level. She pierced Sands and then Owen with a stern glare. "Enough, boys."

Both mumbled something that might have been "Yes, ma'am."

"Troop Master," the commander said, "don't you have a patrol to attend to?"

"I . . . Yes, ma'am." Sands gave them another glower and tapped something on the side of his helmet. Its plates whirled and clicked over Sands's face, forming a fierce dragon's visage. Baden swallowed.

The troop master bounded away.

Apparently satisfied, Commander Verge turned her gaze to Baden. "We need your help."

Baden was perplexed. "With what? You got enough warships to take out a scout. They're damaged, but still. . ."

"Baden, that's not it." Simon moved to his side. "They want the ship in one piece."

Commander Verge nodded. "It has communications equipment valuable to our plans. We need your help to capture it

Baden blinked. He wanted to rattle his head a few times to make sure his brains were still plugged in. "Sorry, my help?"

"Yours. And this young man Owen's too."

Owen whimpered.

"But we especially need your new friend," Commander Verge said.

All eyes turned to Jason.

Jason looked at Baden. "I am a popular one today, aren't I?"

CHAPTER 2

October 2602
Bethel Star System
Bethel, New Grace

The Tiu scout burst through the sundoor from Xiaoji and set off every alarm on the small picket craft left behind by *HMS Bold*, one of the Starkweather warships.

Baden watched with great interest the picket's enhanced visual recording being replayed across a wide monitor. He'd never seen a Martian ship up close. It was not much more than a Raszewski sphere with a tiny command section and crew cabins up front and stubby engines behind. Its bow was studded with what Baden guessed were a plethora of sensors. Somewhere hidden on its dark red and brown hull were doubtless a couple of laser cannons.

Data skittered across the monitor. The picket dumped all its available sensor data into a heavily encoded burst transmission that reached the ships orbiting Bethel less than ten minutes after it was sent.

On the monitor, the Tiu scout angled its trajectory slightly. Then two lights flickered above and below the command section.

The screen blanked into static.

Baden almost jumped in his seat, but he didn't want to make a spectacle of himself in front of everybody else.

He was sitting next to Simon at a wide, round table in a circular room. The Starkweather military folks used it as a generic conference room attached to one of their command cabins on the planet's surface. It had curving prefab walls and a flattened dome for a ceiling. Afternoon sunshine spilled in through the eight windows lining the upper edge of the wall. The decking and décor would have put Baden right at home except for the grass and dirt everyone had tracked in.

Baden glanced around the table and was glad to see he wasn't the only one who seemed nervous. To his immediate left, his dad scratched at his chin—again. His brain must be churning.

Commander Colleen Verge sat next to Simon. She stared coldly at the blank screen. A delver lay abandoned on the table before her. To her left, a tall, lanky man about her same age and sporting the same brilliant red hair leaned back in his chair. His boots wiggled on the table as he hummed a tune under his breath. His face was cheery. He tossed Baden a jaunty salute. Baden eyed the man's pilot wings and the "VERGE" nameplate. Brother? Husband?

Troop Master Benjamin Sands was the thundercloud next door. He had shed his massive suit of armor for a simple mottled green and grey Lancer uniform, but he wasn't much smaller in person. His eyes jumped from person to person, and then to the door. He was making Baden more nervous by the second.

Two more men sat next to him: a young, dark-faced boy with wide eyes and a tall officer with a stern expression and jet-black goatee. The young man wore a plain tan jumpsuit. The officer wore a mottled green-grey uniform with twin silver star insignia and a yellow lightning bolt at the shoulder. Both had "VERGE" on their nameplates. It was a regular family reunion.

The officer cleared his throat. "As you can see, Captain Haczyk, we have a situation."

Simon nodded slowly. "How's about we do names first, Colonel."

Baden was impressed his father got the rank correct.

"Of course. My manners." The officer offered a hand. "Lt. Colonel James Verge, commander of the 21st Lancers Expeditionary Brigade. This is my son, Cadet Trainee Alec Verge."

Son? Baden locked eyes with the young man, who now appeared nervous. Alec swallowed against a lump in his throat and gave a curt nod. Couldn't be any older than seventeen. A kid.

"Troop Master Benjamin Sands, you have already met. He is leading a newly organized troop of some of our best Lancers."

"*The* best," Sands said firmly.

Colonel Verge's lip twitched. "Of course. And next to him, Lt. Connor Verge is the interim leader of Coyote Squadron. His Lynx fighters are providing combat air patrol over the city."

"A pleasure, Captain." Connor thrust a hand across Commander Verge and shook Simon's hand vigorously. Baden imagined he could hear his dad's teeth rattle. "I admired your barge over at the landing pad. Nice modifications. Not as flashy as a Lynx, but—"

"Connor. Enough."

"Sorry, James." Connor offered a jaunty salute.

"And you have also met Commander Colleen Verge—"

"Your sister," Simon said. "The lieutenant's what—your brother? You Starkweatherers always bring the whole bloodline when you do a war?"

Colonel Verge's face froze.

Baden swallowed. "Cool it, Dad," he whispered.

"Whatever." His dad jabbed a finger across the table. "I want to know what's so burning important that you're keeping my ship locked in orbit and my comms jammed so that I can't even find out what's going on on this blasted planet."

The colonel nodded. "Fair enough. As you have no doubt surmised by looking around, there has been a battle here. Martian Tiu attacked us a few days ago. It was an ambush. Our force was decimated. We lost our flagship, a transport, and a destroyer, along with one quarter of our fighter support. Hundreds of soldiers and pilots are dead."

The words pounded into Baden. He glanced around the table and saw the grief etched on all their faces. His dad didn't seem to notice. He must be riled.

"Okay. And what's been on the Reach that you haven't let us see?"

The colonel didn't answer.

"Come on, we've heard the troops talking about it," Baden said. All eyes swiveled his way. "You think we'd plug our ears and go on our way? Oh wait, we can't!"

No one seemed pleased by that remark. Baden caught a nod of approval from his dad. I can play with the big boys.

"The Reach," Colonel Verge said slowly, "has been running a continuous loop of the Kesek commissioner's announcement of a surprise attack on Earth's shipyards. The Home Fleet is destroyed, and the king has disappeared."

All Baden's bravado exploded. The king gone? It was inconceivable. Even his dad, the ruler of the nonplussed, just gaped at Colonel Verge. "How . . . ?"

"Someone kidnapped him, apparently." Commander Verge glanced sidelong at Simon and Baden. His dad seemed to sit up straighter. "We have no more information."

She gestured at the black screen. "And if the Tiu get within scanning range in the next eight hours, they will ascertain the condition of our task force. They can then report back to their masters that we were not destroyed."

Connor grumbled. "And if that happens, you can bet a Collins that every Tiu warship within two tract shifts from here will show up and pound us into atomic particles."

"I'll take a piece of 'em." Sands folded his arms. "Sir."

"Admirable, Benjamin, but I think discretion is what we need here." James folded his fingers. "Captain, we need you and your crew to help us take that ship. We cannot even let the Tiu see us. If we were to attack, they might get a signal off."

Simon nodded his glum understanding. "If they do that, there's no stopping their message. Short of destroying every comm satellite in the system before they can shift their message to the next star. But if you capture the ship without incident, you can . . . send faked replies right from their own transponder—or whatever else you please."

"You understand. We must do this quietly." Colonel Verge gestured. "Hence Colleen's plan."

Baden looked at her. Her cheeks reddened—he wondered if that was because of their sudden scrutiny or the odd smile

Simon gave her. Smile? Baden shook his head. His old man was getting weak in the knees.

"Wait a sec." Baden tapped the tabletop. "Why can't your own people stop them? You don't need us, really."

"We do, actually, to maintain the pretense of our defeat," Commander Verge said. "Your ship will close the distance with the Tiu scout and pretend it is on a cargo run. They will demand you surrender to be boarded, and you will agree."

"We will?" Simon asked.

"Yes. When they board, our soldiers will neutralize their boarding party. At that point, your people will neutralize their armor suit comms. Then you will go aboard the Tiu ship to negotiate your 'surrender.' A scout ship such as this only carries a crew of four beyond its soldiers."

"And who are my people in this?" Simon asked.

"Well . . ." Commander Verge cleared her throat. "Baden here as the ship's representative and negotiator, your man Owen for the jamming portion, and that intriguing stranger of yours to neutralize the bridge crew."

"You mean Jason," Baden said.

Simon rolled his eyes. "Thanks. I caught that."

"Hey, don't get on my—"

"Stop it."

Baden fumed and sat back in his seat. He caught the boy—what was his name? Alec, maybe—watching them. "You got a problem, dirt-sider?"

Sands started to push out of his chair. "Don't talk to the cadet—"

"It's all right, Benjamin." Alec's tone was deep and cool. He locked eyes with Baden. "This Expatriate is having trouble with the concept of family honor. He needs education."

Baden's fist tightened. "And you need a boot in your—"

"Enough." Colonel Verge pushed off from his chair slowly. He planted both hands on the table and scanned the room. Everyone either met his gaze or looked away. Baden tried to keep his chin up but wound up bowing his head when that powerful stare met him.

Simon, he noticed, didn't flinch.

"I don't need this," Colonel Verge said. "I have a king I must save. And I need your help to do it." He tapped the table. "What do you say, Captain Haczyk?"

"Depends. What do I get?"

"For starters, amnesty from your crimes."

Baden's stomach tightened. They knew. They'd seen the Kesek warrants.

"Those are trumped-up charges," Simon said.

Commander Verge slid her delver toward him. A holographic image of a warrant sprang into the air above the unit, with rows of tiny smiling faces staring at Baden—the faces of the *Natalia Zoja* crew. Scrolling text detailed their crimes and identified their ship.

"*Zepsuty*," Simon swore.

The door creaked open behind him. "Spoken truly."

The new voice had a heavy accent. Baden recognized it immediately. Rozsadesh.

Oh, boy. This was going to be bad.

Simon stood from his chair so quickly that he knocked it over. He whirled to face a man in a crimson-edged black uniform. The right sleeve and glove were pure white. Simon's face contorted with hate.

The steely-eyed soldier bared his teeth, but it didn't look to Baden like a happy grin. It looked like an I'm-going-to-eat-your-firstborn-son grin. "Haczyk. So. The rats come running to the refuse." The soldier spat on the floor.

Simon's hand went for his gun. Baden slapped a hand down on top of Simon's. "Dad! Don't!"

Colonel Verge had already come around the table. "Ah . . . Captain Haczyk, this is Major Branko Mazur, commander of the Berdysz—Ninth Cohort of the Ninth Fusilier Legion."

The two glared at each other. Neither offered a hand.

"It has been a long time, Expatriate dog." Branko spat the words.

"Not long enough for me," Simon growled. "Should've been longer."

"You look as ragged as I remember."

"And you're getting fatter, Branko."

Baden looked between the two. "You've . . . met?"

When Branko refused to comment, Simon filled in the blank for everyone. "Lieutenant Mazur was one of the fusiliers who arrested my parents on false smuggling charges. They broke down the front door of our tenement on Rozsada and dragged them off. I never saw them again."

Branko crossed his arms. "Criminals and thieves, both of them."

Simon took a step forward. Branko's hand slipped instinctively to his sidearm, but Colonel Verge seized his shoulder. No one restrained Simon, so he punched Branko square in the jaw.

Branko staggered backward, but he wasn't stunned for long. He grabbed Simon and threw him against the wall, then punched him in the gut.

Baden leapt up and rammed into him with all his weight—which, unfortunately, was not much. Branko shoved him aside.

"Stop!" Colonel Verge planted himself between the two men. Sands was right behind him and had a massive handgun in his raised hand. "Major, sit down! And Captain—

"I was five," Simon said. "You hit my mother with a baton when she screamed my name."

Branko glared at him. "Is his involvement necessary, James? Expatriate scum."

"We have a particular need for his ship, Branko, and I have determined he must be made fully aware of the situation here, yes." Colonel Verge was firm.

Baden was impressed that Branko seemed to back down after that. He didn't think anything short of a shipboard laser turret could get that guy to back down.

"Gentlemen, again . . . sit."

Branko made for an empty seat next to Colonel Verge's. Simon watched him go.

Baden tugged on his arm. "Nice friends, Dad," he whispered. "Can I join this fan club?"

Simon gave him a withering look and finally slumped into his chair.

Commander Verge tapped the delver. Its holographic array of warrants flickered. "It says here your crew is wanted 'for illegal possession of a text-in-violation as per the Charter of Religious Tolerance.' What do you have?"

Simon didn't look up from the table.

Baden decided to go for honesty. After all, these people had bigger guns. "I, uh, salvaged a Bible at Muhterem."

He might as well have told them he was planning to dance on the table with his pants tied around his forehead and his boots dangling from his ears. Lieutenant Connor Verge, the pilot, stared open-mouthed at him. Alec looked as if he might faint. Sands actually stopped scowling. Even Branko seemed moved. "By the ancient saints," he whispered.

"I see." Colonel Verge cleared his throat. "Well . . . I see. No wonder they've raised the reward."

Baden glanced at the numbers flickering under the warrant. Yeah, they sure had.

"So you want me and my boy to be your decoys so you can take this scout ship?" Simon grunted. "I don't like where this is going."

"In addition to granting you amnesty," Colonel Verge said, "we will compensate you and your crew, and provide what protection we can."

Simon scratched his chin. Baden's ears perked up. They looked at each other. Payment. Better than nothing, as far as Baden was concerned. "Dad, I'm in. We could do this."

"Are you crazy? We've got enough to worry about without stepping in the middle of their fight."

"If they can get us out of trouble with Kesek, it'll be worth it!" Baden shrugged. "Besides, Jason can handle this kind of stuff."

"He certainly seems able," Alec said. When Baden glared at him, he continued, "We've all seen the Reach footage from Puerto Guijarro."

"Mighty impressive." Sands sounded appreciative.

Baden turned to Simon. "C'mon, Dad. We need these guys."

His dad stared at Branko. "No. That's my final word."

• • •

In a few hours, *Natalia Zoja* was underway out of Bethel's orbit. On the ship's half-cylindrical bridge, Simon sat in front of the curved drive controls. He glowered at the main monitor sprawling before them.

Baden sat at the navigation console to Simon's right. He tried not to smile as he perused the four screens vying for his attention.

Simon glanced over his shoulder. "What?"

"Whaddya mean, 'What?'"

"You're making a face."

Baden turned away. Now he was grinning. "So much for 'my last word,' eh, Dad?"

Simon grumbled something unintelligible.

"I do not think it wise to provoke him in such a mood." Emi Akai sat at the comm/weapons console behind Baden. Her slender hands flew across the console as she prepared the ship's few hidden weapons systems for action, should they be needed. Her short black hair gleamed under the dim bridge lights.

"Not my fault. Colonel Verge just showed him the smarts behind this scheme."

"And probably showed him a great sum of money too."

"Well, yeah."

"Why don't you get down to the cargo bay and make sure your buddy knows his role?" Simon said.

"My buddy?" Baden wondered what Jason would think of that new title.

"Will you get moving?" Simon snapped. "Or are you going to sit there and repeat my orders back to me?"

Baden unstrapped from his chair and pushed off from the console. "Whatever you say, Captain."

He'd stomped only a few steps when Simon called out, "Be careful."

Nice touch. Worried about me now, Dad? "Why don't you worry about your ship for now?"

"That's what I mean. I don't want you and your buddy to damage my ship."

Baden looked back over his shoulder at him.

"You nervous about flying that Tiu rust bucket?"

"Just a bit," Baden said. "Can't say I've flown anything beyond barge size. I hope Jason can help."

Dad offered a grudging smile. "You'll be okay. Someday maybe I'll even let you fly *Natalia*."

Baden couldn't help return the smile. "You got it."

Baden pounded down the stairs at the back end of the cargo bay. It looked even more wide open than usual with most of its cargo transshipped to Bethel's surface. Catwalks stretched along the sides of the curving bulkheads and across the main deck. The lights blazed overhead, illuminating the ship's barge at the forward end of the bay. The six-wheeled Suhesky and rows of hefter robots sat patiently in their cubicles.

The soldiers made the only movement below Baden.

They were the newly created Troop One, Echo Company, a collection of survivors from decimated units. Baden didn't see any of the famed railer guns in their possession—he was glad for that. Railgun accelerated projectiles would punch right through the ship's hull. Instead, they carried short, bulky assault rifles and handguns that Baden recognized as Hunsaker Black Bulls. Somewhere he'd seen a tech article that mentioned the large shells they fired could pierce the weak points of combat armor.

He admired their variety of helmets, including three bear's faces, two glowering warrior masks, and a hawk's hooked beak. He spotted Troop Master Sands's brilliant green armor amidst the rest. "Hopefully Ozzy's down there too," Baden muttered to himself.

He took the stairs to the main deck. The Lancers were busy surveying the bay—for what, Baden couldn't be sure. "Troop Master?"

Sands turned. "What? You lost on your own ship, kid?"

"Cute." Baden wasn't about to be bullied by this dirt-sider in his own home. "I'm looking for Ozzy—guy with the blond goatee. Probably tearing a delver apart."

Sands waved a hand dismissively. "He was hiding over by the barge with your bodyguard."

"What are these guys doing, anyway?"

"It's called taking up defensive positions," Sands said condescendingly. "Whoever those Marties send aboard are going to be in for a surprise."

"Aced."

"You and your pals just find a place where you won't get shot."

"I know my part, Troop Master."

"You better." Sands turned his attention to one of his Lancers.

Baden found Owen and Jason crouched down around the side of the barge, tucked away from soldiers checking their weapons and looking over what Baden assumed were the defensive positions Sands had just mentioned.

Jason glanced up at him. "Where is the Bible? Is it safe?"

"Gail has it. Planetside." As if Baden would have it anywhere near him in the face of danger like this.

Owen smirked at Baden. "Hack, you ready for this?"

Baden's heart was hammering double time under his ribs, but he wasn't going to tell Owen that. "Yeah, I guess. What've you got?"

"We have a way to disrupt the Martians' suit units once they board." Jason gestured with a delver in one hand. "Once they are sealed off from their own ship."

"Hey, what's this 'we' business?" Owen shook his head. "It's my skills at play, boss. You're just along for the ride with your smackdown abilities."

Baden chuckled. He was about to add to Owen's comment when he felt the vibration in the deckplates increase. "We're accelerating. It won't be long now." He hunkered down with his friend and Jason. Baden watched the timer on his delver anxiously. The Tiu scout should be hailing *Natalia Zoja* soon.

Sands and his Lancers had secreted themselves among the stored hefters, behind the Suhesky, and in any other hiding spot they could find. Baden watched them make tiny hand motions to each other. They were maintaining comm silence, as were Baden and his companions. Nobody made a sound. Only the creaks and pops of the hull interrupted the moanings from the ventilation system.

Baden could hear the groan of the ship's engines as *Natalia Zoja* slowed. He spotted Sands's hiding place and saw him tighten his grip on his lance.

It was not long after that the engines fell silent.

A tremor ran through the hull. It shuddered up through Baden's body, rattling his clenched teeth.

"Docking clamps," Owen whispered. "It's them."

“Shhh.” Baden reached down to the small Hunsaker Wasp pistol at his side. “Get ready.”

The noises shaking the hull increased. Some less secure items in the cargo bay shifted out of place before the rattling finally died out. Baden peered around the barge toward the main cargo hatch.

This was it.

CHAPTER 3

October 2602
Bethel Star System

Lights flashed around the rim of the cargo hatch, indicating a good seal. Indicators along the seam blinked, and with a pop, the hatch hissed open.

It had barely split a couple of meters when two eight-legged robots skittered out into the middle of the hold, weapons bristling. Baden shivered. They were silvery nightmarish beetles, as long as a man was tall. Each octet did a nervous dance on the eight spindly legs jutting from its hemispherical body. Twin eyestalks rose from that body about an arm's length. The eyes were turned at sharp angles as they scanned the interior of the cargo hold. A pair of autocannons rotated with keening whines on struts midway back on the torso.

The octets communicated with each other in chittering bursts as they separated to take up sentry positions by the open hatch. Four more octets came scurrying out after them, roach-like, clattering farther into the bay.

Baden's throat tightened. Beside him, Owen made a quiet whimper.

Jason inched up next to them. "Stay steady." His voice carried steel behind it.

On cue, four Tiu soldiers strode through the hatch, assault rifles leveled. Baden's eyes widened. Two were tall and slender, wearing plain opaque facemasks and lightly armored exoskeletons. Baden figured they must be the ones sent to check out the *Natalia Zoja*'s corridors and bridge.

The other two sure wouldn't fit anywhere but the cargo bay. They were just as huge as the armored Lancers. Their armor was bulkier, less streamlined, and covered with strange curving designs that Baden figured must have some tribal significance to the Tiu. Masks of flat reddish metal with flat black visors surveyed the cargo bay. The soldiers spoke aloud over suit speakers. Baden couldn't translate their harsh language. He had a hard time assuring himself that the beings inside the suits were human. He knew they'd been raised in one-third standard gravity and had been heavily modified with genetic tampering.

Gunfire erupted like thunder.

The Lancers opened up on the Tiu soldiers and their robots. The bear-helmeted Lancers raced at them from the left, firing pairs of heavy handguns. At the same time the main cargo hatch came slamming together.

Shouts hammered off the walls as the Lancers leapt from hiding. The primary lights in the bay died, plunging the close-quartered world into near darkness. But Baden could still follow the firefight in the feeble glow of the orange auxiliary lights as the man-made lightning of muzzle flashes tore through the gloom.

His mind finally unfroze. He shoved Owen. "Their armor suits' comms, Ozzy! Jam 'em!"

Owen grappled with his delver. It emitted a series of beeps and chirps. Green lights flashed along its surface.

Flashes lit up the artificial night as the soldiers opened fire, catching the two octets nearest the cargo hatch by surprise. They tried in vain to return fire but were shredded and crippled by the blasts in seconds. The Tiu soldiers immediately dove for cover, screaming Martian oaths as they fired at random. Baden saw one Lancer's back arch as shots pierced his chest.

"Cut them off!" Sands's amplified voice echoed throughout the hold.

Owen's delver beeped once more. "Aced! Got it, Hack!"

Baden couldn't tell if the jamming devices hidden throughout the cargo hold had worked or not. He edged forward a bit more but froze when one of the two Tiu soldiers turned and looked right at him. Fear paralyzed him as the armored soldier screamed his frustration. "Uh, guys . . ."

Troop Master Sands slammed into the deck behind the Tiu soldier. The Tiu whirled and fired off a few shots before realizing his gun was out of ammunition. "You're out, Martie." Sands raised his own weapon and jerked the trigger.

Empty.

"Blast it all!" Sands tossed the gun away, groping instead for his lance. The Tiu saw his move and flexed his armored claw. They collided with a deafening ring of metal on metal, Sands barely getting his unextended lance into place to block the Martian's blow.

Sands shoved back. He swung his lance sharply to block the second blow. It drove him almost his knees. The Martian growled something in his guttural tongue and took another swing.

"I think you're pretty too, thanks for asking," Sands snapped as he lashed out with his lance. The strike forced the Tiu back a few steps.

The Martian swung again, but this time Sands leapt up. This was no hop. He sprang thirty feet straight up—nearly to the ceiling. Baden couldn't believe his eyes. Artificial muscles, maybe? Aced.

Sands arced toward a bulkhead, then shoved off with a motion that looked like it wrenched his arm. He barreled down into the Tiu, knocking him aside as the two rolled across the deck.

Pushing apart from the Tiu as he came out of their roll, Sands gained enough distance to flex his lance and extend its blade. The Martian yelled and charged the short distance. Sands jabbed with his lance, and the Martian parried with his claw.

Locked together with the lance blade stuck between the claw, Sands reached down and yanked the Tiu's own unused pistol from his utility hook. He rammed it against a flexible part of the armor—and fired.

The Martian went instantly limp.

Sands planted a boot against the Tiu's chest, pushing him down to the deck and separating his lance from the claw. He turned to Baden, who could only stare. "You could say thanks, kid."

"Th . . . thanks."

Beyond Sands, Baden could see under the feeble glow of the emergency lights that the other Lancers had destroyed all the octet robots and killed two of the other Tiu soldiers. It looked like two of the Lancers were down. They lay on the deck, their comrades hunched over their still forms.

One Lancer approached with a prisoner. It was a Tiu in the light armor. "Sir. This one is apparently in charge. Caught him trying to get up to the crew decks."

Sands grunted. "Nice one, Private. Lose his mask."

The Lancer pulled the mask off the Tiu's face. Baden gasped. Owen let loose a string of colorful profanity.

The Tiu's face was long, drawn, and pale. If Baden hadn't just seen them fight he'd think the man was ill. His eyes were ghostly grey-blue and his narrow head was shaved bald. But it was the swirling, jagged tattoos of red and maroon on his cheeks, forehead and nose that drew Baden's attention.

"You!" Sands held the blade of his lance under the man's chin, forced him to look at Baden, Owen, and Jason. "Take them to the bridge of your ship. Pretend they are your prisoners. Got it?"

The Tiu looked at him. Perspiration beaded his brow.

"Prisoners. Bridge. You tell about us, you die." Sands waggled the lance. "Got it?"

Baden swallowed hard. How did they even know this guy spoke something other than Tiu?

"Understand," the Tiu said tonelessly.

Sands shoved him hard forward. "Get moving!" He glared at Baden. "Don't foul this up, Expatriate. I don't wanna come chasing after you without my armor."

Baden looked at the cargo hatch. God, don't let me die now.

The Tiu, whom Baden figured must be some kind of officer, led them into a short, squat docking tube. It was made out of what looked to Baden like six different pieces of older docking tubes. He was glad he had an emergency breather mask in his pocket.

Natalia Zoja's cargo hatch banged shut behind them. Baden jumped at the sound. He kept his Hunsaker Wasp pistol trained on the Tiu's backside.

Jason whispered, "Now, open the hatch. No alarms."

"No alarms." The Tiu's command of their language was precise, clipped, and heavily accented. He opened the hatch into the Tiu ship.

Owen nudged Baden. "This goes wrong, Hack, we're dead men."

"Shut up, Ozzy."

Baden followed Jason and the Tiu over the threshold. He almost stumbled as he stepped into the dimly lit interior of the scout ship. Gravity here was one-third of standard. Every step felt like he was going to hop. But he got used to it soon enough, thanks to time spent in variable or zero gravity aboard ships and stations.

The corridors here were narrower but slightly taller than aboard *Natalia Zoja*. Their ribbed support struts were painted dull, rusty ochre and the bulkheads were deep grey. It made Baden think unpleasantly of being inside some great creature. Swallowed whole. He slipped his gun into a pocket.

The Tiu led them down the corridor to a spiral staircase. They ascended slowly.

The bridge was, by contrast to the corridors, a bowl of light. It was a half-circle set on its side with curved walls reaching to the deck. At the bottom of this half-circle an oval main monitor showed a breathtaking view of space about three meters across. Three stations were arranged around the perimeter, all of them bearing screens and consoles that looked vaguely familiar to

Baden. Perhaps the Tiu weren't as far afield from other races as he had thought.

The three Tiu at their stations wore form-fitting dark orange jumpsuits emblazoned with black symbols. They turned almost as one to face the new arrivals. Baden noticed they had fewer and less elaborate tattoos on their heads than the Tiu soldier had.

In the center was a throne-like black chair. It turned to reveal a man slightly taller and heavier than the other crew, in the same orange uniform shirt but wearing brown trousers with red triple stripes down both legs. He wore a small cap atop his head and had darker, olive-toned skin. He rose and said something in Tiu.

"He wants to know who we are," Jason whispered.

The Tiu soldier answered.

"He is telling the captain we are prisoners from the cargo ship," Jason said.

The captain looked directly at Baden.

Baden cleared his throat. "I'm Baden Haczyk, representing the crew of *Natalia Zoja*. We are here to offer our surrender."

That was when it all went bad.

The Tiu soldier turned on them suddenly and grabbed Jason's arm. Bad move. Jason wrenched out of his grasp and flung the man headlong into one of the seated crew.

The captain pulled a nasty-looking sidearm from his chair. Baden had his gun out faster and fired. The shot grazed the captain's shoulder and sent him toppling onto the deck.

One of the remaining two crewmen leapt at Baden and tackled him to the floor. They both promptly bounced off the deck. "Ozzy!" Baden yelped. "Get the comms!"

Owen dashed for one of the consoles. The soldier and the man he'd been thrown into were out cold. Owen shoved their tangled bodies aside and slipped into the seat. "What? This don't look like a comm . . ."

"The next station over!" Jason grabbed the Tiu captain's gun and aimed it at the remaining crewman. The Tiu stared at him wide-eyed. "Get out of that seat now!"

The Tiu jabbered something in his language and punched at his control board. An alarm shrieked.

Baden shoved the Tiu crewman aside. He flew into a bulkhead strut and cried out in pain. "Did he send a message?"

"No way, Hack!" Owen had his delver poised over the middle console. Wires snaked down inside the board. "I got it trashed. They ain't sending nothing."

"Then what—"

Jason pistol-whipped the last Tiu. "Laser cannon. He fired on *Natalia Zoja*."

Baden's heart fell as Jason brought up the image on the scanner. There was a dark gash across *Natalia Zoja*'s hull.

"She's returning fire," Jason said.

A beam leapt across the void and struck the Tiu scout. Baden grabbed for the bulkhead as the deck swayed. He grabbed his comm from his pocket. "Dad! Hold fire! Stop! We got the bridge!"

He felt his dad's relief echo through the comm. "Stars above, Baden. Are you okay?"

"Yeah. Just bruised."

"You shot at us."

"Ah, no, Dad, that was the bad guys."

"Right. Just get back over here."

Baden looked around the bridge. Jason was stacking the Tiu crew up like so many pipes. Then it occurred to him, "Hey, Dad?"

"Yeah?"

"Didn't mean to nick your ship."

He swore he heard his dad guffaw before he snapped off the comm.

Cadet Trainee Alec Verge stood amidst the ruins of the Starkweather camp. He ignored the torn and burnt cabins, staring instead up at the blue sky.

He was at war with himself. Part of him wanted to be up there in orbit, helping Benjamin Sands fight the Tiu on the scout ship. The other part of him recoiled at the prospect of engaging in combat. Of having to kill again.

He felt sick.

Pushing those feelings aside, he turned back to the task at hand. He sat astride a deactivated hexambler robot. It was a bit like riding a giant, armored beetle. Alec pulled aside the access panel and dove into its control circuits. The robot had been rendered inactive during the Tiu attack. Alec figured he would put his tech training from the academy to good use by trying to get it restarted.

He reached into his uniform pocket for a control circuit. As he did, his arm brushed against the container hanging on a strap around his neck and arm. Ah, yes: the recon imager. Alec looked up from his work and across the ruined camp. He hoped she'd agree with his proposal.

After a few minutes of tinkering with the circuitry, Alec blew out a frustrated breath. So much for training. It was obvious he hadn't paid as close attention in that class as he'd thought.

"You're Alec?"

He almost dropped one of the control connections. The young woman was standing at the base of the hexambler. Her name was Gail. She had the Bible in her hands. "Thank you for coming, Gail."

She smiled. Quite pretty. But Alec had seen the way she looked at Baden and he at her. The cadet had no plans for making any rash moves. It amused him to think of Benjamin's reaction to this meeting. He'd certainly crow.

"You're welcome," Gail said. "I thought your idea was a good one. I'm happy to help. Are you busy?"

"Er, not at the moment." Alec slapped shut the hatch on the hexambler. He'd tackle this problem later. He slid down the robot's armored carapace and thumped his boots onto the dirt.

"Why didn't you ask Baden, though?" Gail held up the Bible. "About copying it?"

"Well, I didn't know how he'd take the idea," Alec said. "He seems torn by this book."

"That's for certain. I'm not sure I should let you borrow it, considering he trusted me to hold on to it for him."

Alec held up a hand. "Don't worry. It will never leave your possession. I just think we need to take further steps to secure its contents."

"Maybe. But . . . why do you care? Are you a Christian like the Bethelites?"

"No. I just don't believe the Realm should suppress knowledge of any kind."

"You're not going to turn me in and take it, right?"

"Gail, do you realize the devastation Kesek has caused our battle group? Our Kesek officer tried to assassinate my father.

I'm pretty sure they're responsible for my uncle's death. Believe me, I have no interest in helping Kesek get anything they want."

"Well, I suppose that means you won't turn me in."

"Please, follow me."

He led her toward one of the ruined cabins. A pair of Lancers were tearing down damaged bits of the walls and assessing the strength of what remained. One of them gave Alec a thumbs-up.

He gave them what he hoped was a sufficiently cold glare.

Next to the cabin was a half-burnt table. Alec gestured. "Set the Bible there and open it to the first page, if you would."

Gail did so. "How fast do I have to turn the pages?" she asked with a hint of amusement.

Alec drew the recon imager from its case. The device was about half the size of the Bible, dull green, with eyepieces at one end and a scanning scope at the other. Alec checked the charge. All lights were blue. "As fast as you like. The imager will match your speed."

He positioned himself over the Bible. There was a certain thrill to participating in this illegal act, defying Kesek like this. Alec smiled. Let them try to arrest him. He aimed the imager and held it steady. "Go."

It clicked and a double red light flashed. One page down. Hundreds to go.

Alec and Gail stood there in silence as the imager whirred and Gail turned the pages. All the while, the recon imager's data sorter was cleaning up the images it took and separating out the information for storage. A pair of lightdragons flitted by on diaphanous wings, their finger-length bodies shimmering brilliantly in the sunlight. One landed on Alec's hand. Its bristly legs tickled.

"None of that now. Shoo." He blew and it flew off.

"I hope this isn't all for nothing," Gail said. She flipped to the next page.

"One can only hope," Alec said. The imager clicked and whirred.

"The Bethelites would say, 'One can only *pray* and hope.' That's what makes them so wonderful to me."

Alec nodded. "If I only knew more about this God of theirs, I would understand them better, I think."

Gail turned another page. "You know where to look, don't you? Just listening to Baden speak has done some strange things to me. Ideas I never considered before."

"Such as?"

"That God loves me." Gail turned another page.

Alec sighed. That was an idea that would take some getting used to. There was nothing of that sort in the Union Synoptic Church, the Kesek-monitored church to which his family and most aristocratic bloodlines belonged.

His imager whirred again. From off in the distance, Alec heard faint singing coming from the town.

Yes, he'd have to read more closely.

Commander Colleen Verge stood at the command chair, supervising as the Starkweather navy personnel took over the bridge of the Tiu scout ship. She'd thanked Baden, Owen, and Jason, but had instructed them to stand aside so her crew could get busy. Now only one of them remained on the bridge.

HMS Herald had followed *Natalia Zoja* out of orbit after the successful capture and had transferred personnel between the three ships. Colleen watched as two crewmen from her ship, *HMS Herald*, calibrated the scout ship's controls. The gravity was still set at one-third standard. She couldn't very well increase the ship's gravity field and crush the Tiu prisoners.

She'd made one concession. Baden Haczyk sat at the helm/nav console, next to Ensign Jeffrey Belus on the comm. Colleen had invited him to stay and try his hand at flying this bucket. She could've brought her own people. She could have flown it herself, actually, and even thought about it. But the young man had come such a long way and played his part well in the capture of the Tiu ship.

"Do you think you can handle her, Mister Haczyk?"

Baden went a little red around the ears. "Ah, yeah. It doesn't look too complicated. Drive controls are pretty much the same as *Natalia Zoja*'s, just fancier."

He was right. The control panel in front of him didn't look that different from the one aboard *HMS Herald* or most merchant ships Colleen had seen. Even the drive control off to the right had similar contours. "By all means, then, get her underway to Bethel. Quarter speed, please."

"Got it, Skipper." Baden reached for the drive controls and, his eyes closed, eased back on them.

The scout lurched underfoot but smoothed out soon afterward. Baden made a couple of quick adjustments to the thrust.

Colleen smiled. "Nicely done."

"Thanks." He returned the smile.

James Verge came onto the bridge in slightly bouncing steps. "Good to see you have things well in hand, Colleen," he said, sounding bemused.

"She's a clanky little ship, but she has good engines." Colleen gave the command chair a spin. "The comm center is all set up for your message."

"Good. Let's get this done." James strode over to the station. Ensign Belus nodded nervously. James pulled a delver from his uniform pocket and handed it to the comm officer. "When you're ready, Ensign."

"Yessir, Colonel." Belus downloaded the message from the delver to his console. A series of green lights dribbled down one side of the routing screen. "It looks good, sir. Ready in the queue."

"Send it."

"Aye, sir." Belus punched the code.

Silence pervaded the bridge. Baden swiveled in the helm chair. "Is that it?"

"Yes, that's it." James turned to Colleen. "So it should take about ten minutes for the signal to reach the comm satellites at the sundoor."

Colleen ran the calculations in her head. "Yes, ten minutes there. The comm message ferry won't collect the satellites for another six hours. Then the ferry will tract shift to the next star system and release the satellites, sending the signal on its way."

"And you guys want whoever sent this thing—" Baden indicated the bridge— "to hear it?"

"Certainly. We recorded a message using this ship's transponder code and the Tiu captain's personal encrypt to broadcast a report. I'm gratified that we've gotten this far in our plans without being discovered by whatever Tiu forces may still be lurking about. That report will tell this ship's masters that the four ships sent a few days ago succeeded in destroying the Starkweather-Rozsada task force. No survivors were left."

"Giving us the time to plan our next move," James said. "That move has to be to Earth. We must lend help to whatever loyal forces remain."

"But you said the Home Fleet was destroyed," Baden said. "Who else is left?"

Colleen wondered that too. There had been no word from any other roaming task forces. "The only news we have is that some task forces have been attacked at Muhterem and Rozsada. But we don't know how many ships were lost or how widespread were the attacks. We have not attempted to contact anyone for fear of bringing more Tiu forces down on ourselves."

"I'm taking our task force remnants to Earth," James said. "That is where we need to be. Colleen, you have some information indicating that Congress was not entirely unprepared for this action?"

She hesitated. James didn't know much about her secret pact with Representatives Gostislav Baran of Rozsada and Carina Sulis of the Expatriate Cooperative. Several other highly ranked naval officers were in on that pact. "The arrangement I have made with some . . . let us call them *loyal planners* . . . is to return to Earth and take a stand against Kesek."

"So there might be some help when we get there?" Baden asked.

"It is a leap of faith," Colleen admitted. "Surely you're familiar with the concept."

Baden winced. "Oh, you bet."

"Either way, we have cast our lot with the king." James's tone was steely. "We go to his side and fight."

Colleen looked out the main monitor at the stars. Yes. There was no doubt in her mind.

They would fight.

CHAPTER 4

October 2602
Earth Star System
Earth, North America, Wyoming

The third day in the Verge family's secluded cabin dawned cold and overcast. Tara Douglas-Verge made herself a steaming mug of cider and wrapped a blanket about her winter clothing. She stepped out the front door, closing it quietly behind her. There was little sound in the clearing, save for the cracking of overhead branches under the weight of snow. A pair of rabbits stood stock-still a few meters from her, deciding whether to run.

She knew how they felt.

The door whispered open behind her. "Good morning, Professor." Najwa stood in the open space. Her voice was soft, almost musical. She seemed utterly unconcerned by Tara's predicament.

"Good morning." Tara blew steam off the top of her cider and took a sip. "Are you planning on telling me whether we can leave today or not?"

Najwa raised an eyebrow in a quizzical expression. "I am told that it is best to remain until further instructions are given."

"Further instructions." Tara repeated it with disdain. "Then tell Representative Baran I grow weary of waiting for his instructions. You do work for him, don't you? Representative Gostislav Baran of Rozsada?"

"In a manner of speaking. Now I am at your service."

"And how can you serve me?"

"By safely guiding you and your daughters to those who have also signed the accord," Najwa replied.

"And I can trust you?"

"My oath is to the king, as is yours. That, and you do not have much of a choice."

"Am I supposed to take your orders then?"

"If you would prefer to think of it that way, yes."

Tara sighed. "Well, we're obviously going nowhere with this line of questioning. What *can* you tell me?"

"There are those in the governments of the Five who are aware of the . . . oddity of recent events." Najwa closed the cabin door behind her and stepped past Tara into the snow. Her boots made a muffled crunch as they sank in. She took a deep breath. "A very cold place, this. Nothing like my home." She shook herself from her reverie. "I apologize. Since the Hamarkhis attacks, Kesek has moved swiftly to arrest members of Congress and alternates. This all came at the time of the commissioner's announcement, which I gather you saw."

"Yes."

"Let us say that these individuals, including some of those who signed the accord, were preparing elements that will restore the government and the king to his throne." The serene beauty of Najwa's aristocratic features, especially her eyes of almost total black, made Tara wonder where Baran had recruited such a well-cultured assistant. "But first, we need the support of the military, and that is a problem." Najwa started ticking off points on her fingers. "One: the destruction of the Home Fleet. Two: the coordinated attacks on various task forces. Three: the recall of many elite combat units to the European continent here on Earth."

Tara blinked. "Why Europe? The palace and government buildings are in North Africa."

"Yes, but Kesek's headquarters are in Europe."

As Tara's eyes narrowed, Najwa nodded. "You see now why this is a very worrying situation."

"That's putting it mildly."

Najwa was about to respond but stopped. She raised one hand and looked to the sky. Tara gripped her mug tightly. "What is it?"

"Low-level craft." Najwa closed her eyes. "Two transports. Coming from the west."

Tara's voice quivered. "Who is it?"

Najwa's eyes flew open. "Get inside, quickly. Get the girls."

"But—"

"Move!"

Tara obeyed. Her mug slipped from her hand and poured its steaming contents into the snow. "Bridget! Julianna! Get up!"

Before she could get back inside the cabin, the whine grew in sudden intensity. A pair of black jetcopters burst over the clearing at treetop level.

"Attention!" a voice boomed over a loudspeaker. It echoed about the clearing. "This is the Royal Stability Force. Stay where you are or we will shoot!"

The first jetcopter dropped like a rock to the ground but eased into a landing at the last second. Kesek shock troopers leapt out even before it touched the grass. They fanned out around the cabin, assault rifles at the ready, and sealed off all routes of escape.

The second jetcopter settled farther up the hill. Another horde of Kesek men deftly navigated the boulders on the hill to reach their positions on the right flank.

The inspector in charge kept his pistol aimed straight at Tara. "Don't move," he ordered, "or you will die."

Najwa slowly raised her hands. Tara did the same.

His eyes flicked from side to side, body rigid. "Where are the girls? In the cabin?"

When he received no reply, he angled his gun slightly and fired off one shot, the bang echoing off the hills. The ringing was still fading from Tara's ears as he turned the barrel back toward them. "Bring them out."

"By whose order?" Tara asked.

The Kesek officer flashed a badge in his free hand. "Detective Inspector Konrad Toers. I am tasked with your arrest, by order of Commissioner Gironde, on the charge of sedition." His gun barrel flicked to one side. "The girls, please."

Quickly scanning the men surrounding them, and seeing Najwa frozen in apparent fear, Tara obeyed.

The girls followed her out with wide eyes. Younger Bridget clung to her arm, but Julianna strode defiantly right up to the inspector and spat on his boot. "Traitor."

Toers smoothly holstered his gun, never taking his eyes off her furious expression. He snapped his fingers, and two agents scurried up, seizing Julianna's arms. "You will pay for that," he murmured. "Bind her."

Two constables dragged her off, screaming. Tara dove at them, but more officers grabbed her. Bridget stood by, holding her hands to her face as tears poured down.

"You leave her be!" Tara shouted. "Don't touch her!"

Toers swiveled in her direction. He slapped her hard across the cheek. "I'll do as I please, Professor."

The constables finished binding Julianna's arms and legs, then threw her roughly against the cabin wall. She staggered in the snow but remained upright, glaring at them.

"What are you going to do?" Bridget asked quietly.

Toers turned to her slowly. "No need to fret, dear."

Tara winced as a constable bound her wrists, and Najwa's too.

"Well, I must say, I never thought we'd find you here, Professor Douglas-Verge," Toers continued, holstering his gun. His breath came out in ghostly wisps. "Most of the other representatives were much easier to locate. They at least didn't go running into the mountains like cowards."

"Let the girls go," Tara demanded.

"I think not. They make excellent leverage." Toers stood very close to Tara and brushed a hand across her jaw. "As I was saying, we did find most of your Congressional counterparts, but Representative Baran has seemingly vanished. I want to know where he is."

Tara said nothing.

"Disappointing." Toers sighed, then snapped his finger at the two constables. "The rude one, please."

The constable reached for Julianna.

Najwa shouted, "Wait!"

All eyes turned toward her. She was staring at Toers with what appeared to be abject terror in her eyes. "I will tell you anything you want," she whimpered. "Just do not hurt us."

Toers beckoned again to the guards. They left Julianna. "You would do so willingly? Without . . . persuasion?"

Najwa nodded.

"Good, though I don't know who you are, so I suspect I shall have to arrest you. But tell us what you know and perhaps I'll have my men leave you be."

Tara pressed her eyes shut. This couldn't be happening. Her last flicker of hope that Najwa could somehow negotiate them out of this mess went out. Why had Representative Baran sent a spineless lackey? Better to have no help than to be betrayed. Now she feared for the Realm's very survival.

CRAACK.

One of the constables screamed.

Tara looked up in time to see him collapse, his left arm bent at an unnatural angle. Toers's face was a study in amazement in the split-second before Najwa's elbow hit his jaw, sending him staggering backward.

Toers belatedly raised his pistol, but there was a flash of metal. He yelled and dropped the weapon. He reached with both hands toward the knife now protruding from his shoulder. By then, Najwa was on him.

Two swift blows later, Toers lay in a silent heap on the snow-covered ground. The shock troopers raised their guns.

"Now!" Najwa yelled. She tackled Bridget and Tara to the snow.

Weapons fire erupted from all directions.

Tara pressed her daughter into the snow. The flashes of scrambler blasts zipped overhead. She could make out ghostly white shapes moving silently amongst the snowy trees.

The Kesek officers panicked. They yelled in confusion, their assault rifles rattling and blazing into the woods. But the ambushers were coordinated and prepared. Within seconds, silence reigned.

Najwa helped Bridget and Tara to their feet. Her shackles lay beside Tara's face. Tara stared open mouthed at her.

"RG," Najwa said, her voice a thousand times steelier than it had been earlier. "Resolution Group. Rozsada."

Tara rushed to Julianna's side and removed the binders. She squeezed her daughter in a hug, ignoring her protests.

"I'm fine, Mother!'

"I know, I was just so worried . . . Why did you have to do that?"

"Um, Mother?"

Tara followed Julianna's gaze. Eight hooded men in white and grey winter camouflage emerged from the forest like ghosts. One lifted a med-scanner toward Bridget and swept it across her. The seven other soldiers came into the clearing and trained their scramblers on the downed Kesek officers.

"Who are they?" Tara asked.

"They are loyal to the king." Najwa kicked the gun away from where Toers lay unconscious. "As loyal to the king as these Kesek scum are to their beloved commissioner."

"But what were they doing here?" Tara's arms shook. The adrenaline from the confrontation was wearing off. "They couldn't have been just passing by. They had to have been in position for—"

"Eight hours," Najwa said. "You were fortunate we moved as swiftly as we did."

At Najwa's wave, the soldiers began securing the Kesek men in binders. They also covered their eyes with straps.

"What are they doing?" Bridget asked.

"They are getting our prisoners ready for transport. We can't very well have them see or hear us, nor do we want them to know where they are going," Najwa explained.

One of the camouflaged soldiers stopped in front of Najwa. "*Prosz' pana. Cy pani gotowa?*"

"*Tak. Zaraz sprawdz.*" Najwa rested a hand on Tara's shoulder. "Professor, you and your daughters must come with me. We will take you to Representative Baran and safety. RG has units in place across Earth, safeguarding the remaining representatives and waiting for their directive on what action to take."

"What do you mean, what action?"

"Action to save the king and restore the monarchy." Najwa's expression turned cold. She glanced at the prisoners. "Kesek is obviously in some way involved in this move against the Realm, though we do not know what the commissioner's intents are. They cannot be good. We will try to get word to loyal military forces off- and on-world as soon as we can, but those decisions will be left to you and your peers."

Tara nodded. "If we can contact James—Colonel Verge—and my brother, they can get their Lancers here. I hope."

"We will do what we can."

A buzzing alerted them as another pair of transports rounded a nearby ridge. These were a mottled grey and white. Their insectoid bodies floated on four turbofans as they lowered into the clearing. The soldier near Najwa shifted his position. "Kestrels are here. We must go," he said, his Rozsadesh accent thick.

"*Tak.* Load the prisoners into one of the Kestrels. Make room for us in the other. Move!" The soldier bolted off to relay her orders.

Najwa shepherded the Verge women aboard the waiting Kestrel.

Tara took a last look at the cabin through one of the stained, scratched portholes as the transports thundered into the sky. "Now this is in our hands," Tara said, making eye contact with Najwa.

Najwa, seated between two RG soldiers, shook her head. She looked suddenly very tired for her young age. "We will make full speed to our sanctuary, *insh'allah*," she murmured. "God is great. It is in his hands."

Tara felt her insides churn. Oh. She was one of *them*. "Muslim?"

"Is that a problem?"

"Not so long as you keep your superstitions to yourself." Tara didn't want to say anything further. There was no point arguing with one of the religionists. While she didn't like how they were treated under the so-called Charter of Tolerance, Tara personally had little tolerance for their rantings.

"There will be no proselytizing on this trip," Najwa said wryly. "My people forbid it."

"Smart of them," Tara said.

Toers saw a white blur. Then he felt the pain throughout his body. Everything ached. His head rang like the ancient courthouse bell from his hometown.

He struggled to his knees. His hands scratched at hardscrabble ground and coarse brush. Wind blew across his face and his body. He tore at the blindfold. "Blast."

He found himself kneeling on a vast, wide prairie with the rest of his team. Where was the cabin in the snow? Most of his men were still blindfolded and apparently unconscious. A few stood about, assessing their situation—no comms, no weapons, no delvers. Only their clothing and badges.

Toers looked up at the sun in the cold, cloudless sky. Midday. He craned his neck and scanned the horizon. There were low hills to the west, and nothing for kilometers but open plains in every other direction. Wait. No, there was a tiny town to the southeast. "Ten kilometers," he muttered.

No jetcopters. No mysterious soldiers in white. No mountain cabin.

No Professor Tara Douglas-Verge.

But he and his men were not dead. That indicated his enemies intended to humiliate him. Toers struck the ground in frustration. They'd succeeded. When word reached the commissioner of this debacle . . .

Toers decided he'd better start walking.

King Andrew II sat on a low bench. He was stripped of all his royal signifiers and was clad in a powder blue jumpsuit, devoid of any markings or decoration. Looking himself over in a small cracked mirror, he decided he looked surprisingly dignified, if somewhat haggard.

That's how he looked. How he felt was naked and afraid.

The cell was not Spartan, but decorated comfortably like a middle-class apartment. Besides the bench on which he sat, it had a simple bed, a chair and desk, access to a computer system, and a tiny bathroom through a door off to one side. The walls were a comfortable muted peach color. It even had two wall screens that showed city scenes, mimicking a window. They were meant to alleviate any feeling of claustrophobia.

King Andrew took no enjoyment in them. He stared instead at the cold metal cell door before him. He didn't dare touch the wire mesh window. Flexing his right hand, he looked down at the burn mark on his fingertips. So much for experimenting with escape.

He'd also tried gaining information from the computer. But it had turned out to be a closed system. It wasn't much more than an encyclopedia of historical, biological, and astronomical data. Nothing useful for Andrew in his situation.

His reverie was interrupted by a clanking sound. He felt his cell shift slowly. His body swayed a bit, a similar sensation to riding in an elevator. The clanking stopped. A series of thuds came from behind his cell door. King Andrew sat up straight and braced himself for whatever was coming through.

The door opened. Kesek Commissioner E. H. Gironde stood just over the threshold, smiling.

It was a galling sight. That smile had been at his side for years, offering advice that had always seemed prudent and wise. Now that smile had a mocking edge. The eyes were dark and cold, as usual—the face, charmingly handsome. His grey hair was perfectly combed and not the least bit out of place.

"I hope the accommodations are to your liking, Your Majesty," Gironde said, brushing lint from his immaculate grey uniform. "I gave you our best, after all."

King Andrew bolted to his feet. "Traitor! I should have known. Why I didn't listen to those who advised me of your schemes, I will never know."

"Yes, that was rather stupid of you, wasn't it?" Gironde folded his arms. "You only listened to one advisor. Though

I must admit, I always thought you picked the best of the lot."

King Andrew lunged forward. Gironde brought his leg up. A sharp pain erupted in King Andrew's kidneys. He collapsed to the metal floor with a grunt, falling across the threshold.

Vision hazy, the king looked up to see two Kesek guards in black body armor. They had automatic rifles at the ready. Gironde waved them off. "A clumsy move. He tripped."

The guards looked at each other, then Gironde, and turned away.

King Andrew tried to rise, but winced in pain. Gironde had one boot on the small of his back. The soft click above him made him freeze.

"This is my favorite KM3, Your Highness. Please don't give me the satisfaction of using it just yet," Gironde said. "You have no idea how easy it would be for me to shoot you here, with no witnesses, and then slaughter your entire family, and the only version of events anyone would hear would be my own. Your line has long squandered the sheer power at your fingertips, using it only for the wealth it produces. But I alone have the vision necessary to wield this power for the absolute control it will bring."

He knelt down onto the king's back. King Andrew gasped under the pressure. He felt the cold metal of the gun's muzzle against the small of his neck. "All I needed was to take a few simple steps. Your Starkweather and Rozsade allies needed to be dealt with—the Tiu were all too willing to oblige. You see, Your Highness, I have found that all men can be bought for a price."

"The Tiu will never be your allies!" King Andrew said. "They hate us too much."

"No, you see, that is where you are wrong. They hate you—or more specifically, the royal house. It was your ancestors who waged a bloody war to push them off their sacred world, your ancestors who raised the army of Lancers against their war machines, and your family who banished them from the civilized Realm. But I have welcomed them back."

For a moment, King Andrew could not fathom what he meant. Like the sunlight creeping around the edge of a planet, the truth dawned on him. "You'll let them have Mars back."

"Not all of it, Your Highness. It is still the property of the Realm and will remain such. But the Tiu will be allowed to worship and maintain a presence there. Their Hamarkhis cousins, of course, have been implicated in the attacks, and I will strike back hard against them and encourage reprisals, keeping them from interfering with the Tiu."

"How can you possibly rein them in without the Home Fleet and the task forces? You've butchered our men and women and left us with nothing!"

"Nothing is too broad a description." The pressure thankfully eased. King Andrew took several deep breaths. "Get up, please, this embarrassment has gone on long enough."

King Andrew grunted as he pushed up off the floor. The comfortable interior of his cell spun wildly before his eyes. He staggered sideways and reached swiftly for the cell wall to prevent himself from teetering.

"Much better." Gironde had put his gun away. "As I was saying, the Realm will not be left with 'nothing.' Not all the task forces have been reduced. There is still Earth's task force, which is soon to return from its routine piratical patrols. As I understand it, many of the pirates we have pursued for years have seen fit to accept my new offers of amnesty."

"Amnesty?" King Andrew bristled at the thought. "And what price do they pay for this amnesty?"

"Service. To me, and to the Realm. Legitimate armed merchant vessels are much more profitable, are they not?" Gironde said. "So you see, ships are not a problem."

King Andrew gritted his teeth. He yearned to strangle the man, but the pain in his side and back from the previous foiled attempt was still fresh. "You are ruining the Realm my family has preserved for centuries, through partnership between the Five and the Expatriates—"

"Preserved? Don't flatter yourself. It has survived only because of Kesek's strength. Your precious Five would have torn each other apart before the Realm was even through its infancy, if the Koninklijke Stabiliteitskracht had not held it together in its firm grip. And now, thanks to your failures, we will keep it so for centuries to come."

"And what of myself and my family? Somehow I can't believe you came down here just to gloat."

"Actually, I did come to gloat. It is most enjoyable." Gironde's eyes narrowed. "The Tiu, as I mentioned, have an undying hatred for you and, as I also mentioned, everyone has a price. You, Your Highness, are my price."

"What?"

"You will not be here much longer. Soon I will hand you and your family over to the Tiu, where you will face the charges of genocide and war crimes they levied against your ancestors. They have never been able to prosecute, of course, until now."

King Andrew felt his face blanch as sudden fear raced through his mind. The air in his cell seemed as thick as fog now. "Madman!" The accusation had an edge of terror to it, rather than the anger for which he was hoping.

"Perhaps. I will, of course, make a case for leniency, but I understand the Tiu are experts at gravity torture, and they do love an opportunity to expand upon their skill. You are right, however. I do have another purpose to my visit." Gironde drew his delver from its case on his belt, handing it over to the king. "Sign this. Now."

King Andrew read the document that was displayed on the screen, dumbfounded. "You want control of my family's share of MarkIntech? You cannot—"

"Do not dictate to me, Your Highness!" Gironde's pistol hand shook. Andrew flinched from the rage. "You will sign over to Kesek the Markham family's fifty-four percent of the shares of MarkIntech. It is a step that should have been taken long ago."

"If I refuse?"

"Then there is no hope for you to escape from the Tiu."

Fear and anger warred again in King Andrew as he read the glowing words on the delver. If he signed this, Kesek would gain the political and economic power to bring destruction to his Realm. It would be a dark age. Billions would suffer. He blinked at the document. Long ago he'd vowed he would sacrifice himself willingly to save his people from such a fate. Though if he refused, it would certainly cost him the lives of himself and his family. But this too was a cold arithmetic he had tallied long ago.

He'd never dreamed such a scenario would come to pass.

Then something occurred to him. Gironde was seeking his cooperation. "Wait, you will need me to stand before the board of directors to win their favor for your actions. There is no other way, is there?"

Gironde's eyes narrowed. "How very astute. True, I need you alive. For now."

He shoved the delver aside. “Then I will never sign. Nor will I try to convince anyone to help you, least of all the board. Go ahead and kill me now.”

“And your family?”

King Andrew bit his tongue.

“Hmm. I would not want to endanger my good associations with the Tiu by depriving them of their reward.” Gironde lowered the pistol. “I consider myself patient. You have one week to sign this agreement. Indeed, it may work more to my advantage to give you to the Tiu. After all, could I not take over MarkIntech in your stead after your assassination at the hands of the Martian barbarians?”

“People will find out the truth,” King Andrew said. “You can’t hide it forever.”

“The truth? What truth?” Gironde jabbed a finger at his own chest. “The only truth that matters is mine. Whatever I make it to be, it will be so.”

King Andrew bowed his head. What more could he do? Surely Gironde would find a way to gain control of his company. With or without him.

“Oh, don’t sulk.” Gironde stepped lightly past him through the cell entrance. “I will take good care of the Realm.”

CHAPTER 5

October 2602
Southcrown Star System

Detective Chief Inspector Nikolaas Ryke was alone in his cabin aboard the battle corvette *HMS Interrogator*. He leaned back in his chair with legs extended and his boots crossed over one another underneath a desk. His fingers drummed a steady beat on his tan uniform pants. He'd left his maroon jacket unsealed—it was too blasted warm in this cabin.

Ryke looked around disgustedly. He thought this was the ugliest set of quarters he'd ever had on a ship. Four plain, pale blue bulkheads, one charcoal-colored deck, a bunk, a small bathroom, a narrow desk, and three maroon chairs. Not even a viewport or a piece of artwork on the walls. Navy brass would hear about this from the Kesek home office.

He returned his attention to the image glowing on his delver screen. All he really knew was that the man was called Jason. "You've been busy," he murmured to the screen. "Once I figure out what you've been up to, you won't get away."

Ryke turned from the image and considered the data displayed on the other monitor at his desk. His ever-loyal partner, Detective Inspector George Cotes, had compiled all the relevant case files and data he'd requested, both from Cotes's own analysis and from the Kesek home office. It made Ryke infinitely more curious.

It seemed that Cotes's initial findings about the resiliency of the DNA and cellular structure were correct. Whoever this Jason was, something had been done to not only strengthen his body but also increase his longevity. Both kinds of treatment, to this radical a degree, were illegal. Ryke had never seen anything quite like it. Not even the hated RG did this to their field operatives. He reveled in the number of charges he could bring against this man—provided he brought him in alive, of course.

The most interesting part of the home office analysis was that the DNA from these multiple theft instances all shared similar traits. It was almost as if a family of genetically enhanced thieves had struck in various places throughout the Realm over the recent years.

Ryke tapped a finger on the desk. "Curious. What were you looking for, I wonder?"

He scrolled through the reports, reading the synopsis of each. The estate of a wealthy but reclusive retired merchant . . . the offices of a black market trader . . . a criminal cartel's hidden freight depot . . . a small community museum. Ryke narrowed his eyes. Well, there was a connection—all of them were known to keep antiques of some manner on display. But that made no sense. Unless, of course, Ryke considered recent events.

This Jason had latched onto the boy with the Bible. And people bearing similar genetic structure to his had committed thefts from places holding antiques. That pointed to some organization looking for religious artifacts—perhaps just Christian artifacts, though Ryke had dismantled a couple of groups of fanatics that pledged to defend "history's integrity," as they called it. He chuckled as he remembered those arrests. They were all still in prison, or dead.

His cabin door buzzer sounded. "Enter."

Cotes entered. Broad-shouldered and dark-skinned, his face was a mask behind a thick black moustache. He stood stiffly by the door as it slid shut behind him.

"Ah, Cotes. Have you seen the broadcast on the Reach from our dear commissioner?"

"Yes, sir."

"And? What did you think?"

Cotes hesitated.

"Come on, I'll not have you shot for your opinion," Ryke prodded. "I must say, this all took me by surprise. It is rather convenient to our situation to have the commissioner as the biggest link in the food chain, as it were. It makes opening doors even easier."

"I want only for the Realm to remain intact," Cotes said.

Ryke knew that was the closest to unvarnished opinion he'd get out of his partner. "Fine, well, let's leave it at that. What did you want?"

"Sir, I have the background data you requested."

Ryke eyed him suspiciously. "I'm flattered you brought it in person, Cotes. But I did just see you at mealtime."

Cotes fidgeted. "Yes, sir. I opted to bring it with me rather than transmit it because of its sensitive nature. Only my eyes have seen it, sir."

"What are you prattling about? Give me the delver."

Cotes reached into a coat pocket and pulled out a purple data stick. Ryke snatched it up and plugged it into the delver on his desk. The delver pulled the information off and projected it into the air in a blue hologram. Ryke maneuvered it with a wave of his hand.

A young man's face appeared, much slimmer and paler than Jason's. Next to it, text spilled down the transparent screen, baring every detail of Baden Haczyk's life—ailments, grades, meals, delver reading habits. "Ah, good Mister Haczyk the Younger," Ryke said. "What's the problem then?"

"The family, sir. You'll recognize her."

The display flashed a smaller image of Captain Simon Haczyk in one corner, spelling out the familial relation, and then the image of a beautiful woman appeared in the space next to his head.

Ryke froze.

No wonder the name had seemed familiar.

"It is Hannah Haczyk, sir, isn't it?"

Ryke nodded slowly. His mind was churning. He barely heard Cotes sigh.

"I thought so. Sir, I would request you hand this case over to another chief inspector. Perhaps before we leave Southcrown the office here would be willing—"

"No!" Ryke's own vehemence took him aback. "No," he repeated, more subdued. "The past is irrelevant. We will handle the Haczyk men as we do others in a case of this magnitude. Possession of a religious text-in-violation is a capital offense, Inspector Cotes, and we must pursue the criminals with all means at our disposal."

Cotes nodded. His face looked even more dour, if that were possible. "Yes, sir."

"You're worried about me, then?"

Cotes said nothing.

"I'm touched, but there's no need." Ryke forced some of his typical arrogance back into his voice. "The woman is dead—at the hand of pirates, according to my own official report, remember?—and if her men aren't careful, they will follow her soon. You're dismissed."

Cotes left.

Ryke magnified the image of Hannah. That peaceful, beautiful face. Of course, by the time he'd finished with that face it had not been so pretty. The interrogation had been long and brutal, more psychologically terrifying than physically brutal, Ryke thought dispassionately. Overall, he'd been pleased with his work.

But what had stayed with him all these years was the sheer steadiness of spirit with which Hannah had borne the terror. Ryke had never seen anything quite like it.

Which was why he kept the recordings of that particular interrogation. Cotes was trustworthy beyond measure—if a little naïve, Ryke thought crossly. He knew of these recordings and the potential trouble they could bring his superior. That was why he had brought Ryke the Haczyk family information in person. There was always the chance another Kesek officer aboard *Interrogator* would monitor data transmissions between Ryke and Cotes, even if they were Ryke's subordinates.

Even amongst their own, Kesek did not trust.

He pulled the purple memory stick and tossed it aside. It clattered across his desk. He dug into his own pockets and retrieved a small folded knife. Its pearl white handle was barely as long as the palm of his hand. Ryke pressed down on one end and a short rectangular segment popped free. He slid this segment out and plugged it into his delver. Ryke supplied the password.

Before it could play, though, he yanked it out. He looked at it closely, twirling it between his fingers. Did he really want to do this to himself? It had been no different than any other interrogation. Why should he review something so mundane?

Ryke tossed it onto his desk. He got up and paced the deck of his cabin. He needed distraction. Or a drink.

He went back to the desk and retrieved his delver. There, his secure notes from the current investigation were still on the screen. Ryke tried reading them. He didn't look down at the memory stick on his desk.

It would be easier if he could go on operating as usual. Focus like a laser on his targets, incinerate them, and move along. That was what he'd been doing. Until the Haczyk boy had shown up.

Ryke pounded the table with his fist. Just when he'd managed to forget her. Just when he'd shoved that data stick away from his mind.

A snarl of disgust built at the back of his throat. He scooted into his chair and seized the data stick. Again he plugged it into the delver. Again the password request came.

This time he let the file play. He closed his eyes and listened to the audio as the memories came streaming back.

"Who else do you communicate with? Come now, we have your access codes. Where do they meet?"

"I won't . . . won't submit them to this. My brothers and sisters will escape you."

"You seem so certain about that."

"I have faith in my God, and His Son has promised we will never be taken from His hand. That's all that matters. I won't help you torture them in this world."

"Then you will bear their pain."

A pause. A barely audible thrum bled through the audio feed. Hannah cried out, and in the modern day Ryke nodded approvingly at her anguish, his eyes still shut. Direct neural stimulation—he always saved the best for last. No need to get one's hands dirty when it was much simpler and cleaner to hook microscopic tendrils into the body's nervous system and manipulate its local pain receptors directly.

He opened his eyes, and there she was.

The holographic image of Hannah Haczyk bound to a chair made his breath catch. Her long, brown hair was disheveled and her beautiful face marred by cuts. Defiance and strength burned clearly in her dark eyes, even in a hologram no larger than Ryke's hand. He stared as a miniature of himself strode into view.

"That wasn't fun, was it? We should avoid any further pain. Your diagnostic readings are not good, you know. Just tell me where they are, and you can walk away."

"Liar." She had so wanted to disbelieve him, Ryke mused.

"Often I am, yes, but not in this case. I am very pragmatic. If letting you go nets me an entire enclave of these fundamentalists, then I am perfectly willing to drop all charges and pretend we never crossed paths. Of course, you would have to disavow your faith's exclusivity and affirm our Charter."

Ryke watched Hannah raise her bruised face to meet his own stare, and that look in her eyes unnerved him even across the years. *"You cannot tell me what to believe. My heart is the Lord's to guide, and my conscience will stay clean."*

"You will not relent? Not even for your son or your husband?"

"God . . . will help them understand."

"I hope so. Because you have exhausted the last of my patience."

And then, the part he could never reconcile.

"Then God forgive you."

His own laughter was tinny and grating in the recording. *"Forgive me? For what, doing my duty? Serving my Realm? For protecting it from zealots who would see it crumble in fire?"*

"You are a murderer and a liar. God showed us the way in His own Son when He forgave His enemies as He died nailed to a cross, and for what you have done to me . . . I forgive you too."

So certain. So peaceful. Ryke gritted his teeth. He could not understand her.

He yanked the white data stick out and threw the delver across the room. It clattered against the bulkhead. Though the release satisfied him, Ryke hoped he hadn't broken the device.

He needed a drink.

He unlocked the narrow locker set aside for his meager personal belongings. Inside was a single slender bottle of amber liquid. Ryke unsealed the lid. The aroma wafting from the neck made him close his eyes and smile. Laojiang—Old River, vintage 2567. Fine Xiantian whiskey that shared his birth date. Yes, Nikolaas Ryke needed that drink. He needed to get raging drunk.

He was three tumblers closer to his goal when the door buzzer sounded yet again. Probably Cotes again. "Thousands of constables and officers, and I get paired with that *domkop*," Ryke growled. He managed not to throw the glass. Setting it instead next to the bottle—without spilling it, a feat that impressed his fuzzy brain—he wove a path to the hatch.

He slapped at the release. It took two tries to trigger the lock. "Cotes, this is borderline stalking," he slurred. His clever train of thought careened off track when he saw a very amused

Captain Goro Sasaki standing in the hatchway. The shorter man stood ramrod straight in his black uniform. "Ah. Captain," Ryke said. "Do come in. Care for a drink?"

"No, thank you. I could come back if this is a bad time, Detective Chief Inspector." Sasaki spoke the title with respect, but the laughter was plainly visible in his eyes and cheeks. Even inebriated, Ryke could see it.

"You must find me amusing, Captain." Ryke sank back into his chair. He grabbed the glass and took another swig. The warmth spread through his chest. He closed his eyes. Blasted fine Laojiang.

"Your investigative skills are astounding." Sasaki took a seat near Ryke. "I thought you'd like to know that we've made significant progress with the new cooling vanes."

"Good." Ryke took another drink. "No rocks bashing these off, I take it?"

"The installation is complete, but repairs and testing will take four days. Then we can get underway."

"Four days?" Ryke spluttered his whiskey. Amber liquid dribbled onto the clean white front of his shirt. Why had he left the jacket unsealed? He was a sloppy drunk. "It's already been three days, Captain."

"Yes." Sasaki's lip twitched. "Four more will make seven."

Ryke growled, slamming the glass down on the table. Or at least he tried to—he missed and it clunked to the floor, spilling the dregs. His anger washed away just as suddenly, replaced by weariness. "I don't suppose there are any other ships—more reliable vessels—nearby?"

Sasaki chose to ignore the dig. "Not unless you'd like to charter a merchant navastel or a pirate vessel."

"Hmph." If only Sasaki had paid closer attention to Ryke's contacts. He did have a pirate ship at his beck and call, as a matter of fact. "So, more waiting."

"Yes. You could send a commnote ahead to the Kesek officers in the other systems."

"The officers in the other systems? Hah!" Ryke threw his head back and rubbed his eyes as he looked to the collection of ductwork and wire bundles running along the ceiling. "Oh, Captain, you know so little of the wondrous policies of the Kesek commissioner! There are no officers between here and Bethel."

"None?"

"Zero. You see, our dear commissioner prefers the fear of the unknown to constant interference, at least where these zealots are concerned. Kesek leaves the smaller settlements alone for weeks, even months at a time, and then spends a few days gathering intelligence before sweeping in to conduct mass arrests and raids. Then we blaze away, leaving shattered towns and hopefully wrecked societies in our wake."

Sasaki's expression was a study in disgust. "You sound so proud."

"Shouldn't I be?" Ryke laughed. His throat hurt. "Behold the sheer power of the Koninklijke stabiliteitskracht!"

Sasaki rose. His face was stern. "I had enjoyed quietly mocking you, Ryke," he said, leaving his title off. "But you're no longer entertaining."

"Neither are you. Go fix your ship so I can continue my pursuit." Ryke offered a bitter smile. "And hope I don't decide your arrogant behavior warrants a formal report, Captain. I'm sure I could find all manner of tidbits in your delver."

The door slid shut. Ryke fumed. He pushed off from his chair and staggered across the room for his delver. Then he stopped, thought about it a moment, and dug his comm out of his pocket.

"Cotes!"

"Sir." The response was crisp and immediate.

"What was the last we heard from Captain Bell?"

"Captain Bell?"

Ryke gritted his teeth. "Yes, Cotes, our own pet pirate who has failed twice now to bring me the Bible and its owners."

"Ah. Our last communication indicated she had secured a covert tracking device and was en route to Bethel to secure the Bible."

"Promising?"

"I think so, sir. The tracking device was my own design and is quite simple. Whenever the Bible's possessor accesses the Reach, the device emits a shrouded signal burst that is undetectable by conventional means."

Ryke's mind refused to translate most of that. "That had better work. If she fails again, Cotes, I'll give Captain Sasaki the chance for more target practice."

A pause. "Yes, sir. Is that all?"

"Go away." Ryke snapped the comm off. The cabin was suddenly silent.

Except for the echoes.

I forgive you too.

He swept the bottle off the table. It crashed to the floor. "Blast you!"

• • •

Captain Charlotte Ruby Bell wanted to blink but couldn't. Time was motionless in the millisecond of her ship's shift through the touch tract region surrounding the Gurjarpuri star.

Everything suddenly came unstuck, and her ship was some fourteen light-years away. At Bethel. Green indicators flashed on the flickering monitor attached to her command chair. The Raszewski sphere at the core of her 200-meter navastel *Golden Orchid* had successfully created a quantum singularity, breached space-time, and leapt the ship between two distant points.

Bell sneezed hard. She sniffled but avoided wiping her nose on her already grubby grey and brown work jacket. A patch near the sleeve was working loose. She sneezed again. And twice more. The image on the wide main monitor looming before went fuzzy for a moment as her eyes teared up. Stars, she hated tract shifts.

"You okay, Skipper?" The missile tech stood at his console to her left. He looked queasy.

"Same as usual." Bell gave in and wiped her nose. She scratched the top of her ragged black hair. "You'd think I'd be able to find a doc who could tell me why . . . why . . ." She sneezed hard. "Blast it! Why I sneeze after every single tract shift!"

The missile tech snickered. At the station in front of him, the comm tech whistled a tune as he cycled through comm channels on his board. Bell glanced to the right at her gunner, a lanky fellow with a cybernetic replacement for a left eye and a wiry brown beard. She called him Dennis—he'd never given her a real name. But he was trustworthy enough to be her first mate. As trustworthy as pirates went. "How're we looking?" she asked.

Dennis gave each of his six screens a cursory glance. "No targets, Skipper."

"Good. I . . ." Bell sneezed. She moaned and rubbed the bridge of her nose. "I don't want any surprises."

"Skipper?" The comms man was frowning at whatever he heard on his earpiece. "Got a message floating around out there. Sounds like it was transmitted from Bethel orbit."

Bell winced. Floating around out there. Bad choice of words. She was reminded of her recent imprisonment in a cargo crate after *Natalia Zoja*'s crew got the jump on them. There was a major backfire, if she'd ever seen one. At least Dennis had had the presence of mind to fish them out of space in short order. "What kind of message?"

"Sounds—well, sounds Tiu."

Bell frowned. "Okay, we heard that on the Reach. Some task force got jumped here, or something like that. Can you translate it?"

"My Tiu's rusty but it says something about 'complete destruction' and 'no survivors,'" the comms man reported. "Nothing much beyond self-congratulations."

Bell rubbed her nose again. "So the coast is clear."

"The what?"

"Never mind." Bell looked forward at her helmsman, whose face reflected the glow of several holo-displays. "Take us in. Not too hot—no need to panic 'em."

"Aye, Skipper."

Bell felt the thrum of the antimatter engines through the deck plates and relaxed into her chair. She would feel much more relaxed once they caught this kid and turned him over to Kesek. She shook her head.

"Problem, Skipper?" Dennis stood at his console, eyes still fixed on his displays.

"Yeah. This whole mess." Bell waved her hand as if she could brush it all away. "This dumb book we have to go hunt down for Kesek. Meanwhile we get ourselves shot at, my ship gets holes punched in it, and we get stuffed in crates and set adrift. For what?"

"Three hundred sixty thousand," the gunner said.

Hearing that number raised goosebumps along Bell's arm. "Yeah, well, I've only seen thirty of that. And it's secured away in an account we won't be accessing anytime soon." She sneezed hard.

"Bless you."

"Thanks." She rubbed her nose. "Dennis, we need cash, and then we gotta go hit a few unarmed cargo haulers or something less dangerous."

"No argument there, Skipper." A light flashed on his console. His stoic face cracked with a smile. "Now there we go."

"You got something?" Bell pushed out of her seat. "Let me see."

Dennis stepped aside so Bell had an unobstructed view of his console. She squinted at the red circle flashing on one screen. "That's it. It's still working."

"Someone must have gotten on the Reach." Dennis reached past her and manipulated a control. "It's definitely coming from the planet, though, not orbit. We can tell at this range."

"What do we know about what's in orbit?"

"Not much. I'm picking up a few ships, but no one has their engines lit. Can't tell at this range what they are. Looks like *Natalia Zoja*'s just hanging about in orbit. But she has to be there, if the tracking device is still on the Bible."

"I can't wait to see their faces when we show up."

She sneezed again.

Her anticipation waned a bit over the next several hours. But soon enough *Golden Orchid* was coming up on the planet. Bell kept one eye on the navigator's display that showed her ship flipping end over end and firing off its main drive. The blazing white flare slowed the vessel as it approached Bethel.

The proximity alarm blared. "We got a contact coming around the planet, Skipper!" the navigator called. "Looks like a six-brace."

He manipulated his controls. Bethel appeared as a brilliant blue ball a couple hands widths across. A small silver object peeked around one edge. The navigator pressed more buttons, and the silver object leapt in magnification. Bell grinned. She remembered that ship.

"Running scans now," Dennis said.

"Good. Comms, ring 'em up. Let 'em know we're here."

"You got it—"

"Ah, Skipper?" The navigator's voice carried much less enthusiasm. And he looked nervous. "We got a problem."

"What?"

The navigator pointed wordlessly at the screen.

Another ship was entering the magnification frame around the *Natalia Zoja*. It looked like a dead ringer for the Kesek ship that had tagged along with the pirates at the beginning of this fiasco. Except Bell could see it was not painted matte black but rather a dusky blue-grey.

Dennis answered her pending questions. "Battle corvette, Starkweather flag. ID comes up as *HMS Herald*, attached to Seventh Royal Task Force. Skipper, I've got three more ships coming around behind her."

Bell's heart was in her gut. Two more battle corvettes swung around the planet in tight formation, followed by another more massive ship—a carrier of some sort.

Blast Kesek and their cursed book chasing!

Dennis cleared his throat. "Captain, their armament—"

Bell held up a hand. "Don't even say it, Dennis."

"Aye, Skipper."

"What about that Tiu message? Remember? They said 'total destruction' or some such."

"Looks like it was a decoy."

"Super." Bell sighed.

The comms man tore his wide-open eyes away from the screen long enough to pay attention to his earpiece. "Ah . . . they're hailing us, Skipper."

"I suppose they know who we are?"

The comms man nodded. "You ain't gonna like this."

Bell gave him a furious glare.

"One Commander Verge is requesting our surrender," the comms man said nervously. "She wants us to join her for a discussion with Captain Haczyk."

"Of course she does." Bell wilted in her chair. Her nose was stuffed up, her ship was being targeted by four warships, and her quarry had managed to find bodyguards. Perfect. "Open a channel," she said wearily. "Lemme see if I can get us out of this mess."

CHAPTER 6

October 2602
Bethel Star System
Bethel, New Grace

Baden was having way too much fun. He couldn't wait to tell Ozzy.

He was back in the Starkweather officers' conference room down on the planet's surface, but this time Captain Charlotte Ruby Bell was the object of everyone's attention. The last Baden had seen of the pirate captain, she was out cold and being unceremoniously dumped into an empty cargo crate by Cyril.

She didn't look much better now. Her face was drawn and pinched. She looked like she had swallowed something unpleasant.

Baden figured she looked that way because she was seated across from Colonel Verge and his sister, Commander Verge. Troop Master Sands and Major Mazur stood on either side of her, still as statues. Jason sat on Baden's right, his face expressionless.

"Nice to see you again." Simon leaned back in his chair at Baden's left. He glanced at Baden and winked. Baden wished in the sappiest way possible that he'd had more times like this with his dad—albeit minus the angry pirate.

"Shut it, Haczyk," Bell growled. "You know I ain't got no choice."

"No, you do have a choice." Simon nodded at the Verges. "It's a pretty easy one."

Bell grimaced at him. Baden heard tapping—he realized it was Colonel Verge kicking his boot against the table leg.

"We have accessed all your comm records and questioned your crew," Colonel Verge said.

"Uh huh." Bell folded her arms. "They tell you anything?"

Major Mazur chuckled. It was a hard, cruel sound. Baden shivered. He saw Simon's jaw tense. Easy, Dad.

"They did, but your comm records told us more." Colonel Verge folded his hands atop the table. "Your dealings with Kesek are all there."

"So?" Bell snorted. "It's all legal. I mean—not our profession, maybe, but the contracts. Kesek can do whatever they want, right? And these two were breaking the Tolerance law or charter or whatever. Since when does Starkweather give a rip?"

"You seem to have no qualms about accepting this . . . assignment."

Bell shrugged. "Ain't the first time Kesek's come to one of us with this kind of offer. I've run into a few other captains who do pretty regular work for them. Pays well too."

Commander Verge made a disgusted noise in her throat. "I'd heard rumors of Kesek hiring pirates for their dirty deeds. The king doesn't allow them many of their own ships."

"They don't need 'em with us around." Bell spread her arms wide. "We get it done. Most of the time."

Baden had to cover his mouth. This was so nova. She had no clue.

Her sharp eyes locked on him anyway. "What's so funny, kid? You wouldn't be laughing if Kesek had their hooks in you."

"Yeah, well, they don't." Baden unfurled his grin. "And you—"

"Baden, enough." Simon waved a hand in front of him. "Let the colonel talk."

Baden snapped his mouth shut. His anger pushed any satisfaction out of the way.

"I believe what the young man is trying to say, Captain Bell, is that neither I nor Commander Verge here feel any loyalty toward Kesek." Colonel Verge's eyes narrowed. "Considering my sister and I both survived assassination attempts at their hands."

The arrogance disappeared from Bell's face. She sat up a little straighter in the chair. Baden could almost hear her mind spinning. Major Mazur leaned down by her shoulder. "You see the problem? So. You have choice."

"It is simple. Kesek has not paid you. We will."

Bell tilted her head. "Go ahead."

Colonel Verge nodded. Sands bustled by the table and out the door. Baden waited in the stony silence that followed. He didn't bother to look at Simon—probably trying to make eye contact to see if Baden was okay.

When Sands returned, he carried a slim silver container in both hands. He set it on the table in front of Colonel Verge. "Thank you, Troop Master," Colonel Verge said. Sands took up his post next to Mazur.

Colonel Verge turned the case around. He unsealed the front fasteners. Bell leaned forward ever so slightly. Baden took his eyes off her just for a moment so that he too could see what was inside.

The colonel lifted the lid. Simon whistled low. "Aced," Baden murmured. Bell's eyes went big and round.

The case was full of money. Purple banknotes and orange ones. Mostly purple. Baden had never seen that much money in one place. He had a sudden urge to take it, get on a ship with Gail and Ozzy, and get as far away from Bethel as he could.

"One hundred fifty thousand," Colonel Verge said. He sounded to Baden like he was reciting navigation charts, but his mouth curved into a hard smile. "Cash, of course. Directly from our payroll safe. All yours, if you like. No waiting for Kesek to complete a deal on which they will never follow through."

Bell put on a face that conveyed supreme disinterest. "Uh huh."

"This is yours for the taking. Right now. In return, we ask you to tell no one of what you have seen here."

"That's it? No life-threatening tasks?"

"That's it." Colonel Verge closed the lid with a click. "From me, anyway. Baden?"

All eyes swiveled to search Baden's face. He hoped his cheeks weren't as red as they felt. Simon's stare was especially unnerving. Watch me now, Dad.

"You take this money, and I've—well, *we've* got a proposal for you." He shared a look with Jason.

Bell's eyes went wide. His dad scowled. "What the blazes is this? What are you talking about?"

"Dad, do me a big favor right now." Baden gritted his teeth and hissed out the words. "Shut up."

Simon's face paled. Dangerous muscles worked in his jaw. Before he could burst into whatever tirade he had planned, Commander Verge spoke up.

"Captain Haczyk, your son has a solution that may solve both our problems," she said in her soft but firm voice. "We have no interest in dragging along a pirate captive—"

"Gee, thanks," Bell muttered.

"—and he has another use for her."

To Baden's utter shock, some of the ice on Simon's expression melted. "Let's hear it," he said in clipped tones.

Baden's mouth flapped wide open. He sucked air like a faulty ramjet. "Uh . . . okay. But I need to do this in private. Colonel?"

Colonel Verge nodded. "I don't know the details of his option, Captain Bell, but I suggest you take it and the money. Consider the alternative."

"Like what?"

Major Mazur leaned forward. "Unpleasant. The colonel is good man, yes? I am not. So."

Bell swallowed. She didn't look at Mazur. "I think I get it."

"Good." Colonel Verge stood and gestured everyone from the room. "Captain Haczyk?"

Simon gave Baden one more quizzical yet hostile look. "You better know what you're doing."

"Save it, Dad." Baden locked eyes with him. "I'm getting rid of that book just like you wanted. So stay out of it."

Simon left without another word.

Only Jason remained. "Why's he get to stay?" Bell asked. "Not planning to gas me again, are you?"

"Only if I am provoked," Jason said.

Baden fidgeted in his chair. "So, you just got a great bucket of cash, right?"

Bell drummed her fingers on the tabletop. "Looks like it, kid. Remains to be seen whether I get to enjoy it."

"How's about I add something to it."

"You? Like what, an old pair of boots?"

Baden ignored her condescension. "More like a room full of antique books."

Bell's mouth parted a fraction, but no sound came out. Just like Baden had hoped. That's it. Get greedy.

"A cache of books?" she asked. "What kind?"

"Ancient manuscripts, religious writings." Baden pulled the Bible from his pocket and set it on the table. "Lots more of these too."

"I dunno." Bell pushed back a bit from the table, her eyes on the Bible. "Kesek's awfully keen to get their hands on that kind of stuff. I ain't looking to get in their way."

Baden put on what he hoped was nonchalance. That way she wouldn't see his teeth chattering. "Yeah, but if you get to the goods first, think what you could do with it. Collectors want this stuff—people with real banknotes. They'll pay."

Okay, so he was making that all up. But he caught Jason's very slight nod. They could tell Bell was hooked.

"If books are too great a liability, keep in mind that artwork may also be among the items in this cache," Jason said. "Paintings and sculptures can pass more easily through Kesek's filters."

Bell chewed her lip. "Guess so. Where do you want me to take it?"

"To a safe place. We have the coordinates."

"This safe place got a name or just numbers?"

"It's called Alexandria," Baden said.

"Oh, yeah?" Bell wagged a finger at them. "Heard something about that. Some rumor about a gold mine of relics—but that's a myth. Usually you hear it from drunks."

"It is not a myth," Jason said. "We have coordinates. We need you to take us there."

"Hold up." Bell jabbed a finger at Baden. "I thought you were on some kind of mission with that bibble."

"Bible. B-I-B-L-E."

"Whatever."

Baden ran his hand across the cover. Some kind of mission. Yeah, that about summed it up. He'd wanted only to pawn this thing off; instead he'd run smack into a planet full of people who viewed him as some kind of herald. "I guess I am. But I—we need to get to this Alexandria place. And you got a ship. This way, we can slip by."

"Okay. So you want me to take you two to this place and load up the cache."

"You got it."

"And how do you know Kesek won't just track you down again?"

Jason leaned forward. "Because you will take care of whatever tracking device you planted on *Natalia Zoja*."

Bell nodded slowly. "So that's what the cash is for."

Baden's throat tightened. He hoped this was all worth it. The idea of dealing with pirates made him sick. They'd killed his mom, after all.

But he didn't think she'd want him to die for this book.

"So, what do you say?" Baden held his breath.

Bell chewed on her lip. Her face didn't look nearly as pale with the late afternoon sun streaming in the conference room windows. "I do this, I walk away with the money, right? And whatever I want from this cache?"

"Within reason, Captain. I trust we can agree on that." His voice brooked no argument.

Bell's eyes went unfocused for a moment. No doubt she was remembering how Jason had dealt with her boarding party and wiped the floor with the Kesek officers. "Yeah. We can deal."

Baden exhaled. "All right, the tracker. Where's it at?"

"Gimme the book."

Baden hesitated. He slowly pushed it toward her. Bell stood from her seat and reached for it. She flipped it onto its backside, revealing an indentation. Baden squinted. "What the blazes?"

"Never noticed, huh?" Bell dug a slender pocketknife from her coat. Jason visibly tensed. "Relax, pal, I ain't that stupid," she said. Instead she dug the blade into the cover. A sliver of white about the length of a finger slipped out onto the table. Bell skewered it with a deft stab. A tiny wisp of smoke curled into the air.

Baden peered at it. "That's it?"

"That's it." Bell eyed it admiringly. "Kesek made a beaut. Got it matched to my own special tranq pistol. You guys didn't even see me do it."

Actually, Baden did recall the silent gun she'd fired at him aboard *Natalia Zoja*. He'd thought it was a tranquilizer gun, like she'd said.

"Well, I suppose I'd better get this to the commander." Bell slipped the knife and the tracker into her pocket. "You'd better make good on this. Last thing I need is Kesek on my hide. Get me my money and I'm out."

"Of course. Thank you, Captain," Jason said.

She left with a considerable swagger to her step. Baden exhaled, his body deflating into the chair. "Man, are we spaced or what?"

"Indeed."

"We don't even know what's there. At least we know where it is."

"I have thought about that. I believe the coordinates are to sundoor."

Baden shivered with excitement. "A new sundoor? That'd be an amazing find, if it's true."

"It makes the most sense for Alexandria. If no one ever saw a ship tract shift there, it would remain utterly hidden. But I still do not like giving her the location for Alexandria."

"Hey, it won't matter much when we load up the whole cache."

"You are assuming we will be able to load it all. I have no idea how much is there. It could take days or weeks to move."

"I don't like the sound of that."

"We must be prepared for that possibility, Baden. Perhaps your friend Owen could help us with their navigational computers." Jason got up from the table. "Are you coming?"

Baden nodded. "Yeah. I got an appointment to keep."

"Oh? With whom?"

"With Heng. Since I'm taking the Bible with me, I'd better make sure they've got something to remember it by."

For all his complaining, Baden found it somehow peaceful to be back in front of a crowd at the New Grace town square.

There were fewer wrecked robots here now. Local workers and Starkweather Lancers had spent much of the day clearing away debris. It left room for more people to pack the square. Baden tried estimating but lost count somewhere around six hundred. The setting sun lit the whole crowd with murky yellows and oranges. Long shadows stretched out behind them.

He stood on a meter-high makeshift platform. Heng waited off to one side, his face beaming. Baden had no doubt he'd made the man's year by offering to read from the Bible again.

Baden cleared his throat. His stomach was churning. He looked about for the crew and was relieved to see them standing off to one side under a set of half-burnt trees. Owen grinned and gave him a thumbs-up; he waved his modified delver aloft. Gail stood by him, her eyes aglow. That was enough to wipe away Baden's nerves.

His dad leaned against the tree with Cyril standing behind him. Baden made eye contact with him for a moment. He'd debated telling Simon what he'd learned about his mom, but this was a rough time for both of them. Besides, Baden knew how much trust his dad placed in Jason—next to none.

It didn't matter. Baden opened the Bible and leafed through its pages. He wasn't doing this for his dad, or even for Heng. Sure, he wanted to help out the Bethelites. But this was more than that. He was doing this for his mom.

His finger came to rest on the Gospel according to John. He figured that was a good place to start, for now. There was always more to read later. If he read the whole thing he'd be standing here for three days, at least.

"Okay, so, uh . . ." Baden gestured vaguely. He didn't know what to say. "Guess I'd better get reading. 'In the beginning was the Word, and the Word was with God, and the Word was God. He was in the beginning with God. All things were made through him, and without him was not anything made that was made. In him was life, and the life was the light of men. The light shines in the darkness, and the darkness has not overcome it.'"

He read on through the chapter, his thoughts blurring in the text as he followed the people through the ministry of this Jesus guy. The crazy man John, dressed in woolly animal skins and shouting proclamations from the middle of a river—now there was devotion. Baden went on, ignoring the chill in the air and the dimming light. He didn't even notice time slipping by until a light suddenly illuminated the text.

Baden looked up, puzzled. Jason held a small lamp over the Bible's pages. "You may need this," he said with a smile.

Baden was abruptly aware that he had a sharp pain in his neck and a throbbing sensation in his feet. "How long have I been at this?"

"About three hours."

"Three hours!" Blast, no wonder he was tired. Baden looked out over the crowd. It had grown even larger. Most of the people were now seated on blankets and mats; it gave the square the appearance of an old quilt. Their faces watched him, glowing dimly under the lights around the edge of the square that were blinking to life in pairs.

He looked down at the Bible. Blazes, he was almost through the next book—something called Acts. How'd he lose track of time like that?

It reminded Baden of the times he heard the words in his head. He looked up at the darkening sky. The stars were just appearing. They looked strange—muted and dim when viewed through a thick atmosphere. Not like the shining jewels he saw from *Natalia Zoja*.

Are You out there somewhere, God? What are You doing to me?

Baden blinked and looked back at the crowd. That's when he noticed Gail was gone. Suddenly he felt the urgent need to talk to her, or at least be near her.

"Are you all right, Baden?"

"Where's Gail?"

Jason tilted his head. "She left with Assemblyman Heng. I believe they were headed for the harbor."

Baden pocketed the Bible. He got down off the platform, then stopped. The crowd was still waiting. "Um, that's all for tonight. So . . . good night."

Most of the crowd applauded and cheered. A few groans mixed with the celebration—latecomers Baden had seen drift in to the sides of the crowd. Owen made his way through the masses. "Got good audio on that, Hack." He held up his delver. "Gonna get some cash out of this for sure."

"Ozzy, can't you just give it to them?" A chill breeze brushed past Baden's face. He really wanted to find Gail.

"What, at no cost?" Owen made a face. "No profit in that."

"Ah, we have company." Jason pointed over Baden's shoulder.

A crowd of some dozen Bethelites had gathered in silence behind him. Another two or three dozen men, women, and children of all ages were making their way over to the knot. They must have stayed after Baden finished reading. "Oh, boy. Who are they?"

"Your fan club," Owen snickered.

"Shut up."

"Mister Haczyk." A tall, elderly man near the front addressed him. "We were wondering . . . could you answer some of our questions?"

Baden stared, befuddled. "Questions?"

"Yes. About the Word." The man cleared his throat, looking unsure how to proceed. "Well . . . what does it say about the body of Christ?"

"Must it be bread and wine?" someone piped up toward the back.

"Should we baptize our little children?" asked a mother holding a red-cheeked infant.

"What about the dead? Do we pray for them?"

"Can we pray *to* them?"

"What does it say about the Holy Spirit? Is it a being or a power, a force?"

"Please, what does it say about . . ."

"Can you tell us about . . ."

"I want to know . . ."

Baden stumbled back as the questions came faster and faster, one and two on top of each other. "Whoa, hey, wait a microsec!" he yelled. "Stop it! I'm not some preacher! I just read it to you. I don't have answers."

The elderly man held his hands together. "But you have the true Word! Please, you must share the meaning!"

"Please, yes!" others implored.

They moved closer. Jason interposed himself between Baden and the crowd. "You must leave the boy be," he said, his voice loud and commanding. As one body, the crowd flinched. "Do not expect him to bring you wisdom. That is from God alone."

With that, Jason hustled them away from the crowd. Baden couldn't help looking back over his shoulder at the expectancy on their faces, especially that of the elderly man.

"Why do they want to know what's in there so badly?" he whispered. "I mean, I've read it all . . . and it's . . . I just don't know."

"You have been given a great gift, Baden, and I pray you will soon understand it," Jason said as they hurried toward town.

"The gift of a colossal pain in the rear," Owen said.

The trio made their way into the downtown. Baden couldn't figure why Gail had disappeared on them. They soon found several people running toward the harbor. "What's wrong?" Jason asked a passerby.

"One of the offworlders! This way!" The man sprinted on.

"Gail?" Baden broke into a run. "Gail! No!"

"Baden, wait!" Jason and Owen took off after him.

Baden ran as fast as he could. He kept the other man in his sight, desperate to find Gail. If anything happened to her . . . He shook the thought from his mind. In his fear, he tried something new. "Please, don't let her be hurt," he murmured.

He reached the pier just ahead of Jason and Owen. His boots skidded as he came up short at the water's edge. No, not what he expected to see at all.

A few scattered dock lights illuminated the shallow water at the end of a landing ramp. Heng was standing in the water, his work clothes wet up to his stomach. He was grinning like it was his birthday. He was pulling something up from underwater. Bethelites lined the docks. They cheered and raised their arms to the sky. Some were on their knees and had their eyes closed. A few were singing. Baden longed for the simplicity of his Duke Ellington collection.

"Rise from the dead, our new sister in Christ, and live!" Heng said. "Let the Lord God Almighty wash away your sins with the blood of the Lamb!"

He raised a very wet and very happy looking Gail Salpare from underwater.

Baden scarcely took it in. "What happened?"

Jason trotted up beside him. Owen came soon after, panting and red in the face. Jason looked down into the water. "Baden, my friend, she has been baptized."

CHAPTER 7

October 2602
Earth Star System
Earth, North America, New England Coast

Cold ocean waves hammered the rocks along the tree-trimmed coastline. Winds whipped up whitecaps as rain pounded down from the clouds, soaking the trees and forming tiny ponds among the gnarled roots of pines. The town huddled around the harbor was quiet this morning, in the midst of the storm, with most people secure in their offices, shops, and homes, avoiding any unnecessary travel outdoors. It was far too unpleasant, and even after centuries of living in the same communities, most Mainers didn't like it.

Tara Douglas-Verge pulled her gaze away from the rain-spattered window not far from her chair. Her mood matched the foul weather perfectly.

She sat at a long, creaking wooden table with twelve other women and men of varying ages. They wore an eclectic collection of clothes—flowing Muhteremi robes, exotic Tiaozhanese floral cloaks, plain Rozsade suits, and colorful Terran garb. They were the last members of Congress, the only ones who'd managed to avoid Kesek arrest. Tara credited the secret pact they'd all signed with providing advance warning—the pact to preserve the Realm of Five in the event of a Kesek takeover.

The hastily arranged boardroom was an old parlor. Dust-covered portraits of men in high collars and women in severe hairdos made Tara wonder about the history of the house. Peeling and faded wallpaper hung limply from the walls. Only a row of brand-new, soft lights were different. She was thankful the old house was nestled deep in one of the less-traveled neighborhoods, among nearly identical houses of similar vintage.

"Our discussions are pointless until we have proof of the deception," one elderly woman said. Tara listened with interest to Tze Biyu, the senior representative from Tiaozhan and the only member of Congress from that world to escape the roundup. There were three other Congressmen in the group; the remainder were alternates like Tara. "Planning for our next steps is unwise unless those next steps include acquiring this proof," Tze said.

"I wouldn't advise holding our collective breaths," Devereaux Garrison said. The normally suave chairman of the Congress of Worlds looked haggard. His dark skin had taken on a sickly pall. He appeared to have not shaved in several days, and there were deep shadows under his eyes. He, at least, was not alone here—two Earth alternates to Congress were seated to his left.

"We cannot argue. Nothing will be done." Representative Gostislav Baran of Rozsada shifted his bulk uncomfortably in his chair next to Tara. "Is nonsense. Kesek is hunting for us.

All we agree on is what we should not do. This is not progress, yes? So we are failures."

"What can we do? We have limited resources, Representative Baran, especially since our names are all affixed to Kesek warrants," Garrison said.

"We must enter into direct negotiations with Kesek," Tze said.

"What? Pah. That is lunacy." Baran rubbed at his moustache.

"They can be reasonable," Tze said implacably. "With the proper acquiescence and application of funds . . ."

"Just a moment—you would have us buy Kesek off?" Garrison looked incredulous. Tara knew how he felt, but she held her own tongue. "No, that will never work. They would stab us in the backs as soon as the money ran out. I suggest we contact the commandant of the Earth Rangers Corps."

"Yes, wonderful." Baran's voice was heavy with sarcasm. "Gironde has already brought them into his camp."

"And how would you know that, Representative?"

"RG is never wrong on such things. So. It is true, Mister Chairman."

"I suppose your pet terrorists would do the job for us, then?" Garrison snapped.

"Their existence is an affront to our king," Tze said.

"You insult my people!" Baran said. He rose from his chair. "Rozsada will not stand for this!"

That started up a fresh round of accusations, counter-accusations, and name-calling. The tempo increased until Tara's rising temper got the better of her. She slapped the table. Water glasses and delvers bounced. The sound echoed through the room and her hand stung. "Stop!"

The combined noises cut off all the arguing. Everyone stared at her. Only the rain rattling the slanted roof interrupted. Tara glared around the table at them all. "This is shameful and a waste," she said. "We have more than enough ideas in this room to proceed with a coherent plan, and all you can manage to do is argue about whose idea is the best and why it should take precedence."

"Perhaps my colleague would like to take a moment to reflect on the situation." Jerome Abernathy was the senior of Starkweather's Congressional representatives. His family was the most influential commercial force on Starkweather and long-time allies of the king. He smiled politely. The overhead lights gleamed off his brown balding head as he brushed his immaculate black moustache. "There is much to consider."

"I've done enough reflecting, thank you, Representative," Tara said. Ignoring his stricken expression, she continued, "The situation is simple: Kesek now runs the Realm. They have further tightened their restriction on communications access, have increased arrests of so-called 'dissidents,' and have illegally detained the majority of Congress."

"And the king," Baran said.

"Of course! How silly of me!" Tara's sarcasm brought murmurs of discontent from some of the alternates. "We are all fairly convinced that Kesek is behind the abduction of the king and his family. Representative Baran's sources have all but confirmed it. I doubt very much the Hamarkhis planned these attacks on Trebizond Base and the task forces. If we can prove this, we can bring Kesek's sympathizers over to our side."

"So Kesek has sympathizers now? Pray tell, who are they?" Abernathy said.

Tara ticked off the list on her fingers. "The Earth Rangers Corps, the remnants of the Home Fleet and Admiral Sutar's returning ships, the new so-called 'armed private merchantmen' our dear commissioner has made out of his amnesty deals with pirates . . . Is that enough for you?"

"Relax, my dear," Abernathy said. "I was merely asking for proof."

"There is proof." Baran inadvertently bumped the table with his stomach. Abernathy reached to steady his glass of water. "RG has confirmed these things."

"So Rozsada's Rezolucjagrupa has done its research," Abernathy said. "Very convenient."

"There's no need for that," Tara said. "If it weren't for RG, few of us would be here right now. Yourself included, Representative Abernathy."

The others chuckled. Abernathy looked miffed but held up a hand in surrender. "Point well made."

Tze leaned forward to speak. "What course would you advocate, Professor Douglas-Verge?"

"Madam Representative, we know the commissioner is a meticulous record keeper who prides himself in his secrets. Somewhere, he must have recordings or data of his actions. We must get them. It's that simple."

"It's hardly simple," Abernathy said. "Do you want to be the one who walks in there and requests it?"

"No." Tara looked at Baran.

Baran drummed his beefy fingers on the table. "Ah, yes, we do have assets who could—theoretically—accomplish this task."

"What?" Abernathy asked. "You can get someone in and out?"

"*Nie ma problemu.*" The representative leaned forward, gestures becoming animated as he explained. "The difficulty is finding where commissioner keeps his records, yes? Next part is finding transmission station to send message to rest of Realm, so they know of Kesek's betrayal."

"Oh. How do your assets intend to accomplish that?" Abernathy asked.

"With money. And other assets."

"Remind me to send a thank-you commnote to the RG director when this all settles down."

"Of course." Baran's bushy moustache twitched. "*Dzi´kuj´ bardzo.*"

"What news do we have of the other representatives?" Tara directed the question to Garrison.

"None. There is absolutely nothing on the Reach." He gestured to Baran. "Nor do our Rozsade friends have any details."

Baran confirmed this with a curt nod. "There is no news. Kesek has them—we know nothing more. I have heard rumors the representatives may be executed."

The gloom intensified. Tara couldn't bear to look out the window at the increasing rain. It drummed heavily on the roof above. "Regardless of what has happened, we have to agree to this action," she said firmly. "If we can convince the military and the powerful families that Kesek was behind the attacks and the king's disappearance, they will be more willing to rise against them when the time is right. In the minds of the people, the king represents all that is well with the Realm, and Kesek symbolizes all that is terribly wrong. I don't know about you, but I'm tired of hiding myself and my daughters in a safe house, dreading every commnote."

Garrison nodded. For the first time in the past few days, he looked refreshed. "You're right. We are the king's Congress, after all, and we have more right to rule than Kesek ever will."

Within moments, the thirteen had cast their lot with Tara's plan. Now all that remained was for RG to make it happen.

The house had been swept clean of cobwebs and scanned for eavesdropping devices prior to the secret Congress's arrival. But in this old a structure, there were still nooks and crannies through which dedicated vermin could scurry.

One such vole had sat silently on its haunches, hidden in a hole behind the thin wall of the meeting room. It listened to every word.

At the conclusion of the meeting, the vole squirmed its way through bends in the framing and gaps in insulation to a hole in the foundation. It burst into the rain at a dead run, sprinting across the street and down the slippery sidewalk. It did not stop running until it reached the end of the block, then dashed around the corner to a waiting navy blue groundcar. Detective Inspector Toers waited patiently by its door.

This was a far better situation than his unceremonious awakening in the plains—of Nebraska, it had turned out—a few days before. And as he'd predicted, the commissioner had been less than pleased. It was only Toers's prior exemplary record that had kept him from being executed outright. He breathed a sigh in relief for the umpteenth time. Now he'd been given a chance at redemption.

Very well. Last time he'd gone for overwhelming force and had been foiled. This time he chose finesse. That was why he wore no uniform, just a simple brown jacket and blue trousers.

The vole stopped at his feet. Toers lowered a cracker smeared with peanut spread. It nibbled happily on its snack and let Toers scoop him up carefully. The inspector took care to harm neither the animal nor the organic recording device he knew was implanted in its body. He opened the driver's door of the groundcar and slid in, taking a moment to wipe rain from his jacket with his free hand. "Good boy," he said. He set the vole gently into a clear container on the passenger seat and sealed the lid. "Now, let me hear it all."

Toers activated the translation system in the portable system secured to the floor of the groundcar. A series of lights implanted around the lid of the container strobed, and the vole stood on its haunches, seemingly mesmerized. The lights flickered, and then changed color from yellow to green. Toers manipulated another set of controls, and sound poured forth from the tiny speakers.

After several minutes of dampening, sorting, and cleaning, the translator had turned the recording stored in the vole's body into human-recognizable speech. Toers smiled broadly as the entire secret meeting of the resisting Congress aired in his groundcar.

"Success." He grinned broadly and transferred the data to his delver. Then he punched the transmit button.

NO SIGNAL.

Toers stared at the device, incredulous. He punched the control again. Harder.

NO SIGNAL.

"Not possible. Unless . . ." He inquired of his delver to define the signal blockage.

There was a dead zone emanating from his groundcar. And only his groundcar.

Toers cursed and smacked the steering controls. Someone knew. He didn't know how they had tracked him, but they'd put some kind of signal blocker in or under his rented groundcar. He shoved the door open angrily and stepped out into the rain, anxious to find the source of his troubles.

He came face-to-face with a woman.

Not just any woman. Even without her aquiline profile partially obscured by a forest-green cap, he'd know her. "You."

The woman smiled back. She gestured politely for him to get back in the groundcar. Toers caught a glimpse of the slender knife blade in her hand. "Please. Let us get inside. I do not like the rain."

Toers gritted his teeth but got in. Before he could think about pulling his concealed pistol, the woman slipped into the rear passenger seat directly behind him. The slamming of the groundcar doors cut off the gentle hiss of the rain. Only the drops drumming on the roof filled the silence.

Toers did manage a peek in the rear view mirror. A pair of lovely dark eyes stared back from a cold, composed face. "You were there, in the mountains," he said.

"Flattery," the woman said. "Could not forget a pretty woman like myself, could you? I didn't forget you either, Detective Inspector Toers."

"Najwa. That's what they called you. Who are you with?" Toers demanded. "Does Congress have its own spies?"

"Now, no answers to those first two," Najwa said. "That is a professional secret. I have been watching you for, oh, three or four hours. I find meditating on the sutras of the Prophet a peaceful way to pass the time. Takes the mind off muscle cramps."

Toers gripped the controls. "You planted the blocker in this car."

"Such a bright student." Something cold and sharp pressed against the back of Toers's neck. He swallowed. This was no way to die. "Now, drive. Take us out of town, along the coastal route. North."

Toers complied. He guided the groundcar through the town streets, past a handful of pedestrians running to get out of the rain, and right below the granite steps of the local constabulatory. It was galling. Soon they were on a rising, winding road lined on both sides by thick trees. Toers caught sight of the ocean and wave-splattered rocks through gaps in the tree line.

"Ingenious, and diabolical," Najwa said from behind him. Toers looked again in the mirror. She gestured with the tip of the knife at the vole in its case and its accompanying hardware. "No doubt this is how you circumvented security at the house. It is a shame I will take it with me. You, on the other hand, are a liability."

He went cold inside. So much for redemption. He'd failed his commissioner, and Kesek.

They came to a sharp curve in the road. Toers smirked at the sight. Perhaps . . .

He wrenched the controls to the left, then right again, ducking against the door as Najwa's blade whipped through his hair, grazing his scalp.

She reached for him, but he had already sent the car into a wild spin, the motion slamming her against the rear passenger window. Toers hit the seat release and leaned back hard, pinning her legs down. She yelped. The knife clattered to the floor.

Toers slid the groundcar across the road, scraping its right side against a guardrail next to the rocky hillside. Sparks flew as it screamed in protest along the rail. Toers took advantage of its relatively secure trajectory to twist about in his seat and punch Najwa in the face. She wriggled to avoid him, trying to block his blows as she maneuvered for more room. She brought her feet up against the back of the lowered seat and shoved hard against it. Toers grunted as he was smashed against the console.

This sent the groundcar skidding across the wet pavement in the opposite direction. A hovercraft coming in the opposite lane blared its warning horn in alarm as the two vehicles nearly collided head-on. Toers was unable to react, but the hovercraft driver did not have his own face smashed against his console—he desperately tried to gain altitude. The hovercraft almost rose above the groundcar but failed to clear it by a few centimeters.

The long, jarring scrape sent the groundcar into a spin even as the hovercraft glanced off the roof, arcing into the trees and tumbling twice end over end before slamming flat on its belly on the ground.

Toers pushed back against the seat. He gritted his teeth as he inched himself away from the console. With his free hand he groped for his gun, still sandwiched in its holster. He pulled it free as Najwa wriggled from behind him.

He turned and fired, the bullets piercing glass and the composite sides of the groundcar. One lucky shot nicked Najwa's arm, causing her to yelp.

Toers's glow of victory dimmed when the view of rainy skies swirling outside the rear windscreen was replaced by the wet bark of a very thick elm.

The groundcar's right rear corner bashed into the tree, banking the vehicle sharply off to one side and sending it careening down a shallow embankment. It narrowly missed more trees as it tumbled toward the rocks along the ocean. Toers had an instant to brace himself before it landed with a titanic crash and his vision went black.

Najwa shook herself awake. Her ears were ringing. She made a quick inventory of her injuries—minor scrapes and abrasions, a deep cut on her forehead, severe pain in her left forearm.

Manageable.

A gentle rain played a tune on the groundcar. The winds had died down, and a pervasive mist was settling outside. Najwa pulled herself out of the groundcar. It sat crumpled, torn, and beaten against boulders at the ocean's edge. Hydrogen hissed as it escaped from the fuel cell exhaust vents. Other than that, and the pounding of waves against rocks, there was silence.

She saw the battered driver's side door propped open. A trail of muddy bootprints led up the hillside toward the tree-lined road. Najwa watched Toers stumbling up. He cradled the container with the vole under his right arm and a gun in the other. She couldn't let him get away.

Najwa sprinted up the hill, ignoring the pain in her arm as she ran. Toers was reaching for something in his pocket—a comm or a delver. Either way, her alarm increased. The signal blocker extended its influence a ways from the groundcar, but not very far.

He was raising it to his face when she barreled into his back.

Toers cried out. Najwa wrenched him around, ignoring his shouts. The delver tumbled down the hillside. They grappled for the gun. Toers pushed her back toward a stand of trees. His face was twisted with rage and pocked by red slashes where glass had shredded his cheeks. His eyes flicked to her hurt arm.

Before she could dodge, he struck at the injury like a viper. Najwa groaned but immediately switched her grip. Toers dropped his precious box and pushed her against the trees.

Except for the intermittent grunt and the heavy breathing, they said nothing, made no demands and offered no negotiation. They struggled against each other, arms straining, hands clenched about the gun, until Toers kicked at her. Najwa backed away. Toers aimed the gun and pulled the trigger.

Nothing.

He gawked at the weapon. Najwa threw the ammunition clip aside and lashed out with her fist. Toers went sprawling. He rolled over and came back up with a small serrated knife.

Toers thrust with the blade but found only air. He gasped as Najwa struck him in the center of his chest. This time her hand wasn't empty. She'd drawn her own blade.

Toers stared down at the protruding hilt. Blood seeped around its edge. He looked back up at her, but his eyes were blank. He crumpled to the ground.

Najwa stood there in the rain. She clenched the knife in her hand and panted for breath. She closed her eyes and let the cold drench her body. "To God belongs the east and the west," she whispered. "Whichever way you turn there is the face of God. *Allahu ahkbar.*"

She repeated the words her grandfather gave her. They helped somewhat, but not enough. Najwa knelt and rifled through Toers's pockets for his comm, feeling a twinge of regret at disturbing his body. She found it and secured it in her own coat pocket. Then she scooped up the box containing the vole and Toers's delver. Her hands shook as she checked the delver's signal queue.

Relief flooded her. Toers hadn't got the signal out past the blocker.

Sirens howled in the distance. Najwa spotted smoke drifting above the trees, probably from the hovercraft they'd run off the road. No telling when the authorities would spot the gash Toers's groundcar had left in the hillside.

Najwa grabbed Toers and heaved him up over her shoulder. Gritting her teeth, she staggered under his weight but kept moving, not stopping until they were behind a trio of round boulders. Each was the size of a large table. She eased Toers's body to the ground. Sparing only the slightest glance at his still form, she took off through the woods.

There was a protocol in place for this scenario. Najwa hoped it was ready.

A buzzing sound echoed behind her. She ducked behind a gnarled elm and hazarded a glance back. The trees shielded her from view of the road, but she could still see the wreck. She couldn't tell what was going on at this range until she dug a pair of binoculars from her belt. She wiped the rain from her face as she looked through.

A pair of drone minicopters hovered over the wreckage like huge metallic bees. Their two pairs of rotors beat at the damp air and churned up the grass as beady red optic sensors scanned for footprints. Najwa could imagine them conversing in code as they followed the muddy trail to the edge of the woods. There they buzzed closer to the ground.

Najwa watched as a small hatch cracked open on the smooth underbelly of one drone. A quadramount about the size of a canine dropped down to the ground. It lowered its sharp-edged head close to the grass and dirt. Najwa swore. If the antennae on its back were any indication, it was linked to a human handler somewhere nearby. Its sensors were calibrated to track human DNA—especially blood.

The quadramount's head snapped up. It pounced forward into the woods. There was no doubt in Najwa's mind—it would find Toers's body in seconds.

She crept off into the mist.

Tara was staring out the window of the meeting room when Baran approached her. Everyone else had reconvened to other rooms following the conference. "Professor, there is a problem."

"That's not what I want to hear, Gostislav." Tara sighed. "What?"

"One of our operatives intercepted a Kesek man down the street. He monitored our meeting."

Tara closed her eyes. Fear wrenched her insides. Not only for herself, but also for her daughters. "He has certainly transmitted what he knows. We must—"

"*Nie*," Baran said. "He has not yet transmitted message. Operative intercepted. She is . . . engaged with him."

"Can he be stopped?"

"Perhaps. Now we see if she returns, yes?"

Najwa pulled up behind a shallow ledge. Her breath came in ragged gasps. It was no use. She wasn't going to outrun that thing.

Twisting to one side, she peeked up over the ledge. She took care to hide herself behind a large curling tree root.

The quadramount burst into view from behind some bushes. Its glowing blue optical band glared unfeelingly at the surroundings. Mud streaked its normally unmarred charcoal grey and green body. Najwa watched as it began a slow encircling of the immediate area. She groped into a pocket for the gun she needed. She had only one shot.

She threw a rock hard to her left. The quadramount froze. Its head snapped immediately in that direction. Najwa steadied a slender, pale blue pistol on the ledge and fired.

The shimmering pulse looking like a heat wave on a hot paved surface struck the quadramount on its antennae-covered back. It lurched and twitched as sparks rippled over its body. Najwa pulled herself over the ledge and pounded across the clearing. The stun effect was temporary—she had only seconds.

She grabbed the quadramount by its articulated neck and pulled it back. Bracing herself, she jabbed her knife deep into its optical band.

It jolted in her arms like a spooked horse. Convulsions wracked its body. Then it abruptly went still. The blue light faded from its optical band.

Najwa exhaled in a shuddering gasp. She sagged to the ground. The quadramount lay still in the mud. She yanked her knife free.

Staggering to her feet, Najwa crept up the hillside toward the road. She peered along its winding stretch.

A hovercar approached. It was a plain white civilian model, completely ordinary.

Najwa watched as the hovercraft slowed just around the next bend, out of sight of the police. It had barely stopped when she bolted from the ragged hedges along the road. She tumbled into the open side door, gasping, "Go!"

She rolled back into a low bench seat as the hovercraft sped forward. "*Jak leci?*" The female driver's stern voice was barely audible over the hum of the fans.

Najwa winced as she held her arm. Blood trickled from her forehead. "I have been better. You did not encounter any trouble?"

The driver was a thin, blonde woman with pinched face. "Pah. They did not need one of us from RG for this. A girl with more cleavage than sense would have fared as well with police roadblock back there."

Najwa could not hide a chuckle. "Could I trouble you for a bandage?"

"Under your seat."

"Excellent." Hoisting herself up onto the bench seat, Najwa secured her restraints. She pulled the box containing the vole from her coat and tucked it beside her. The creature looked scared and perplexed, but unhurt. Najwa found the med-kit and pulled a small tube from it. She positioned it over her cut and squeezed. The milky gel oozed across the wound. She waited a moment as it hardened. She tested it—a solid seal.

"Thank you."

"Welcome. Hold on, we are on scenic route to house."

At that, the hovercraft veered abruptly off the road to the left. It buzzed up an embankment and onto a near-abandoned dirt track through the trees. There was barely room for the vehicle.

Najwa allowed herself to relax. The dirt track made a wide loop around the town and would bring her back to the safe house. She ignored the slap-slap of pine branches against the hovercraft's windows and closed her eyes. She needed the rest.

• • •

Tara chewed her lip as she watched the local news report play out on the holo display in the living room of the meeting house. The suave commentator's voice confirmed her fears.

"Authorities will not comment on the status of their investigation, except to say that the inspector died on impact when his groundcar slid down an embankment . . ."

Behind her, Baran rumbled, "Nothing more than official line. Even news agencies are in Kesek's grip."

"How can they be anything else when Kesek controls all the information channels?"

Tara turned her gaze to Najwa, seated in a wooden chair at the back of the room. She looked a great deal different from the poised, elegant woman who'd rescued her from the Big Horn Mountains—a sealed cut marred her forehead, as did numerous scratches, and her left forearm was wrapped in a bandage. Najwa cradled a mug of steaming coffee in both hands and had her own eyes locked on Baran as he paged through the confiscated delver.

"Excellent work." He nodded, satisfied with what she'd discovered. "And this animal you found . . . it is extraordinary."

Najwa plucked a bit of cheddar off the tray of food set before her. She dropped a crumb into the box at her side. The vole gobbled it up greedily. "I only regret I could not retrieve the translator device from the groundcar wreckage. It would have made an easier job for the boys in Analysis."

"Do not worry. You kept our secrets from Kesek. This leaves us with matter we discussed earlier, then." Baran spread his hands apart. "Your operative-in-charge has already given us clearance to acquire your services."

"I see." Najwa hesitated. "There are many ways this idea can go wrong."

"Optimist, aren't you?" Tara took a seat opposite Baran. She eyed Najwa's tray. "Not hungry?" she asked. When the operative shook her head, Tara plucked an apple off a plate.

"Najwa says what I have already pointed out," Baran said. "There are many dangers in mission we have tasked her. It comes so soon after she risked her own life on our behalf."

"Well, I'd say that's part of her job description." Tara took a crackling bite, chewed on the apple for a bit, then swallowed before continuing, "We're all in the business of risking our lives, for now. If you can get us the information, we will transmit it."

"If I may?" Najwa's tone was firm. "I would be honored to undertake this mission for Rozsada and the Crown. This must be left to RG."

"We are in your debt, Najwa. Doubly so now." Tara said. "Thank you."

The slender woman rose, and bowed at the waist. "It is mine to serve."

"And will you serve us as well as you serve Allah?" Tara still wasn't comfortable with having a potential fanatic on her hands. She advocated tolerance and freedom, true, but it was different when facing one of the Realm's more superstitious citizens.

Najwa, to her credit, didn't bat an eyelash. "His will is the one I seek. But I have pledged myself to uphold the Crown."

"Make sure you keep that in mind," Tara said sternly.

• • •

An hour later, Tara stood in the greenhouse along the south side of the house. She watched as Najwa departed in a brown hovercraft—this one was a different model from the one that had brought her to the house. Tara absentmindedly fingered the petals of nearby begonias. With the other, she raised a mug of fragrant coffee to her mouth. It was a Tiaozhan blend called *Ning*. It was a precious commodity on the interstellar trade routes.

"Mother?" Bridget and Julianna stood in the doorway. Bridget fingered the sleeve of her red blouse. "What's going to happen now?"

Tara reached out for her youngest child's hand and drew her near. "We wait and we pray, Bridget. I have faith your father and Alec and all our family will survive this."

Even as the words left her mouth, she harbored doubt. Julianna frowned at her. She was dressed more casually than her sister, in a work shirt and pants. "You don't really mean it, do you?"

"Stop it!" Bridget was near tears. "You don't know that something's happened to them!"

"I know they walked into a trap, we haven't heard from them, and Kesek is after us!" Bridget swiped at a begonia and decapitated the blossom.

Tara released Bridget's hand and put her hand on Julianna's face. Some of the tension bled from her face as Tara said, "I know you're troubled too. Don't worry."

"I'm trying not to, but you know me." Julianna patted her mother's hand. "I'll be fine, Mother. Especially once we receive news."

"Perhaps I may offer some." Baran eased into the doorway.

"Have you heard from James?" Tara asked.

Baran hesitated. "No. RG intercepted a transmission from Tiu forces at Bethel, reporting on their assault there."

Bridget grabbed her mother's arm. Tara's blood froze. "What did it say?"

"Professor, you should understand . . ."

"What did it say?" Tara snapped.

"They reported success," Baran said bluntly. "Starkweather forces were defeated, utterly. So they say."

Tara leaned heavily against the glass. She tilted her head back, resting it against the cool surface. "And James?" she whispered.

"We don't know specifics. No prisoner counts, casualties. Typical Tiu bragging," Baran said.

"Then they could have been captured."

"I do not know."

Bridget sniffled, and Tara was relieved that Julianna put her arms around her sister. Tara turned to face the rain again. Her breath fogged the window. She had to get in touch with James, somehow. She had to know he and Alec were safe. "I must get word through."

"You cannot. We do not know if the Martians are in control of the system or not. It could be intercepted. Message drones will doubtless be intercepted."

"There has to be some way RG can get a message through. I refuse to believe you don't have some kind of trick up your sleeve, Gostislav."

"I am sorry. It is a risk we cannot take. You must understand. We must stay hidden. So. It is too dangerous."

Tara sighed. She knew he was right. But she was desperate for some news. Any news. It only made her determination to overthrow Kesek intensify. "Of course. I'm sorry I pressed, Gostislav."

Baran smiled warmly. He touched her arm. "*Nie martw si ́*, Professor. I will ask my ancestors to guard his soul."

Tara watched him leave. She took a sip of her coffee. It was starting to grow cold.

Bridget hugged her. "I'm sorry, Mother."

"It's all right, dear." Tara hugged her with her free arm. "It will all be all right."

She prayed to the apparently uncaring universe right then for James and Alec, her brother Jonathan, and James's siblings—she feared terribly for them all. Had they truly been annihilated?

Twenty-four hours and half a world away, Najwa peered out the dingy window of a rundown apartment complex in the city of The Hague. It was in one of the older and less attractive neighborhoods, however, it offered a fine view of the towering spires of downtown. Several silvery towers rose into the sky. Their sharp edges contrasted with the long, smooth curve of the massive seawall protecting the city from the encroaching ocean. But Najwa was more interested in the five black spires that stood off to the northeast.

Kesek command headquarters.

She turned to face the small-wheeled robot waiting behind her. It roused itself from an apparent sleep mode. "Rent is 85 per day." It waved its two pairs of spindly metal arms about. "Rent must be paid by 1700 hours local time each day. The room has facilities for eating, sleeping, bathing, and relief of bodily functions. Is it acceptable?"

Najwa surveyed the drab accommodations. There was one bed, one desk, one chair, one food storage unit, one small computer, and a doorway to a bathroom. Everything was varying shades of dirty white and cream. "You are quite the salesman, aren't you?" Too bad robots could not determine sarcasm.

"Is it acceptable?" the robot repeated.

"Yes, it will do." Najwa paid the robot—cash, of course. The unit deposited the money in a compartment on its cylindrical body, locked it, and then handed over the electronic key. "Enjoy your stay in our fair city," it said.

Najwa looked back over her shoulder to the towers out the window. "I think I will."

CHAPTER 8

October 2602
Bethel Star System
Bethel, New Grace

Baden knew his dad would be upset about his plans to use the pirates as transport to Alexandria. It didn't make it any easier to argue the point with him.

"It's perfect," Baden said. "There's nothing to worry about. The colonel's got them paid off, and they've got the promise of more money once they get us to Alexandria and back to you guys."

Simon folded his arms. "It's insane. You saw how willing Captain Bell was to ignore the Kesek assignment. What makes you think she'll keep up her end of the bargain with you?"

Baden shook his head, exasperated. He turned his attention to the *Natalia Zoja*'s barge. It sat quietly nearby on the singed circle of earth that was an informal landing pad on the plains outside New Grace. A dozen or so Bethelites were working in tandem with a rusty and run-down-looking hefter robot to load crates up the barge's ramp. They contained local pottery and refrigerated soft-feather duck meat for the interstellar markets. Baden knew Hamid ibn Thaqib, owner of al-Azhar Shipyards and a frequent customer of *Natalia Zoja*'s cargo hauls, had the contacts to seal a deal for Simon.

"There's nothing to worry about." Baden smirked. "I'll have Jason along."

"That will probably help." His dad squinted up at the sun. "But you're assuming I'll let you go."

There he goes again. I'm just a kid to him. "Dad, you're not going to stop me."

"You think you can just go traipsing off with this Jason *kretyn* without my permission?" Simon jabbed a finger angrily at him. "You have responsibilities. Not just to me, but to everybody else on my ship."

"Your ship? Don't forget—I own 33 percent of the shares, Dad. Have ever since my eighteenth birthday."

"That doesn't give you the right to go against my orders. I'm the captain."

"And I got my own life!" Baden snapped.

Uh oh. Dad's cheeks reddened. Not good. "I'm still responsible for that life! Blast it, you don't seem to get it. You're my son, and I don't want anything happening to you."

The hefter thumped back down the landing ramp with two Bethelites in tow. They chattered on about one of the crates being off balance, but Baden shook the distraction away. "Like what happened to Mom?" It was cruel and unnecessary, but he didn't care. He was furious that his dad didn't trust him to handle himself. Baden just wanted his dad to hurt. Like him.

Simon looked stricken. "Your mother's death—there wasn't anything I could do."

"Just keep telling yourself that." Enough, Baden! Leave him be. But he couldn't stop.

"You have no call to talk to me like that," Simon said. His voice shook. "I've done my best to take care of you. And so have Renshu and Emi and everybody else on that ship. You owe them."

"Like I owe you?"

"That's not what I meant!" Simon's shout startled the nearby Bethelite workers. Even the hefter slowly turned its massive head. He grabbed Baden's shoulder and pulled him aside, away from the loading activity. "You just call this stupid deal off and find some other way of getting rid of that book."

"Well, Bell's gotta get a vote from her crew, first."

"A vote?"

"Yeah, apparently that's the deal when you change jobs midway. So she says, anyway." Baden shrugged. "She could be planning a double-cross, for all I know."

"Instead you're standing around reading the blasted thing like this was a concert tour. How long were you at it last night?"

Baden sighed. He rubbed his eyes. He was still tired from the marathon session. "Three hours the first round. Didn't even realize it. Then I went looking for Gail—"

"Yeah, I heard about that." Simon put his hands on his hips. Baden looked away to the hefter now bringing another pair of crates up the loading ramp of the barge.

"Why are you doing this?" Dad didn't seem mad this time, but genuinely curious.

"I . . . I'm not sure." It was the truth. Something about giving these writings to the people made him feel—better? Special? He wasn't sure. "It just seems . . . right, you know?"

"You have to give this up." Dad scratched his chin. "I told Jason he should have just taken it off you and be done with it."

Baden's ire increased. "Nice. Nice, Dad. Just forget about it. We're going to Alexandria, and that's it!"

"No, you're not!"

"C'mon, Dad, you should be happy—you get rid of that book and you get a few days without me!"

Baden stormed off, brushing past the Bethelite workers.

"Baden!" his dad shouted. "Get back here!"

Not likely. Baden had wasted enough time as it was. Now he was late.

It happened again.

For the second time in as many days, Baden read aloud through a part of the Bible and completely lost track of time. Four hours, gone in a flash. He'd read through the Gospels of Matthew and Mark and was into Luke.

It was approaching local noon. The sun peeked from behind one of the scattered, wispy clouds scooting through the sapphire blue sky. Shadows skipped across the crowd packed into the square—more than a thousand people. Young, old, women, men, and even injured soldiers from the Starkweather and Rozsada forces.

Gail stood at the front of the crowd. She was positively beaming. Owen stood next to her, giving her sideways glances. He didn't look comfortable with her new status. Baden hadn't even tried talking to her about the baptism yet.

Simon and Cyril were nowhere to be seen—they had planned to make trips to and from *Natalia Zoja* with cargo. Baden wasn't surprised his dad was avoiding him.

But there were newcomers to this reading. Baden spotted Commander Verge standing a few paces back from Gail, near a restored park bench. Her red hair stood out like a beacon. Next to her stood the young cadet—another Verge, Baden remembered—who had an eager expression on his face. Troop Master Sands, however, was grimacing as if he had a toothache.

Heng touched Baden's shoulder lightly. His Asian features were etched with concern. "You may want to rest, Baden. We are so thankful you are giving this time, but we do not want you to fatigue yourself."

"Uh, thanks." Baden's throat hurt. He coughed a few times. "Yeah, I think I'll quit for a while."

Heng took his arm and helped him down off the makeshift platform. The crowd roared its appreciation. Baden wished they wouldn't. Besides creeping him out, it reinforced the headache now throbbing through his skull.

"Baden, that was wonderful!" Gail squeezed him in a tight hug. Baden's headache receded a bit. "Are you okay?"

"Yeah, I think so." Baden eyed her curiously. They hadn't really spoken much about her dunking in the harbor—baptism, he reminded himself. "Are you?"

"I am."

"Sorry I wandered off on you last night." Baden ran a hand through his hair. "I didn't understand . . . I needed some time away from everyone."

"Even me?"

Whoops. Now he'd done it. "Uh, well . . . Yeah. Sorry."

"It's okay. You looked kind of overwhelmed."

"No kidding." Baden sighed.

"Hey, you're doing great, all right? Don't worry about it." Gail smiled again.

Crisis averted. Baden cleared his throat. "So . . . what was that all about last night?"

"It's kind of hard to explain." Gail looked around at the dispersing crowd of Bethelites. "These people—they're just like us, in most ways, but many of them have a peace inside that I couldn't comprehend. They tried explaining to me, but there wasn't much they could say."

Baden felt a stab of heartache. "Let me guess. They told you to read this." He held up the Bible.

Gail nodded. Her expression brightened. "When you were reading last night, it was . . . I don't know, something just lined up. It was right there for me, as if God were reaching out a hand just to me."

Owen sauntered over. He slipped an arm over Gail's shoulders. "Hey, man, I told her she had a loose thruster, right? But she wasn't gonna listen to me."

Gail shrugged his arm off. "Owen . . ."

"Sorry, sorry. Didn't mean to trigger the old proximity alert." Owen grinned. Then he swooped in to kiss her cheek.

Baden didn't know if he was more surprised or if Gail was. She pushed Owen back. "Stop! Please." Then she moved closer to Baden.

Owen's expression darkened. "Whatever."

Baden was in no mood to joke. "You can't believe all this stuff," he said to Gail.

"Can't I?" Gail folded her arms. "Do you think I've lost my mind just because I saw my need for a savior?"

"A savior? You didn't need saving from anything! You didn't do anything to anyone."

"I'd rejected God. I never even saw a need for Him. That changed yesterday."

Her matter-of-fact tone infuriated and placated Baden all at once. He didn't know what to make of the turmoil between his head and heart. He knew only this: he didn't want to see Gail hurt. No matter what.

Before he could voice that, however, the young cadet and his ever-present companion, Troop Master Sands, approached from the crowd. "I must say, that was a great bit of reading," the teenager said. "There are many here with questions for you. I'm one of them."

"You better just give Hack some space." Owen interposed himself between the two groups. "He ain't liking all this attention, if you hadn't noticed."

"Well, he certainly seems to be making little effort to avoid it."

"Don't matter." Owen poked the cadet's shoulder. "Heave to, chief."

It was a mistake. Sands had his fists bunched up in Owen's collar a half-second later. "You best not lay a hand on the cadet, Expatriate," Sands growled. "He's on my watch. You want a reminder?"

"No! Nope! I got it!" Owen's face was deathly pale. His voice came out a squeak. "I ain't messing with him, boss!"

"Corporal, that's enough." The cadet grabbed Sands's arm. Baden thought he must be brave or an idiot—Baden wouldn't come even close to touching this brute.

"He's a pest, kid. Let me squash him down a bit."

"I asked you to stop it, Benjamin."

The tone brooked no further argument. Sands muttered something vaguely obscene and dropped Owen. He staggered back and made an exaggerated effort to smooth out his shirt. "You got it, Alec."

"Thanks." The teenager turned to Baden and extended his hand. "Sorry about that. Alec Verge."

Baden took it and matched his firm grip. "Baden. Haczyk."

Alec looked at the Bible. "Did you really find that in a wrecked ship?"

"Yeah. It was . . ." Baden thought back to that moment. It seemed like years ago rather than weeks. He could still feel his heart hammering and the sweat pouring down his face. He'd felt nothing like it—the power and peace, all at once, for a brief second that had actually lasted far longer. "It was something else," he finished lamely.

"Could I . . . ?" Alec held out his hand tentatively.

"Yeah, okay." Baden handed him the Bible.

Alec's eyes widened. "Stars." He ran a hand softly over the cover. Grabbing the corner gently, he opened the Bible and flipped through a few pages. "I never thought I would ever see one, let alone touch one."

"You'd better not let the colonel see you with that," Sands grumbled. "It's illegal."

"So I've heard." Alec closed the Bible and handed it back to Baden. "Thank you for letting me hold it again."

Alarms rang in Baden's head. "Again? What do you mean, again?"

"Uh, Hack?" Owen looked sheepish. Baden didn't think he'd ever seen him look sheepish about anything. Even the time he'd stood up to ask for the comm frequency of a particularly voluptuous holo-game attendant and realized he'd forgotten to wipe the marinara sauce off his goatee. "It was kinda my idea. Don't get mad at him or Gail."

"Gail?" Blazes, what was this all about? Baden glared at the prim cadet. The one who idolized his father. Vac-head. "What was Ozzy's idea?"

"It was quite simple." Alec gestured to Gail. "She flipped the pages and I took still pictures with a recon imager. Then I downloaded them to a delver."

"You did what?" Baden didn't know why he was getting upset. Maybe it was the idea of more people putting themselves in danger over this Bible. "Yeah, and what are you going to print it out with?"

"We were just going to disseminate the image files," Alec said slowly. "Is there a problem?"

"Illegal," Sands said.

"I am not trying to dissuade you from preaching, Baden—"

"It's not preaching!" Baden pointed back toward the crowds. They were heading back to their tents and moving off into the streets. Heng was among them. "You want preaching, go talk to him!"

Alec held up his hands. "I tried asking more about this faith, but he seems to think you hold the key to the true faith. Listening to him and some of his people, I'm inclined to agree. Their beliefs are a muddle. This—" he pointed to the Bible—"is straightforward. Laser-cut."

Laser-cut. Didn't Baden wish. "Look, Alec, you want a free Bible study, you'll have to find somebody else."

Gail put a hand on his arm. "Baden, he didn't mean any harm. You've already shared so much with everyone else here. Why not take a moment with him?"

"I would like to hear more as well." Commander Verge joined their little knot. Baden saw that the square had about half emptied—large groups of people were still joined in earnest discussions. Small clusters were on their knees with eyes squeezed shut and hands pressed against their chests.

"So you're crazy too, huh?" Baden asked. He felt a strong urge to lock this thing away. But the draw it exerted on people all around him was enrapturing. Baden felt like his soul was being torn in half. It hurt.

"No, just . . . considering." Commander Verge smiled a kind smile, and for a moment, Baden's aching heart recycled an image of his mother. "I've heard many philosophies and religions in my life, not the least of which is the Union Synoptic Church. But they are all like a match's flame compared to the fire in those words. I want to know more of it."

Baden rubbed his forehead. He couldn't deal with this. Not now. Not ever. "Just—go away, okay?" He backed away from them. All of them. "Bell's gonna convince her crew soon enough, and then we're out of here! No more waiting around." He had to breathe. Darkness seemed to press at him, even though the late morning couldn't get any brighter. Birds were singing from the rooftops—birds!

"Hack, you oughta know." Owen kicked at some dirt. "I been sending out the recordings to the other delvers. Your recordings and the images Mister Cadet here put together."

Baden eyed him. "What other delvers?"

"The other ones. The ones I been rigging up while you've been preach—er, reading."

"You rigged more?" Baden's head was starting to hurt again. "How many?"

"Oh, I dunno." Owen waved his hand about in the air, as if to conjure up the right answer. "Fifteen. Twenty, maybe. Or more."

"So what, are we just all racking up felonies for Kesek to nail us on?" Baden snapped. "You're gonna get yourself spaced!"

"Ain't like it matters now!" Owen shoved Baden hard on a shoulder. Alec took a step forward, but Sands placed a halting hand before him. "You got us into this by bringing that blasted thing back, man! You coulda just left it out there! But no, not Mr. Hack-man, the history ace! You had to have it. And you couldn't wait to show it off to Gail! Look what happened to her mom because of that, Hack!"

Baden clenched a fist and took a step toward him. He'd never wanted to hit anyone as badly as he wanted to sock Owen right now. But Gail was right there, her own eyes on fire. She put both hands on Baden's chest. "You stop it right now!" Her voice was permacrete. She whipped her head around to Owen, her short hair flying furiously. "And you leave him alone! The both of you are being stupid! Baden was meant to have the Bible, and now that he has it, it's his call on what to do with it! So deal with it, instead of crying like children!"

Shame flooded Baden. He looked at Owen and saw some of the heat flee his expression.

This book is no good.

It wasn't the usual voice Baden heard. It was softer, friendlier—and convincing.

Look what it's doing to you. And your friend. If he is really your friend.

He couldn't believe Owen's behavior. If he really was his friend, he'd help Baden out. Maybe this advice was right . . .

He is a liar and the father of lies.

The force of the statement pushed Baden almost to his knees. Gail was right there to grab his arm.

This time Alec ignored Sands's restraining arm and reached for Baden's other side. "Easy. Take it easy."

Baden shuddered. It was like the rest of the mind-numbing words he heard, but with greater strength. And he had the feeling the speaker wasn't talking about Owen, but about the softly insinuating statements that had come earlier.

"I just need to go." Baden carefully extricated himself from Gail and Alec. "Please."

He left with tears brimming.

Alec joined Benjamin Sands in the cleanup work still left to be done. They set about disassembling a cabin that looked as if it had taken a direct hit from a Tiu rocket. Its roof had been torn off and only three walls were left standing. Two of those walls were full of more holes than a vegetable strainer Alec remembered from the Verge estate's kitchen. The charred walls still stank of burnt plastic resin. Benjamin stood inside, looking up at the destruction.

"Nothin' much worth salvaging," Benjamin said. His always dour face was etched with deep disgust as he peered through one of the larger holes in the cabin wall. "Gimme a hand here, kid, and we'll rip it down."

Alec was on the other side of the wall, arc torch in hand. "Always ready to follow your instruction, Troop Master."

"Yeah, I'll bet. Especially now that I'm an officer and you're still just a kay-det." Benjamin snickered. "Hey, get your goggles on first! I don't wanna have to tell the colonel I saved your butt in combat action against Tiu warriors but let you fry your eyeballs with a demolition torch."

"Understood." Alec tossed him a mock salute. He pulled a pair of mirrored goggles from his uniform pocket and slid them over his eyes. He activated the torch and turned it toward the wall. The dazzling blue-white flame sizzled and threw sparks as it cut into the resin. Alec stared at the cut as he led the torch slowly down the surface of the wall. The torch flame was hypnotizing. In his mind's eye he saw bright light of a different kind—the actinic flash of a railer.

It was as if he was back on that dark, rainy battlefield of downtown New Grace. The screams of helpless Bethelites were real. The shouts and agonized cries of Lancers were real. The guttural barks of Tiu warriors were real. The lance was in his hand, and the Tiu in terrifying war-painted armor was before him. He stabbed with the lance.

Blood.

His vision blurred and his head swam. "Alec!" The voice sounded as if it were coming through a mask. "Kid, you okay?"

Alec blinked his eyes open. He was on his back, in the grass. Benjamin was kneeling at his side. The arc torch lay abandoned beside him. It had apparently burnt the grass, judging by the brown circle on green. "What happened?" It came out as a croak.

"You were cuttin' the wall and just kinda went rigid. Then you keeled over like a hexambler with its power axed." Benjamin reached a hand beneath his back and grabbed his arm with the other hand. "C'mon, get up. Easy, now."

Alec's legs were still a little wobbly as he straightened. Suddenly he broke out in a cold sweat. His stomach tightened. He heaved and—

Benjamin wrinkled his face. "Easy, kid."

Alec wiped vomit from the corner of his mouth. "It was terrifying. I was right there again, in the fighting. I don't know if I can face that again. And there's Uncle Jonathan . . ." He couldn't go on. He was almost in tears.

"Major Douglas was a good man and the best Lancer. He wouldn't want you moping after him." Benjamin leaned against the cabin wall. A flight of Lynx fighters roared past. Benjamin pointed. "See? This ain't over. You gotta pull yourself back together and hold it in. We got work to do at Earth. Can't let Kesek and the Tiu tear it all to bits. But you can get a med exemption, probably, if you want."

Alec exhaled. "No. No, I'll be fine."

"No, you won't." Benjamin sounded almost regretful. "You'll never be fine. And if you are fine with the killing and the death, well, then there's something wrong in the old database." He tapped the side of his head.

Alec considered this. He wanted to please Father and continue on as a Lancer in the king's service, but it was hard. More difficult than he had imagined. Not just physically, but mentally. "Thanks, Benjamin."

"No prob. And don't worry, I won't tell anyone about the old heave-ho there." Benjamin slapped him roughly on the shoulder. "You gotta stay in good shape if you're coming with me back to Earth."

Earth. Alec hoped his mother and sisters were all right. There was no telling what Kesek might do. "Do you think we'll see it again?"

"Blasted right we will. I have to get back."

"Do you?" Alec raised an eyebrow. "Oh. For Carol, isn't it?"

Benjamin's mouth twisted. "Yeah. Carol." He dug a delver from his pocket. "Kept her last message with me. She didn't like everything I've done, you know? But I dunno. I want her to respect me . . ."

"And to love you," Alec guessed.

"Hey, now, don't go putting words in my mouth."

Alec smiled. He retrieved his arc torch from the grass. "Let's finish our task or your dear Carol will have to be content with a hologram of you for the rest of her days."

Benjamin returned the grin. "Lead on, Cadet Trainee."

The Gold Beasts fighter wing based on the carrier *HMCV Crossbow* had taken heavy losses during its fight with the Tiu warplanes. Nine planes were destroyed and five in need of major repairs. That left barely enough for three squadrons to patrol Bethel's skies in case more Tiu showed up. It also left vacancies in the command structure.

Lieutenant Connor Verge mulled over that situation as he brought his Lynx fighter, Coyote 11, out of a steep bank over the ruined Starkweather encampment. Those vacancies put him into the leadership role of Coyote Squadron. He'd imagined one day commanding a full twelve fighters instead of just four in a flight, but this wasn't how he wanted to gain the role.

"Terrible sight, isn't it, No-Joy?" Connor angled his fighter toward a wide plain of baked earth a half kilometer from New Grace. The rest of Coyote Squadron's planes were lined up on a makeshift landing circle ringed by tents and prefab cabins.

Chief Warrant Officer Logan Joy, his sensorman, sighed over his helmet comm. He sat behind Connor in the long cockpit. "It is, Conman. Breaks my heart. Those guys had it far worse than we did."

"Yes, no doubt." Connor's heart ached as he thought of Major Jonathan Douglas. The two had so enjoyed playing dueling instruments at family gatherings. He'd miss Jonathan's music. "That's why we get to patrol endlessly rather than lounging aboard *Crossbow*, to make sure we're not caught unawares."

"Lucky us."

Connor spotted the flashing red and green landing beacons at the airstrip. He eased back on the throttle. The Lynx's engines cycled back to a dull thrum, and a new whine of hoverjets cut in. He eased the fighter down into a billowing dust cloud. The landing pads thudded against the dirt.

"We're down. Another spectacularly smooth landing! Thank you, no clapping." Connor disengaged the power systems and unsealed the cockpit hatch. A crewman in a bright red jumpsuit came running over with a folding ladder under one arm. She held tight to her red cap. *Crossbow* fighter techs had been shuttled to Bethel's surface to service those planes still on groundside patrol.

Logan groaned. "Don't you ever get tired of yourself?" He removed his helmet, revealing cropped silvery hair. He clambered out of his seat.

"Never. I'd think you'd know that by now."

"Yeah, you'd think."

The technician clanged the ladder against the Lynx's fuselage. Connor pulled himself up and out of the cockpit. He got a good look at the tech. She was the same one who'd prepped his fighter before they'd departed *Crossbow* after arriving at Bethel. Connor grinned. He pulled his helmet off and ran a hand hastily through his red hair. "Well, I am glad to see you again."

She tipped her cap back. Her eyes were deep brown, set off by pale skin and jet black hair tied up in a ponytail. The corner of her mouth tipped up. "Lieutenant. Did you manage to take in the sights?"

"I did, but now I've found something more worthwhile to observe." Connor stepped backward down the ladder, careful not to catch his blue flight suit on the rungs. He hopped lightly to the ground before offering a slight bow.

"Betcha never used that line before," the tech said dryly. She walked by him. "How's the autocannon behaving?"

Connor appreciated the view. Logan cleared his throat. When Connor looked at him, he shook his head. Connor waved him away. "No problems. Of course, I didn't have to shoot anything this time."

"How awful for you."

Hmm. This was not going satisfactorily. Usually he received a more pleasant response to his inquiries, and his looks, for that matter. "Perhaps I could be of more assistance if I knew whom I had the pleasure of addressing." There. Much better.

"Petty Officer First Class Donna Pramanik."

"Lieutenant Connor Verge."

"Already knew that, Conman, sir."

Hmm. She didn't sound amused by this at all. He checked her finger for a ring. None. New tactic then. "Look, why don't you let that wait until later?" he said. "Chief Joy is headed into a game of kanat with my wingman. Join us, why don't you."

Donna stopped tinkering with the autocannon. She looked him over. "Okay. If that's not an order, Lieutenant." She smiled.

Connor grinned. "I'll make sure it's an order, so as to keep you out of trouble."

They walked over to one of the tents at the edge of the landing field. Logan was already settling into a folding chair, accepting a stack of triangular cards from Flight Officer Giacomo "Pants" Pantusa. He sat at a battered table with his sensorman and two other technicians. Pantusa was wearing his dark brown uniform. His head was shaved bald and he had a thin black moustache. "Conman! Pull up a chair. You and your guest."

"Thanks, Pants." Connor straddled one of the folding chairs. He was by far the tallest person at the table. Logan dealt him his seven cards. "What's the call?"

"Starships are double," Pantusa said. "Penalty is minus three for ringers."

"Minus three? Well." Connor fanned out his cards to assess his hand. Yes, he did have a card with a ringed planet on it. Lucky him. "That makes it interesting. Everyone ante?"

"Yep." Pantusa tapped a little pile of bright yellow and red banknotes at the center of the table. "Fivers only."

Connor sighed. "Small change. All right, then." He dug into his flight suit and tossed a crumpled five into the mix. Donna, seated next to him, did likewise.

Pantusa dealt the cards. The four players went quiet as they considered options. "Ladies first," Pantusa said.

Donna tossed a pair of cards onto the table. "Two. You fellas see anything interesting on your patrol?"

"Here's your two." Pantusa drew cards from the top of the deck and passed them her way. "Negatory. Unless you count a flock of Nathan geese."

"Four," Logan said in a grim tone. "We came up empty on our run too."

"Yeah, well, what do you expect? There's no stinking Martians left on this rock." Pantusa gave him his cards. Logan cringed.

"Chief, you gotta do a better job at hiding it than that," Donna said with a laugh.

"No Joy is incapable of masking his disgruntlement," Connor said. "And speaking of disgruntlement, have you heard the latest off the Reach?"

"You mean the attacks at Earth?" Pantusa made a sour face. "'Course. Blasted Martians."

"C'mon, sir, you really think the Hamarkhis had anything to do with that?" Donna said. Connor was surprised by the sudden vehemence in her voice.

"Why not? Those Martians are all insane. They'd do anything to kill us off and take their bloody Mars back," Pantusa said. He dealt himself three cards. "Ante."

Connor made no move. Donna, still staring hard at Pantusa, pulled two more banknotes from her pocket and put them into the pile. Connor followed suit, and so did Pantusa.

Logan quietly set down his cards. "Out."

"Didn't see that one coming," Pantusa said.

"Sir, the Hamarkhis don't do stuff like that suicide attack with pilgrim transports," Donna said firmly. "They're pacifists. Devout pacifists. They'd see it as the ultimate sacrilege."

"I'll bet." Pantusa threw down his cards. "Triple mark."

Connor swore. He put his own cards down. "Old fleet. No good." He turned to Donna. "Where did you grow up, if you don't mind my asking?"

"Harendra Desh. Starkweather frontier." Donna set her cards down primly. "Gold nova."

"Blazes!" Pantusa put his hands to his forehead. "Beginner's luck."

Donna collected all the money, a smile brightening her face. "There's a lot of Hamarkhis on Harendra Desh's moon, Conman," she said. "We learned to live together. It's the Tiu you've gotta watch out for. They'd kill their own cousins for the so-called 'glory of Mars.'"

"I don't doubt it." Connor smiled her way. "Congratulations, Petty Officer Pramanik. May I escort the winner to the commissary?"

"Certainly."

Connor flashed Pantusa a thumbs-up. "Later, Pants."

"You too, Conman."

Logan rolled his eyes. "I'm going to get a shower."

Connor followed Donna away from the table. She was already halfway to the commissary cabin. "You know, I don't care if they're Tiu or Hamarkhis," Connor said. "Martian is Martian, in my flight regs."

"Maybe you shouldn't be so by the book, sir," she said.

Him? By the book? Connor thought about that. No one had ever made that accusation.

He glanced at Donna. Beautiful, and strong. Maybe he'd have to reconsider those regs.

October 2602
Bethel Star System
Bethel, New Grace

Baden fled the square south. He followed a sidewalk past a few bombed-out houses and found a tiny street corner park. It was tucked alongside a pair of three-story prefabricated commercial buildings that had managed to escape major structural damage in the fight between the Martians and Lancers. The park was full of flowering bucina trees, their pale blossoms brilliant in the sunlight. Baden ducked behind the tall, thick shrubbery and collapsed onto a black metal mesh bench. It sagged a bit.

He put his face in his hands. "Why me?" he whispered. "Why can't it all just go back to the way it was?"

Even as he said it, he knew it was impossible. His life would be forever different, whether or not Kesek got him.

"Baden?"

Gail stood at the narrow entrance to the park. She had her hands folded in front of her. "Can I sit with you?"

Baden pulled his face out of his hands. He nodded.

She settled down quietly beside him. She didn't ask any questions, but just sat next to him. Her blue eyes watched him, and she waited.

"Gail . . ." Baden blew out a breath. "I'm sorry I got upset. There's no excuse . . . This thing just has my brain muddled. And I thought . . ."

"You thought what?"

"I don't know." Baden ran a hand roughly through his hair. "Maybe Owen's right. This Bible's getting people hurt. Kesek's after us and—well, I don't want anything to happen to you."

He said the last part rapid-fire. He couldn't quite believe where he was going with this. It was hard to maintain his self-imposed mope when Gail sat next to him looking so beautiful and being possibly the best friend he had in this galaxy. And she was gorgeous. Which Baden realized he'd noticed twice in three seconds.

Gail stayed quiet. Baden smacked his hand against the bench. "Geez, I'm no good with this stuff. Look . . . you know . . . I've always . . ."

"Baden." Gail scooted closer to him. "You need some help with this?"

Baden swallowed. Her eyes were shining, either in his imagination or in the dim light. "Um . . . okay."

She lifted up his arm, draped it around her shoulder, and squirmed right up against him. Baden was sure everyone on the street—and in the city, for that matter—could hear his heart screaming in his chest.

"I know you care about me. A lot," Gail whispered.

"Yeah . . . uh, I do." Baden couldn't move.

"You don't have to worry about me. I haven't lost my mind." Her voice shook a bit. "This is where I was supposed to go, don't you see? If I hadn't come with you, I never would have known. God showed me the way. And you were there to help."

Baden wasn't sure it was true. But it somehow didn't seem too crazy. It was very difficult to concentrate right now.

He swallowed hard. "You've always been a good friend, and you've always been . . ."

"What?"

He hesitated, then blurted, "Beautiful."

She ran a finger ever so lightly across the back of his neck. "Why didn't you say anything?"

Baden bit his lip. Hard. "I guess, maybe, I was afraid of messing up what we were. You know, friends."

"So, can you tell me now? About how you feel, I mean."

He looked down at his boots. He thought about all they'd been through in the past few days, how they could have easily died in that chase off Serhat, all the risk and terror.

Then he looked back at her, his friend, a person he'd confided in just as much as Owen, yet when his mother died she was the only one who seemed to share in his grief, separated as they were by light-years. There was no talking to his father about that, but Gail had always listened. She had always been there for him. He wanted to tell her all this.

Instead, he kissed her.

She showed no surprise, but she returned the kiss with more energy than he'd expected. He reached his arm beneath hers to pull her closer.

For a while neither of them heard anything—not the soft chatter of passersby, not the chirping of striped sparrows, not the scream of a flight of Lynx fighters that soared low over New

Grace. For just those few moments, there was no other place on any world around any star.

When they did finally open their eyes, Baden saw that while neither of them had changed, something quite different existed between them.

They didn't get to the landing field until later in the afternoon. Baden wasn't paying much attention to anything—save for Gail. He ignored his buzzing comm. There was only the vaguest of memories of how the two had walked through town, talking, laughing, and a sharing a frosty Ice Tower from the local watering hole. Baden would have thought himself drunk, or at least tipsy, save for the fact that an Ice Tower contained no alcohol.

It was the crowd gathered at the barge's landing spot that shocked him back to his senses.

Simon was standing at the foot of the ramp with Colonel Verge and his sister, Commander Verge. Alec and Troop Master Sands stood off to one side. It seemed Alec was trying to engage Cyril and Jason in polite conversation. Baden snickered—the former was simply staring at Alec with a quizzical look. At least Jason answered in his stead.

Owen came sprinting up to them. He looked far more irked than Baden figured he should. "Hey, where you two been? Our ride's been asking about us."

He jerked a thumb over his shoulder. Baden spotted the hawk-like, slender atmospheric shuttle—called a skipjack, by some archaic tradition—perched on a rise maybe one hundred meters from the barge. He could just make out the sharp figure of Captain Bell. Even at that distance her eyes pinned him to the spot.

"Yeah, well, they can wait. I gotta talk to Dad first." Baden grasped Gail's hand tightly.

Owen's mouth twisted. "That's new, Hack."

"Hey, man, I'll fill you in later."

"Yeah. Sure." Owen fell into step with them. He was oddly subdued, but Baden chalked it up to their earlier argument. He'd get over it. He always did.

Simon was deep in conversation with Commander Verge when they approached. With the wind whistling through from the south, Baden couldn't hear what his dad was saying. Commander Verge laughing, her bright blue eyes squinting. Simon returned a lopsided grin.

Grin? Baden's jaw fell. His dad, grinned? At a woman? And not just any woman—a mighty good-looking one from a whole other social class.

Gail poked his ribs.

"Ow! What?"

"You were gawking." She smiled.

Baden's cheeks burned. "Sorry."

Simon noticed them then. Baden watched his eyes do the same scan of his and Gail's clasped hands as Owen's had. "Where've you guys been?"

"In town."

Gail pushed up possessively beside him. Baden blushed furiously.

"Okay." Simon looked as though he might say something but thought better of it.

"What have you all been doing?" Baden indicated the group. "Got plans I should know about?"

"Depends on whether you're coming with us." Simon folded his arms.

"I asked you first," Baden said.

"Fair enough. Colleen . . . er, Commander Verge wants to get the task force back to Earth." Baden watched the red flare along his dad's cheeks. Commander Verge didn't seem to notice the slip, but her brother the colonel raised an eyebrow. "Anyway, she figures that having *Natalia Zoja* along will give her group the appearance of a protected convoy."

"If we make some alterations to our antimatter drive emissions and keep our accelerations down, of course," Commander Verge said.

"Of course." Baden had no clue what she meant.

Colonel Verge cleared his throat. "I also need a transport to bring some of my men along. We lost one of ours."

Baden looked at his dad. Simon didn't appear entirely comfortable. "And you're okay with this?"

"It's going to pay well. Colonel Verge has some money available—and assuming he can get his assets unfrozen by Kesek if this all goes well, he'll get us more. Plus we'll have the corvettes along if there's trouble." Simon scratched his chin. "I'm taking them up on the offer. We're taking *Natalia Zoja* to Earth."

No need for my opinion, then, Baden thought. "So that's all settled."

"Guess so. Now are you ready to go, or what?"

There was an awkward silence. Baden glanced over at Alec. He took in the entire proceedings with interest. Baden saw obvious admiration on Alec's face as he looked at the colonel. Must be nice to have a dad who doesn't treat you like a toddler.

"I'm ready." Baden pointed to Jason. "We're going to Alexandria. With Captain Bell."

Simon gave Colonel Verge a dirty look. "Thanks for giving him that brainwave."

"It was Baden's suggestion, not my own." Colonel Verge tapped his booted toe against the barge ramp. "He will be just as secure aboard Captain Bell's ship as aboard this barge."

"As long as your money keeps her distracted." He crooked a finger at Baden. "Come here."

Baden followed him a few paces away from the barge. He looked over his shoulder. Alec, Colonel Verge, and Sands were walking away from the landing area. Commander Verge waited for a moment longer, then went with them.

"Leave the book here."

Baden blinked. "What?"

His dad gritted his teeth. "I've had just about enough of this," he grumbled. "You need to get rid of that thing before it gets all of us killed, you understand?"

"Yeah, and that's what I'm doing—I'm getting rid of it."

"By riding off with that pirate?" His dad shook his head. "Baden, I don't trust her."

"Me neither. But Jason's going along." Baden tried a smile. "He's pretty handy. C'mon, Dad, let it go, it's just a book." Even as he said it, he didn't quite believe it.

"Sure it is! That's why Kesek's chasing us across half a dozen star systems and why those freaks down there are treating you like some messenger from on high!" Simon snapped. He poked Baden in the chest. "I thought we agreed to sell it."

"In your own brain, maybe, but I never said I would," Baden said. "Besides, Heng's not gonna pay for it."

"What?"

"He said it was best for the Bible to not stay on Bethel." Baden waved a hand behind him.

"I don't believe this . . ."

"This is my call, Dad, and I don't need you telling me what to do with it," Baden said. "What are you so scared of anyway?"

"Scared? Who says I'm scared?"

"Come on, Dad, you've been a bit possessive. Does this have to do with Mom?"

"Of course it does!" His dad grabbed his shoulders. There was more anguish than anger in his eyes.

The silence was deafening. The gusts of wind buffeted the two of them, howling as they brushed under the barge's wings. "Those pirates?" Baden asked. "They're working for us now."

Simon turned aside. His expression rippled with sorrow. Something wasn't right.

Then it slammed into Baden like an asteroid. "You don't mean the pirates. It was someone else."

Simon didn't answer. His face took on a faraway look.

"Man, why am I even trying!" White hot anger burned Baden's insides. "You couldn't even save her! You just let her die!"

"I tried!" Simon roared.

Then his dad wept. Not just a tear or two, while preserving a manly aura. No, he flat-out cried. Baden felt like he'd run face-first into a bulkhead and bounced off in zero-gee. His body was numb.

Simon rubbed the heel of his hand across his face. "We were at Reynolds Station," he said softly. "Your mom loved it there. She said it shone like a comet's tail in the twin suns. Like jewels.

"There'd been warnings of pirate activity in the area. We didn't pay it much mind. Pirates generally steered clear of us, 'cause we had Hamid's patronage. They knew better. So we put in on the outer ring of docking hatches." His dad looked at him with red-rimmed eyes. "You know what we brought? We were carrying flowers. Flowers! Fresh tulips from Barneveld. She loved the smell. And she knew they'd bring a good price."

Baden couldn't speak. His heart was hammering in his chest.

"We sent the rest of the crew on leave. Just me, your mom, and Renshu. He's the one who heard them at the airlock." His dad turned aside. Baden followed his gaze down to the town of New Grace. It had probably been pretty and tranquil, before it was trashed by the Tiu. The wind rustled Simon's jacket.

"They knocked him out pretty bad. I thought it was pirates. I shouted at your mom to hide, but you know how she was—she had her gun out and was two steps ahead of me. I caught up with her at the airlock."

"Renshu was on the deck, out cold. And there were six of them."

"The pirates," Baden said quietly.

"No. No, Baden." Simon turned to face him. "Kesek."

Baden's jaw dropped. They had found her. Somehow, they'd found her—and the Seventy didn't know that.

"They put her under arrest for violating the Charter of Tolerance. She grappled with them and managed to shoot one through the foot. I fought them . . ." Tears ran down his dad's face again. He clenched his teeth so hard Baden thought he'd break them. "Blazes, I fought them. Fought them until my knuckles bled. But they beat on me until I blacked out. She called out for me . . . and I couldn't save her. I just couldn't save her. And then two days later, they sent me a commnote. Said she was dead. Just like that. Gone."

Baden shook. His dad put a hand gently on his arm. "Baden, they covered it up. Threatened us with arrest and impoundment if Renshu and I ever talked. They said . . . they even said they'd kill you.

"I couldn't let that happen," Simon said. "I love you, son. Your mom was my one and only, but she was gone, and you were all I had left. It was hard to show you that. I tried to, like she would have wanted, but I know I wound up hurting you instead."

Now Baden was crying. He couldn't help it. Dad had never spoken like this to him. Even before Mom died. He couldn't stand it. "Dad—"

His dad hugged him. Baden returned the gesture, folding into his arms, sobbing as he thought of his mom. There wasn't anything he wanted more than to revel in this moment.

"Look." His dad wiped his face. "I know you've got to do this. I'm sorry I tried to make you stop. I see it now. You've got to go to Alexandria and get the cache from there. Even if it means going with Bell and her pirates."

"But Dad, I can't leave you." Baden surprised himself with the admission.

"No. It's what she would have wanted." His dad pointed. Baden followed his arm. Gail was running over to them. Owen, Cyril, and Jason remained by the barge, watching intently. "Gail's going with you, I think."

Gail skidded to a halt next to Baden. She looked upset. "Baden, Simon . . . are you okay?"

"Yeah. I think so." Baden dug into his pocket. There was something he needed to do. He pulled out the Bible. "Dad. Please, read some of this. Look it up on one of the delvers that Alec has. It's—it's what you need. I think it's what we all need."

"No. I can't." His dad pushed it away abruptly. Baden lost his grip and it tumbled to the dirt. A page ripped.

"Baden, I'm sorry. I didn't want this to come between us. I didn't want anything to come between us."

Baden stooped down and picked up the Bible. He brushed dirt off it before he met his dad's eyes. "I know, Dad. It's okay. But I can't leave you now."

The wind blew dust clouds by their boots. "Baden, you need to do this," his dad said. "Do it for your mother."

"And I will come with you, Baden," Gail said. She intertwined her fingers in his.

Footsteps scuffed in the dirt behind them. "Hack's gonna need more than you to wipe his nose." Owen clapped a hand on Baden's shoulder. Cyril and Jason were with him.

"Thanks, Ozzy." Baden cleared his throat. "Dad—"

"Don't worry about it, son. We're done with it now."

"No, Dad. I need to say this. I love you, and I don't hate you. Sorry I've been scum all this time."

His dad hugged him again. Gail sniffled. Owen tried to put an arm around her shoulders, but she wriggled out of his grasp.

"All right. Okay, I'll do it." Baden wiped his eyes.

Simon waved. "Cyril! Baden's leaving."

The giant with the blond moustache came directly to Baden. He seized him in a crushing bear hug that pressed most of the air from Baden's lungs and had him dangling a half-meter off the ground. "Be safe," he boomed.

Everyone stared at him as he went back to the barge.

"Tell Earth I said hey." Baden held out his hand. "Good luck, Dad."

"You too, son."

• • •

Baden shielded his eyes against the dust as the barge roared into the morning sky. He sighed. "So that's that."

Gail kissed his cheek. "I think he sees what's at work here."

"I am always amazed at the Lord's hand," Jason said. "He works His will in mysterious ways."

"Yeah, well, His will must be for you to stay busy as my bodyguard," Baden said.

"That's gonna be a full-shift job for all of us now, Hack," Owen said. "You sure about this craziness?"

"Yeah, Ozzy. Sure as I'm gonna get."

"Can't say I like it. It's stupid." Owen held out his hand. "But let's do it, anyway, boss."

Baden grabbed his hand and squeezed.

Gail pointed past him. "Here comes our other captain."

Sure enough, Bell was striding down the hill from her skipjack.

"There's our ride," Baden said.

"Haczyk!" Bell's grating tone dug at his nerves. "We voted. Had to knock a few heads around, but it was unanimous on the second try. We're taking the job. So gimme the coordinates to this Alexandria place, and we'll go grab that cache."

"Sounds like a plan. Ozzy's got 'em. You'll get them once we head out of orbit."

"Don't trust me?"

"Not particularly."

"Smart, kid. C'mon, get on my boat."

The five of them clambered aboard the skipjack. It was cramped inside, but there was room enough for Baden and Gail to squeeze onto one of the two bench seats after they moved some backpacks. Owen didn't look comfortable wedged up against Jason, though.

"Hang on, boys and girl." The skipjack leapt into the air under powerful engines and soared up through the atmosphere. Baden tore his attention away from the inspiring sight of the frail edge where sky meets space to assess the damage done to the Bible.

When he came to the torn page, Baden let out a deep sigh. He thought about rifling through whatever passed for a med kit on the skipjack for some adhesive tape. Then his eye fell upon the passage the rip had bisected. He smoothed the two halves back together and read:

"Do not think that I have come to bring peace to the earth. I have not come to bring peace, but a sword."

Baden slammed it shut. He hoped God made exceptions.

CHAPTER 10

October 2602
Earth Star System
Earth, Europe, The Hague

There were few people still working in the Kesek headquarters building downtown at this late hour. No more than twenty technicians and inspectors were still on the premises in the central tower, which was more an administrative structure rather than one dedicated to law enforcement.

A few clouds darkened an otherwise bright, starry sky. Najwa walked nonchalantly down the stately paved pathway to the central tower. It rose glistening and ominous far above her. She refused to let the sight scare her. Instead she hefted the large duffel bag in her right hand over a shoulder.

Two heavily armed security robots stood outside the glass doors. They had a pair of tracked treads for legs and no arms, but a flat optical scanner for a head with two machine guns perched on ersatz shoulders. Najwa held up her wrist. A white personnel-tracker bracelet hung loosely. One robot pivoted its head and its optical band blinked at the tracker. "Temporary evening maintenance tech Gina Sanchez. Clearance granted. Proceed."

Najwa caught sight of herself in the mirror-finish doors as they split to admit her—black hair tucked under a blue-grey cap, body slight in a baggy and rumpled blue-grey work coverall spotted with unidentified stains, the temporary false irises that changed her eyes to blue. She nodded at the smudges on her cheeks. A nice touch, she must say. No sign of Najwa here.

The cavernous entry foyer was mostly empty. Everything was white marble and gleaming metal. The floor was a glossy black speckled with silver. Two guards sat hunched over their delvers, paying scant attention to the banks of security monitors and holo-displays arranged in a three-quarters circle around their station. Shift change was in an hour and a half. Najwa had little time.

"Can't wait. I missed that soccer match between the Tiaozhan Terrors and the Corazon Conquistadors," the older of the two guards said. He had thinning grey hair and two chins.

"Hey, no worries, they've got the playback filed on the Reach." The younger was Hispanic and had a curly black mop that no doubt incited jealousy in his partner.

"Yeah, and how much you think getting access will cost, hmm? My wife will have my head on her spotless rug if I pay that much."

"Ah, but it won't cost you a bit if you know someone who's already paid up."

"Evenin', fellas." Najwa grinned broadly. That was an odd sensation.

The younger guard waved his hand as she approached the desk. "Evening." He let her place her palm on the handheld reader and used another device to scan her optical print. "Eyes and fingers match. Gina Sanchez. Temporary replacement in maintenance."

"Thanks for checkin'," she quipped. She set her bag down. "Need to scan this too?"

The older guard took it carefully. He fed the bag into a large receptacle recessed in the desk. "Won't take but a second."

The scanner accepted the bag and spun it in a spherical container, probing its contents from all sides. "Green light," the older guard called.

Gina took the bag back from him, hefting it over her shoulder. "Thanks, fellas. I got a long night ahead of me, and those 'bots ain't gonna make it any easier," she said in her rough voice.

The younger guard gestured toward the two hulking units at the door. "Hold on, let me activate your PT before you go too far."

"Oops, almost forgot." Gina lifted her arm. The guard held her wrist up and pointed a thin white wand at the ribbed white band below her hand. A blue light started slowly marching around the band's circumference. "Now you can spy on me when I go to the can, eh?"

"Him, maybe, but I'm far too genteel," the older guard said.

"Hey, who's doing the flirting now, chief?" the younger guard protested. "Get outta here, Gina. We'll catch you later."

A door to their left slid open. "Yup, have a good night if I don't see you on my rounds," she said. "I can't wait to get outta here and watch the Conquistadors wipe the field with—"

"No, no, don't spoil it!" The older guard pressed his hands to his ears. "Don't you dare!"

Najwa gave a little wave as the lift doors closed.

She pressed the destination button for the 77th floor. As the lift rose, she set her bag on the floor. It contained an assortment of tools the scanning computer had decided were no threat. But as she dismantled several of them, she offered a quick prayer of thanks to Allah that those security robots were fairly dumb units—at least, dumb as far as RG's standards went. They did not recognize that five could be dismantled, components of each rejoined into a compact scrambler weapon, and then reassembled into working tools again.

She placed the assembled scrambler in one of her many pockets. A light blinked at her from her belt's tiny watch. Twenty-two thirty five. Plenty of time to prepare for the recalibration.

She stepped out at the 77th floor. One of the analysts still working hurried past with only the briefest of waves, a cup of coffee cradled in one arm and delver flashing a stream of data in the other. She cracked a grin, switching effortlessly back into character.

Gina, she reminded herself. Not Najwa.

She headed for a maintenance closet.

Three floors above, Kesek Commissioner E. H. Gironde was ensconced in his luxurious office on the 80th floor. He watched the replay of the ReachWrit newscast from earlier in the evening. It went exactly as he'd scripted.

" . . . today encouraged Realm citizens that there was no need to fear the recent and surprising Tiu landings on Mars.

Commissioner Gironde stated that the Tiu have agreed to provide a temporary security presence in the Earth system until such time as the Earth fleet can summon other warships to guard against any further incursion. This of course comes shortly after the Hamarkhis betrayal in their destruction of most of the Earth fleet during their so-called pilgrimage . . ."

Then Gironde's own face beamed out of the display, replacing the newscaster's. "Not bad," Gironde said.

"We welcome the assistance of the Tiu government and have signed with them a temporary treaty allowing them settlement of a small portion of Mars for military and religious purposes," his broadcast self said firmly.

Gironde applauded himself as he shut the recording off. "Nicely put," he purred. "All of it false—with the exception of the treaty, of course. That is all too real. And not the least bit temporary."

He took his glass of Merlot and rose to look out upon the city. Lights sparkled like shimmering jewels, ending at the black expanse of the sea. Only the towering, segmented seawall keeping the ocean back ruined the scenery. Still, Gironde found the view inspiring—the seawall was such a grand accomplishment of human might, a monument to the defiance of the species that faced the rising tides of centuries before and refused to buckle.

Gironde took a deep drink. It was that same defiance that drove him to tighten his grip on the Realm. Soon, Kesek's control would be complete. Then he could rewrite the accounts of the recent weeks—and author the coming history, for that matter—to suit his purposes.

Such power. Gironde liked that.

• • •

Najwa hunkered over the last of the maintenance robots to come through her station. They reported in periodically for updates to their orders, resetting of systems that malfunctioned due to common software glitches, or minor repairs. One of the ten-wheeled units had come in lamenting the loss of its antenna.

Najwa slapped the access hatch on the curved body shut. The robot, resembling a half-meter-long beetle sporting ten wheels balanced on independent axles, quivered to life and scooted out the small hatch in the base of the wall by the maintenance station.

"Excellent," she said. She slid a modified delver from her pocket. Her left hand drew a long, slim film from its side. It stretched out before her, lighting up as it revealed the visual input from more than a dozen cameras she'd installed in a dozen robots. She'd need them to keep tabs on the goings-on in the building when the time was right.

She had her own herd of spies.

Najwa concealed the device and stepped out into the hall. She walked along with her diagnostic kit, scanning the light fixtures and wiring in the walls for malfunctions but ignoring the results. She counted the doors until she reached the one home to the lone technician she'd seen on this floor. She peeked inside and saw a tall, rangy man, his skin swarthy and his hair jet black, staring intently at a monitor as his hands manipulated the control board. The nameplate on the desk identified Thomas Direnc as an Analyst First Class.

She stuck her head in the door and waved. "Hey. Mind if I poke around?"

Direnc looked up, momentarily baffled. "Oh. Sure." He gestured aimlessly about the room, as if her presence only distracted him from his work. "Go ahead."

"Thanks." Najwa continued her scanning, smiling to herself as she recognized his accent. "You grow up around here?"

"Ah . . . no. Istanbul."

"Hmm. Used to call Veracruz home, myself."

"Oh?" Direnc looked her way, noticing her fully for the first time. "I haven't been there myself. Are you new?"

"Gina. Temporary maintenance, while the regular guy's out." True enough—the regular maintenance man was out on sick leave. The fact that Najwa had caused that illness was something she didn't need to tell Direnc. "Surprised they let me wander around as much as they do." She moved to scan the wall closest to Direnc, stretching as tall as she could to check on a motion sensor.

"Well, uh, the personnel trackers make it near impossible for unwanted visitors to enter the tower." Direnc was having trouble focusing on his work; Najwa's coveralls were not baggy, and her reaching around tightened them in places he could appreciate. "And all the systems are so well encrypted . . . Well, I shouldn't say more."

"Gotcha. I won't tell."

At that moment, one of her modified 'bots rolled through the door and started vacuuming. Its appearance drew Direnc's eyes away from Najwa, and humming vacuums were loud enough to disguise sound as she drew the scrambler from her pocket. She glanced down at her watch, which displayed the time but also showed a flashing timer, one that had a few seconds remaining.

Right on schedule, the red light on the tiny cameras in opposite corners of the ceiling winked out. "Ah, forgot they were taking the security cams down for a software upgrade," Direnc noticed.

Najwa fired the scrambler. Direnc gasped. He slid out of his chair and onto the floor as his muscles failed. Najwa knelt beside him, gently administering a soporific. "I did not forget."

The robot kept vacuuming, unperturbed.

Najwa sealed the door using the control on Direnc's console, then checked the man's pulse. Steady. She checked her watch again. The cameras would be down for twenty minutes, according to the maintenance tech whose place she'd taken. That gave her little time.

Using a makeshift device from her pocket, Najwa removed Direnc's personnel tracker and then her own. She slipped his on to her wrist before securing her tracker inside the access panel of the 'bot, which protested with whining wheels as she interrupted its vacuuming. Its protestation stopped when she activated the new software she'd programmed in its computer. Shutting down its vacuum, the 'bot rolled to the door, waited as it opened, then slipped out.

Using her delver, Najwa sent the 'bot on its preprogrammed course to several locations that a maintenance tech of her assumed status would visit on this floor. With the cameras down, the security systems would see "Gina" visiting these locations. No one else was working on the floor, and after the 'bot completed its rounds, it was ordered to return to the maintenance station and putter about, making it look like "Gina" was working there. The other robots she'd reprogrammed to return every once in a while so that "Gina" could check on them.

There was a risk of someone seeing the 'bot and corresponding "Gina's" tracker with the 'bot's location, but since the only ones authorized to do so were the security squad—and they were all downstairs with another tech uploading the new camera software—Najwa was not concerned. She had her sights set on the 80th floor, where maintenance technicians were expressly forbidden.

Analyst First Class Thomas Direnc, however, had the proper clearance.

Making sure the door was again secure, Najwa slid into Direnc's seat. He had logged onto the Kesek mainframe with his own password, and the computer had not been dormant long enough for it to automatically log him out. Taking advantage of this free access, Najwa activated the tower's internal messaging system and then slipped a tiny data stick from her pocket. It fit neatly into one of the drive slots on the front of the computer. Watching the lights on the opposite end flicker, she waited anxiously as it downloaded a new program.

The computer, however, was not aware of this. Instead, the data stick's espionage software convinced the computer that what was being downloaded was a set of high-resolution images in one packet. Najwa was amused by the thought that computers, like people, could lie.

The new program, once in place, gave Najwa supreme access to the messaging network. She could send a message to whomever she wanted and make it appear to come from whomever she wanted. The catch was that her downloaded program could only allow this access for a few minutes before the computer realized that the so-called images were behaving like a program.

Eyes glued to the screen, she typed out new orders from the commissioner for Direnc to run an analysis on the political affiliations of all suspects apprehended by Kesek in the last eighteen months. For that work, Direnc would need to use one of the offices in the commissioner's suite of rooms on the 80th floor.

She finished the message, posted it to Direnc's board on his computer, and then withdrew the data stick, deleting the downloaded program in the process.

She paused. No alarms sounded from the hallway. No alerts flashed on the computer screen. No security warnings echoed over the intercom. She allowed herself to breathe again.

Rising from the chair, she considered Direnc's prone form. She couldn't hide him in the supply closet—the PT would show him in that precise location, and the security guards would wonder why a highly ranked analyst was lounging in his closet. She opted instead to prop him up in his chair, strapping him there with a spare length of wire from her belt. "I do apologize for the inconvenience," she murmured as she rifled through his pockets for the door key.

She left him slumped there, still unconscious, as she locked the door behind her.

Najwa pulled out her delver. It lit up, showing her the location and names of everyone in the building. How she loved Kesek's personnel trackers.

It was nice knowing the commissioner was not here.

Gironde locked his personal office for the night and entered his private lift.

The lift had started its high-speed descent to the basement levels when his delver beeped. Gironde frowned at the sound—the melody indicated a message sent from the device. Odd, considering he'd composed no message recently. Pulling it from his pocket, he flipped open the cover and read the notice.

Then he slapped the emergency stop button, jerking the lift to a bumpy halt.

Direnc's security clearance code unlocked the main door to the commissioner's suite of offices. She made sure it locked again behind her—if she were to be found out by security it would buy her some time.

Searching out the proper records terminal in one of the several offices in the suite, she used Direnc's key to get into the database she needed. All the analysis computers on this floor could be accessed in that manner. Once in the network, however, Najwa unhooked Direnc's PT from her wrist and set it on the chair. All she needed was for security to see that Direnc was in the database and on the 80th floor, while she attended to other matters.

The lock on the commissioner's door was simple enough for her electronic pick to handle, but she knew there were a series of other alarms in place that would be triggered. Najwa did not consider this a problem—she had someone to help her get in.

Using her delver, she summoned one of the maintenance 'bots working on this floor. It used its own access code to enter the suite and beamed another code at the commissioner's locked door. A second later it popped open, and the obedient 'bot started its cleaning routine inside.

Normally the maintenance robots would not open a locked door with humans present unless given specific authority to do so. Najwa took care of that difficulty in her reprogramming, and so it ignored her.

She made for the commissioner's main computer. She tried a series of different programs to hack past the security, watching the timer on her belt out of the corner of her eye. Finally the fourth program worked—it let her in.

Breathing deeply, she set about searching all the databases and files. There were endless memos, self-congratulatory press releases and images, but not the data she needed. Then she stumbled onto something—a photograph that didn't fit. All the rest were labeled with a brief subject and a specific date; this one said only "Sacred Red." She opened it.

It wasn't an image, but a collection of data files disguised as one. Pages popped open as she flipped through the data. Contacts made with Tiu warships. Coordinates and intercept times for Realm task forces. Daily security settings for Trebizond Base. Payments made to pirate cruisers in exchange for their loyalty. Arrest records. The whole vast project was there for the taking.

Fumbling with a data stick, Najwa jammed it into the drive and waited. The files dutifully marched off the screen into her icon, copying onto the stick. She continued to read, leafing through the arrest files. "They're here," she murmured. "Congress, and others. Underground—right under the tower."

A file opened that made her gasp. King Andrew, bereft of his royal garb, in a room that was labeled with a prison cell number. "He's with them," she said breathlessly. Further reading made her sick, as she discovered the commissioner's plans for the king. "He can't—"

"There's very little I 'can't' do right now, young lady."

She froze. Gironde stood in the office doorway. He held his gun low, aiming for her head. He was smiling, but it was not a pleasant face he made. She could see the fury.

"You've done a superb job infiltrating this building," he said. "Maintenance. I'll be you had something to do with the hospitalization of our normal man, eh? No matter."

"You shouldn't be here."

"Ah. You've been tracking us?" Gironde shook his head. "My silly girl, I don't wear a PT. What a rookie mistake. So, you've busied yourself with some reading in my absence. Opinions?"

Najwa yanked the data stick from the drive. "You will be stopped."

"Yes, and who will do that when you're dead, hmm?" His smile vanished. "RG perhaps? They've grown more mature and seen the folly of sending Rozsade everywhere, recruited you off-world."

He stepped closer, gun steady. "Listen well. This Realm is mine. It will remain mine. When my power here is consolidated, Rozsada is first on my list. An ecological 'accident,' perhaps. Or another terrorist attack. And then the rest of the worlds will bow to me."

"My clan has a name for your kind." The scrambler was tucked in her open pocket. She didn't dare grab it with him staring right at her.

"What?"

"Blasphemer."

The fury exploded onto his face. "Why, you . . ." His finger tightened on the trigger . . .

And he jumped suddenly. He looked down at his leg. The 'bot was diligently sweeping and had collided with him.

Najwa drew the scrambler and fired, its pulse rippling the air. Gironde jerked to one side. The pulse grazed his gun arm—it fell lifeless. His gun clattered to the floor.

Najwa braced herself against the chair and vaulted across the desk. She lashed out with her foot to kick Gironde—but to her shock, the commissioner seized her ankle with his good arm and twisted, sending her crashing off the corner of the desk.

"You underestimate my abilities," he said in a cold, quiet voice. "Take some solace in knowing you are not the first."

The stirrings of fear intensified. She was up on her feet as he advanced, throwing a solid punch. Najwa deflected the blow, counterattacking with her own swipe. Gironde's reflexes were up to the task—they traded punches and kicks, each causing some damage to the other but neither gaining the advantage. Najwa found it vaguely comical, with his limp arm slapping against his side. Then Gironde struck again. It hurt badly.

He swung a punch. This time Najwa caught his arm, spinning around to slam him up against the wall.

With a grunt, Gironde bashed his head into her face. Najwa flinched. She deflected the blow to one cheek—the impact would have otherwise broken her nose. But her grip loosened enough for Gironde to break free. He struck once across her face, a second time in the shoulder, and a third to her chest to knock her back over the desk.

Gironde stood there, panting. He spotted his gun on the floor and scooped it up. "You have some nerve, young lady. Slithering in here like a serpent, challenging me, striking me. I will take great pleasure in killing you. But not here. I think I'd rather see you suffer first."

Najwa shuddered to her feet. She leaned back.

Against the window.

Fear trickled away. Najwa lifted her chin. "That's only because you couldn't kill me now. Incompetent."

Gironde snarled, a fierce growl, and fired.

But Najwa was already out of his line of fire. The window shattered in an explosion of flashing shards. Cool night air blew in.

Gironde shielded himself from the glass.

Najwa turned and leapt from the window.

The wind roared by her ears as she plummeted headfirst. She caught a breathtaking view of the sparkling city lights reflected off the sea. She pointed her wrist at the smaller tower fifty meters away. The grappling claw shot out with a burst of compressed gas and a jolt to her arm. Its cord cut through the air behind it. Najwa reached for the arm-mounted launcher and held on tight.

The claw imbedded itself in the masonry surrounding the windows. The cord yanked hard, jerking Najwa's arm. She grunted against the pain. Her fall suddenly became a curving loop as she arced around the second tower. She timed her inertia carefully, calculating just the right moment to prepare her body for impact . . .

The cord wrapped more tightly around the building until she kicked out her feet, crashing through a window on the 45th floor of the adjacent tower.

Najwa tumbled across the table, pulling herself up out of the roll. To her relief, it was an empty conference room, devoid of any major obstacles—except of course, the marble-surfaced table she'd just traversed.

It was at that moment that she heard the faint sounds of alarms from the central tower, carried across the night air.

• • •

Najwa made it halfway to the ground floor when her lift jerked to a halt. A display screen prompted her for her security ID before she would be allowed to disembark. Snorting, she dug in her coverall pouch not for the ID but for her plasma torch. Making sure the lift was indeed stopped at the 22nd floor, she lit the torch, shielding her eyes in the process. She made a smooth, slow sweep with her arm and cut herself her own exit.

Najwa was halfway to the next lift shaft down the pearl white and steel grey corridor when she spotted a camera's light flashing. She had a half-second to leap aside into an alcove shielded by a pair of fan palms.

The pair of cameras, one above each lift and aimed down the hall, had begun their slow rotations. Najwa cursed. She knew she still had a couple of minutes on her timer, which means someone had ended the software update ahead of schedule. Gironde reacted fast.

There was no way to the lift except past one of those two cameras, either of which could detect her at the moment. Najwa pondered her next move and was halfway through her short list of options when footsteps broke her reverie.

A lone guard was walking toward her from the recently opened lift. She peered at him through the ferns, watching the cameras out of the corner of her eye. He would see the cut door at any moment, and she knew she could only act when he was out of view of the cameras.

She waited. The second camera turned away, as the first started its rotation back, creating a momentary blind spot.

Najwa threw her plasma torch across the hall. The guard's head snapped to his lift, tracking the projectile . . .

And Najwa was on him, hand clamped over his mouth, arm fastened around his neck. She gritted her teeth as she held him against his struggling. He soon slipped into unconsciousness.

She managed to drag him back into the alcove before the camera turned back.

Panting from the exertion, she crouched as low and as far back as possible.

The cameras continued their sweep, unperturbed.

Najwa sagged against the wall. She turned to the collapsed guard and checked his pulse first—it was still strong. She dug his ID badge from its clear pocket on his chest and yanked his pistol from his belt. Loaded. Two extra clips. She pocketed those too, grimacing slightly.

She'd need that gun, if worse came to worse. She'd lost her scrambler in her tussle with Gironde.

But her first targets would cause her no remorse.

She waited, calmly this time, until the cameras were pointed away from her position.

Then she bolted.

She was at the end of the corridor instantly. The cameras turned back.

Najwa started cutting the next lift door.

"Any sign of her?"

"Nothing yet. She may have taken the lift shaft."

"Blazes. Uh oh." The shift commander hopped to his feet. His subordinate followed suit, saluting just in time as Commissioner Gironde stormed through the doorway. "Sir!"

"Where is she now?"

"Ah . . . we're having some difficulty tracking her, Commissioner. She has no PT, and is avoiding most of the cameras."

Gironde glowered at the shift commander. "Flood the shafts with carbon dioxide."

"Yes, Commissioner."

Najwa was rappelling down the lift shaft when she heard the hissing of gas. The car beneath her was stopped at the second floor. She increased her pace rappelling down the shaft, well aware that the carbon dioxide would settle to the bottom of the shaft and elbow the available oxygen out of the way, filling the lower levels first.

At the third floor, she dug again for her torch and cut through the closed doors.

The front door was still well guarded.

Four security robots formed a cordon in front of the wide glass doors. A pair of human guards wearing maroon body armor paced in front of their line. Each one bore an assault rifle.

Najwa leaned back around the corner of the side corridor. Far too much firepower awaited. She needed another way out. But she was out of exits.

She thought about cutting her way out a sidewall. She dismissed that idea. The security around the perimeter was tightened beyond the normal two guards on each side of the tower's base—Najwa knew Kesek protocol well enough.

Najwa sighed. She looked down at the gun in her hand and the spare weapons in her pockets. She pulled out her spare scrambler. If she could take out the two men first . . .

The distant staccato of gunfire drew her attention. Peering back around the corner, she saw the two guards race out the doors, a pair of robots trailing them. More guards were outside, arrayed about the entry courtyard in a loose semicircle, firing from half concealment. Firing skyward.

Najwa murmured a prayer of thanks and bolted from her hiding spot. She heard a shout from behind her—someone must have just come down the stairs—but she was already shooting with both guns at the robots.

One series of shots pierced the robot's thin armor by its neck, severing the head from the body before it could react. The second was turned halfway and firing with its own weapon when her bullets cut through a central electricity supply. The upper half of its body went limp, as it continued to roll about on its treads.

Najwa continued firing in a seemingly random pattern at the glass doors, which the guards had locked. Her shots brought the glass on both doors cascading to the floor. They crashed and tinkled in an almost musical tone. Alarms shrieked as she burst into the courtyard. One of the remaining two security robots spun her way. It aimed a machine gun at her head. Najwa was quicker. A point blank blast with a scrambler pulse fried every circuit in the robot's artificial skull.

The human guards—a half dozen of them, Najwa belatedly noticed—finally realized they had a threat behind them. They wheeled about to fire.

Najwa finally saw what had occupied their attention. A smaller, more compact version of a jetcopter hovered overhead. Its single autocannon sprayed white-hot projectiles at the ground. Whoever was firing didn't aim directly at the guards but sent them running. Then it swiveled its aim and blasted the remaining robot into metal shards.

The jetcopter dropped suddenly to the courtyard. It stopped in a hover less than a meter off the ground. A hatch on one side opened. Najwa figured that was all the invitation she'd receive. Running across the dirt, she fired her scrambler as she went. A body's length away she dove into the compartment. Her side crashed against an empty seat. "Go!"

No pilot responded to her command, but the jetcopter roared off the ground. Its autocannon continued to scream as its flight path curved its way perilously close to a stand of trees. The hatch slipped shut. "We're hit!" Najwa called out, staggering to the cockpit.

No one was at the controls. There were no visible controls Najwa could see, only a set of status indicators and screens.

ENGINE DAMAGE REPORTED. The tinny voice came from a small console grid. LOSING ALTITUDE. ATTEMPTING TO LEVEL FLIGHT PATH.

Robot-piloted. Najwa nodded. RG planned well.

She withdrew her delver and jabbed at the transmit button. It started sending. She exhaled. The data from Gironde's files was on its way.

Another voice spoke out of the console. "Whisper, this is Monitor One. Report."

"Charlie Six Bravo," Najwa said clearly.

"Countersign: Delta Niner Foxtrot," the voice answered. "Proceed."

"Data retrieval was successful," Najwa said. "But there's more than we expected. We need to get the news out as soon as possible. I've started transmission to your frequency."

"Good. We will have Mom and Dad send it out. You're being followed. There's no time for rendezvous. Go to Bed. Monitor One, out."

Najwa snapped her jaw shut as the jetcopter bounced its way through the sky. Mom and Dad. RG must have helped Congress find a transmission station so they could get the information out onto the reach. And "Go to Bed" meant she'd have to find her own way out of this mess.

The jetcopter lurched. Its engines were suddenly much quieter. Najwa saw on one flashing red screen that this was because it had lost one of its engines.

The craft rose and fell unevenly as the robot pilot did its best to stay aloft. Out the cockpit window, Najwa could see a city park growing in the distance. Aiming for a soft landing, she guessed.

Skidding across the open field, the jetcopter banked off a set of playground equipment, mangling the climbing rack and throwing Najwa against one side of the compartment. Metal squealed against dirt as the aircraft dug a deep furrow through the smooth surface of the grassy field. It finally shuddered to a halt at the edge of a glade.

LANDING . . . ACCOMPLISHED, the robot pilot stammered. DAMAGE CRITICAL. PURSUERS CLOSING IN FIVE MINUTES. IMPERATIVE . . . MUST NOT BE ALLOWED TO RECOVER . . .

The voice faded into a hiss of static. All the displays went dark, save one—a timer that started its countdown.

Najwa stripped off her coveralls. Underneath she wore a short-sleeved flower-print blouse and casual pants. She discarded her boots, opting to go barefoot—shoes were not an immediate concern.

She opened the hatch and ran for the cover of the glade. Sirens whined in the distance. The delver rode snugly in her pants. Najwa continued her mental countdown, hoping she remembered correctly . . .

The thunder of the explosion momentarily deafened her. She saw the trees silhouetted by the flames and knew there was nothing left of the jetcopter to point authorities to her or RG.

All the while, her delver continued transmitting its data.

Kortenaer market square was teeming with people and riddled with booths containing all manner of diversions this night. It was an annual festival. Dancing, talking, laughing, drinking—they were having their party, and nothing would dissuade them.

Swarms of Kesek officers burst into the square. They looked perplexed by the sheer quantity of people. Some revelers tried offering beverages to the officers. Gironde, standing at the fore of his men, angrily shoved them away. "Find her!"

Thirty meters away, Najwa sipped on a glass of cold cider as she mingled with the crowd.

CHAPTER 11

October 2602
Bethel Star System
Bethel, New Grace

Simon's folded arms and deadpan expression were meant to intimidate, to enforce his answer. Neither had any effect on his engineer, Shen Renshu.

"I'm not letting 'em in there!" The shorter man was no less passionate in his statement. His Asian features were animated with outrage, and his normally slicked back, grey-streaked black hair was coming undone from its ponytail.

Renshu's comments echoed loudly in the cargo bay of *Natalia Zoja*. Simon always found its sprawling interior comforting, but now he stood by the wings of the barge ruing the day he agreed to this half-insane idea. Unarmored Lancers trucked weapons and ammunition down the barge's cargo ramp. The sight of all those guns made him uneasy. If it wasn't for Colleen—Commander Verge, he reminded himself—offering the down payment for services and promising future pay, he'd never have signed up for this.

He supposed he'd have to have Colonel Verge visit *Natalia Zoja* and see if everything was to his liking. Might not be too bad if he brought his sister along . . .

"Simon! Are you listening?"

"Of course." By that Simon meant not at all.

Renshu planted his hands on his hips. He shook a greasy tool in Simon's face. "You know they've got their techs fooling around with my ship's innards?"

"Your ship? Stars, Renshu, it's mine!"

"Don't change the subject. They're talking about upgrades and rewiring circuits and something about the efficiency of the Raszewski sphere . . ."

"Renshu . . ."

" . . . never let anybody else touch those drives, I told you . . ."

"Renshu . . ."

" . . . if they think they're going to change one screw without my permission . . ."

"*Renshu!*"

The engineer choked off his tirade. "What?"

"Don't worry about it. Just glare over their shoulders the whole time and show them who's boss, right?" He clapped Renshu on the arm and turned him aside. This wasn't getting any easier.

"You wouldn't say that if you weren't so goggle-eyed every time you mentioned Commander Verge, Skipper."

"What's that supposed to mean?"

Renshu twisted around. "Simon, you're a great friend but you're a terrible liar."

Heat rose inside Simon. "Are you saying I'm interested in a royal fleet commander who's probably what, ten years younger than me?"

"It doesn't mean you're dishonoring Hannah." Renshu spoke in a lowered voice.

Simon wondered at that. He had to admit, he had paid quite a bit of attention to the commander. Why not? She was an impressive woman—and pretty. But his guilt over Hannah's death overwhelmed him at every turn. Maybe someday that would change.

Simon snapped himself back to the present. "You changed the subject on purpose."

"You're a smart one, Skipper. Now promise me you'll keep these fleet techies out of my engine room!"

"No, I won't."

"Blast and blazes . . . !"

"Calm down! You've got the final say on these changes." He had to get back to work. Anything to stop thinking about Commander Verge. "Like I said, just keep your eagle eyes on them. I'll make sure they listen to you. Hey, we need them—they got the gear we could only dream of."

"Well, they have fixed those hull breaches a lot faster than we could." Renshu turned morose. "We just can't do that intense work. Sure, we patched them up after the asteroid run at Serhat, but their stuff will last longer. And they're very tidy—no mess when they're done . . ."

"See? It's working out." Simon eased him toward the stairs at the rear of the cargo bay. "Now go straighten them out. You're in charge, got it?"

"Right. I'm in charge. We'll work on it." But Simon could still hear Renshu's grumbling fade away: " . . . think they'll retune *my* drives, do they?"

Simon rubbed his hand over his face, weary. Crew troubles. That thought made him remember Baden. That boy was as stubborn as anyone. Come to think of it, he was as bad as his mother.

He watched the Lancers shoulder their armor down the barge ramp. One of the younger soldiers wore a tan uniform instead of the mottled grey-green. He was a lot slimmer than the well-muscled bunch. Simon recognized him as the colonel's son. "Where do we put these, Captain?" the teen gasped.

"There's room in the back." Simon gestured vaguely behind him. "You need a hand, Cadet?"

"Alec, Captain. No need for civilians to call me by rank. I don't even have a real one yet."

This kid was okay. Very respectful. Again Simon thought of Baden. Maybe that would change too.

"We're converting some space at the back into makeshift bunks for your guys," Simon said. "It's gonna get pretty crowded with more than seventy of you—plus those hexambler robots. Your officers already got dibs on the few spare cabins we carry."

"Thank you, Captain."

Troop Master Sands stomped up behind them. He balanced a sinister-looking staff over one arm and hefted a heavy assault rifle in the other. "You getting settled, kid?"

"Yes, thank you, Benjamin. The captain was just offering his assistance."

Simon didn't like the look Sands gave him, one he himself had reserved for pirates. "You probably should steer clear of the captain," Sands said.

Alec gave him a curious look but obeyed. They both walked toward the stairs. As Sands passed, he muttered to Simon, "Stay outta the way, Expatriate."

Simon burned a glare into his back. This arrangement was getting better and better. "Zepsuty," he swore.

Alec climbed the stairs behind Benjamin. He shifted his duffle bag onto his other shoulder. Down below in the cargo back, Captain Haczyk was watching them. "You didn't have to be like that to him, Benjamin."

Benjamin snorted. "Like what?"

"Like yourself."

No answer came to that.

Alec followed him up into the crowded corridors of the six-brace. He looked around in fascination. The only ships he'd traveled on had been Verge family liners and military transports. This was entirely different. Everything had a worn edge to it, from the deck plates right up to the flickering lights. Despite the wear and tear, and the lack of uniformity, the ship felt warm. It felt lived in.

Benjamin stopped before a hatch. "Home sweet home for a week or so."

He shoved it open. Alec's mouth twisted into a suppressed smile. It wasn't quite a cabin. More of a converted storage space. A bunk cot was squeezed into one side of the room. Boxes and half-open containers lined the other wall. Alec figured he could lay on the floor with his head under the bunk and touch both walls. The room wasn't much longer.

"Roomy, ain't it?" Benjamin chucked his bag onto the boxes. They apparently were secured by straps, because they didn't fall over. He threw himself onto the bottom cot.

The whole bunk cot swayed ominously. Benjamin looked up in alarm. "I don't think you should try that again, Troop Master," Alec said.

"Yeah, duly noted, Cadet Trainee." Benjamin unfastened the top closure of his grey-green uniform. "Man, look at this. Where do you think we go to empty the old cargo hatch?"

"What?"

"You know, the little boys' restroom."

"Cargo hatch?" Alec made a face. "Thank you for that image. I'd imagine there's a crew bathroom down the corridor somewhere. Perhaps we should call down to the planet and make sure a few camp units make it up to this ship."

"Not a bad idea." Benjamin swung his feet over the edge of the cot. He started rummaging through his bag. "Come on, get your gear set up."

Alec wondered how to do so in this closet. So he just tossed his bag down next to Benjamin's.

"You got the idea, kid. Ah." Benjamin pulled out whatever he was looking for. Alec stared at the curved silver object, smooth all over save for a tiny control panel. It reminded him of half a bowl. A black strap hung loosely from its edges. The inside was covered with smooth padding and a sheen of gold bristles.

"Where did you get a neural sim?" Alec asked in quiet admiration.

"From the good colonel." Benjamin threw it to him. "Catch."

"Benjamin!" Alec caught the device. He cradled it as one might a newborn. "Do you have any idea how much this costs? You cannot just buy a device that links directly into your mind for pocket change, you know."

"Definitely can't buy it on a corporal's pay. Put it on. Your daddy wants to make sure you're ready when we hit Earth, and seeing as how you're the only one without advanced drop training . . ."

"I've had drop training. I ranked highly in my class."

"Do I look like I care?" Benjamin scowled. "This ain't no standard drop, kid. Put it on."

Alec eased the device over his head. The curved silver portion covered his vision, plunging him into darkness. There was a tickling beneath his hair and across his scalp as the neural bristles made contact with his mind. Alec kept his eyes squeezed shut as colors flickered and flashed beyond his eyelids. Some people could stand looking at the startup procedure. He got dizzy and had fainted once in class.

PROGRAM READY. The words appeared like a marquee against the darkness.

He opened his eyes.

He stood at the threshold of *Natalia Zoja*'s cargo bay, fully clad in his armor. More than that, his armor was coated in a thick layer of ablative foam. He could feel the jumpsuit against his skin, and the armor beyond it. The familiar smells of sweat and plastics irritated his nose. So real.

A quick check of his heads-up display showed he was equipped with a railer, a lance, a machine gun, a breather pack and . . . Wait a microsec.

An aerowing?

Alec looked out the cargo bay. He could see the star-speckled expanse of space curving over the vast blue curve of Earth.

Stars above!

He ran the mental commands to cut the program. After a whirl of images flew by his eyes, he wrenched off the device. Benjamin was grinning at him.

"What kind of a drop is Father planning?" Alec was aware he sounded breathless.

"The kind that you get killed in real quick if you don't practice. The kind where you can turn into a mini meteorite even if you do it right." Benjamin stood up. "I'm supposed to help you out on this. I'll link my comm into your neural sim and talk you through it."

Alec swallowed. "I guess we'd better practice, then."

Commander Colleen Verge was trying, at that moment, to not pine for what she saw as the simple life of a six-brace captain.

She sat at a black mesh and grey paneled desk in her small office. The cabin had just enough room for two chairs, the desk, and a row of computer and holographic displays. It also had the door to a small restroom off to one side. The only thing brightening the dull tans and metallic finishes of the bulkheads was the brilliant green creeping vine she had growing from an empty storage bin in one corner. Colleen was amazed as anyone else that it was still alive.

She relinquished her attention to the delver glowing on her desk. Crew manifests. Colleen sighed. Since the battle that devastated her ship and its companions the week before, she'd had to do some major juggling of crews to make up for losses in various departments. There were still gaps to be plugged.

Her hatch buzzer sounded. It grated on her nerves like an irritating insect. "Come in."

Lieutenant Lucia de Silva entered. Colleen nodded at her first officer. She could see the bustle of activity on *HMS Herald*'s bridge just beyond. "Hello, Lucia. Come to stir me to action?"

"Seems you might need it, Skipper." De Silva shut the hatch. She handed a delver to Colleen. "I thought you would like my update on the crew levels."

"Thanks. I think." Colleen accepted the device and scrolled down the pages. Now, here was some good news. "So the Bethelites are willing to provide volunteers."

"Yes. It seems they feel indebted to us for fighting off the Tiu. We managed to get several dozen for our damage control slots."

"Good. That's where we need them the most. You saw the work they did?"

"It's impressive." De Silva took the chair opposite Colleen. "Our own people commented to me on their skill. We should consider ourselves lucky."

"Lucky, indeed." Colleen felt some of the weight of her work drop away. She linked de Silva's delver to her own and transferred the report. Tiny lights trickled down one side of Colleen's delver as it accepted the data. "You wouldn't happen to have assignments for them all, would you?"

"Not yet, Skipper. But the day is young." De Silva accepted her delver back. "I did take the liberty of divvying up the ones with the most experience between *Herald* and *Algiers*."

"Good. Make sure we get a few barges down to the surface to collect the volunteers from the planet. In fact, I'll probably go along myself." Colleen rubbed her eyes. De Silva hadn't made a move to leave. "Was there something else?"

"Well . . . yes." De Silva cocked her head slightly. "I wanted to make sure you're all right, Captain."

"Is this an official inquiry?"

"As your exec and friend, I suppose so." De Silva rapped her delver on the edge of the desk. "Out with it. You have to be under some strain."

"Oh, there is that. Becoming commodore of a five-ship task force in a split-second adds stress," Colleen said wearily.

De Silva nodded. "You know the other officers and I will do everything we can to share the burden, Skipper."

"Of course." Colleen was thankful for the crew she had. Her heart warmed at the verbal confirmation of her own faith.

"Is there . . . anything else?"

"Lucia, what are you fishing for?"

De Silva fidgeted in her seat. "There's some talk about you and . . . this six-brace captain."

Colleen stared at her for a moment. Then she laughed. "Have you come in here to update me on rumors about my personal life?"

De Silva smiled back. "Not really. Mostly I wanted to warn you so you wouldn't be surprised. You know how the rumor factories work on starships."

"Yes, they never stop."

De Silva waited. Colleen laughed again. "That's none of your business, Lieutenant. Captain Haczyk is . . . an interesting man. That's all."

"I see. Forgive the intrusion, Skipper. But my concern is that you have a lot going on right now," de Silva said. "I just want you to know that if there's anything else I can do."

Colleen waved a hand. She rose from her chair and stretched. Stars, her back ached. She reached out with one hand and ran her fingers over the coarse leaves of her creeping vine. "It has been hard," Colleen admitted. "But there are things that have helped. Right before we arrived at Bethel, I had—a strange dream."

De Silva turned toward her. Colleen could almost see her brain accessing old files. "Was that when you requested the picket launch? Late that night?"

"That was." Colleen shivered at the memory of the dream. The pangs of fear, the flickering wreckage, and the warning. "It was almost a message of sorts. I don't know how to explain it. Or rather, I didn't know how to explain it until we met the Bethelites. And that boy with the Bible."

She saw de Silva tense. "Don't worry, Lucia, I'm not planning on breaking any Kesek laws at the moment."

"It's not that, Skipper." De Silva fiddled with her delver. "Something about these people strikes me deep in my heart. *La paz de Dios.*"

"Yes. You do see it," Colleen said. She thought she might be the only one—though her nephew Alec had excitedly talked with her after one of the outdoor Bible readings. "I have no patience left for the Union Synoptic Church, Lucia. There is nothing there to sustain me. And I could care less if Kesek's official church has my membership or not."

"It isn't mandatory."

"Oh, but you know as well as I do the social and political benefits," Colleen said. She reached for the wall intercom. "Captain to hangar bay."

"Hangar bay. Deck officer here."

"Ready a barge for me, deck officer. I'm going down to the surface to meet with the Bethel volunteers."

"Aye, Skipper. How soon?"

"Twenty minutes."

• • •

Simon got several commnotes from Major Branko Mazur, the last person in the galaxy he wanted to speak with. He finally tracked Mazur down at the combined Starkweather and Rozsade camp in Bethel's hills.

He left *Natalia Zoja*'s barge amidst a half-dozen armored Lancer guards. Simon didn't want to hang around long. The Lancers, standing three meters tall in their full powered armor, unnerved him.

Dust whipped around his boots as he stalked off through the camp. Clouds had rolled in, blanketing the area in cold, grey weather. It cast a pall over the ruined camp. Simon cringed at the sight of crumpled barracks walls, torn and burnt cabins, and wrecked combat robots. Grey-green suited Lancers and Rozsade fusiliers in black and red were everywhere, closing down cabins and moving weaponry. None of them wore their armor. They were busy breaking down camp.

"Haczyk!"

Simon recognized the booming voice immediately. Branko Mazur thundered through some of his own men. The fusiliers almost dropped the ammunition boxes balanced in their muscular arms. "Hey, Branko, nice to see you."

Branko scowled. The scar across his face rippled. "You have ignored my notes, yes? I want to know the arrangements you made for my men."

"What arrangements?"

"Aboard your rusted bucket, Expatriate. My two most elite maniples will accompany Colonel Verge's troops."

"Your what?" Simon clenched his fists. Suddenly Branko's irritation wasn't funny anymore. "Your men too? I thought I was taking the colonel's company! That's seventy-two guys in armor plus their robots!"

"Do not raise complaints with me, Haczyk," Branko said. "It is done. Your barge will be replaced by one of our assault shuttles. Roomy and armored."

Simon gritted his teeth. "Look, this isn't the deal I made with Colonel Verge."

"Pah. James is my superior in this mission."

"Why my ship? You have your own transports, don't you?"

"You will have to ask James."

Simon took a step toward Branko before he remembered the other man's immense size and probably considerable fighting skills. "You tell your colonel I'll decide who goes aboard my ship," he said.

Branko's face went cold. "So. You would do well to remember your place, Expatriate. This is a military operation now."

That was enough of that. "See you around, Branko. Don't load your shuttle yet."

"Haczyk! You will see me again!"

Not if I can avoid it, Simon thought.

As he continued down the hill toward the bottom of the camp, he spotted a trio of military barges, black-edged white triangles with smoothed edges. They stood ready on their quintets of landing legs. Each bore the blue ring and white stars of Starkweather.

Several lines of Bethelites streamed toward each shuttle. Simon figured there must be at least ninety, if not more. He couldn't tell who was who from this distance, but he could tell the ages varied. Most seemed younger, but there were several of middle age. Clustered about the shuttles were pockets of people in tan—Starkweather navy personnel. The bright red hair of one in particular stood out to him.

As Simon approached the first shuttle, he could see the line of crewers was stopped. The Bethelite recruits were entering one at a time. It seemed it would take forever to load them all.

Commander Verge noticed him. "Captain Haczyk." She sounded surprised. "Did you need assistance?"

How to tell her that he was just glad to be able to talk with her, uninterrupted, for a moment? Simon decided not to mention it. Hannah's memory was still with him. "I came down because Branko's been harassing me," he said instead. "And then I found out why."

"Ah. I take it he's going to be a guest aboard your ship."

"Yeah. At least for a while. But after running through an asteroid field I guess I can put up with Branko for a few days."

She laughed. Simon tried not to grin but failed. "Looks like your loading process got bogged down."

Colleen's expression turned more serious. "It's a delay I'm willing to make. Listen."

Simon realized now there was a person standing at the front of each line leading up the shuttles' ramps. The shuttle nearest had a stout, white-haired man who wore a plain green worksuit. He held a small bowl in one hand and a bronze chalice in the other. Simon listened.

"Take and eat. This is the body of Christ."

The middle-aged woman at the front of the line accepted a tiny wedge of bread from the man in green. She bowed slightly, then ate it with apparent reverence. The man offered the bronze chalice. The woman accepted it and took a sip, eyes closed.

"Take and drink. This is the blood of his sacrifice, shed for the forgiveness of your sins," Heng said. "Go in peace to love and serve the Lord."

"Amen."

Simon watched as the next person and the person after that repeated that scene. He'd heard those words somewhere before. Something Hannah had said to him.

"Assemblyman Heng said it is a practice the people here had abandoned long ago," Commander Verge said quietly. "Some still upheld it, but until your son read of it from the Bible, it was viewed as an irrelevancy."

Simon swallowed. He couldn't tear his eyes from the people going through this ritual. Their faces were determined and happy. Like Hannah. And all this because of something Baden had done?

He realized abruptly there were tears in his eyes. He wiped them away, furious at the weakness. "It's . . . something."

The commander stood closer. "There is a love there that I don't understand."

Simon looked at her. She was holding herself tall in professional posture. Her face, however, was a study in longing. "But you'd like to," he said. "Understand it."

"I am grateful your son's recordings and the imaged Bible were available so quickly." She looked down at her boots. "I have a copy of both on my delver."

"Really?" Simon didn't know whether to be appalled or impressed that she had so willingly broken the law for something as strange as this religion.

Of course, so had he.

"Not long ago I made a silent plea to a God I considered uncaring and perhaps nonexistent," Commander Verge said.

"These people did not view Him as nonexistent. They see Him as being right here among them."

The suggestion troubled Simon. They stood in silence as the loading continued. A light mist settled over the area. Water glistened on the curved surfaces of the shuttle. Simon considered offering Commander Verge his jacket but thought better of it.

"I'd like to spend more time with you." Simon blurted the words before he had a chance to stop himself. Blast, he felt like a vac-head teenager all over again.

Commander Verge didn't say anything.

Simon cursed himself. "Sorry, Commander, it was a dumb thing to—"

"Please. Call me Colleen."

"Of course." Simon smothered a grin. "Colleen. I'm sorry if that seemed forward. I didn't know what else to say. But it's true."

Colleen looked down for a moment, and Simon was struck by the distinct impression that this warship commander was shy.

"Thank you, Simon, for your kindness. If these were different circumstances . . ."

Simon shook his head. "Being with you has been a nice change from my self-imposed mourning." He cringed at the bitterness in his own voice.

"We will have a chance, if you'd like," Colleen said softly.

"I certainly would."

"So would I."

They stood close for a moment as the soldiers and crew bustled about. Simon noticed a few of them muttering amongst each other and casting curious glances their way. Colleen abruptly cleared her throat.

"We will have much to discuss once our ships are underway, Captain." Her tone was formal, but Simon saw the smile curving her lips. "I trust you will find time for me in your schedule."

Simon nodded, playing the studiously neutral game. "I will indeed, Commander."

Colleen turned and walked off to one of the shuttles. Simon could only stare and wonder what in blazes he was doing.

Natalia Zoja's bridge was far too crowded when Simon returned to the ship.

Emi was at the nav station. Her raven hair bobbed as she manipulated the charts and plotted a course for *Natalia Zoja* to Bethel's distant sundoors. From those points around the star, they and the ships of the task force would tract shift to Xiaoji, and then from there to Earth.

Baden should be at that station. Simon tried not to remember his son's smart-aleck comments—and then realized that he missed the banter.

Emi was not alone. Branko and Colonel James Verge stood toward one side of the bridge. Perfect, Simon thought. More for the party.

Branko spotted him first. "Haczyk! You take too long. We are ready."

Simon elbowed past him. He may have accidentally jostled the major. "Get off my bridge, Branko. I've work to do. Go play with your guns."

"*Niepotrzebny*," Branko snarled.

Simon sat down in the helm chair. The main screen sprawling before him offered a breathtaking view of the ships riding in orbit behind *Natalia Zoja*, above the semi-crescent jewel of Bethel. The trio of sleek battle corvettes—*HMS Herald, Algiers,* and *Bold*—rode in a loose triangle in the lead. The bulky and massive transport *HMT Randall Keach* was behind them, with the carrier *HMCV Crossbow* drifting off its starboard. The two Rozsade transports—olive drab, ugly and stark to Simon's eye—took up the rear.

"It's quite a sight," Colonel Verge said. "Though three short of what we started with."

Simon looked at him. The officer's stern face framed sad eyes. "You lost a lot of good people."

"I did. But we made the Tiu pay."

No doubt, Simon thought. He tapped a button on his console.

Colonel Verge sighed. "Well, Captain, your ship is fairly stuffed full with our men and weapons. I suppose we are ready."

"Right. You gonna tell me exactly what I do with your boys and Branko's once we get to Earth?"

Colonel Verge shared a look with Branko. The latter's wolfish grin did not reassure Simon. "The details are being worked out," Colonel Verge said.

Somehow Simon didn't believe him. He tapped a button on his console that transferred the comm and weapons station functions to his own master board. Then he smacked the intercom. "Renshu, you good?"

"My baby's ready, Skipper. Say the magic words and she's all yours."

"Deal."

No sooner did he shut off the intercom than the main comm light blinked on his console. "Captain Haczyk. Go ahead."

"This is Commander Verge aboard *HMS Herald*." Her voice was all business but it still made Simon's heart skip a beat. "Are you ready for departure, Captain?"

"Of course, Commander." Simon tried not to grin. "See you at the sundoors."

"Looking forward to it. *Herald* out."

Okay, so he let a small grin slip. But then he remembered his audience included not just Emi but Colonel Verge. Here he was, mooning over the guy's sister.

Simon cleared his throat. "Okay, folks, we're off."

He eased the curved handle of the drive control forward. Subtle vibrations in the deckplates told him the antimatter engines were running smoothly. On the main screen, the task force ships followed suit—brilliant white flares erupted from each.

As they got underway, Simon thought of Baden leaving Bethel the day before aboard the pirate ship. He wished things had gone differently with his only boy. Now that he dwelt on it, though, he came up with a way to possibly heal some of the hurt.

He dug into his pants pocket and dug out a worn, dirty datastick. It was the size of his little finger and dull green. Simon slipped it into an access port under the console. In a second he had sent the contents in a message to Baden's Reach access account.

Simon exhaled. Hadn't even realized he'd been holding his breath. Kesek might track the contents, but at this point that didn't worry him too much. He just hoped Baden would actually read it when the signal caught up with him.

"Haczyk." It seemed to Simon that every time Branko said the name he was trying to spit. "My officers need more room."

"What do you want, Branko, sleeping bags in the galley?" Simon looked over his shoulder. "Maybe if you deflate your ego a bit—"

Branko took a step toward him. Simon was out of his seat and had his hand resting on top of his gun holster. It was unnecessary. Colonel Verge planted himself between the two. "No need for any of that, gentlemen," he said firmly. "We have work to do."

Branko glared. He actually did spit on the deck. Then he turned sharply on his heel and stormed off the bridge.

Colonel Verge gave Simon an apologetic look. "Don't say it, Colonel," Simon warned. He plopped back into his chair and spun it halfway around. "Just enjoy the ride."

CHAPTER 12

October 2602
Southcrown Star System

Baden was exhausted.

He'd spent the past several days doing little more than eating, sleeping, washing, and reading the Bible out loud into his delver's audio recorder. Finally he finished the Old Testament in the middle of the day shift aboard *Golden Orchid.*

Baden thought about Jesus's claim that all Scripture pointed to Him. So he'd gone through the Old Testament expecting a raft of references—laser-cut, as Alec had put it back on Bethel. The hints about a coming redeemer were easy enough to spot. Didn't seem like he'd found much else really, though he was suspicious of God's giving Abraham a ram so he wouldn't have to kill his kid.

What a nav course that was. Baden leaned back in a fairly uncomfortable metal chair and blew out a deep breath.

His audience was still waiting. Five pirates stood crowded in the hatchway to the galley. Baden found it funny that these burly men and lithe women, dressed in outlandish combinations of fancy and utilitarian clothes, looked tough enough to take on any three Kesek officers single-handedly, but they wouldn't enter the galley while Baden had been reading aloud.

He was the only one sitting in the long room. The chipped and dirty false wood paneling and pale yellow paint on the walls only reinforced his loneliness—there was no one around to block his view of the horrible décor. Owen, Gail, and Jason were back in the cabins Bell had set aside for them on Golden Orchid. Gail and Jason had wanted to come hear him record the last section, but Baden felt this was something he wanted to do on his own.

Owen hadn't shown any interest.

"No encores, guys." Baden hoped they'd like the joke. It sounded as feeble as he felt tired. He waved a hand at one of the four empty tables, including his. All were bare except for the delver sitting on his table. "Wanna read?"

They all stared at him. Then a sharp whistle made them scatter. "This ain't feeding time at the zoo, boys and girls," Captain Bell snapped. "Get back to your posts!"

They obeyed. Baden noted how they all avoided touching Bell, even as crowded as it was in the dim passageway. She stepped into the brightly lit galley with two ornate drinking glasses in her hands. The burgundy liquid in each barely sloshed as she walked. Baden was surprised how easily she carried them—good balance.

Bell's mouth curved upward. "You look like you could use one of these." She offered him a glass.

"Uh, thanks." Baden accepted. The glass was chilly to the touch. "Not much of a wine drinker."

"Come on, it's the best." Bell wafted it under her nose, inhaling lightly. "'Eighty-eight Xeng. Fresh from Liberty's finest freighters."

Baden hesitated with the glass at his lips.

"Aw, I didn't kill nobody to take it." Bell took a swig and drained nearly half the glass. "What a minor you are. Just cut their cargo bay open after we disabled 'em."

"Hey, I live on a ship like that," Baden said.

"Oh, right." Bell finished her glass. She belched. Loudly. "'Scuse me. No offense intended."

Baden took a sip. Whoa! Nasty stuff. Bitter, but hold on—kind of warm going down his throat. Baden wasn't sure if he was comfortable with contraband liquor. But . . . maybe one more sip. "So what did you want? Your own reading? Or just looking for excuses to yell at your crew?"

"Don't need an excuse to yell."

"You're pretty good at it."

"Thanks." Bell thumped down into a chair. She propped her scuffed boots up onto a table with a metallic whunk. "I practice. Look, I don't mind you holding your churchy stuff in here—"

"Hold up." Baden raised his hands defensively. "This isn't church stuff. I'm reading into my delver. Just finished the audio clips. See?" He tapped the delver on the table.

"Yeah, whatever. It's interrupting the flow of work on my ship."

Baden choked on a laugh.

"What's funny?" Bell sipped noisily at the dregs at the bottom of her glass.

"You said 'work.' I got the impression pirates didn't do much work. Sure doesn't look like it."

"Maybe you missed the repairs we've been making because of a certain laser strike from a week or so ago," Bell said. All humor was gone from her voice.

Baden hadn't missed. *Natalia Zoja* had inflicted some nasty hits. "Well, I'm done recording, so I won't bother your hard-working crew," he said dryly.

"Good. Guess it wasn't too bad for them. They could use a little civilizing."

Baden found that funny. But he decided against saying so. Bell hadn't taken his last joke so well. "Hey, it's been nice that they haven't messed with us since we came aboard. They're not so bad."

"That's 'cause I told 'em anybody who even looks cross-eyed at your girlie there gets to sleep suitless in an open airlock," Bell said cheerfully.

"Oh." Baden took another careful sip of wine. So much for civilized.

"Don't look all shocked and awed. I got my own code aboard here." Bell leaned forward, left hand extended. With her right she ticked off on her fingers. "One: Any woman captive or passenger is not to be touched or you get smacked. Two: Men can be smacked around, but only if I say so. Three: Paying customers get better treatment than captives, but only if they ain't mouthy."

Baden decided to mention that last one to Owen. "Pirates with a code. But you still steal things and kill people, huh?"

"So what?" Bell snapped. "How's that different than Kesek, or the fleets?"

"The fleets don't take from anyone—"

"Except pirates."

Baden closed his mouth. No sense arguing that one. "Weird."

"What's weird?"

"You are. For a pirate. Rules and all." Baden patted the Bible. "Like you got your own set of these regs. The people on Bethel look at this like it's all they need."

Bell considered that. "A lot of my gang, they don't got anything. Expatriates, for the most part—tossed outta their families or worlds. Nothing to lose." Bell jerked a thumb at her chest. "Me, I got citizenship. And family."

"Family? What planet?"

"None of your biz." Bell ran her finger around the top of her glass. She looked about the galley, seeming anxious to find a new topic. "Blazes, the color in here's awful. Why I ever let Dennis talk me into fake wood—anyways, I got things to protect. So I stick to my rules. For the most part. Someday it'll all catch up with me, I guess, so I figure the more civilized behavior I got under my belt, the better."

Baden sighed. "You picked a strange line of work."

"It picked me, kid. And I like the adventure. The killing—" She shrugged. "Not so much. But that's the way. What, was I gonna lead a boring life on some dumpy cargo ship?"

Hasn't been too boring lately, Baden thought. He raised the glass to his lips. "So why'd you really want to talk to me?"

"Huh?" Bell smacked her forehead. "Listen to me yammer. Right, anyway, I came down to tell you we're being followed."

Baden sprayed fine wine across his shirt and the table.

Bell didn't look amused. "You're wasting it."

• • •

Bell led Baden to the bridge. As they brushed by pirates in the dingy passageways, Baden didn't know which was more disturbing—the fact that the pirates eyed him with hunger or distrust, or the fact that he was used to those looks.

"Where they at, Dennis?" Bell asked as they stepped through the bridge hatch. Baden blinked under the brighter lights—even at their pale setting they were an improvement on the passageways.

The first mate consulted his console. Baden tried to lean forward for a look but Bell planted a hand on his chest.

"Maintaining distance at six light-seconds, Skipper," Dennis said. "They've increased acceleration to match ours."

"Where are we accelerating to?" Baden asked.

"Away from the Southcrown sun."

Baden looked at Bell. Anxiety turned his stomach. He now wished Gail had come with him to the galley, and up to the bridge, instead of staying in the cabins with Owen and Jason.

"Easy, kid. I'm looking to lose whoever this is before we go through the Whelanport sundoor on our way to al-Qamar and your Alexandria hideaway. You just better be sure your coordinates are right."

"Hey, I told you, Ozzy got you the right coordinates. It's not that hard to get to al-Qamar, either."

"Yeah, I know the route." Bell grimaced as she peered over Dennis's shoulder. "Huh. No read on our follower yet?"

"Nothing. Could be military, could be civilian. Drive trail's heavily modified. No active comms or ID."

Bell's eyes went wide.

"What?" Baden didn't like being left out of this conversation. He was the one in trouble here. "You need to tell me what's going on."

"I need you to shut up is what I need," Bell snapped. She folded her arms. "Forgetting who's the passenger and who's captain, aren't ya?"

Baden gritted his teeth. "They why'd you blasted drag me up here?"

Bell gave him a hard shove on one shoulder. "So you know how serious this is. It's not some game you can keep playing, like you did with those yokels on that rock. Kesek plays for keeps."

She turned to Dennis. "How's traffic? Can we ditch 'em in there?"

"Hold on. Nav, bring traffic up on the big screen."

"Aye." The navigator worked his console. The main screen, filled by a vast field of stars, blinked to show a simple graphic of the Southcrown system layout. The sundoors around the giant, searing white star were busy as usual. Baden knew it was the nexus of seven links between trade routes and was one of the major hubs on the Tiaozhan Path. By his count there were at least three dozen ships within the sensor range of just one light-minute of the *Golden Orchid.*

The ships were marked by bright blue pips. One was flashing red.

"They're at least an hour behind us, Skipper," Dennis said.

"Okay." Bell walked a bit closer to the massive monitor. She put her hands on her hips as she looked up. "Overlay courses and projections."

"On all those ships?" the navigator asked.

"No, just on the ones you can read from my mind." Bell reached over to swat the man on the side of the head. He winced. "Yes, all of them, you gene-crossed inbred vac-for-brains!"

A bewildering array of red, yellow, and green arcs rippled across the screen. Baden's eyes hurt as he tried to see which ships were headed where at what velocity. It reminded him of his own nav screens aboard *Natalia Zoja*, magnified a hundred times. That was a mistake—he was instantly homesick.

Bell pointed. "There. Those two. See that navastel and kansen? Oh, about ten light-seconds off, on parallel tracks?"

"Ah . . . got them, Skipper."

"Looks like they're headed in to a course change." Bell pivoted. "You see it, little Haczyk?"

Baden liked "kid" better. "Sure. Takes them right around the second planet, that gas giant."

"Yep." Bell looked pleased as she stomped back up to Dennis's console. "Gas giant's got about twenty or thirty moons, don't it?"

"Forty-three," Dennis said.

"That's the neighborhood we want. Watch those ships. Keep on our course, but in 20 minutes, shut the main drive down and drift. Then use thrusters to get us on a gradual intercept."

Dennis's hands flew across his console as Baden tried doing the computations in his head. "We're gonna ride with them," he said.

"That should do it," Dennis said. "Skipper, we'll wind up right at their heading just before they enter the outer moon orbits."

"Beautiful."

"Skipper . . ." Dennis gave Baden a funny look. "What do we do if Kesek calls first?"

Bell ran a hand through her hair. "Ignore their calls. Then stall. Until I think of something else." She gestured to Baden. "Meanwhile, you and your little company stay out of sight."

"So what, we're confined to quarters?"

Bell stepped up close to him. "Remember my third rule? The word 'mouthy'?"

Baden nodded and left the bridge.

His company, as Bell called them, took the news about as well as could be expected.

Gail greeted him with a kiss, but she looked crestfallen about his announcement. Owen grumbled but went back to fiddling with a delver. Jason's mouth twitched, but he said nothing.

"Sorry, guys. That's what the captain says," Baden said. He brushed his hand along Gail's back.

"That's a problem," she said. "There's a couple of pirates who had some questions for me."

They were sitting in a grungy cabin that Bell had set aside for her passengers. It was fairly big—at least, it had room for two double-decker bunks on opposite walls, plus a tiny bathroom stall. Many small boxes were crammed into the storage lockers tucked into the bulkheads. Everything was the same dingy brown and streaked with grease.

"About what?" Baden asked. He leaned against the open hatchway.

"She's been preacher-woman in your absence, Hack." Owen sat on the top bunk, his long legs dangling over the edge. He didn't sound pleased about it. He sounded downright irritable. "You been off reading that book in the galley and she's been spreading the good words to anybody who don't tell her to jump down a black hole."

"Cut it, Ozzy," Baden said. He was worried, though. "That's probably not safe."

"Probably not, but they need to know the truth," Gail said firmly. She sat on the lower bunk across from Owen.

Baden had a bad feeling. He looked at Jason, seated next to Gail. "Did you tell her that?"

"She asked. I informed her that this path is not an easy one." Jason stared back at him. The calmness in his gaze unnerved Baden like always, but now its similarity to Gail's expression irked him. "You should know."

"You mean, like Mom," Baden said.

Gail frowned. "Like your mom?"

Baden sighed. "Look, can we talk?"

"Sure," Gail said.

Baden rapped his knuckles on the bunk frame. Owen glanced up. "I kinda meant in private, Ozzy."

"Yeah, okay. Whatever, Hack." Owen shoved off the bunk and landed roughly on the deck. His cheeks were flush with irritation as he faced Baden. "I got nothing else to do. Maybe I'll go orbit with the pirates." He shouldered past Baden.

"Hey!" Baden grabbed him. "What gives? You got a malfunction?"

Owen yanked his arm free. "Go have your churchy time."

He stalked off, leaving Baden stunned.

Jason cleared his throat. "I will keep an eye on him. Surreptitiously."

"Yeah. Thanks." Baden slumped onto a bunk. He didn't notice Jason leave until Gail quietly closed the hatch.

"He's feeling outnumbered, I think," Gail said. She sat beside Baden and put her arm around his middle. "You've been . . . concentrating . . . so much on the Bible."

"You mean obsessed with it," Baden said glumly.

"No. You have a purpose, Baden, and I think it's from God."

Baden thought about this. "It's just . . . now I feel like I can do something other than wreck my links with Dad, you know?" He pulled the Bible from his pocket. "There's something about this that just . . . Blast, I can't even explain it."

"Christ is working on you, Baden."

Baden fanned through the pages. The smell—stars, he loved that smell of paper. Then his fingers caught the page that had ripped when his dad had thrown the Bible back on Bethel. It tore at his heart. "Everywhere you look in here, God keeps telling His people that He will be with them, no matter how badly they mess up. I guess I kinda hope that means me too."

Gail smiled at him. "I'm pretty sure it does."

"But this is all one crazy, awfully big leap. I mean, to believe that some guy rose from the dead."

Gail shook her head. "It's more than that. You know it's true, Baden. You've read it, and . . . well, you've seen it."

Have I? Baden wondered about his visions, or hallucinations, or whatever you want to call them. He thought perhaps they could be messages as Jason suggested, given Emi's diagnosis that there was nothing wrong with his head. And if this book was right, there were people who'd seen strange things in their day—Ezekiel and his wheels within wheels, for one. And Isaiah the hot-coal eater.

And there was Mom. Baden's heart sank. She'd never said anything about weird sightings. She hadn't said much at all, at least not directly.

Until Simon's message.

"Gail, you gotta listen to this." Baden slid his delver out of another pocket. "Dad sent me this file through the Reach after we left. I picked it up late last night. You guys were all asleep when I came back from the galley."

"What is it?"

"It's . . . from Mom."

Baden triggered the audio play and closed his eyes. He had no doubt Kesek had used it or something like it to find reason to lock her up. There came the faint glimmer of admiration at his father for having hung on to it this long.

"Someday I hope you'll understand," Hannah's soft voice said from the delver speakers. Baden missed that voice terribly. *"The joy I have in Christ is difficult for me to explain to you, but the best way I can put it is that there is peace. No matter the circumstances of my life, there is peace in knowing that all this will pale in comparison with the life eternal. It doesn't mean I don't value this life—no, it helps me cherish it all the more. It means love is that much more important, the love I have for you, Simon, and my dear Baden."*

Baden blinked back tears. He wasn't sure he wanted to hear it all again. Gail held on to his hand with a strong grip. "She believed, didn't she?" he whispered aloud. "She followed Him. And . . . He let her die."

"No. He took her home, Baden. He didn't abandon her," Gail said. "God promises to be with us always."

With us always . . . The words rang in his head. From the delver his mom said, *"My heartfelt prayer is that my two men would come to know this faith, to find this peace, and even if I die before I see it with my own eyes, I pray it will happen nonetheless. I will love you always, And God will never leave you if you go to Him. Remember that."*

Baden rested his head against the bulkhead, hot tears running freely down his face. "Mom. What do I do? I want to believe, but it's hard."

And even as he tried to think about all the reasons why he should or shouldn't believe, he saw . . .

The storm.

Roaring winds, thunderous clamor, crashing waves, and cold water. A small group of men in a rickety boat, struggling with the oars and rigging, crying out in terror. Everything was noise and chaos and sweat and fear.

Except in the back of the boat. There, a young man rested silently, deep in sleep as if He were comfortable at home on a spring evening. His followers, finally noticing this serenity amidst their calamity, could bear it no more. They roughly shook Him awake, their adoration and admiration for this man forgotten in the moment. "Teacher! Master! Do You not care that we are perishing?" they cried. "Save us, Lord!"

He opened his eyes, met their raving stares with a calm compassion, and poured out peace on their anxiety. "Why are you afraid?" He asked, sounding almost curious and yet utterly empathetic. "Where is your faith? Do you still have none?"

There was nothing they could say to that. They pressed away from Him as He eased to His feet, made His way forward on the tossing vessel, and planted one foot firmly on the bow. Then, in a voice that blasted sound like the rush of a waterfall, deafening even over the storm's rage, He demanded, "Peace! Be still!"

It was no suggestion, but an order, as from a captain to a crew, but with infinite authority. Like a curtain rising, the clouds shriveled. The wind died from a blasting tempest to absolute calm. The churning sea rolled to a halt, smoothing out like a silk cloth settling to the ground.

He turned to face the men, and though their fear of death abated, there was a new terror, a terrible awe that seized them. One of them murmured, "Who is this, that the winds and sea obey Him?

Here the image froze. Baden felt himself drawn into it somehow, as if he were standing alongside that boat, no longer staring in at another world but part of it. But the man at the bow saw him, and smiled—somewhat sadly, Baden felt. There was such love in that expression that Baden fell to his knees, his heart overwhelmed.

"I would never have left them alone," the voice boomed. It rang in Baden's ears and whispered in his mind, all the same. "Only for a time did I depart, to do My Father's work, and bear the terrible cup meant for you, the children."

He held forth His hands, and Baden could see jagged holes at the wrists, blood oozing forth. Yet there was no sign of weakness about the man, only strength. With the sight, Baden was overcome by intense guilt and sorrow. "Please forgive me!" he found himself asking, and when he questioned himself why, he realized—it was bad stuff. The Bible called it sin. The junk that lived in him like a chronic illness, a dark companion. His own misdeeds and the inherited guilt of mankind. Before this man Baden wanted only to recoil.

But instead of wrath, there was only a smile. The man gestured again with His hands. "It is done, long ago and today, forever. Come, and I will give you peace. I will make you a fisher of men."

Baden rose to his feet, stepping forward on . . . air? Water? He didn't know and didn't care. He reached for the outstretched hands, and as he did, a glow grew in the chest of the man, and the light grew until Baden could see nothing but that light. Through it, though, he felt a warm embrace.

And the voice whispered to him, "My son, your sins are forgiven. I am the way, and the truth, and the life. Come, follow Me."

Then Baden was back in the bunk.

Gail was staring into his eyes. She held his shoulders tight. His entire body was shaking. The tremors made him drop the delver to the deck with a clatter. "Baden! What happened?" she urged. "What did you see?"

Baden tried to speak. His throat was thick with emotion. "It was . . . Him."

Gail's eyes went, if possible, even wider. "The Christ?"

Baden nodded.

She hugged him. Her own tears mingled with his.

"He gave me faith, Gail."

Faith. The word that eluded him all these weeks had an entirely new meaning. Certainty like he'd never experienced was suddenly and totally there.

Baden exhaled a ragged breath. "I know it now. I feel it. And I gave myself to Him."

She leaned forward and kissed him. Baden thought, Blast, I am really in trouble.

They found Owen and Jason in the galley. A handful of pirates were engaged in a raucous game of cribbage. Baden had seen the game played among Expatriate merchants and company crews before, but the pirates added two novel elements—copious food and sharp knives.

Owen greeted Baden's news with a blank stare. Jason clapped his hands and wrapped Baden in a bear hug. His strong arms yanked the young man off his feet and spun him twice. Jason laughed after finally depositing Baden, dizzy but happy, on the deck. "I never thought I would be able to call you brother, Baden. This is magnificent! Come, you must be baptized."

"Baptized?" Baden's stomach churned. "Where? Bell hasn't stolen a river last time I checked."

"Let's get down to the cargo bay," Jason said. "I have an idea."

Owen had a grimace carved on his face. Baden didn't get to ask about it before Jason and Gail ushered the group out the hatch.

He found himself wondering what his dad, on his way to Earth with the Starkweather and Rozsada troops, would think of this.

"You must be insane," Bell said. "You want me to do what with a cargo container?"

"The auxiliary lines run directly over your aft cargo hold," Jason said with maddening calm. "If you let us siphon one off—"

"Shut up." Bell slapped the hatch of her cabin. She was standing outside in the corridor with Baden and his group. She glared at him. "We're driftin' to run along with those other ships, you know. Our follower is still on us."

Baden swallowed against a dry throat. "Kesek?" Owen asked.

"Probably. Unless you got admirers with a hot starship, Goatee Boy."

Owen muttered something unintelligible. He fingered his goatee.

"Our request is minimal," Jason said.

Bell rubbed her forehead. "I just keep tellin' myself, 'One hundred fifty thousand cash, plus loot. One hundred fifty thousand cash, plus loot.' Insane."

Within a half hour, the *Golden Orchid*'s crew had set up an empty cargo crate in the hangar bay and filled it with frigid water from the ship's tanks. Baden stood waist-deep in that water, shivering. The grey shipsuit he'd borrowed from a pirate's locker didn't keep him nearly warm enough.

Gail and Owen stood to one side of the tank. She wore a beaming smile, but Owen scowled as if he could use his facial expressions to burn a hole in the hull. A knot of six pirates loitered a few steps away. Baden recognized them as eavesdroppers from his Bible recording sessions. Under the handful of brilliant overhead lights, the small area of the massive cargo bay was like a sanctuary from darkness.

Jason stood at his side. "It is water, plain and simple, but combined with the promise of God's Word, it embodies the gift of salvation," he said. Baden closed his eyes and dipped his head low. Jason filled his cupped hands.

"I baptize you now in the name of the Father, the Son, and the Holy Spirit," Jason said as he poured the water down the front of Baden's head. "You have asked His forgiveness, and He has called to you repent of your sin. His promise is thus—your sin has been washed away, never again to be counted against you. Jesus has paid your debt."

He held Baden by the shoulders. "You were dead in your sin—" Then he leaned him backward until he was underwater.

It was wet and dark and murky sounds. Baden's mouth and nose were pinched tight against the water. He had a flash of panic. Drowning would be a horrible way to come to the end of his life. Without redemption—

Jason's strong hands lifted him and he burst in a gurgling rush back into the light. Baden gasped and wiped water from his bleary eyes. "Now arise alive in Christ," Jason finished.

There was no magical burst of light, no ringing music filling the air, but Baden found he was suddenly, inexplicably happy. It was just . . . right. He was surprised at the depth of his own feeling as he said, "Amen."

Gail clapped loudly. Baden looked around and was surprised to see even a couple of the pirates grinning his way. The rest looked curious.

Owen was the only one glaring at him. "Ain't that great. Church team adds another player."

"Hey—" Baden sputtered water. "What gives, Ozzy?" His friend should be happy for him. What was his problem?

"You gotta think too hard about that one, Hack!" Owen yelled. His voice echoed off the bulkheads. "Don't be stupid! You buying into this junk, it's just one more leaky fuel cell in the hull, you know?"

"Delete it!" Baden's old familiar anger came bursting back. "You just can't stand it that Gail's not picking up your comm signal!"

Owen went rigid. "You think so. Blast it, Hack, you go play with your Bible and leave me out of it!"

He stalked off. Gail reached for him, but he was gone.

Baden closed his eyes in pain. So where's the magic now, God?

• • •

He wasted little time drying off and getting changed. He had to talk to Owen.

Baden found him lingering by a public screen in the corridor outside the bridge hatchway. The bright screen flickered as news stories from ReachWrit sloshed and slipped across its surface. Owen poked at one—it shimmered and expanded.

"What's that?" Baden asked.

"News. On a talk board from Puerto Guijarro. Says Ravenna's out of Hamid's clinic. The writer wants to know when Kesek's gonna pay the med bills." Owen chuckled. It was a bleak sound, not his normal laugh. "It's funny, Hack. Seems like years ago since we went blazin' out of there, right?"

"Yeah." Years. Since everything was normal. Since they were just two guys talking about girls, comms, ships, and food. "Like forever."

"Yeah." Owen seemed to deflate. "You come here to cheer me up?"

"Nope. But we gotta talk."

"Hmm. Figured you'd done all that with your new Bible club."

"Ozzy, will you space it!" In a heartbeat, Baden felt like he was back to his old irritable self. "This thing I believe—it doesn't mean we're not friends. You've had my back for years, and I've had yours. That ain't gonna change."

"Except now God's got your back," Owen snapped. He rounded on Baden. They stood nose to nose. "You and Gail and that Jason freak. And what do I got?" His voice shook. "What does Ozzy got?"

Baden opened his mouth to reply, but he couldn't. Owen didn't need a sermon. He changed tack. "Look, man, you're right. God is important to me. But so are you, okay? None of the teachings I read so far say you gotta turn your back on your best friend when you sign on to God's crew. I'd invite you aboard too, but I know you're not on to that."

Owen's face softened a bit. "It still ain't fair."

This wasn't going to be easy. Not like their past arguments about dumb things. Like girls and ships. "We're gonna work on this, okay?" Baden said. "You gotta be there for me while I get this all straightened out in my head."

"Okay. I'll work on it too." Owen folded his arms. "It doesn't mean I like it, Hack. I don't like anything about this mess."

Baden smacked him playfully on the arm. "Hey, Ozzy, I don't like large parts of it either."

The hatch sprang open. Captain Bell's eyes were wild and her hair was tousled. Baden didn't like the appearance.

"Get your butts in here," she snarled.

Bell fidgeted before the small comm screen attached to her chair. "That ship that was following us? She gave an ID."

"Oh. And?" Baden asked.

"*HMS Interrogator*," Bell said sourly. "Our lovely black-hulled battle corvette. Home to your favorite pal and my cranky boss, Detective Chief Inspector Nikolaas Ryke. They caught up with us a little bit ago. Ryke called and wanted to chat."

"Where is he now?"

"Oh, they're coasting along about a light-second behind us. No guns out. Yet." Bell scratched her head. "I, uh, put him on hold for a sec."

On cue, her comm monitor chirped. "He's through waiting, Skipper," Dennis said.

"Thanks. I figured." Bell took a deep breath. Baden was impressed how fast she could pull herself out of despair and put on a ramrod stance that made him a bit nervous. "Here goes."

She triggered the comm. "Sorry, Inspector, had a glitch," she said cheerily.

"Ah. I see." Ryke's face filled that tiny screen. Even that small his sneer made Baden shake. He wanted to hide under a bunk, but he stood off to one side of Bell—along with Owen, Gail, and Jason—out of Ryke's view. He looked ready to kill.

"Inspector, I ain't got a problem. We just ran right around the *Natalia Zoja*, but relax—my tracking signal picked her right up again. She's just got ahead of us a bit, is all."

"I grow weary of your incompetence, Captain Bell, and one way or another, I aim to terminate your employment."

"Look, I know, we fouled up," Bell said. She sounded genuinely apologetic. "But we got 'em! We got 'em right where—"

She abruptly stabbed a button on her console. The comm screen went black. "Now!"

Dennis and the helmsman attacked their controls. Baden swayed as the *Golden Orchid*'s deck lurched under his feet. He caught Gail's elbow. "Accelerating," Owen muttered.

"Shut up and watch!" Bell snapped her fingers. The view on the screen flickered and Gail gasped.

The slender, dark form of a battle corvette was receding rapidly. Even as Baden wondered if *HMS Interrogator* was about to shoot at them, a quintet of brilliant flashes peppered space between the camera view and the ship. "Blazes! What was that?"

"Nuke flutter mines. Havoc with scanners." Bell's mouth curved wickedly. "They got a lot of dead sensors right now."

"It is likely they are not dead sensors but temporarily scrambled sensors," Jason said.

"Killjoy." Bell spun in her chair. "Dennis, they try to blow us up yet?"

Dennis consulted his readouts. "Nope. No guns or missiles. They've got their main drive up. You surprised them good, though."

"Beautiful. Get us back in that system traffic." Bell looked at Baden. "This book—it's a big deal, eh?"

Baden nodded.

"You'd die to protect it?"

He looked at Gail. She didn't flinch. Tougher than him, for sure. "Yes."

Bell grunted. "You may get your chance."

CHAPTER 13

October 2602
Southcrown Star System

Nikolaas Ryke wanted blood.

Unfortunately, his mission dictated otherwise. At least, for now.

He stood on the bridge of *HMS Interrogator* with his hands wrapped around the command deck railing and did his best to leave indentations. Anger surged through his mind. "Blast it all, Cotes, I want to shoot them all through the head. Messy but satisfying."

Detective Inspector George Cotes stood silently at his side.

"You're no fun." Ryke slapped the railing. "Captain! Captain, we are not matching their speed! This is intolerable!"

The seven bridge crewmen were busy scurrying from console to console as the screens flickered and sparked. Some of the instrument panels reminded Ryke of laser optic shows as their monitors flashed a rainbow of colors under the dim lights of the hemispherical bridge. The pirate ship's flutter mines were a dirty trick and had interrupted most vital systems save for life support. Things seemed to be calming down a bit; at least the helmsman seemed to be seated and in control once more.

Captain Goro Sasaki turned slowly in his command chair. The bridge lights gleamed off his balding pate and the sweat beading across his brow. "We will match their speed, Detective Chief Inspector. Seeing as how they have a head start on us, you may have to be patient."

Ryke was irritated to see that his irate display had no affect on the captain. Perhaps it was further needling for catching Ryke drunk a few days ago. No matter. "Keep in mind, Captain, whose mission this is and whom you serve."

"I serve the king," Sasaki said stiffly.

Ryke waggled a finger. "Ah, now, the king is indisposed. Commissioner Gironde is ruling in his stead. You know where that puts Kesek in the chain of command, now don't you?"

Sasaki paled. He turned his chair back toward the rest of the crew consoles. "Helm, increase acceleration."

"Sir, we're already at maximum."

"Then give me some more than maximum!" Sasaki snapped.

Much better, Ryke mused.

"Sir." Cotes sounded quizzical. "Are you certain the pirates already have the Haczyk boy?"

Ryke waved a hand at the large main monitor. It showed a bright glare of a starship's main drive against a starry background. "Why else would she drop those mines and bolt?"

Cotes shifted. "Perhaps she did not want to face your not-inconsiderable wrath."

"My wrath? Cotes, you are wicked. All right, you make a fair point. Perhaps she did not want to face certain atomization under *Interrogator*'s guns. But to be honest, I would not have incinerated her ship."

"No?"

Ryke looked hungrily at the monitor again. "No. I want them alive. For awhile."

"How're we doing?" Bell paced the bridge. She weaved a path between the consoles.

"Not good, Skipper. She's definitely gaining."

"No surprise there. Military compensators are way better than ours. What acceleration's she pulling?"

"Fifty-two gees."

"Blast." Bell picked at something caught between her teeth. "Well, we ain't gonna out-accelerate 'em. What's our speed?"

"Five forty five kilometers per second and rising."

"Thanks, Dennis." Bell looked across the bridge at Baden. "You got any suggestions?"

"Gee, lemme think." Baden made a show of rubbing his chin. "If I'd known this was happening before now I might've come up with something. But it looks like all you've done is left us one choice—run!"

Bell scowled. "Mouthy kid."

Jason stepped forward. Gail and Owen stood against the back bulkhead, near the bridge hatch. "We have prayed," Jason said.

Bell rolled her eyes. "Super. Might as well stow the guns and lock down the missile tubes then."

"I have targeting prepared, Skipper," the missile tech said from his station.

"Prepared for what? I'm not lettin' a missile down Ryke's throat when he's got a warship on my tail, thank you very much. Moron." Bell gave him a dirty look. "What we need to do is get mixed in."

She rubbed her chin. Baden looked again at the main monitor, which had an updated view of the starship traffic around Southcrown's sundoors. The bulk of the ships were arrayed in three overlapping rings taking them to one of the seven sundoors. "We should hide in there, get mixed in with the rest of the merchant ships if we can," he said.

"Thought of that," Bell murmured absentmindedly. "But it will take too long to get into an approach vector . . ." Her voice trailed off. She looked at Baden.

"What?" he asked.

"You thought it was funny pirates had rules."

"So?"

"So, I don't need any stinkin' approach vector." Bell sauntered over to her chair and flopped into it. She spun three times before planting her feet and jerking the chair to a halt with a rusty creak. "Get as many gees out of us as you can, Dennis. Put us right in the middle."

"Aye, Skipper."

Sasaki peered over his navigator's shoulder. "What is she doing?"

The officer shook his head. "Looks like she's running head-on for the sundoor traffic. Cooking at a bit more than 31 gees."

"Not lining up for approach to a sundoor?"

"Negative."

Ryke joined them. "She's trying to hide from us."

Sasaki shook his head. "No, if she were trying to hide, she'd be shaping a course to mimic one of the other merchant-ers. She's got something else in mind, I think."

"Put a warning shot at her, Captain. I don't like her attitude."

Sasaki gave him a dour look. "Is that an order, Detective Chief Inspector?"

"Consider it a strong recommendation." Ryke leaned for-ward on tiptoes and pinned on his nastiest smile. "A very strong recommendation."

Sasaki matched his glare for a moment. Then he ordered, "Ready missiles."

The tactical console howled in alarm. "Two fish out!" Dennis said. "Coming in fast from *Interrogator*!"

He punched up a small holo-display that showed a tiny blue rendition of *Golden Orchid*. A pair of red arrows streaked into view.

"Counter-fire when they reach range!" Bell said. "Drop a porcupine on my mark."

The missile tech's hands flew over the console. "Weaps standing by."

Bell held her left hand up. Baden wondered how she could stand living like this all the time—just a few weeks of being hunted down was enough to give him a serious case of anxiety.

Bell caught him watching. "Kid, when those missiles come at us . . ."

"Yeah?"

"Try not to scream like a baby," Bell said. She snapped her hand down. "Go!"

A muffled whump echoed throughout the hull. One of Bell's screens and the missile tech's main display showed the same thing—a silvery orb studded with black ridges that went tumbling away from *Golden Orchid.* When it was too distant for the imagers to see, the computer rendered it as a green flashing dot.

"Porcupine coming into range of the missiles—in sixty seconds."

No one on the bridge spoke. Baden stood right beside Bell's chair. He grabbed the rough padding of an armrest. The pirate captain ignored him, her eyes flitting from tactical screen to nav holo to the main monitor. Baden looked back at his friends. Owen was pale but flashed Baden a strained grin—better than nothing. Gail wrapped her arms tight about herself. Jason placed a comforting hand on her shoulder.

You didn't tell me it was going to be like this, Baden thought in a quick prayer. Don't know if I'd have signed up.

Dennis said, "Porcupine detonation in five . . . four . . . three . . ."

Baden inhaled.

"Two . . . one . . . Go!"

A sharp yellow flash burst onto the main monitor. Then it was gone.

"That's it?" Owen made a disgusted noise in the back of his throat. "Man, what are you vac-heads throwing out your back hatch, old robots?"

Bell swiveled slowly in the chair. "You're a mouthy one, ain't ya?"

Owen's sneer slid off his face.

Before Bell could remark, a pair of mismatched explosions lit up the monitor. The twin red arrows disappeared from Dennis's hologram. He pumped a fist in the air. "Neutralized, Skipper."

"Little bits of hot metal!" Bell crowed. She turned back around. "Porcupine explodes and throws off a big ol' sphere of shrapnel and accelerated positrons. Nasty ball for any missile to run into at twenty thousand kilometers a second."

She crooked a finger at the monitor and beckoned with it. "C'mon, Ryke, that the best you got?"

Sasaki grunted. "Porcupine. Not surprising, but nicely executed."

Ryke was not impressed. "Please refrain from praising our prey," he growled. "Shoot at them again."

"When I am ready, I will." Sasaki turned to his tactical officer. "Ready full spread. Four disablers, two nukes. Crippling effects only, please."

"Aye, sir, four disablers, two nukes. Stand by."

Sasaki offered Ryke a half bow. Ryke was certain it was done out of sarcasm. "Is that to your wishes?"

Ryke lifted his chin.

"I'll see."

"Missiles armed and ready, Captain!"

"Launch all," Sasaki said evenly.

The six missiles raced out from *Interrogator* like six new stars added to the heavens.

"We're getting awfully close to the in-system traffic to be launching missiles, Skipper," the navigator said.

"I know it." Sasaki put his hands behind his back. "We'll have to think of something else soon."

Ryke coughed into his hand. "And why, Captain, is that?"

Sasaki gave him a familiar look—the same look he'd pasted on his face when Ryke was falling-down drunk. Ryke was growing tired of the man's insolence. "We don't want to risk hitting civilian traffic, Detective Chief Inspector."

Speak to me like a child, will you? Ryke fumed.

This time he gave his full attention to the tactical officer. "You will maintain your rate of fire until that ship stops running, or I will bind your wrists and find you a wondrous new home on a penal colony."

Sasaki balled his hands into fists. "Now, just one moment—"

Ryke lashed out with his hand. It whipped into the crook of Sasaki's neck, right at the shoulder. The captain cried out and collapsed against his chair. A pair of officers rose from their seats. Ryke pulled his gun and pointed it at one.

"Sit down!" he thundered. The barrel snapped from person to person, almost alive in its intent. Ryke's chest heaved. "Sit down and keep your blasted hands off your precious captain! We have criminals and traitors to pursue. I do not have the luxury of worrying about every civilian ship we may or may not singe with our weapons fire!"

The crew slowly returned to their seats. Ryke holstered his gun. "Cotes. Call up the rest of our men. Position three outside each of the two entrances onto this bridge, and send the other one inside with us. I've been far too lenient."

"Yes, Inspector." Cotes had his gun out too. He swept the comm out of his pocket and started issuing orders.

Ryke reached out a hand to Sasaki. The captain gasped for air and refused to take it. Snarling like a beast, Ryke seized his collar instead and yanked him nose to nose. He spoke four words like bullets.

"Get me that ship."

Baden thought they were dead the minute those six angry red arrows showed up on *Golden Orchid*'s sensors.

The ship's defenses were up to the task, for the most part. The point defense laser—just the one, for the second was still down thanks to *Natalia Zoja*'s attack—took care of one. Dennis's expert deployment of a bevy of sandcaster canisters unleashed glittering clouds of particles right into the path of the remainder. Three exploded like blooming white-hot flowers; two maneuvered through.

Those two made it close enough in to detonate. The tamped energy from the nukes ravaged the ventral hull, rocking the ship violently. Baden hung on to the back of Bell's chair as Owen grabbed on to Gail's shoulders. Jason, in turn, pressed them both against the bulkhead and gripped onto stanchions to keep them from being tossed about.

Alarms shrieked in dismay. "Hull plating buckled across sections seven and eight!" Dennis said over the cacophony.

"Shut them off!" Bell said.

He complied. But now flashing blood-red lights vied for the crew's attention. "Anything broken?" Bell asked.

"Handful of minor injury reports."

"I meant on my ship, dummy, not the crew. They got bandages."

"Right. No hull breaches. Electro-static shields off-line on those crumpled sections. Hamsters deploying for damage control."

"Peachy." Bell rotated a shoulder. "Blast. Must've wrenched it."

"I can get the doc up here—"

"I said 'wrenched it,' not 'tore it bleeding from my socket'! Blazes, calm down!"

Baden straightened. "They missed us."

"Yeah, you got that right, kid. We'd be dead and floating if they'd hit center on." Bell grinned at him. "You might be playing the harp then."

From the back of the bridge, Jason spoke up. "They're trying to capture us. Those warheads do not have the capacity to destroy the ship without direct impact."

Bell rolled her eyes as she swiveled to face him. Baden scooted out of her way. "Thank you, Mister Weaps Tech. Why don't . . ." She trailed off as she saw the stanchions. "What'd you do?"

Baden followed her gaze. Jason's firm grip had left mild indentations in the metal. He hoped Owen and Gail didn't bruise easily.

Jason smiled at Bell. "Forgive me. I could repair the damage."

"Uh . . . No, no, that's okay." Bell turned back, but gave him one more look. "That's okay."

"Skipper? We're coming up on the sundoor traffic."

"Good." Bell waved at Baden. "Now watch close, kid. We're gonna jump right down in there and hope we don't hit nothing."

Baden didn't like the sound of that.

• • •

The *Interrogator*'s tactical officer avoided Ryke as he reported, "Missiles expired, Captain. Two delivered their payloads, but damage must have been insubstantial—target shows no change in velocity and only a minor change in heading."

"Yes, they took care of them well enough." Sasaki's voice was scratchy. Ryke enjoyed the sound.

"Launch another six."

"Ah, Skipper . . ."

"I know about the civilian ships!" Sasaki barked. "Launch now!"

"Aye, Captain!"

The deck vibrated as six more missiles raced off.

"Well done, Captain," Ryke said.

"More missiles?"

Bell sounded incredulous. Baden couldn't blame her.

They huddled over Dennis's console.

"Sure it ain't too late to give them the book, Hack?" Owen asked. He sounded as if he were only half joking. He wasn't smiling.

Baden shot him a withering glare. It didn't help that he'd been contemplating just that fact.

"Those missiles are going to follow us right down into the traffic," Dennis said solemnly.

"No kidding." Bell sighed. "Shoulda known that Ryke wasn't running on all thrusters."

She stomped down to the navigator's station. "Get up."

"Skipper?"

She grabbed him by the shirt and hauled him out of the seat. "I'm driving."

According to the *Golden Orchid*'s navigational computers, the average speed of the more than fifty ships converging on Southcrown's seven sundoors was 350 kilometers per second.

Bell calmly disabled every one of her ship's proximity alarms as she pushed it ahead at twice that speed.

"Missiles closing," Dennis reported.

Bell didn't answer.

Baden didn't really want to look at the main monitor. But it was so huge it was hard to avoid. He didn't want to see how close they were going to get to the other ships. He squeezed his eyes shut as the slim hull of a 400-meter kansen zipped by just 35 kilometers away. Somebody gasped.

"Bet that woke them up," Bell muttered.

"Southcrown traffic control requests—" The comms man stopped, then started up again. "It isn't pretty what they request."

"Tell them to stick their heads up my main drive," Bell snarled. "Then shut the comms down."

She wove a deft course through the traffic toward the Whelanport sundoor. *Golden Orchid* breezed by a pair of navastels, 30 kilometers away. "Awfully close for this speed," Baden said nervously.

"Kid. Shut. Up."

"Missiles closing! Do you want sandcasters?"

"No!" Baden grabbed Bell's shoulder. "You do that you'll hole every ship within a hundred kilos!"

Bell looked at his hand as if it were a squashed insect. Baden removed it quickly. "Wasn't going to. Go with point laser, Dennis. And get the particle guns up."

"Particle guns? At this speed?" Owen gaped. "You can't hit the broad side of a moon with cannon at this speed."

Bell corkscrewed *Golden Orchid* past a bulbous MarkTel communications ferry. Baden winced and read the flickering numbers off a display screen. That was 20 kilometers. They could sneeze and blast into one of these ships if they went any faster.

"Missiles coming into range," Dennis said. "Cannon up and ready."

"Try not to shoot anybody, will ya?"

"Do my best, Skipper." Dennis paused. "Missiles in range!"

"Fire!"

Ryke could not believe it.

The impertinent pirates were actually shooting down his missiles while they were winding their way through the merchant ships. And they'd managed to hit three! With particle cannon!

Sasaki let out a low whistle. "I can see why you hired them."

"Hmph. Yes." Ryke beckoned Cotes closer. "This is not getting results," he whispered. "Get down to their signals box, hook yourself into the Reach, and stop that ship."

Cotes's eyes gleamed with anticipation. "Understood, Chief Inspector."

He bustled off the bridge.

Ryke turned back to Sasaki. The captain watched him suspiciously. "You keep firing," Ryke ordered.

Baden's spirits buoyed again. Three of the six missiles were gone, thanks to Dennis's expert shooting. One of the missiles detonated and disabled the wrong ship.

He pointed a finger at the nav display as a heavy ore transport went limping off course. "They got one."

"And there goes another," Bell said. A second missile exploded behind *Golden Orchid* and directed its fury at an unregistered six-brace. "Gonna be some unhappy merchanters out their today."

"Skipper! The last missile's closing! Point laser can't get it!"

"Brace yourselves!"

The explosion ripped along the *Golden Orchid*'s port side. Lights and computers flickered and flashed. Baden held on to the navigation console and urged the ship, Not now. Don't stop.

The lights steadied and came back up. But some of the nav screens stayed black. "Blast it, I lost ventral sensors!" Bell smacked her console. "What's my distance to the Whelanport sundoor?"

"If we're planning on going through, you gotta brake in six minutes, Skipper," Dennis said. "We have to slow down enough to get into the touch tract and engage the Raszewski generator before we can make the shift."

"Got it. Get damage control to get me something for ventral—I don't care if they gotta strap Ian to the hull with a telescope in one hand!"

"Aye!"

But before Dennis could comply, his hands froze over his console. Owen raced forward to join him. "Man, you got problems now," Owen said.

"Dennis?" Bell kept her eyes glued to her readouts as Baden went up the steps to the back of the bridge. "Dennis, I don't like that. That 'problems' word."

"Skipper—somebody's in our systems. In the mainframe. Weapons, comms—they're taking the works apart."

"What? Where's Ian?"

"You sent him out with damage control."

"Blast and blazes! Get someone else in to stop this!"

"No time! Change your course." Owen elbowed Dennis aside and cracked his knuckles with a flourish. "Behold the skills."

Owen yanked his delver from a pocket and pulled two bright green wires from its backside. He felt around for something under the console. "Aced." He jabbed both into access ports beneath his fingers. "Where you hiding?"

"What are you doing?" Baden watched as a dizzying array of symbols scrambled across all of Dennis's screens at once.

"Somebody's transmitted a nasty digger into their mainframe," Owen muttered. "Probably came in over the Reach. Yeah, there we go. Disguised as a system nav buoy update. Not too shabby, by even my elite standards."

"Can you kill it?"

"Sure can." Owen offered a sly wink. Despite his fear Baden was happy to see a little of the old Ozzy again. "Just gotta do it without breaking all the life support and nav works too. Before the missiles get us."

"Heard that!" Bell hollered.

• • •

Ryke paced behind the command rail on *Interrogator*'s bridge. Cotes appeared at the bridge's upper hatch, breathing hard. "Well?"

Cotes held up a hand as he caught his breath. "Come now, Cotes, you're not paid to be comfortable," Ryke said.

"The digger was delivered successfully. You should see results . . . soon," Cotes panted.

"Excellent." Ryke beamed. "This is why you're my right-hand man—you're borderline competent."

"Thank you, sir."

Kesek Constable DeVoors trotted through the hatch. He sealed it behind him before saluting Ryke. "Sir, as Inspector Cotes ordered, I have our officers positioned at both hatches," DeVoors said.

"Good. Prepared for payback for that little escapade at Puerto Guijarro, Constable?"

DeVoors shifted his stance. "Ever since they shot me in the leg and left me locked in a box, sir."

"Well said."

"Captain!" The tactical officer sounded overjoyed. "Target is altering course. Acceleration is variable. Looks like their engines are malfunctioning."

"That's a good thing for us," Sasaki said.

Ryke smirked at Cotes.

Owen's hands savaged the console in front of him like claws. Baden thought he might tear it apart—he'd already removed one panel to get at some of the innards.

"Stop staring at me, Hack." Sweat dribbled down Owen's temples. "You're making me twitchy. Twitchy ain't good."

"Sorry." Baden turned instead to Bell and Dennis, both of whom were hunkered over the nav console. A brilliant explosion on the main screen startled him. The missile tech whooped.

"What's the racket?" Owen complained.

"Porcupine got another missile, I think."

Bell pounded the console with glee. "Make that two. But we got four more."

"We're not far off from the sundoor, Skipper," Dennis said. "If you can get us into position—"

"Love to! But I got engines that don't want to fire when I say fire! And Goatee Boy back there ain't working fast enough!"

"Hey! I already kept it out of life support and comms!" Owen said. "Gimme a break! This ain't no low-level digger . . . Ha!"

"'Ha' better be good," Bell said.

"Oh, yeah. The digger's dead." Owen gave a slight bow. "Yes, thank you, ladies and gentlemen!"

"Super. Now put my gunner's console back together." Bell manipulated her own controls. "Nova. We got helm responding again."

"Those missiles are getting awfully close, Skipper," the missile tech said. "I've got counter-missiles out, but it ain't looking good."

"Time to intercept?"

"Two minutes . . . Skipper! One of the missiles got a navastel!"

Baden caught a glimpse of a green dot on the navigation display go curving off from the rest of the traffic around Southcrown's sundoors. It came uncomfortably close to another ship.

"Hold tight! We'll make it!" Bell said. "Decelerating now!"

Baden's stomach lurched a bit as the *Golden Orchid* flipped end over end and lit off its main drive. If they timed it right, they'd slow enough inside the sundoor to Whelanport to activate the Raszewski and make the tract shift before *Interrogator* caught up with them. If the generator wouldn't fire up, sitting at the sundoor was no different from any other patch of empty space.

Even as he considered it, Baden had his doubts. Gail came up next to him. "What are you thinking?"

Baden patted his pocket. "I'm thinking I need to get rid of this."

"The Bible?" Gail asked with alarm.

"No. Something else." Baden's gaze roamed to the comm station.

"Your men are quite adept at disabling innocent civilian ships," Ryke said. "Thank goodness there hasn't been a collision."

Sasaki glared at him, but only for a moment. "Prepare another spread," he ordered. "Hold fire until I give the word."

"Aye, sir."

Baden tapped the *Golden Orchid*'s comm tech on the shoulder. "Bell wants to talk to you," he said. "She didn't sound happy."

The man looked at him in puzzlement but went down to the nav console to investigate. Baden pulled his delver from his pocket and started the download. He looked at the missiles closing on the screen. Gail interposed herself in Bell's line of sight.

Just needed a few seconds—there. Message sent, the comm board confirmed.

"Get back to your post, vac-head!" Bell didn't sound pleased by the interruption. The bewildered comms man came hustling back up to this console not two seconds after Baden vacated it. Please don't notice.

The comms man perused the board. His eyes flicked over to Baden. "What did you . . ."

"Counter-fire missed! Three inbound missiles!" the missile tech cried.

"Dennis?"

"On it, Skipper." Dennis brought the laser turret and particle cannons into position. "Commencing counter-fire."

Dennis's screens lit up with flashes as he switched to the external cameras. The particle cannon threw gouts of energy at the oncoming missiles, but Baden could see on the tactical display that the red arrows of the missiles continued on unfazed. Finally one succumbed to Dennis's gunnery skills.

"Detonation range!" he said.

This time the assault shook the *Golden Orchid* vigorously. Owen and Jason toppled against a bulkhead. Gail slid in to Baden and knocked him over. She managed to grab his arm and then hold on to a console to keep them from sliding completely across the bridge. From her nav console, Bell swore vociferously.

Screens flickered, and this time, died all as one. The deep thrum of the engines through the hull went silent. Emergency beacons blinked orange and steadied, casting peculiar shadows around the bridge.

Nobody spoke for a moment. "Everything's down, Skipper," Dennis said quietly. "Guns, shields, missiles . . . We have gravity and air, that's about it. We're inside the sundoor but the Raszewski generator's dead. We're not making tract shift anytime soon."

"That's bad," Bell finally said.

Baden watched marines in black and violet body armor burst through *Golden Orchid*'s cargo airlock and swarm into the hold. Bell had apparently decided not to fight, however, and had her entire crew of seventeen standing in three rows. Their guns lay visible on the deck.

Bell stood with Dennis and her four guests in front. She held up her hands. "We ain't armed," she said calmly. She had to pitch her voice loud to be heard over the rumble of boots. "We surrender—"

She was cut off when a marine planted an assault rifle butt in her abdomen. Bell collapsed to her knees with a grunt. Dennis took a swing at the marine but was immediately tackled by another. The pirates started shouting and punching. A few sharp whines from scrambler stun weapons, though, and no resistance remained.

"You four! On your knees!" The marine jerked his rifle barrel at Baden. He complied. Gail, Owen, and Jason did likewise.

Nine more men came out of the hatch. Kesek officers. Baden took one look at the bald man in the lead and moaned.

Ryke walked right up to him and smiled. A cold dread crept through Baden.

"Hello," Ryke said pleasantly.

CHAPTER 14

October 2602
Xiaoji Star System

Simon usually enjoyed his mealtime in peace and relative quiet aboard *Natalia Zoja*. His crew knew better than to bother him while he was eating. Doing so was a surefire way to draw his wrath, likely in the form of some undesired cleaning or maintenance duty. Not even Renshu was willing to complain about his ship when Simon was eating.

Today they left him be. But that did nothing to assuage Simon's sour mood, because today the galley was packed to the bulkheads with far too many people.

There were fifteen soldiers in there. All were Rozsade fusiliers—much to Simon's chagrin—and half were officers. He found it unsettling to see their black and red uniforms contrasted against the soft amber hues of the galley walls, completed with stenciled green vines. Simon just hoped they'd brought enough rations to prevent them from raiding the food lockers along the back wall.

The worst part was that Branko Mazur was there.

The Rozsade major had spent most of the meal casting dark looks Simon's way. It seemed he ignored most of his officers' conversational remarks, even the ones intended for him. Simon kept his head down and tried to similarly ignore his own fuming temper. As a result his appetite suffered.

Eventually, others took notice of the tension and started drifting from the room in twos and threes. Simon made himself look up only once from his tray of stale noodles. Branko glared right at him. Simon took care to look Branko firmly in the eye, then returned his attention to his plate. He poked at his food with a fork.

Soon they were alone.

Finally Simon sighed and set down his fork. "You know, Branko, you could just toss a knife at my head and we'd both be a lot happier, instead of you sitting there looking like you're constipated."

Branko kept his eyes locked on Simon. He leaned a bit to one side and spat on the deck.

"Yeah, the timeless Rozsade expression of contempt. Wipe it up before you leave."

"Contempt is too mild a word," Branko growled, "for a dog such as you."

Simon pushed off from his table. He leaned back in his chair and thunked his boots on the top. "What, don't you speak the mother tongue off-world, Major?" Simon clasped his hands over his stomach. "No *dzien dobry* for your brother?"

"No brother of mine." Branko pounded the table angrily with a fist and leapt to his feet.

Simon's hand instinctively dropped to his pistol holster. "Careful."

"You get no greeting from me, Haczyk," Branko said. He pronounced Simon's name like a curse. "I know what you are."

Simon's eyes narrowed. "Really."

The pair fell silent. Only the whir and occasional clank from the ventilation system interrupted. Branko said one word with absolute venom: "*Niewdzeczny.*"

Simon's insides went hot. His pulse quickened. He forgot his lifelong promise to himself that he would never take such insults seriously, and clenched both fists.

"Ungrateful?" he snapped. "You call me ungrateful? For what, Major? For a home that had no place for me? A nation that looked at me as a failure before I even had the chance to prove myself? For a world that disowned me?"

"Your family denied its honor!" Mazur jabbed an accusing finger across the room. "They made choice to turn their backs on family name—stealing and smuggling and filching. Worthless criminals, both of them. Best thing for Rozsada was to make them Expatriate. You have no place on mother world. Is no honor for you or your son."

"Don't say that!" Simon's vehemence surprised himself. Judging by Branko's expression, it did for him too. "My boy will earn his way, just like I did. He'll bring his own honor to his family—Haczyk, our own name—and to me. I won't let him be cast aside as a worthless orphan like I was."

"You are a prisoner of your own pride, Haczyk." Branko stood slowly from his seat to leave. "I will enjoy watching you fall. Like your lunatic son who hears voices in his head."

Simon rounded the table. Branko's body eased into a fighting stance. Simon saw and relaxed himself, arms akimbo, ready for a spacer's brawl. "You shut your mouth."

Branko sneered. “Close it for me.”

“Sure.” Simon jarred the table with a flick of his leg and sent his tray crashing to the deck. The racket distracted Branko long enough for Simon to lunge. His right fist surged past Branko’s jaw as the other dodged. The fusilier ducked a second blow and threw two of his own. Simon gasped as they caught him in the gut.

He staggered backward and braced himself on the table. Branko grabbed his jacket collar and pulled back a fist. Simon brought his knee up into Branko’s stomach, just above his groin. Branko bellowed. Simon slugged him hard across the jaw and winced as something in his hand that he hoped wasn’t important cracked. Branko’s face snapped satisfyingly around.

And then to Simon’s dismay, Branko turned right back to face him. Branko bared his teeth. Blood stained a few teeth and his lip. “So. Our dog bites.”

He battered Simon with blows. Simon desperately blocked what he could but was unable to fend most off. He knew it was an unfair matchup—Branko was trained in brutal hand-to-hand combat while Simon’s fighting was limited to zero-gravity encounters and barroom brawling where more finesse than brute strength was required. He received another gut-wrenching punch, then a sharp strike to his face that hurt like lightning. Simon slumped against the wall, panting. Blood dripped freely from his nose.

Branko loomed over him. He grabbed Simon’s hair and pulled his head up. “Expatriate.” He spat again. “You learn respect now.”

“He learned what a beating is, anyway.”

Simon blinked away the bleariness and saw Troop Master Sands leaning against the open hatchway. His stance was casual, but there was a dangerous look about his face. "I don't think James had this in mind when he said we were all to communicate."

"Pah! You hide behind his weakness and bow to these space scum." He jerked Simon's head higher. "I teach with pain."

The cadet kid, Alec, stood stiffly next to him. "Major, Captain, there must be some other way to settle this. The colonel—"

"*Zamknij si*'!"

Simon winced. Sands took steady strides over to them. "Tell the boy to shut up again. I wanna hear it."

Branko straightened. He pulled on Simon's hair as he did. Simon was pretty sure he lost a few follicles in the process. "Dog. You speak to me this way. I must get back to my pupil."

"You want a lesson too? I'm a good teacher."

Branko snorted and returned his attention to Simon.

Sands wrenched him around and slammed his fist square into Branko's face.

The blow sent Branko reeling. His hand came away from his face, blood between the fingers. Simon pulled himself up off the floor and saw wild-eyed disbelief—but not fear—on Branko's face. "You . . . struck me."

"You needed it!" Sands snapped. "Go sleep it off, Major, and nobody needs to find out about it. Especially not the colonel."

Simon raised a hand limply. "Hello? I vote for that solution too."

Branko snarled and leaped at him. Simon yelped and got out of the way—he wasn't interested in getting further injuries. Sands swept his knee up into Branko's leg. The fusilier tumbled to the floor. He tried to roll over, but Sands was already on him. He hauled Branko to his feet before landing a blow on his jaw.

"You should've stayed back, Major!" Sands growled. He punched Branko again, slammed both hands down on his raised arm, blocked a punch, and slugged him yet again. Sands went on hitting him, pummeling his body . . .

"Stop! Get off him!" Alec grabbed on to Sands's uniform to hold him back. He managed to pull Sands back some, but Sands tried to push him away. Alec shoved between Sands and Branko. Then he stood there.

Sands stopped. His left fist hovered back over his shoulder. Simon saw it waver. He wondered if he'd punch the colonel's kid too.

"Corporal! That is enough!" Alec snapped.

The kid might not be an officer anytime soon, but he's learning to sound like it, Simon thought.

Sands's chest heaved. He looked down at Branko, then up at Simon. Simon shook his head slowly.

"Back down, Benjamin. Please." Alec pulled on his arm. Simon watched him, expecting to see a scared boy. Instead he saw a stern confidence. Kind of like the little bit he'd seen of the colonel.

Branko coughed. He was on his knees with his face to the deck, breathing hard. He looked up, and the defiance was still there. So was a flicker of fear. Simon saw it before it disappeared.

Sands exhaled. He lowered his fist. His fingers flexed.

Branko tottered to his feet. "So . . ." He spat yet again. Simon was going to have to get a rag. This time, though, something clattered to the metal grating. A tooth. "You have . . . put me in my place, Captain," he said to Simon. "I will not disrespect you aboard your vessel again."

Simon gaped, then winced. It hurt too much to gape. He looked at Sands and Alec. Apparently Branko was going to keep Sands out of this mess. "Uh . . . Yep, well . . . just you remember that. So I don't, you know, have to smack you around again."

"Yes," Branko rumbled. Simon decided not to needle him further.

"This need not be reported," Alec said.

"It will not, officially," Branko said. "But James, he will know."

Simon watched as Sands's jaw worked. Stars only knew what was going through his head. "Yeah. I figured."

He stalked off out of the galley.

Alec and Branko followed. Simon was left alone. He cataloged the hurt—it was a long list.

This wasn't a fun trip so far.

Branko was true to his word.

Alec and Benjamin stood stock-still at attention before Colonel James Verge. The three of them were crammed into the small cabin set aside as Father's quarters and office for the voyage. There was one bunk recessed into the bulkhead, with a row of cabinets underneath. A tiny desk had been bolted to the floor, and a chair secured behind it. Alec and Benjamin had just enough room to stand side by side, at arms' length from Father's desk.

Father slid his delver aside and looked up at the two of them. His boot drummed a steady beat against a desk leg. "What am I supposed to do with you?" he asked. His voice was tinged with sadness.

Alec kept his mouth studiously shut. He glanced at Benjamin. The hulking troop master wouldn't make eye contact with either of them.

Father abruptly pounded his tiny table with a fist. Alec flinched. "Blast it, Troop Master, I asked you a question and you will give me a response!" Father said.

"Sir." Benjamin spoke in a terse monotone. "My conduct was . . . irresponsible."

"That's putting it mildly."

"I've abused your trust. It makes me unfit to be an officer. I will submit to punishment as you see fit."

"Of course you will." Father sighed. "That is not the problem, is it?" He waved a hand. "At ease, the both of you."

Alec relaxed his stance. "Colonel, maybe I can explain—"

Father lifted a finger in his direction. "I will speak with you later, Cadet Trainee."

Alec stopped cold.

"And enough of the 'sirs,' Benjamin. This isn't a formally reported incident." Father leaned back in his chair with his delver in one hand. "I didn't get you out of the royal prison just so I could throw you in the brig."

Benjamin's lip twisted.

"Major Mazur was quite sparse in his details of this incident. But he seems to think your action was not out of line. Just the . . . severity of your reaction."

"Understood, sir—er, James." Benjamin started to say something else but stopped.

"Go on."

"Blast, you know he had it comin'!" Benjamin said. "Branko's been looking to take a piece outta that Expatriate since departure. I figured he needed to taste his own medicine, ya know?"

"But you were hardly the appropriate one to administer it, Benjamin, being one of my junior officers. And a provisional one at that." Father tapped the delver. "This message from Branko is the truth, I take it?"

Benjamin nodded glumly. "Yeah."

Father glanced at Alec. "Do you have anything to add?"

Alec straightened. "No, sir. Major Mazur's account is accurate."

Father frowned. He rubbed at the delver absentmindedly with his thumb. Finally he asked, "Do you need help?"

The question surprised Alec. He didn't think Benjamin would take it well. The troop master jerked his head upright. "What do you mean?"

"I think the question is straightforward. You could see one of the Benevolents aboard the battle corvettes."

"Like Friend Marsano? No thanks. Your sister . . . er, the commander . . . didn't seem impressed with him. I don't think I need that junk."

"Fair argument. I can't say as they have ever been helpful to me. So do you need to see a medic?"

"No!" Benjamin turned twice, apparently intending to pace. He stopped when it became apparent there wasn't even room in the cabin for him to take four steps in any direction. "Why do you keep asking me that?"

"Because of your record, Benjamin," Father said. "Not the number of altercations, though that is troubling too, but the severity of them—the severity with which you punish your opponents."

"Nobody seems to mind when it's Tiu," Benjamin countered, crossing his arms.

"But Major Mazur is not a Tiu!" Father snapped. "Nor was your sergeant this summer, nor were the drunken men in that bar last year. They were not combatants, and those fights didn't take place on a battlefield. These outbursts of rage are entirely inappropriate. You're supposed to maintain control of yourself, Troop Master, and if you're going to continue as one of my Lancers, you will have to do so. Keep in mind too that you're supposed to be providing an example for a certain impressionable cadet."

Alec blushed furiously. He was beginning to feel like he'd failed his end of the assignment—to keep an eye on Benjamin and keep him from trouble. "Sir, if I may, Troop Master Sands—"

"Is reckless." Father finished the sentence, though not with the words Alec intended. He returned his attention to Benjamin. "Take heed. If it occurs again, I will not protect you. Someday this anger will burn too long, and against the wrong person, and it will get you cashiered out of my brigade—and worse."

"I understand, sir."

"I hope you do. Dismissed."

Benjamin left Alec standing in the middle of the cabin. The silence closed in on him. "Father," he said quietly. "I'm sorry about this."

"It's not your fault." Father rubbed a hand across his face. "Perhaps it was too much for me to ask of you—to try to mellow Benjamin. He is a good man but far too volatile for his own good."

"In all fairness, he has done well," Alec said. "Aside from this."

"And the fight with the Bethelite tavern-goers," Father added.

Alec winced. So he'd heard about that fight. It was a good thing Father hadn't been there to see Benjamin put the stops on an unruly, drunken Bethelite angling for a fight. "That was a matter of self-defense."

"I won't disagree." Father smiled. He clapped his son on the shoulder. "Branko had good things to say about you, though, both about your conduct during the fight in the galley and during the combat on Bethel."

Alec felt the stirrings of pride, but sorrow quickly washed over them. Many men had died on Bethel, including his uncle, Major Jonathan Douglas. "I keep thinking there should have been something I could have done to save Uncle Jonathan," he said. "It's foolish."

"Not so foolish." Father's face fell. "Don't think you are the only one, Alec. I was right there when he died . . . and there was nothing I could have done."

"I know." Alec didn't want to think of his uncle, especially of the shattered body buried on some other world. It made him wonder, though. "Have you heard anything from Mother?"

"No. I haven't attempted a message, either. It's too dangerous. We don't know if there are more Martian ships waiting for us. The presence of that scout ship at Bethel means we may see some here."

"So we don't know if she is all right."

"Don't worry." Father gave him a half hug. "Your mother is strong. She will not be easily stopped if Kesek comes after her."

Alec really didn't want to consider that.

He found Benjamin off by himself at the back of the galley. A troop of Lancers were digging into their own meal of combat rations at three of the tables toward the front. Benjamin had a delver out on the table before him. It projected glowing blue letters into the air, but the troop master wasn't looking at those—he was staring out the observation window.

Alec joined him at the table but didn't say anything. He casually scanned the galley but didn't see any signs of the brawl. Captain Haczyk must have tidied up.

He too watched the *HMS Herald* cruising relatively nearby. Some gleaming specks further beyond might have been the rest of the task force. He held up his hand, framing *Herald* between his fingers. In his imagination his hand was a protective shield around his Aunt Colleen's command. If it were only that easy.

"Careful. You might squash it," Benjamin said.

Alec smirked at him. "So you are conscious. I thought you might need a medic."

"Or a Benevolent?" Benjamin turned back to his delver. "Not funny, kid."

"Maybe so." Alec sat beside him. "What are you reading?"

"Well . . . I was thinkin' more about what the colonel said. Figured I might take a look at some of that stuff the Haczyk kid was preaching."

"Oh." That was surprising. From his determination Alec thought Benjamin was going to say he'd been reading the latest hand-to-hand combat regs from the academy.

Benjamin eyed him curiously. He poked a finger through the holographic words, making them waver like a mirage on a hot engine surface. "You should recognize it, Cadet. It's the pages from that Bible."

"What?" Alec looked more closely. Yes, they were indeed the same pages he'd scanned with the recon imager back on Bethel. "I didn't know you put a copy on your delver."

"I didn't. It's on the Reach. Started out on some dinky message box the Expatriates use. But it keeps gettin' deleted."

"So somebody put the pages I scanned out there for all to read."

"Guess so."

"Where is it now?"

"Ah, who knows. ReachWrit says it's 'terrorist propaganda.' Whoever's deletin' it can't do it fast enough—keeps hoppin' around to other message boxes and posterboards." Benjamin chuckled. "Expatriates are keepin' it alive. You gotta give it to them, they got guts."

"They never have played by anyone else's rules, especially Kesek's." Alec gestured at the floating text. "May I?"

Benjamin swiveled the delver a bit.

It was a section Alec had heard Baden read on Bethel to the teeming crowds: "And Peter said to them, 'Repent and be baptized every one of you in the name of Jesus Christ for the forgiveness of your sins, and you will receive the gift of the Holy Spirit. For the promise is for you and for your children and for all who are far off, everyone whom the Lord our God calls to himself.'"

Benjamin grunted. "Do we count as 'far off,' ya think?"

"It's possible. That's certainly what it sounds like."

"This Peter guy who said this stuff—he was in other parts of the book, right?"

"He was." Alec clawed back through his memory for what Baden had read. "He was one of the primary followers of this Christ."

"Yeah. And he was a hothead. Chopped a guy's head with a sword—"

"I think it was an ear."

"Whatever. He even told off his boss. Then he sold him out so he wouldn't get spaced." Benjamin shook his head. Alec saw his own amazement mirrored in his rough face. "And then you get to this part. The guy's preachin' his head off and don't care who he riles up. What the blazes happened to him?"

There was longing behind the question. Alec didn't need special training to hear it. "He was transformed, somehow. Changed for the better."

"Huh." Benjamin rubbed his chin. "You buy this stuff?"

"Buy it?"

"Believe, kid. Do you believe it?"

Alec hesitated. He had tried praying—repeatedly—since they'd departed Bethel. He wasn't sure what kind of response to expect. But something about the words from the Bible called to him. "I'm not sure."

"Yeah. Well, me neither."

Suddenly a red haze descended over the text. Tiny letters raced across the uppermost border: WARNING-TEXT-IN-VIOLATION. CRIMINAL OFFENSE. DELETION COMMENCING.

Alec watched in stunned silence as the words shivered and disintegrated. Benjamin swore. He smacked the delver. The hologram disappeared. "So much for that."

Alec drew his own delver from his pocket. "Fortunately for you I have the entire scanned copy here."

Benjamin looked at him. "Really? That's risky carrying that around."

"Please. Kesek can feel free to take it from me after I restore the king that they overthrew," Alec said sternly. He turned on his delver.

Benjamin laughed. He slapped Alec hard on the back. "That's my cadet trainee!"

The intercom squawked to life. "Colonel Verge, please come to the bridge." The voice was feminine and cool. All professional. "Repeat, Colonel Verge, please come to the bridge. We are receiving a distress signal from a Rescue Corps cutter."

Alec shot the troop master a look. "What do you think that's about?"

"One way to know, Cadet."

CHAPTER 15

October 2602
Xiaoji Star System

Colleen Verge strode onto *HMS Herald*'s spherical bridge. The wide main monitor of the two level command center showed a stunning view of Xiaoji's sun and the stars around it. There were no other ships visible, since *Herald* was running point for the convoy. "What's the word, Ensign Belus?"

"Emergency signal from Rescue Corps cutter, Skipper." Ensign Jeffrey Belus turned his tall, thin frame partway in the comm station's chair. His console was on the upper level of the bridge, along with Colleen's station, Lieutenant de Silva's console, and Chief Warrant Officer Abraham Lake's tactical station. "It went out to all the ships of the convoy. I already passed it along to Colonel Verge on *Natalia Zoja*."

"Where is this cutter, Chief?"

"She's about four light-seconds from out track, Skipper." Lake's bass voice echoed in the confines of the bridge. "Looks like a small one, 120 meters long. ID comes up as *HMRC Anaconda*. And they've got another one with them, following in tandem. Might be a small in-system liner. Call it a half-hour intercept at this speed, 600 kilometers per second."

"Hmm." Colleen watched the courses in the holographic display tank on the lower level of the bridge, under the main monitor. "Helm, take us out of formation, and put us on a direct intercept course. Boost speed to 700. I want to talk to this cutter as soon as we're within a light-second."

"Aye, Skipper." Second Lieutenant Isabel Travers brought *Herald* into a slow roll onto its new heading, then smoothly engaged the antimatter drives. "We're on our way."

"Jeffrey, get me the colonel, please."

"Aye, Captain."

The bridge of *Natalia Zoja* filled part of the main monitor. James stood behind Simon and a slender Asian woman. Colleen tried to avoid eye contact with Simon. She didn't want her brother to see her grin like a fool.

"You're headed off to investigate our visitors, I presume?" James asked.

"I am. We'll send you a signal once we see what the problem is. Do you have anything specific you want me to say about our little convoy?"

James frowned. "Let's keep it vague for now. The less they know, the less they may let slip to outside parties."

"Right. We'll see what we can do. *Herald* out." Colleen made a slashing motion with one hand for Belus to cut the signal.

"What do you think, Skipper?" De Silva asked. "A trap?"

"I doubt it." Colleen looked down at the holo-tank. The green curve of *Herald*'s course was now repositioning to intersect the red course line of the cutter *Anaconda*. "But we'll know soon enough."

HMRC Anaconda called first when *Herald* was within a light-second. Colleen looked at the small, angular cutter displayed on the main monitor. It was painted the gleaming white and blue of Rescue Corps. The ship floating nearby was indeed an in-system liner of a fairly generic variety. Neither was equipped with a Raszewski sphere for traveling between star systems.

"Do you want the signal on visual, Captain?" Belus asked.

"I'd rather know to whom I'm speaking first, Jeffrey." Colleen shared a smile with de Silva.

"Ah. Right." Belus's pale cheeks burned red. "Ah, Lieutenant Rich Bayers, captain of *HMRC Anaconda*."

"Go ahead."

Belus manipulated his controls. The upper half of a burly, smiling Rescue Corps lieutenant filled a section of the monitor that was roughly life-sized. Colleen was pleased Belus hadn't magnified him up to fill the entire space. The officer wore the white shirt that marked him as captain, with the black Rescue Corps vest over top. "Captain Bayers. How may I be of service?"

"We're hoping you can take some refugees off our hands, Captain," Bayers said.

"Oh?" Colleen saw de Silva step up beside her. "Of what variety?"

"Of the Hamarkhis variety."

Colleen blinked. She heard Chief Lake mutter something she was sure was inappropriate. "I didn't realize there were any Hamarkhis refugees in the vicinity," she said.

"Well, they weren't refugees up until a week or so ago. They had their own settlement on Xiaoji III. It's similar to Mars, a lot warmer, but with almost zilch for atmosphere and about a third of standard gravity. It's also home to about two thousand colonists from Earth who aren't so keen on sharing the planet since they saw what happened at Trebizond."

"You mean the suicide attack with the pilgrimage ships."

"Yeah. That." Bayers's brow furrowed. "Look, I don't think it really was the Hamarkhis. It just isn't how they work. Then you got those Tiu ambushes that the Kesek commissioner talked about on the Reach. Something's up."

"That was my impression, in light of other events. Why the emergency signal?"

"Ah. The refugees. They picked up their entire settlement and left, all 300 of them, but on the way out they got jumped by some merchanters with more muscle than sense. The merchanters roughed them up and took most of their goods. Now I have about 80 Hamarkhis who need transport out of this system."

Colleen chewed her lip. "Their ship's too small?"

"Overcrowded. Plus we've got sick and injured." Bayers looked suddenly tired. "Look, Captain, I've got the largest Rescue Corps ship in this system. Between us and the smaller craft among the outer planets, we got our hands full with shipping and mining accidents."

"We can certainly help out, Captain. Let me confer with my officers and we'll let you know where and how to begin transferring the refugees."

"Thanks, Captain. *Anaconda* out."

De Silva approached Colleen as soon as the conversation ended. "Skipper, we can't put them aboard Herald."

"I know that, Lucia. I don't want them on any of the battle corvettes." Colleen clasped her hands behind her back. "And the transports are full up with troops and supplies."

"So, that leaves Crossbow."

"Right. As sad as it is, Crossbow has more hangar space to accommodate barge traffic with fewer fighters aboard." Colleen stepped forward from her chair. "And that's where we'll put them."

"Is that wise, Skipper?"

"I'll not abandon these people to destruction," Colleen said firmly. "Even if it was Hamarkhis and not Tiu who attacked Earth, these settlers did nothing. They deserve protection. Even from our own kind."

She turned to Belus. "Signal Colonel Verge. Have him redirect the convoy to meet us."

"Aye, Captain."

The convoy. Colleen thought about Simon. "And Lucia, have the flight deck get me a shuttle. I'm transferring to *Natalia Zoja* for a bit."

De Silva gave her a sly look. "To confer with Colonel Verge."

"Of course." Colleen smiled.

And if she happened to speak to Simon in person while she was there, all the better.

• • •

Connor stood back from Coyote 11 with a paintbrush in one hand and battered canister in the other. "There now. Doesn't that stir your soul?"

Logan grunted and pulled himself out from underneath the fighter. He wiped a stain from his forehead. "Next time ask me after I'm through with the ventral sensors."

The overhead work lights of the domed hangar provided just enough illumination for heavy maintenance on the fighter. And for painting. Connor glanced about the dome, just big enough to accommodate the plane and its maintenance alcoves. A ramp led down through a heavy hatch to pilot country. The dome was one of 48 dotting *Crossbow*'s hull.

Connor waved the brush at his handiwork. Six freshly painted red silhouettes in the shape of Tiu Harpy fighters adorned the fuselage. "Not too shabby, eh? Brings our total up to eleven."

"Pretty sad when you consider how many years it took us to get to five, and we earned six in one day." Logan wiped his hands and crouched back underneath the plane.

"You're no fun." Connor set the canister down on the deck and the brush atop the canister. "Now, where's that laminate?"

"Here." Donna Pramanik, walking toward him from one of the alcoves, tossed him the spray bottle. He caught it easily and flashed her a grin. She chuckled. "Why you waste your time with kiddie paints is beyond me. You could've let me work up decals on the hangar comps."

"Oh, yes, and rob me of my connection with this beautiful machine." Connor stroked the fuselage. "Not the same."

"Nice. Get that laminate on there and we'll put more sealant over top so it doesn't all burn off the next time you planet-dive."

"Understood, Petty Officer." Connor shook the bottle.

The intercom snapped to life. "All available flight deck hands, report to Dome 11 for assistance with incoming casualties. Repeat, all available flight deck hands, report to Hangar Eight for assistance with incoming casualties. Gravity will be adjusted to one-third, effective immediately. That is all."

It clicked off. Before Connor could frame a snappy reply, pink lights pulsed throughout the hangar, accompanied by a chime. Connor felt oddly buoyant. He let go of the spray bottle and watched in amusement as it fell at a much slower rate to the deck. "What fun!"

"Come on, Conman, it must be serious." Donna sprinted toward the ramp. Of course, it was a bounding, funny-looking sprint.

Connor took off after her. Logan joined him. "Why the change in gravity?"

"Only one reason I can think of, No-Joy." The idea soured Connor's mood. "It probably has to do with Martians."

"Prisoners?"

"We'll see."

They joined a knot of other technicians and a few pilots heading to Hangar Eight. Donna was far ahead of them. The corridor through pilot country was wide open with dozens of hatches along either side for pilots' cabins and ready rooms. Then Connor saw the first of the stretchers.

He'd been right. The crowd cleared out for two medics in whites and blues as the pair pushed a stretcher with a wounded man. He had his arm in a bloodied sling and wore a torn, muddy green shipsuit. And he was indisputably Hamarkhis—tall, long-limbed, wide, pale-eyed, with a light complexion.

Connor watched them go by, shocked. "Why are they bringing them aboard?"

"Refugees." Donna came through, holding one end of another stretcher. Another fighter tech held the other end. Its occupant was a Hamarkhis woman. "Earth settlers on Xiaoji kicked them off because of the attacks on the king."

Logan made a face. Connor's emotions roiled. He didn't want Martians anywhere near him. They'd shot down Jerry on Bethel and killed Jonathan, James Verge's brother-in-law. That had been Tiu warriors. But then Martians were Martians. Weren't they?

The woman reached out a slender arm and touched Connor's hand. It was cool and clammy. Her eyes were a very pale green. She said something in a halting tongue that Connor couldn't understand, then added, "Thank you."

Donna looked at him. "There's forty of them. Coming in off of a barge in Hangar Eight. Somebody said another barge is bringing the rest to Hangar Ten." Her eyes were hard. "No one on Harendra Desh ever treated them this way."

She pulled the stretcher along with the other technician in tow. The Hamarkhis woman's hand fell away. Connor shivered as he watched them go. More stretchers were coming.

Logan was at his side. "What is it, Conman? You're never this quiet."

"I never knew," Connor said numbly. "They're human."

"We all learned that in bio class, Lieutenant," Logan said gently.

"Oh, I know it." Connor watched as a pair of pilots helped a tall Hamarkhis man carry a frightened child. "But now they really are."

• • •

Simon pulled himself up the rungs of a ladder onto a wide catwalk. Colleen Verge followed. "Well, here we are," he said.

The engine spaces of *Natalia Zoja* were far from glamorous. Simon wondered how they compared against the setup on a battle corvette. Probably were a lot cleaner, with new labels and bright warning notations. Simon surreptitiously rubbed a greasy smudge off a blue coolant line.

Colleen Verge looked around. Her crisp, pressed uniform of khaki and white looked out of place here, no doubt. They stood on the widest catwalk that housed all three sets of drive controls—those for the main antimatter engines, the secondary ion drives, and the auxiliary chemical rockets. She took a step closer to the railing and looked a long way down. Eight meters below were the rainbow jumble of pipes, spheres, and drive casings of the main engines. Simon figured there was more color here than on the stenciled walls of the galley.

"It certainly seems organized," Colleen said.

Simon chuckled. "Renshu would love to hear you say that."

"Boy, would I ever!" Renshu came around the corner by the dorsal airlock nearby. He wiped his hands hurriedly on his coveralls. "Welcome to the most important works of my ship, Commander."

Colleen extended her hand and Renshu dashingly swept her fingers up to his lips for a kiss. "Is this how you treat all of your guests, Mister . . . ?"

"Shen Renshu, ma'am, engineer of *Natalia Zoja*. I only treat important guests this way." He winked at Simon. "Not like the skipper here lets me have many visitors. Mostly keeps me locked away."

Colleen smiled. Simon moved to take Renshu's arm in a friendly but forceful way. "That's mostly so my guests don't hear him talking about this as if it were *his* ship instead of *mine*," he said.

"Thank you for allowing me to view your home, Mister Renshu," Colleen said. She ran a hand over the railing. "I can tell just by listening that she is well cared for."

Renshu looked as if he'd won top prize for engine maintenance. Simon gently steered him back toward the airlock. "You hear that, Simon? Blast, I wish I'd had my delver on 'record.' I'm not gonna let you forget it."

"Yeah. Fine. That's great." Simon leaned in closer and whispered, "Now go tune the sphere or something."

"Don't you want a tour guide?"

Simon looked back at Colleen. She was looking the antimatter drive board over with interest. "Nope. I can find my way around, I think."

Renshu followed his gaze. "Oh. I see." He slapped Simon on the back. "Why didn't you say so in the first place? Don't stay out too late without your chaperone, Captain."

Simon swatted at him but missed.

He took a deep breath and went back over to Colleen. "Sorry about that. He . . . had some other work to do."

"Work that you found for him?"

Simon's mouth hung open for a second. Then he managed a smile. He liked her. "Yeah, you could say that. I have to say, I was surprised when you said you wanted a tour of the ship. She's not much to look at."'

"True, but I heard the way you talked about her and saw the way you looked at her." Colleen reached up and patted a support strut. "She's more than your ship. She's home."

Simon looked around. His throat tightened as he thought of so many years spent laughing, working, playing, fighting, and crying aboard *Natalia Zoja*. So many of the times spent with Hannah.

His ship was his home, and it was also where Hannah had been taken from him.

"I'm sorry." Colleen stood close to him. "I didn't mean to say anything inappropriate."

"You didn't. It's just . . . I lost my wife to Kesek. And it's been difficult without her." There. It was said.

Colleen looked conflicted. "I don't want to dishonor her memory in any way. But I do want you to know how I feel . . . about you."

She stepped closer and put her hands around his waist. Simon's heart was pounding. He wasn't sure about any of this. He missed Hannah terribly. At the same time, he was drawn to Colleen. He put his hands on her shoulders. She kissed him gently on the cheek.

Simon was electrified. He moved to kiss her.

But he couldn't. "I . . . I'm sorry."

Colleen put her fingertips on his lips. "It's all right."

He pressed his forehead against hers. Her hands brushed the side of his hair.

They stood together amidst the hum of *Natalia Zoja*'s heart for a long time.

• • •

James had to admit, he still expected the sleek, curving confines of a warship or transport command nexus. The slightly dingy bridge of *Natalia Zoja* did not inspire him to confidence in their mission.

The only person who was on the bridge was apparently the woman who'd called him, Colleen, and Captain Haczyk to the bridge. She had an elegant look about her, even though she wore a slightly rumpled shipsuit. Her black hair framed a placid, pale face of Asian descent. James was apparently the first one there.

The woman was moving between two different consoles, a harried expression on her face. "Problem, Miss?" James asked.

"The name is Emi," she said softly. "Emi Akai. And yes, the helm's down. Computer link to engineering failed. In times like this I really miss Owen. There, that ought to do it."

Oh, stars. James kept a blank face. What a heap of rust. "I am glad to see we are not in imminent danger."

"It shouldn't be a minute before the main system is online again. The backup has control of the ship now."

"Very good. Where is Captain Haczyk?"

"Ah. Excuse me."

James turned. Simon stood at the entrance to the bridge. He was an aged image of his son, though with less untidy hair and greying whiskers. The sharp grey-green eyes were more watchful too.

Colleen stood next to him.

James was at a loss.

"I believe Captain Haczyk is here," Emi said pleasantly. "Colonel Verge was looking for you, Skipper."

"Figured that." Captain Haczyk nodded as he walked to his seat. "Colonel."

"Captain." James looked to Colleen, but she stood there with an odd expression on her face. "You requested my presence?"

"Sure did. How's your kid?"

What did that have to do with it? "He is well. Though I would rather he not have to intervene in any more shipboard skirmishes."

"Huh." The captain crossed his arms. "So what did you want, Emi?"

"I called you all up to see this. The message was broadcast over the Reach a few hours ago. We just received it now. Not all of it, of course, because somebody—probably Kesek—shut it down partway." Emi reached for her console.

Within moments the main monitor blinked to life showing . . .

The Congress of Worlds. Or rather, part of it.

James stared. He recognized Devereaux Garrison from royal functions he'd attended over the years. Garrison sat alone at a simple table. Standing behind him were several others, though James did not recall who they were—many must be alternates rather than full representatives. Gostislav Baran stood at Garrison's left elbow, looking like an irate bull with a moustache.

Tara stood to the right. James's heart ached. She was alive. And looking determined. At least at the time the recording was made.

"Citizens of the Realm, I am Chairman Devereaux Garrison of the Congress of Worlds and representative of the Freeholdings of Earth." Garrison was stern and strong. "You have doubtless heard the many pronouncements offered by the Commissioner of Kesek made over the past days, proclaiming his special role as caretaker of the Realm while our Royal

Highness is missing. We, the active remnant of the Congress ,are here to shed light on these lies made by the commissioner, who has set his sights on the very throne of the Realm."

"Interesting," Captain Haczyk said.

Emi shushed him.

"The evidence of collusion with Tiu forces is contained in the commissioner's private files," Garrison said. "We have obtained them directly from his office. It was he who enticed them to attack our task forces and orchestrated the deadly suicide raid on Trebizond Base, making a mockery of the most holy pilgrimage revered by the Hamarkhis. The Tiu used Hamarkhis ships to make their suicidal raid."

James shook his head at the sight of the text scrolling alongside an image of the devastation at the Trebizond shipyards. He'd already seen the images in Gironde's announcement several days prior, but it was far more galling to think that Kesek was behind it. "If a Kesek man hadn't tried to put his own knife in me, I would not have thought this possible."

"You obviously haven't seen Kesek in action often," Captain Haczyk said. "They drag Expatriates off to prison all the time, and nobody raises too big a fuss."

"Don't be too sure of that." Tara had yet to speak. James wanted desperately to hear her voice again, to know it wasn't some hallucination.

She gave him his wish.

"We have also learned that it was Kesek that abducted His Royal Highness Andrew the Second and fabricated the story about a Martian abduction," Tara said. "We know now that the commissioner is planning to hand over the king to Tiu conspirators later this week. Our operatives have obtained video evidence that the king, his wife, and their twin sons are being held in a prison facility beneath Kesek's headquarters building at The Hague on Earth. We beg you, the people of the Realm, to voice your grievances and your protests to Kesek at once and with one voice. The Royal Stability Force has lost its true, original purpose and has become a self-perpetuating organ of oppression."

James was immensely proud. "She has waited a long time to say this to those who would listen."

The image now refocused on Garrison. "This is your Realm. We and the Freeholders of your respective worlds are the stewards, but you must assert your power as the people," he said grandly. "To the military forces supporting Kesek, we urge you—"

The transmission blinked out in a hail of static, then cut out entirely.

The silence on the bridge of *Natalia Zoja* lasted a long time. Then Captain Haczyk cleared his throat. "So . . . what do you want to do?"

James was still staring at the screen. Colleen now stood behind him. She put a hand on his shoulder.

"Father. Colonel!"

He spun around. Alec and Benjamin stood just outside the hatchway. Alec wore a look of fierce indignation. Benjamin just looked like he'd rather be elsewhere. "We cannot let this stand, Father!" Alec said. "We have to do something to help."

James nodded slowly at his son. He was truly growing into his heritage as a Lancer. "You're right, of course. Fortunately, Branko and I have a plan."

"Hey, remember the captain?" Haczyk stood and confronted James. "What's the deal?'

James smiled as the outline raced through his head. "We will drop in on them."

CHAPTER 16

November 2602
Whelanport Star System
Whelanport, Dome Eight

Detective Chief Inspector Nikolaas Ryke smiled as he walked slowly around his prisoner. Jason sat under blinding lights in one of the most secure interrogation cells of the Kesek forward operating base. The walls were dark shadows out of the circle of light. Only a long mirror along one wall shimmered. Clamps secured his arms, legs, and body to an upright metal bed. His head lolled to one side, then jerked to the other. One eye was swollen half shut by an ugly bruise. He was clothed but there were bloody tears in his tunic and pants.

Ryke cataloged the damage to Jason with the same contentment that a ship's engine tech might experience over a finely tuned antimatter drive. He had the boy, he had his friends, he had this nuisance Jason, and he had the Bible. It rode safely in his jacket pocket. Once Ryke found out where Alexandria was, he would take immense pleasure in destroying it along with the rest of the texts-in-violation he was sure to find.

"It's always satisfying to see that one's subordinates follow one's orders to the letter," he said. "Hmm. Yes, this work is as fine as any I could have done."

Jason coughed. He spat up blood.

"Oh, well, I suppose you don't appreciate that point of view." Ryke stopped his pace. "This doesn't have to go on any longer than the—how long has it been? Twenty hours?—than the time it has already lasted." He leaned forward, voice near a whisper. "You could just tell me where the rest of your friends are."

"Don't—" Jason coughed again. This time his body was wracked with shaking. When it subsided, his voice sounded only a bit firmer. He pulled at the clamps holding his arms in place. "I don't know what you mean."

"Oh, yes you do, yes you do. Your friends. The Seventy, I believe you call them? How quaint. A perfectly charming picture of the poor, humble souls your beloved Savior sent out to missionize the dregs and the masses.

"I had heard rumblings about their actions, mere rumors from the pirates we have questioned over the years, but never took them seriously," Ryke continued. "I never imagined them to be true. But my good man Cotes was able to data sift several dozen references to the Seventy made during Kesek arrests in recent years. Now I take great pleasure in seeing that he is correct in his analysis."

He leaned in closer. "What does your lovely message give the downtrodden, dear friend? Hmm?"

"Peace," Jason wheezed. "Life."

"Peace!" Ryke laughed, a cold, sharp noise. "You have no peace. You people face nothing but hardship and opposition."

"You'd know," Jason murmured.

Ryke snarled. He backhanded Jason again. "Yes, I would know, because I have hunted your kind for years and grown quite skilled at my profession. I've seen how your kind live, in hiding, or forlorn, unwilling to raise a hand to defend themselves . . . present company excluded, of course. You seem rather skilled in the defensive and offensive arts for a cross-hugger."

Jason said nothing. Ryke drew a short, slender stiletto from a hidden sheath in his sleeve. He twisted it in the light and admired its flawless blade. "Not as brutal as a gun," he mused. "Did you know that all Kesek officers are given extensive combat training with knives during their first month? It is mandatory and takes place well before firearm training. There are just so many situations in which a blade is more effective than a gun."

Ryke slashed across Jason's chest. The blade ripped a shallow cut that blossomed with blood. Jason grunted in pain. He bit his lip to keep a full shout from erupting. "You put on a good show, young man. I have noticed that your wounds have clotted at a remarkable rate," Ryke said. He continued his walkabout. He waved the bloody blade absently. "And maybe I should not call you 'young man,' is that correct?"

Jason turned his head slowly. "What do you mean?"

"I mean that my inestimable Inspector Cotes has done his homework well, once again," Ryke said. "I mean that your body may look like that of a twenty-five-year-old, but you were born more than nine decades ago. The ultimate sin of your Seventy—gross tampering with the human body."

"No. You're . . . wrong."

"Oh, now, don't be so modest. It took many Kesek inspectors dozens of years to compile the information that led us to this discovery. All those robberies, the minute bits of hair and skin samples left behind, all very confusing and pointless by themselves, but when examined as one . . . Yes, it becomes very intriguing.

"For example," Ryke continued, "I now know that the normal levels of discomfort our methods of questioning employ are of little value. That is why I had my men lavish extra care upon you, as opposed to your traveling companions."

"Do not harm them." The warning had steel behind it. Ryke found himself staring down his prisoner.

"If you even so much as try to escape, or use your wondrous fighting techniques against me, I will kill them in the most painful manner available to my imagination." He waggled the knife at him. "You do fascinate me. You seem to have no trouble lying—or beating people senseless, for that matter—when it comes to pursuing your little crusade, eh?"

"It . . . is shameful," Jason croaked. "I had . . . always pushed it aside, but now . . . now I cannot escape that fact."

Ryke clasped his hands against his chest, pressing the dagger hilt there. "I weep for you. Now before we kill you and strip you down cell by cell to learn how you are made, tell me . . . where is Alexandria?"

"You already asked me that question," Jason said.

"Yes, many times, and you've ignored the question each time." Ryke waggled the stiletto again. "Hence the cutting and the bleeding."

"You have no idea what you're dealing with," Jason said, his voice shaking.

"Who, you? The self-appointed superhuman? Or perhaps you mean your God?" Ryke barked a laugh. "Please. I've taken my chances against him for years."

"You should not mock Him." Jason strained at his clasps. "And you can't hold me here forever."

"Why don't you try?"

Jason lunged against his restraints. He screamed in agony.

"Ah, see? There is your answer. Enough electrical current to kill most people—though you are more robust, I grant." Ryke chuckled. The fool. Didn't he know this was Ryke's domain?

Jason slumped against the restraints, and Ryke moved right up beside him. "I think we have you well in hand," he said. "Now, Alexandria . . ."

"I will . . . not . . . say . . ."

Ryke sighed deeply. "Well, I was hoping I wouldn't have to torture anyone else to get that information, but now there is no option."

He turned and strode swiftly from the room. "Your fault, of course," he called over his shoulder.

Jason didn't reply. How delightful.

Ryke made sure to walk through the guarded door he came to with a smile creasing his hard features.

Owen was slouched at the table in the center of the room, alone. It was all metal and plastic—greys and blacks. No comfort. His hands grasped the sides of his head while his eyes were glued to the monitor hanging from the ceiling in one corner. It issued no sound but Ryke could plainly see the girl—Gail Domenica Salpare of Puerto Guijarro, Muhterem system—being questioned by Cotes. Ryke was pleased to see Owen's eyes were bloodshot. Sleep deprivation was one of Kesek's time-honored interrogation favorites.

Ryke sealed the door behind him. He pulled the other metal chair from the small table and eased into the seat. There was barely room on the tabletop for two sets of elbows. Owen leaned back in the chair and put his hands in his pockets, apparently trying to look unconcerned. He failed.

Ryke activated his delver and began paging through his notes—rather, he made those motions to make Owen think he was paging through notes. He was actually scrolling through a Reach junction that highlighted the best watering holes on Corazon for travelers. But Owen didn't know that and began to fidget. Ryke's constant smile dimmed. Owen's fidgeting increased.

Eventually, Owen's gaze drifted back to the monitor. Ryke saw what he was looking for in that stare—desire. He'd seen it before when his men captured the youths. He knew just how to use it.

"She is beautiful, isn't she?" He said it without looking up from his delver.

"What?" Owen snapped his attention back to the Kesek man. "Yeah . . . she's pretty. So? You need a girl?"

"Not that station trash." A flash of anger flitted across Owen's face, and a muscle in his jaw tightened. The response confirmed Ryke's suspicions. "But you . . ."

"I what?"

"You want her." Ryke stared straight into his eyes. Owen looked down quickly. "Yes, it's obvious."

"Shut up."

"Very original. You must have spent hours thinking up that response." Ryke set his delver down and sighed heavily. "Ah, Mister Zinssler, you have so much more to worry about than a pretty pair of eyes and lovely curves. You are in quite a bit of trouble."

Owen didn't look up.

Ryke slammed his fist down on the table. Owen jumped in his seat. "Pay attention when your betters are speaking, boy!" he roared.

"Hey, man, take it easy!" Owen said. "I didn't do anything! You keep me locked up in here and don't even read me any charges, what's the deal with that?"

"Charges?" Ryke slid the chair back so fast it squealed miserably against the deck. He shoved off from his seat and waved his delver in Owen's face. "Here are a few charges . . . aiding the possessor of texts-in-violation, eluding arrest, sedition . . ." He paused smiling. "And, of course, illegal tampering with delver software."

His smile broadened as Owen's face was drained of all its color. Owen stammered, "I . . . I didn't . . ."

"Come now, don't deny it, not such first-rate work," Ryke said. He began to pace about the room, hands clasped at his back. Time to switch sides. "You should really be proud. I've never seen such skill."

"How did you—"

"Find out?" Ryke chuckled. "Let me answer that with my own question: how well do you know your friends, Baden and Gail?"

"They've got my back," Owen said, matter-of-fact. "Baden's my best pal."

"I see. And you trust them implicitly?"

"Duh!"

"Even with their . . . close relationship?"

Something like pain flickered across Owen's expression. Now he was getting somewhere. Ryke homed in on that avenue of questioning. "They do seem very much in love. Cute, if somewhat revolting."

Owen opened his mouth to say something, but stopped. Ryke made a motion with his hand for him to continue. "Well," Owen said, "that's new. But Hack's always kinda had his eye on Gail. It's just . . . She's liked him too, but he never saw it, you know? Or if he did see it, he wasn't gonna do nothing."

"I suppose I don't understand." Ryke took his seat. This was the time to maintain a calm facade in an attempt to draw more out of the young man. "Tell me."

"She always . . ." Owen stopped. He blew out a breath in apparent frustration. "No matter what I said or did, it never made any difference. She was always watching out for him, talking to him about things, especially after his mom died. Never had much to say to me, but I thought . . . I don't know, I guess I wanted it to be different."

Ryke deciphered that last line of code. "You wanted her feel for you what she felt for Baden."

Owen rubbed at a nonexistent blemish on the table with his thumbnail. "Yeah."

"But she loves him, your best friend." Owen said nothing. The crux was here. Ryke could sense it. He leaned in closer as he said in a low voice, "He sold you out, my friend."

"What? Who, Hack?" Owen barked a nervous laugh. "Yeah, nice one. What a comedian."

"I wouldn't lie about this," Ryke said gravely. Inwardly he was delighted. So easy to plant or root out trust when he saw fit. "Ask yourself: How else did I find out about your illegal delver altering?"

Owen shoved away from the table. "No way . . . no way, man, you're scamming me."

"That's for you to decide, isn't it?"

Owen shook his head angrily. Ryke could sense he was trying to work it all out in his head, and opted to keep his tongue—sometimes, with seeds like these planted, it was better to let the subject's own mind do the watering. He would wait for the harvest.

"I can't believe it," Owen murmured. "He did that? What, to save his own skin, I bet."

"Of course."

Owen kicked the underside of the table and looked away. He swore under his breath. "That book."

"Sorry? I didn't catch that."

"It's that blasted book!" Owen yelled, banging both fists on the table. He was near tears, face reddening. "You know I can't even understand him anymore? He and Gail and that Jason freak talk about that thing like it was some pricey cargo, and what happens to Ozzy, huh? He sits around them, trying to talk, and they don't even listen! It's like I'm not even there!"

Ryke repressed the smile curling the corners of his mouth. "You do not share their beliefs, I take it."

"Hey, prize for the top student!" Owen crowed sarcastically. "All that talk about God and sin and dying and heaven—what a load!"

He exhaled in a shuddering breath. Ryke watched him closely for a minute or two and absorbed the warmth of triumph. Then he leaned in and whispered, "I can help."

Owen stared blankly ahead. When he didn't respond, Ryke pressed on. "Baden's fate is sealed. He refuses to give me what I need," he said. Owen didn't need to know that Ryke hadn't even spoken with Baden, let alone questioned him. "If you cooperate, we can keep your record clean. There are other benefits available too."

Owen rubbed his face. "Like what?" He sounded tired. Good.

Ryke pointed at the monitor without moving his face. Owen watched as Cotes continued his questioning of Gail. She gripped the edge of the table in front of her with white-knuckled hands. "I don't get it," Owen said.

"We are a very resourceful agency," Ryke said. "We have all manner of prosecutorial aids at our disposal, and the finest incarceration facilities in the galaxy. Our lesser-known departments, as I'm sure the rumor mills have informed you, can free up space in those prisons by . . . altering our less dangerous criminals."

Ryke lunged for the vulnerability as he saw the understanding dawn on Owen's face. "Selective memory repression is the proper term, I believe. I can clean the hard drive, to put it in terms with which you are familiar, and she will know nothing of what she feels for your so-called friend. If we do it right, she may not remember him at all."

There was a moment of silence. Owen's brow furrowed. "Come now, boy," Ryke purred. "She can be yours. Perhaps we can plant the suggestion."

"No," Owen said firmly.

"No, what?" It didn't sound like an outright rejection of the offer to Ryke.

"She . . ." Owen bit his lip. When he continued, it was in such a whisper Ryke almost couldn't hear. "Don't make her like me. That's not right. But if she doesn't remember him . . ."

"Of course, I understand," Ryke said. Actually, he didn't. Why quibble about that detail if Kesek was going to wipe the girl's mind? A last vestige of compassion, probably. What a waste of energy, this one.

Outwardly he smiled and said to Owen, "You'll tell me?"

"Nobody knows, got it?" Owen refused to make eye contact, but he did steal another glance at the monitor. "Change our names, or something."

"A simple arrangement," Ryke assured him. He leaned back in his chair, practically beaming with joy. So simple, this business of treachery. "Give me the coordinates," he instructed, sliding his delver across the table with one hand.

Owen snatched it up. He stopped, staring at its bright screen. For a second, Ryke thought he might reconsider the deal. That was fine by him—it had been a while since he'd enjoyed a thoroughly fear-filled interrogation. He flexed his fingers.

Nearly half a minute ticked by. Finally Owen bowed his head. He punched a command into the delver.

Holographic star charts leap into the air.

Baden's cell was cramped and dark. It was no bigger than the bare metal panel running along the back wall. There was only a toilet in the corner and a sink on the opposite wall. A lone, sickly pale green light gave off a miniscule amount of illumination.

Baden sat on the edge of the bunk. His hands gripped his hair. This couldn't be happening. Not when they'd come so far and come so close. He finally understood what this was all about and now—trapped.

"Why?" Baden moaned. "I thought it would all be better somehow."

God doesn't hear you. The voice was smooth and soothing. Baden remembered it from Bethel. This time it seemed more insistent. *You're on your own. No one is listening. Except your eavesdropping guards.*

It sure felt that way. Baden sank into his own miry misery.

Face it, you're done. You failed. Not just in this task, but in your life. You've made it a wreck.

Baden groaned aloud. Why won't it shut up?

Then came the power. It splintered the doubting voice into bitter shards.

If we confess our sins, he is faithful and just to forgive us our sins and to cleanse us from all unrighteousness.

Baden shivered, but it was the sensation of warmth washing away cold. I thought You abandoned me. And so soon.

Behold, I am with you always, to the end of the age.

The resonance echoed through his mind. Baden knew that whatever was behind the other voice—the piercing, nagging fears—was not the true power. There was only one God. Baden bowed his head into his hands. He groped for the words.

"Forgive me, Christ, for not believing Your promises," he murmured. "I believe—but it's hard, You know? Keep my doubts out of this, okay?"

His cell hatch banged open. A pair of burly Kesek constables seized him and wrenched him from his slab. "Move it, cross-hugger," one growled.

They took no special care, thumping him along the corridor walls and not avoiding sharp corners. Before Baden could figure out where they were going in the winding maze of identical corridors, they burst into a wide, cream-paneled room. The only furnishings were two steel chairs. Baden's pulse raced at the sight of Gail bound in one of them. "Baden!" she cried. She tugged on the straps holding her in place.

Ryke stood by the door on the other side of the room. Baden pulled against his guards. One thumped him in the ribs with a baton.

"Manners, please, Mister Haczyk." Ryke stepped over to Baden. The constables slammed him into the chair. Baden winced as the metal frame dug into his back. One burly constable strapped him down tightly.

Baden glared back at Ryke. "Where's my Bible?"

Ryke pulled it from his pocket. "Right here, and here it shall remain." He put it away. "You've been a busy boy since last we met, haven't you? You see now there is no point in trying to escape me."

"We haven't done anything wrong," Gail said firmly. "What you're doing isn't right. People should be allowed to read whatever they want and believe whatever they want."

Ryke tilted his head to one side. "Strong-willed. Hmm, and he was correct in his visual assessment." He reached out and brushed a strand of hair from Gail's face. She shivered. Baden's anger surged. "You are beautiful, in your own quaint way."

"No!" Baden wanted to hit the man.

Ryke turned to Baden. A bemused smile creased his face. "That is not one of my favorite words."

Baden strained against the bindings. "You get your hands off her."

Ryke took three swift strides and slapped Baden hard across the face. The impact stung. Baden's cheek began to throb. "Do not presume to order me to do anything, boy," Ryke snapped. "Your lives are in my hands."

Baden expected to be terrified, but the fear he felt was strangely muted. Like a Wynton Marsalis sonata he remembered from his delver. "I belong to God," he said softly. "Why should I be afraid of you?"

Ryke hauled off and punched Baden across the nose, and then grabbed him by the shoulders and drove his knee into Baden's gut. The pain was stunning. Baden's vision blackened around the edges. Don't let me die. Gail screamed.

"Silence!" Ryke flexed his hand.

"Leave him alone!" Gail yelled. "Don't hurt him!"

"My dear, it's a little late to avoid pain." Ryke grabbed a handful of Baden's hair and hauled his head up.

Baden tried to ignore the rage flickering behind those brown eyes. They looked almost like his own or his mother's, but so full of hatred. He had to bargain with this guy. "Leave her alone and take me ... I'll tell you what you want to know."

Ryke stared at him a moment, silent. Then he burst out laughing.

Baden's heart accelerated.

"Tell me what I want to know?" Ryke chuckled. "My boy—my dear, stupid boy—I already know everything of use I need without your narrow mind's help." His smile faded. "I know where to find Alexandria."

The fear rolled over Baden. "No. You can't."

"Oh, yes." Ryke straightened and smoothed his coat. "And don't worry, I don't want your girl." He gestured toward the open hatchway. "But he does."

Owen stepped through the door. Ryke's partner, Cotes, came with him. Owen didn't meet Baden's eyes, but he did look at Gail once.

Baden felt frozen in time. Just like the in-between of a tract shift. It all lurched ahead again when saw Owen bore no bruises.

"A lesson for you, boy," Ryke said. "A lesson in friendship. Do you see the price of your so-called-friend's undying loyalty? A pretty face. You Expatriates have no sense of allegiance."

Baden felt sick. The anger roiling his insides threatened to make him physically ill. He struggled against the roaring voice in his mind. *Tell him! Tell him what a pile of filth he is! Say it!*

"Yes, boy. He sold you out for a girl, and for the promise of his own brain-washed version of her, no less. Courtesy of Kesek's mind-alteration techniques." Ryke's glee only deepened Baden's wounds. "It took a little bit of promising on my part and he was more than willing to give me the coordinates to Alexandria. Why, he even showed me the star charts."

Owen stepped forward. "Baden, I—"

"Shut up! You people and your speeches." Ryke flicked his fingers toward Gail. "Take your reward and get out. The commissioner of Kesek thanks you for your service."

One of Baden's guards unbound Gail. She sat there, motionless. Then she sprang from her seat and advanced on Owen. He recoiled as she slapped him hard across the face. "How could you!" she screamed. "You betrayed us!"

She landed a few more choice blows before Owen caught her wrist. His expression looked pained, but Baden was having difficulty finding sympathy. "Gail! I had to do something! They were gonna kill us! They said they'd let me . . ." He abruptly trailed off.

"Let you what?" Gail's face twisted in disgust. "Have me as a prize? You're insane!"

Ryke's laughter cut through their argument. "You are the prize whether you like it or not, young lady. Only he is still fool enough to think he's walking out of here with you."

Owen spun around. "What do you mean?"

"Come now, did you really think I'd honor our agreement?" Ryke asked. "None of you are going anywhere. Get comfortable."

"But you said . . ." Owen sputtered, then started again. "You said you'd let us go. Me and her."

Baden recognized his omission. Me and her. No mention of Baden or Jason. Gail looked at Baden, then Owen, in horror. Ryke sneered. "Prepare yourself for a shock, Mr. Zinssler—you were deceived. If you want this girl, you may have her, if you can convince her to stay with you. You won't have Kesek's aid in that."

His words found their mark with Gail. She shoved Owen and fled to Baden. The guards at his side tensed, but Ryke shook his head. Gail held to Baden's shoulder. "You can't have expected that to happen, Owen," she said. "I love Baden."

Owen's eyes settled on Ryke. His fists clenched. He growled and lunged.

Cotes drew his gun in a flash, but Ryke had already sidestepped his assailant. He chopped viciously at Owen's lower abdomen. Owen fell with a yelp, grasping at his side. He sucked air through his teeth.

"There is gratitude for you." Ryke drew his own pistol. "Brat."

Gail screamed. "No!" Baden yelled. A guard lashed at him across the shoulder with his gun barrel.

Ryke held the gun on Owen. "Remember this. Your lives are now in my hands. Kesek will decide if you live or die. I'm not inclined to grant you the former."

"How many are you gonna kill?" Baden was furious and confused, and didn't care what anyone did to him. "You Kesek scum killed my mom! You can all burn!"

Ryke locked eyes with him. A smile curled the corner of his mouth. "Boy, the truth is a funny thing, is it not?"

"What?"

"You insolent minor . . ."

"Sir." Cotes looked awkward. "Should you really?"

"Silence, Cotes." Ryke waved a hand at him. "This boy has caused me enough heartburn and liver damage. He deserves to know the lovely truth. After all, he values truth, correct? All right, Mr. Haczyk, here it is: I killed your mother."

There was a ringing in Baden's ears.

"Did you hear me boy? I killed her. The lovely Hannah Haczyk. Trying to do her good deeds by spreading the word. I tortured her. A little knife play, some beatings, mostly direct pain amplification. It was not very bloody. You'll be happy to know she never broke, so I granted her request and sent her to her nonexistent reward. It was simple. The human body can only stand so much agony before it shuts down and dies."

Ryke laughed. "Fools. I stopped her, and I stopped you. I have the recordings and scanned images on your delvers. And I have your Bible. Both will be sent to a very public destruction ceremony. It's good propaganda. The commissioner values such."

Baden's eyes were wet around the edges. But knowing the truth freed him. He wanted to despise Ryke, but something held him back from falling into total hate. He couldn't get his words together, though. There was only chaos.

Gail spoke up instead. "You're the fool. Right before you caught us, Baden dumped the entire Bible into the Reach. Audio recordings, scanned files of the pages, all of it. He did it for all those people you've terrorized."

Comprehension flitted across Ryke's eyes. "No . . ."

"It's probably being deleted from most of the message boards and junctions on the Reach, but you can't catch them all." There was a tremor to Gail's voice, but her expression was defiant.

Ryke's teeth clenched. He pointed the gun at her, then swiveled to face Baden.

"Sir." Cotes came to his side. "We're ready to depart. There's still Alexandria to raid and destroy."

Ryke sighted Baden's forehead down the barrel. Baden swallowed. He was scared, but now that he knew what was on the other side . . .

Ryke abruptly holstered the gun. He smiled, but it was a forced expression. "A nice try. I don't believe you. Not yet. There's no stalling now. We will visit Alexandria and burn whatever might be there to atoms."

He turned and walked to the hatch behind him, Cotes in his wake. Ryke stopped abruptly at the door. "And I will take great pleasure in watching you all die. Starting with that Jason."

There was nothing more to be done. No pleading, no scheming, no negotiating could spare them. Owen tried all three as they were dragged off by two guards, with Ryke and Cotes leading the way.

"Come on, man, I could get you jacked into any finance web you want and the money—man, the money you'd get . . ."

"Shut up," the guard ordered. The group stopped outside an open hatch.

A comm beeped. Cotes reached for it. "Go ahead."

"Sir, Captain Sasaki says the ship is prepped for departure," the tinny voice said.

"Tell him we have business to attend to," Ryke said.

Cotes raised an eyebrow. "Did you hear that, Constable?" he said into the comm.

"Yessir, but Captain Sasaki says, well, that he's leaving for Alexandria now with the coordinates you uploaded and you had better be aboard when he does."

"We will have to remind that man again of what 'obedience' means. Very well." Ryke jabbed a finger at the guards. "Torture Jason a bit more. But leave them alive for me when I return."

The guards saluted. "Yes, sir."

Ryke glared at Baden once again. "Come along, Cotes."

The officers left. The two guards shoved their three prisoners through the hatch, into a darkened room.

Owen lined up next to Gail. She immediately moved around to Baden's other side. He and Owen locked eyes for a moment. They had been friends for a long time, but Baden didn't know what to do. His mind was full of swirling arguments, accusations, and counter-arguments.

Traitor! He would've let you get locked up—or worse!

But they tricked him somehow. They must have! Ozzy wouldn't—

Of course he would. He'd do anything to save his own neck. Wouldn't you?

And don't forget he thought he was getting Gail.

Traitor!

Baden focused instead on the long window in front of him. They were in what he guessed to be an observation room adjacent to an interrogation cell. Right now that cell was pitch black. Their room was barely lit by tiny blue beacons lining the seam where the bare beige walls met textured matte grey decking.

His thoughts still tortured him, until a quieter, yet stronger series of memories began to flow through. They were like a gentle stream carving its way through a desert.

Forgive.

Forgive Owen? For *this*? It was terrible enough to betray his friend, but to want to tear Gail away from him—and then alter her mind . . .

Did I not forgive far worse?

Suddenly he remembered the things he read about Jesus. About the pain and mockery He suffered. Yet He asked for the forgiveness of those who tortured Him.

"Hack?"

He met Owen's eyes. There was something odd there, almost . . . humor?

"Look, man, I know it looks bad, but you ain't gotta worry." Owen's voice was a hurried whisper. "They ain't gonna get Alexandria."

"But you turned on us," Baden hissed. "I can't believe you!"

A shadow of Owen's old familiar grin appeared. "Hack, you are a vac-head. You think I gave that Ryke clown the right coordinates?"

Baden gaped.

"You two shut up!" One constable slapped a wall control. He hadn't heard them. "Eyes up and enjoy the show."

Light flickered behind the window. Gail gasped.

Jason stood before them, bound and wounded.

He cracked open his eyes. Baden thought he looked awful. Any other man would be dead by now. There was no telling how bad it was. Two guards were with him. Both had drawn daggers. One held a small remote.

"He don't look so tough," one constable next to Baden said.

Baden felt helpless. He didn't want to sit here and watch Jason die in this pitiful condition. Not after all he'd done.

Jason raised his head and looked right at the window. Baden wondered if he had enhanced vision and could see him. "I have . . . something to say," Jason murmured. His voice was tinny through speakers somewhere beside Baden.

"We're recording for Chief Inspector Ryke. He was unable to stay for the fun. Go ahead." The guard with the remote gave a mocking bow.

Jason's body suddenly tensed. The life almost visibly flooded back into him. Baden was shocked. "May the Lord forgive me for what I am about to do," Jason said. There was no longer a tremor in his voice.

Then he yanked one hand. It tore the clamp off its backing like so much wet cloth.

CHAPTER 17

November 2602
Whelanport Star System
Whelanport, Dome Eight

The tension in the room became palpable. One of the Kesek constables barked orders into his comm as the other one unholstered his gun. Baden thought he looked unsure whether to fire through the glass.

On the other side of that two-way mirror, Baden could see the two guards standing next to Jason. The one Kesek man with the remote in hand apparently knew just how to react. He thumbed a switch, and Jason jerked in agony. Sparks leapt from the restraints on his legs and other arm. Baden didn't even want to guess how much current was traveling through his body.

Instead of yielding and waiting for the torture to end, Jason lashed out suddenly with his free arm. He grabbed the hand of the guard not holding the remote.

The constable yelled. The sound degenerated into a horrible choking as the current passed into his body. He finally slumped to the ground, arms twitching. Baden saw Jason had the knife in his own free hand.

He flung the knife aside. Its blade cut across the second guard's hand—the one holding the remote. The constable staggered back as the remote clattered to the floor, the knife embedded in its side. He pulled his KM3 pistol but hesitated with terror-filled eyes as Jason wrenched himself free of his remaining bindings.

The silence in the observation room went unbroken, until Owen felt obliged to comment.

"Whoa."

Jason advanced on the constable. He wrenched the gun from the constable's hand and fired into the ceiling.

At the floodlight.

It shattered, showering the room in a fireworks display of sparks as everything went dark.

"Where are the emergency lights?" The guard nearest the window was still aimlessly waving his gun.

The other guard stood behind the trio and to Owen's left. He reached for a comm. "Surge drained the capacitors. Don't worry, it'll be back up in a second."

Gail squinted into the dark. The guard by the window carelessly jerked the gun in her direction. "You see something? Huh? Out with it!"

"Duck."

Baden looked at Gail, puzzled by her pale face. "What?"

"Duck!"

Gail shoved him down. Baden yanked on Owen's sleeve as he went. The armed guard turned back to the window.

Jason's restraint table bashed through the window with deafening thunder.

It showered them all with glass. Baden felt the air brush the back of his neck, heard Owen's curse and the screams of the Kesek men that were suddenly cut off with a sickening crunch. Another loud explosion of sound hammered his ears as the table slammed into the back wall. Bits of computer rained down.

Gail was deathly still. Baden shook her. "You okay?"

She peered out between disheveled hair, wide-eyed. "I was praying."

"Oh. Good idea. Wish I'd remembered to do that."

Footsteps echoed slowly in the cell. Baden rose and saw Jason emerge from the darkness into the hazy pool of light cast from the observation room. Cuts, burns, and bruises marred his otherwise implacable exterior. "Are you hurt?" Jason asked. He might have been inquiring about fresh towels at a hostel.

"No, just really blasted freaked out!" Owen looked back at the crumpled wreckage of the table. Arms and legs jutted from behind it. He shuddered. "Man."

Jason vaulted into the room but stumbled. Baden reached for his arm, afraid for . . . what, his friend? His protector?

Jason had said it himself. They were brothers in faith now.

Baden remembered Troop Master Sands's comment during the fighting against the Tiu aboard *Natalia Zoja*. "Thanks," he said.

"You're welcome." Jason met his look with clear, determined eyes. "There is no time, unfortunately, for further celebration. We must be quick. Follow me."

He pulled the table back from the wall. With one hand. Owen whistled low. Jason slipped a gun from a crushed Kesek guard's holster. That was when Baden saw the handle of another gun and a knife jutting from Jason's pocket. Baden retrieved the other one from the floor.

Owen was uncharacteristically quiet. He was busy staring at Jason, who held the table up with only mild strain evident on his face. "We thought they were going to try to kill you," Gail said.

Baden thought Jason's smile was thin and somewhat sad. "They did try. But they miscalculated."

"Oh."

"Where is Ryke?"

"He took off for Alexandria. And he's got my Bible," Baden said.

Jason's face fell.

"But Ozzy gave him the wrong coordinates," Baden quickly added.

"Ah." Jason smiled. "Clever."

Gail, however, did not look impressed. "You weren't really going to sell us out?"

"Hey, it was game play with Ryke, okay?" Owen backed up nervously.

"Enough, please. There is a service lift on this floor that takes us directly to the shuttle hangar bay," Jason said.

"Wait." Baden caught up to him. "How do you know? Maybe Ozzy should try to hack into their floor plans."

"No need," Jason said. "Kesek uses the same design for all its forward operating bases on airless moons such as this one. It saves them money."

Owen sniggered.

"So, what's the plan?" Baden was puzzled by Jason's behavior. "Something we need to disable before we jet?"

Jason shook his head. “I have none of my usual equipment. I was planning to ride the lift to the hangar bay and shoot our way to a shuttle.”

Baden shared a look with Gail and Owen. “Is that a good idea?” Gail asked.

“Probably not.” Jason stepped out the hatch. “Coming?”

“Wait!” Baden remembered something vital. “We have to get to the other cells first.”

Jason was about to ask why when his face twisted with recognition. “Oh. Yes.”

“Can’t leave without our ride.”

The alarms started as soon as they left. Three guards burst into the corridor. “Halt! Drop your weapons!”

Jason positioned himself in front of his companions. “Give me your gun, Baden.”

There wasn’t any arguing. Baden did so, but slowly. He didn’t want to panic the guards.

“You!” One guard shook his gun at them. “Give me the weapons!”

“Certainly.” Jason took the ammunition clips out of the guns. He held the guns in one hand and the clips in the other. “You would like them?”

“Hand them over, now!”

Baden saw Jason’s arms whirl and two of the guards suddenly dropped to the floor, clutching their heads. Jason had thrown the ammo clips. The third guard stared at them blankly before realizing what had happened. He raised his gun to fire . . .

But Jason had already closed the distance. He grabbed the barrel and, with a wince of exertion, bent it at a shallow angle. Baden swallowed. No way it'd be firing again.

Then Jason punched the Kesek man across the face.

He retrieved the two clips he'd thrown and reinserted them in the guns. He offered one stock first to Baden. "Come on."

Owen grabbed the guns from the two collapsed guards and handed one to Gail. Baden also saw him pull a delver from one guard's pocket. "What's that for?"

"Insurance, Hack."

Jason pointed at him. "Take down their comms. We can't let any ships in system know what we're up to."

"Aye, aye, pseudo-Skipper." Owen started in on his delver.

They followed Jason through a series of corridors. Baden noticed the alerts and flashing lights had stopped. One look at Owen got him an affirming smirk—his handiwork. Three turns later they were at a row of identical, drab bronze hatches. All bore red numbers.

"They should be in these larger group cells," Jason said. "No doubt they are secure."

"Alrighty, stand back, lady and gents." Owen held up the delver he'd confiscated. "Nothin' like having the magic wand in hand."

He punched commands into the delver. The first door popped open.

Captain Charlotte Ruby Bell stepped out. She looked more disheveled than usual. And a whole lot madder.

"'Bout time you slackers busted us out," she said. "First thing's first . . . Where's that Ryke? I owe him pain."

"He took off for Alexandria," Baden said.

Owen rolled his eyes. "C'mon, now, I told you . . . they ain't gonna find it. I gave Ryke bogus coordinates."

"You did?" Bell seemed impressed. "And he bought it?"

"Like an infant. He's gonna be off circling about five star systems too far." Owen grunted. "Ironic, I guess. He spent so much time trying to scam me that he never thought I might pull one on him."

Baden was relieved that his friend hadn't really betrayed them. But the whole bit about wanting Gail as a mind-blank girlfriend? Not time to deal with that now. Gail still looked mad at Owen. "Nice one, Ozzy."

"Thanks, Hack."

"Well, ain't that perfect." Bell's disposition improved. "Got any guns for us?"

That's when Baden realized her entire seventeen-person crew—plus a disgruntled looking Dennis—were crowding behind her at the cell hatch. "Just four."

"Gimme one." Gail handed hers over eagerly. Bell gave them all a disgusted look. "Four. Amateurs."

"Amateurs?" Owen snorted. "Yeah, amateurs who just busted *you* out of your cell. Who's the amateur now?"

"Mouthy," Bell growled. "Let's move it, kiddies! Those Kesek rats got my ship floating around in orbit of this moon somewhere."

"Excuse me." Jason stood aside as the pirates came pouring out of the hatch. "The hangar bay is this way."

Baden could tell Bell wasn't interested in following Jason's orders. Still . . . "Okay, tough guy, lead on," she said testily.

They followed Jason to a set of lifts at the end of one corridor. Bell called out from the back of the crowd, "And find me some more guns!"

• • •

When they exited the lifts onto the hangar deck of Dome Eight, there was only one bored looking technician waiting for them. The paunchy man was standing behind a tall black podium sporting a complex console topped with a long monitor. Behind him, the hangar bay stretched out into a long, wide tunnel curving at a 60-degree bend. Its ceiling loomed more than 20 meters overhead. All manner of craft—ranging in size from two-man skiffs to lumbering trawls—glistened under piercing white lights.

The technician didn't even look up. "Present your ID and badge, please," he said in a monotone. "The next shuttle will be available . . ."

Jason cleared his throat. The tech looked up.

Baden and Jason pointed guns at him. So did Captain Bell and Dennis. The technician's voice trailed off.

"Come here, pasty-face," Bell snarled. "Boys, wrap him up."

The technician offered no resistance. A trio of burly pirates produced conduit tape and quickly had him trussed up like a bundle of wiring. It reminded Baden of some of Renshu's handiwork.

Natalia Zoja. Baden hoped his dad and the crew were all right.

Bell checked the flight control console. "Says *Golden Orchid*'s parked in orbit. So we gotta get a ride up."

"You got a preference?" Baden asked Bell.

"Nope. Bigger is better, of course." Bell jerked her thumb over her shoulder. "I gotta bring all my crew home."

"Then get moving." Jason waved his gun. "Put that man into one of the lifts and send it up."

The bulk of the group sprinted into the hangar bay. Some pirates remained behind with Dennis as he manhandled the technician into the lift. Most of the rest scattered to the lockers along one wall. They broke in and started tossing out medkits, power cells, anything they could get their hands on. One even slunk away to a gig and opened the hatch. Baden sighed. Pirates.

Bell suddenly whooped. “Haczyk! Weapons locker!”

Baden saw it. “Ozzy?”

“No prob, Hack.” Owen peeled off from the group and rendezvoused with Bell.

“Here, girlie, I won’t need this.” Bell tossed her pistol to Gail. She caught it with both hands.

Around the bend in the tunnel, Baden spotted the towering hangar bay doors that led to the airless surface of the moon Whelanport—and two squads of Kesek guards in body armor in front of those doors. Twenty men with assault rifles and six security robots armed with two machine guns each. The robots swiveled their lifeless optical sensors as one in the direction of Baden and the others. A burly man with a blond beard yanked his pistol from his belt and shouted, “Halt! Nobody move!”

Yeah, right. Baden pushed Gail toward a parked gig. Jason and the pirates scattered.

The guards didn’t like this. They raised their sleek black KM705 assault rifles and fired. Bullets ripped through the air and zinged off bulkheads.

“Hope Ozzy can get into that locker,” Baden said. He took a deep breath before leaning around the fuselage of the gig. He let six shots fly. Missed.

“We must get out,” Jason said over the gunfire. Without looking, he put his arm out and fired three quick shots. Two men shouted in pain.

Unreal. Baden shook his head.

"Owen got the comms down, so we should be able to get out of orbit. Right?" Gail asked.

"Theoretically," Jason replied. "One can only hope . . ."

He closed his eyes and slumped against the gig. Baden caught his shoulder. "Jason! You okay?"

"Give me a moment." Jason took slow, deep breaths but kept his eyes closed. His forearms quivered as he pressed his hands against the gig's fuselage. Gunshots ricocheted above them. Baden tried to pray: Please help him.

Jason opened his eyes. "We have to get you to those shuttles."

A smattering of new weapons fire joined the noise. Captain Bell and a few of her pirates, leading a scared-looking Owen, came hurtling down one side of the shuttle bay. She had a heavy KM44 pistol in each hand, as did her pirates. They were firing wildly at the Kesek guards as they split off into two groups. Bell shouted at the top of her lungs as Owen and Dennis ran behind Baden's gig. Bell ducked behind a second later.

"Whew!" She dropped one pistol to the floor and ran her hand furiously through her hair. "Exhilarating!"

"You're spaced," Owen said. His voice shook. "Hack, you see that? Nearly got me killed!"

"Shut up, Goatee-boy." Bell slapped a new cartridge into one pistol. Then she set it down and repeated the process with her other gun. She hefted both aloft. "How we doin'?"

"We are not dead yet," Jason said dryly. He leaned around the gig and fired off a handful of rounds.

"There's a trawl behind those guards," Baden said. "Roomy enough."

"Hate to ruin your idea, but they outgun us," Bell said. She fired both handguns. "Quite a kick to those kiddies!"

"Well. Owen, can you open the hangar doors?" Jason asked.

Owen gave him a disdainful look.

"Never mind," Jason said. He set his gun down on the deck. "Make sure you can do so once everyone is aboard." He walked out around the edge of the gig.

"Jason!" Baden yelled.

"We surrender!" Jason cried. He held his hands up, empty.

The gunfire ceased. The pirates on the other side of the bay peered out from their hiding spot under a long barge. Baden could see their incredulous faces—Bell waved at them to stay put.

Baden watched from the edge of the gig. "I'm not armed," Jason said. He started walking toward the guards. "Let me speak to your superior."

"You hold your distance!" The bearded man in charge held his gun at the ready. Baden saw the other Kesek guards emerge from scattered hiding places. Two robots lay in smoking heaps. At least three guards were slumped against shuttles—two more were sprawled on the deck. Pools of blood glistened beneath them. Baden felt sick.

That still left fifteen men and four robots. Heavily armed. And Jason was walking right up to them.

"You know, I think he's insane," Bell murmured.

"Got my vote," Dennis said from beside her.

Baden shook his head. "Just you wait."

Jason had reached the lead Kesek man. "I'm the detective sergeant in charge here," the man said. His chest puffed out a bit. "Surrender yourself."

Jason raised his hands higher. "I believe I did."

"Well . . . good." The sergeant motioned with his free hand. The four robots trundled forward obediently. "Beta Three and Four, secure the intruders in hiding. Beta Five and Six, hold this prisoner."

The robots rolled off. Beta Three and Four headed off toward both hiding places as their two compatriots took up positions on either side of Jason. Baden held his breath as he watched the security robot rolling toward them. What was Jason up to?

"These robots look heavy," Jason said. "Old and clunky."

The sergeant holstered his pistol. "Hmph. New Sentry-shade models. Weigh a third less than the first production line."

"That is a fine thing to know." Jason turned to appraise one robot. Baden caught his smile. "Thank you."

Then Jason grabbed the torso of Beta Five and with a grunt, swung the robot right into its partner. The resulting crash was deafening. Both robots toppled sideways.

But Jason wasn't finished. He wrenched one of the machine guns off Beta Six and spun it around like the old Reach-vids of discus throwers Baden had seen. Then he let it fly.

The weapon smashed into the sergeant. He flew backwards into a handful of his men. They all collapsed to the deck. The remaining ten guards were stunned in that few seconds.

"Go!" Jason roared.

Bell whooped and raced around the nose of the gig. She emptied both heavy pistols at the Beta Three robot. Its body shook with the impact of the big caliber projectiles. It staggered to a halt before its head blew up in a spectacular burst of plastic and electronic fragments.

The pirates on the other side of the bay ambushed the Beta Four robot in similar fashion, but not before it managed to open fire with its machine guns. A pair of pirates fell to the deck, wounded.

Baden hustled out behind Bell. He tried to make himself as small a target as possible. But he soon saw it didn't matter, because the guards were all occupied with Jason.

Two guards were twisted together in a bizarre entanglement of limbs and torsos. Jason twisted the assault rifle from one guard's hands and struck him down with it. Then he swiveled and fired at another guard, sending him sprawling.

The other guards had spread out and were shooting at Jason and the pirates. None were aiming well as they were trying not to hit each other. Jason took advantage of their hesitance to advance on a tall guard, who fired six shots point-blank at him. All six bullets thudded into his chest, arm, and side.

Blood blossomed from Jason's chest. He collapsed.

"Jason!" No. He couldn't die. Baden needed him.

He stopped to steady his arm and fired his KM3. The shots missed the guard but startled him into running off. Bell shot another guard down. She grunted in pain—blood spilled down from her right arm.

"You're hit!" Baden wasn't sure how to help. He wasn't even sure if she needed it.

"Hands off, Bible boy!" Bell shoved him away with her good arm. She transferred her gun from her right hand to her left.

In seconds, it was all over.

Gail and Owen raced from cover. Gail reached Jason first. She draped one of his arms across her shoulders and heaved them both up. Owen ran right by and popped the hatch of the trawl. "Load 'em up, Hack! I'll get her warmed up!"

"Dennis, give the kid a hand, will ya?" Bell, teeth gritted in pain, ambled off to round up her pirates. Dennis joined Owen at the trawl.

Baden grabbed Jason's other arm. Blood ran down his arm onto Baden's. The man's face was drawn and deathly pale. "Hold on, we'll get you fixed up."

Even as he said the words he doubted them.

A solid whump made Baden turn away. Dennis was standing at the top of the trawl's aft ramp. The pirates, bearing their wounded, trotted inside in a ragged line. A steady hum thrummed throughout the bay as lights blinked on inside the trawl. "Haczyk!" Bell waved with her pistol. "Get aboard!"

Baden and Gail half-led, half-dragged Jason inside. Bell slapped the hatch controls. "Move it, Goatee!"

The pirates sat on long, low benches along either side of the trawl's empty cargo hold. They reached frantically for webbing and restraints in the dark, low-ceilinged confines. Baden watched his feet to avoid tripping over the tie-down latches embedded in the deck. He and Gail brought Jason into the passenger seating area. They set him gently in one of the nine chairs arranged in a square to the left of a narrow walkway. The cockpit was through the hatch at the end of that walkway.

The trawl lurched. "Going up, Skipper!" Dennis said from the pilot's seat. Owen leaned around from the copilot's station.

"He okay, Hack?"

"I dunno." Baden lifted Jason's head back. His eyes were dull and unfocused. He seemed to murmur something, but Baden missed it.

Gail strapped into a seat next to Jason and fumbled beneath it. "Hold on—ah!" Her hands emerged, holding a pearly pouch with a stylized red serpent entwined around a staff. "Medkit. Let me get the medsensor out."

Baden got his own straps secure in the seat on the other side of Jason. Outside his small porthole, the hangar bay whirled as Dennis angled the trawl for the doors. "C'mon, Jason, snap out of it."

Gail's handheld sensor chirped and beeped. She frowned over the accompanying delver. "It doesn't look good. Unless we get him to a medical center . . ."

"There is no time for that," Jason said. His voice was barely a whisper. "Baden . . . listen . . ."

"Somebody better get them blasted doors open!" Bell thundered. She stomped by the trio on her way up the walkway. She tottered a bit as the trawl lurched.

"I'm on it!" Baden plainly heard the strain in Owen's voice. "Gimme half a microsec . . . One more . . . Aced!"

The trawl portholes reflected red flashes. Gail consulted the medsensor's delver and dug into the kit for something she must have thought would stabilize Jason. Baden held on to the man's shoulder and leaned over to the porthole in time to see the towering hangar bay doors crack open. The trawl eased through the open space and hovered in the massive airlock. Baden wondered how long it would take for the inner doors to close and the hatch to depressurize.

Bell stood at the cockpit hatch, both hands braced on the frame. She flashed Baden a grin. "Hold on to your seat."

Gail pressed a subdermal injector to Jason's arm. He hissed through clenched teeth. "Lord God, please save him," she murmured.

Baden saw the outer doors crack open through the cockpit. Stars sparkled like ice crystals on basalt plains he'd seen once on a distant moon. He had a strange desire to grab a delver, turn on some Joel Hollenbeck, and for once, just relax.

The trawl leapt forward into space. The acceleration pressed them back into their seats before the tiny compensators could bring the gravity back to where it was supposed to be. Jason jerked and seized Baden's shirt. Baden held on to his fist.

"I pushed myself too hard . . ." Jason stopped. He gasped for breath. "There is no more strength left."

"Jason, we're gonna get there! Ozzy fooled them—we'll get to Alexandria and the cache." Baden was desperate for him to live. There was so much more he wanted to know, and with his Bible gone . . .

"Baden, I have been such a fool," Jason said. "I have let fear and hate rule me in ways I did not see."

"Never seen you afraid of anything." Don't die. Please don't. Come on, God!

"I feared the loss of Scripture and all it represented." Jason's breathing grew shallower. "The fear that there would be no evidence of Christianity beyond memories and scattered teachings . . . consumed me. That is why I and the Seventy hid the relics we found."

"But they do have to be protected."

"Yes!" Jason coughed. Flecks of blood speckled his pants. Gail held out the subdermal spray but he waved it off. "They need protection, but not seclusion. Baden, you had with you the greatest gift God could give man, but now it is gone. I should not . . . have made you conceal it . . ."

Tears burned Baden's eyes. "Hey, it's all right. They didn't stop us. I sent it all—I sent my audio and scanned pages into the Reach from the pirate ship. It's out there now, and even if they delete everything, someone will hear. That's what Jesus wanted, right? For everyone to hear."

Jason's expression brightened for a moment. "You have more courage than I." He clapped Baden's shoulder. A bloody handprint remained. "The Lord will always protect His Word," he whispered. "With or without us."

Baden's vision dimmed behind tears. "I can't . . . not without the Bible, and you . . ."

Jason leaned his head back against the chair. "It is time to go . . . home."

His eyes drifted slowly to one side, and he breathed his last.

Baden buried his face in his hands. Everything he'd kept back—anger at his dad, sorrow for their lost years, their rediscovered love, grief for his mom, and anguish at the burden he felt pressing on to his shoulders—burst forth. He cried and his shoulders shook.

He felt warm hands around him. "It's okay, Baden," Gail whispered. Her voice was heavy with sadness. "He's out of pain now."

Bell called out from the cockpit, "There she is! There's my ship! Hang on, we'll get him aboard and then—"

She stepped back into the passenger area. Her face tightened. "Oh. Blast. I'm sorry."

Why now, God? Baden didn't understand it. But even in the midst of his anguish, he felt a growing comfort.

Behold, I am with you always, to the end of the age.

CHAPTER 18

November 2602
Al-Qamar Star System

They made it to al-Qamar a little more than a day later.

Baden sat along the back bulkhead of the *Golden Orchid*'s bridge. Gail and Owen sat on either side of him, all three strapped in to fold-out seats. He wasn't paying attention to them. He wasn't paying attention to much of anything. Though the bridge was all quiet activity, all Baden could do was stare at his hands resting on his lap.

Empty hands. His Bible was gone.

Even after more than 24 hours, he was amazed at how incomplete he felt without it. Weeks before, he could've cared less. He'd tried to look up the audio recordings and pages that were out on the Reach, but they'd all been erased. He wondered if anyone had gotten the chance to see them.

It all seemed like a waste.

Gail reached out and grabbed his hand. He made himself look up to meet her eyes. Her always optimistic eyes. Gail lifted her chin. "Don't give up, Baden," she said. "Jason wouldn't have wanted that."

"I feel like . . ." Baden's voice came out as a croak. He hadn't said much lately. He cleared his throat. "I feel like I failed. Like I'm not good enough. And now God's through with me."

"No. None of us are good enough, but God doesn't care—He reaches across to us." Gail squeezed his hand. "We tell Him we can't do it alone, and He carries us."

He knew she was right. But it didn't feel easier.

"Ready for tract shift, kiddies?" Captain Bell spun once in her chair. She looked eager—probably anticipating her payoff in the form of hidden illegal and highly valuable artifacts. Not even having her right arm in a sling seemed to dampen her spirits.

"I don't like her," Gail whispered.

Owen sniggered. "Couldn't tell. You ain't said one word to her."

Gail speared him with a cold look. "I wasn't talking to you."

Owen wilted. Baden hoped they wouldn't keep this going. "Gail, Ozzy already said . . ."

"Ozzy? Ozzy who? I must have had my brain wiped or something, because I don't remember anybody by that name," Gail said stiffly. "I know he gave Kesek false coordinates. That doesn't explain or forgive everything."

Bell whistled sharply. "Hey! Stooges in the nursery! You wanna seal those hatches? I don't . . ." She burst into a series of sneezes. "Blazes! Hate tract shifts. Dennis! Any followers?"

"Nope, Skipper. No sign of *Interrogator*."

"I told you, they're at least a system away by now!" Owen said.

"Yeah, and what if they get their comms back up?" Bell said. "What then, Goatee?"

"Skipper?" Dennis said. "We did vaporize their comm emitter when we left orbit from Whelanport."

"Oh. Right." Bell brightened. "That'll do. Okey-doke, gimme the blue light, Nav."

The normally pale bridge lighting took on a blue hue. "In the bag and ready for tract shift, Skipper."

"Dennis?" Bell sneezed.

"Singularity holding. Engineering reports ready."

Bell wiped her nose with her sleeve. "Tell Ian not to foul us up. If these coordinates are wrong—"

"They ain't." Owen folded his arms in annoyance. "No doubt."

"All right, relax." Bell drummed her fingers on her seat console. "Let out the masts."

The navigator adjusted his controls. A flickering hologram appeared at Bell's right hand. She thwacked the holo-emitter and the image steadied. It was a miniature *Golden Orchid*—a rounded, tapering forward hull and bulky, powerful engines at aft with four rakish cooling vanes. Eight pairs of bright blue tendrils snaked out from the holographic hull. The masts would help open the portal through space that would allow *Golden Orchid* to leap in an instant from this point around al-Qamar's sun to . . .

Who knew where.

"Masts out, Skipper," Dennis said. "Singularity holding. Tract shift at your command."

Bell grinned and cocked a finger at him. "Roll it."

The navigator reached out for his controls and threw the lever . . .

Baden's mind froze solid. Images of Jason flitted through—his eerie face in the dark at Puerto Guijarro—his joy at holding the Bible—his pain as he fought . . .

Everything shook and became noise.

The arrival at their destination rattled Baden. His body wrenched in the restraints. Owen yelped. Bell swore.

"All right, calm down." She grunted and disconnected her straps. Then she sneezed. Twice. "Dennis, how we . . ." She sneezed again. "Blast it all! How we lookin'?"

"Not bad, Skipper." Dennis's eyes roved over his console. "No ships in sight. Wherever we are, we made it."

"Get sun up on the screen." Bell snapped her fingers. "Nav, show me the system map."

A churning orange sphere appeared on the monitor. Simultaneously, a map appeared as an inset against the starry sky. Baden rubbed his chin—then stopped. It made him think of Dad. That made him worry about Simon, headed to Earth with the Starkweather fleet.

"Whatever Alexandria is, it ain't pretty," Owen muttered.

Bell waved a hand at the screen. "Not much here. Two rings of rocks, one dinky planet. Don't suppose you boys brought more directions?"

Baden shook his head. He sank further into his own misery. "There's nothing here."

Bell didn't seem to like that answer. Owen unstrapped from his seat. "Hang on, Hack, there's gotta be something." He sounded agitated. "I mean, there's a reason we're here. Right? There's gotta be!"

Baden looked at him. "You think so?"

Bell sneezed. This apparently didn't improve her mood. "You boys better get your data linked . . ."

"Skipper!" The comms tech had an earpiece up to his ear. "I've got a signal."

Bell tensed. "What is it?"

"Not much. Repetitive beacon. No voice. Coming from the planet."

"More specifically?"

"I've got a fix for Nav if you want it."

"Don't wait for an invite." Bell sighed. "Like infants. Nav, take us in to the planet. Go max."

"Aye, Skipper. Should be seven and a half hours."

"Peachy." Bell rubbed her left shoulder and winced. "Let's enjoy the view."

She sneezed again.

The planet was close enough to its sun to maintain somewhat of a warm and a tenuous atmosphere. Bell scrounged up isolation jumpsuits for everyone who was taking the trawl they'd stolen from Kesek's Whelanport base to the surface—herself, four pirates, Baden, Gail, and Owen. Dennis stayed in command.

Baden stared out a viewport. The small planet was ugly. Mostly browns and purples and greys. It also had very little water, maybe just one good-sized scummy ocean. Everything else was rocky, cratered landmass. Not desirable real estate.

The trawl soared down into the pale violet sky. Below them, mountains and jagged ridges spread in all directions. The signal they'd tracked led them to an ancient impact crater on what the navigation computer deemed the planet's southern hemisphere. The crater sat in the shadow of a trio of snowy peaks. The barge settled to the ground on the flattest surface available, sending clouds of pale purple and brown dust billowing.

"Get your masks on," Bell said. "Sensors say this place has about a quarter the oxygen we like."

They followed her orders. Soon after, the party trudged up to a ledge about halfway up the crater side. Baden squinted into the hazy violet sky and stepped on patches of springy, crescent-shaped patches of purple lichen.

They crested the lip of the ledge. Bell swept a hand-held sensor rod. "Entryway in here," she said. Her voice was muffled through the mask's speaker. "Anybody bring explosives?"

Her four pirates all shook their heads. "Always be prepared," Bell said. She dug into her suit pocket and produced a palm-sized brass cylinder studded with tiny black projections. Three red lights flashed in sequence around the center.

"Whoa!" Owen grabbed her wrist. "You're gonna blow us all to atoms with that thing!"

Bell glared at him until he released her wrist. "No touching, Goatee. I ain't your type."

Gail examined the rough rocky surface before them. "Something about this seems familiar . . . Wait a moment." She ran her gloved hands across the rock. "I thought so. Something's been sealed over. I think it's a door."

"Hmm." Baden started looking further out from the center, feeling the protrusions. "Should be a switch here somewhere."

"You guys be looking for days that way. Budge over." Bell ran her sensor over the rock face. It chirped a double tone every few seconds, repeating the noise until its sensor moved over one of the narrow quartz veins lining the surface. Twin blue lights flashed along one side as it emitted a rapid triple beep.

"See? No prob." Bell pushed on that section of quartz.

Nothing happened.

Her triumphal look melted away. "Blast." She pushed it once more, and when nothing happened again, she hit it. "Ow!"

"Maybe you should try the explosive," Baden said dryly.

"Ha ha." Bell shook the pain out of her hand.

Gail sighed. "Let me try this." She reached past them and held her hand firmly on its surface. To Baden's amazement, that portion of quartz glowed pale yellow. The wall shuddered, and the fine crack Gail discovered began to grow.

She gestured dramatically with both hands. Bell scowled. "Lucky."

"Not really. Puerto Guijarro has private rooms disguised this way. Mom had me and our robots deliver meals to some of our more upscale customers."

"Didn't know the Freighthound Tavern had any upscale customers," Owen said.

Gail elbowed him in the gut.

"Ow!"

The doors trundled to a halt several meters apart. Baden stepped cautiously through into a fully functional, if somewhat outdated-looking, airlock. It was stark white and lined with red lights at the intersection of wall, ceiling, and floor. There was a second, undisguised door ahead of him. It was big enough to accommodate many more than were in the small landing party. "Think it's pretty dumb they didn't lock up the place when they left," Owen said from behind him.

"Maybe they didn't think anyone would ever find the sundoor leading to this system," Baden said. He spotted a more modern control panel by the other door. "Maybe they wanted somebody to find it."

Bell lead the rest of the group inside. She yanked the gun from her hip. "Maybe we better close the outer door so we can open the inner one and quit yakking about it."

As soon as they were inside, Baden punched the control to seal the outer door. Ventilators hissed as the red lights along floor and ceiling flashed. Baden's ears popped at the change in pressure. Finally the lights turned solid green.

Bell pulled a sensor rod from her pocket. "Got air. Ditch the breathers."

Baden pulled his mask off and sniffed. It was stale, dusty, but breathable. He looked back at the group. Owen made a flourish with his hands. "After you, Hack."

"Okay." Baden swallowed his fear and punched the hatch open panel. The doors before them cracked apart.

Owen dropped his delver.

The opening revealed a long, wide cavern spreading before them. Baden figured it was at least one hundred meters to the back wall, and easily twenty meters across. The rocky ceiling curved high above their heads, its darkness untouched by the warm yellow glow from dozens of flat lamps embedded in the smooth-cut floor.

But the most astonishing sight were the rows upon rows of display cases and storage containers. Many had flat black, tan, or white sides. Several were transparent. These latter showed off all manner of manuscripts and books, from crumbing parchment to bound volumes that Baden figured weren't much more than a century old.

"Stars and novas," Bell whispered. She didn't sound at all like herself. Baden saw her slowly holster her gun.

Baden stepped out into the cavern and walked down a short flight of steps carved into the rock. Everything had a golden aura about it. The air was stale. Not surprising.

Gail moved past him to a row of clear cases. "Look! Look at this!" Her excitement poured out as she pressed her hands against the glass. "It says it's from Luke's Gospel!"

Baden joined her. His heart hammered against his chest as he stared through the glass. The massive codex was indeed open to Luke, but the text was so ornate, so magnificent, and the pages embellished with such brilliant designs . . . "Gail, this is . . . They called these 'illuminated,' I think." His voice came out an awed murmur. "More than a thousand years old."

"Hack, check it!" Owen had removed the top of one crate and held aloft a painting sealed in a protective covering. Baden marveled at the sight of a serene bearded man holding his right hand up in a strange gesture. His left hand cradled a clear globe with a gold cross atop it. "Got a label on the covering—says it's 'Salvator Mundi.' And what's a Titian?"

Baden thought he might hyperventilate. "No wonder they wanted these hidden." He grabbed Gail's arm for support. He did feel a bit woozy. "These are ancient relics! They must have been smuggled here from Earth, or from some rich guy's private collection . . ."

"I found delver files too." Gail was pulling small black cubes, each about twenty centimeters on each side, from a larger container. "Looks like each one has data sticks. They've got names . . . 'Commentaries,' 'Orthodoxy,' 'Writings of Polycarp' . . ."

"Haczyk!" Bell stood by a trio of large boxes. Each one came up to her waist. Two of her pirates were pushing the lid off one. "This might be more on your nav course."

Baden trotted over. The box was full of Bibles. They were packed four down, five across and who knew how many deep. Bell reached in and pulled one up. She wiped the deep brown cover. Its gold lettering shone. "This must have been some fella. So was King James one of the guys before King Andrew II?"

"I dunno." Baden took another of the Bibles and opened the pages. He flipped through them. Confusion stole some of his astonishment. "Wait a microsec. This is different than the one I found."

"Doubt it, Bible boy." Bell waggled it in the air. "Says 'Bible' on the side. So did yours. Duh!"

"Shhh! Listen." Baden found what he was looking for. "It's got the same chapters and headings, but . . . Well, this says, 'But I say unto you, That ye resist not evil: but whosoever shall smite thee on thy right cheek, turn to him the other also.' Same idea, but different speech."

"This one reads differently, too." Gail had another Bible. It wore a coarse, torn black cover and had fading letters "RSV" on the binding. "Less of the 'ye's and 'thy's but not the same as the one you had, Baden."

She looked around, concern evident on her face. "There must be some mistake. Is this all a massive hoax? Something Kesek put together as a trap?"

"Don't like that idea," Bell growled. She put the Bible back in the box quickly and looked about the cavern.

"No . . . wait. It does make sense." Baden's anxiety lessened. "The scriptures about Christ came from thousands of years ago, on Earth, right? They wouldn't have been written like this at first. See . . ." He flipped to front inside pages of the Bible he held. "Here! It says the copyright date is 2440 . . ."

"Man. Two hundred years old." Owen pulled another painting out of the box at which he stood. "Nice boat in this one."

" . . . but it gives an original publication date of 1605. And it talks about it being translated from Greek." Baden nodded slowly to himself. "Right. The Jesus followers came from Palestine, on the eastern Mediterranean Sea of Earth, during the Roman Empire's middle years. Greek was the speech of the average guys."

"Score one for nerd-tech," Owen said.

"So these were all translated differently? Is that what you mean?" Gail asked.

"Has to be. Greek ain't easy." Baden smiled, remembering a school course he took on a whim. "They still speak something like it at Nicopolis, I think."

"That's all peachy, kids, but I'm more interested in colors—like purple and orange." Bell patted the box next to her with considerable affection. Her face beamed in the golden lights of the cavern. "It ain't gonna fetch no cash in this dungeon. We gotta get it sold."

"First we have to find out how much of it belongs to legitimate owners," Baden said.

"Kesek probably killed all the owners!" Bell snapped.

"Yeah, well, we don't know that!" Baden stepped up to her. He poked her in the chest. Probably a bad idea. "But we have to find out. Don't worry, you'll still get your cut. There's plenty here."

"Shouldn't we just let it be?" Gail asked. "We don't want to steal it."

"I don't really want to take it, but we can't let it sit here. You know, maybe this is why I found the Bible in the first place. We have to show people the history that's just rotting away and forgotten because of Kesek's stupid laws. And we have to tell other believers in Christ that there is still hope."

"Hack, you got a point." Owen looked unusually solemn as he approached them. He held a dark-toned painting in his hands. "This thing . . . Man, something like this outta be out there for everybody to see, you know? It's . . . nova."

High praise coming from Owen. Baden brushed his fingers across the covering of the painting. Beneath the plastic, the faded image of a boat lifted among stormy waves while frightened men scrambled about its deck called to him. Especially the one man sitting peacefully near the aft.

Follow me, and I will make you fishers of men.

Baden inhaled sharply. "We have to take it. All of it."

Bell's eyebrows flew up toward the ceiling. "*All* of it?"

"Yeah. All of it." Baden gave her a wry smile. "Your guys can do it, right?"

Bell's face took on a haughty expression. She folded her arms and puffed herself up a bit. "'Course we can. Just gonna take a while. Dennis'll get the other barge down. Don't know if that's smart, though, loading it all up into one ship that can get easily shot down ain't my idea of bright."

"We got time." Owen put the painting carefully back in its container. "Even if Kesek figures out they got duped, they don't know the real co-ords for this place."

"Fine. Whatever. As long I as I get my share for me and my crew."

"I don't want to risk leaving it here. If Kesek backtracks our route, they might find it." Baden made the first move by scooping up one of the containers of data stick cubes. "We get these all aboard and then we get out of here."

Bell snorted. "To where?"

"Earth."

"You're spaced. That's eight tract shifts back, kid." Bell sighed. "We're all gonna be mighty wiped after that. I'm assumin' you don't wanna take the scenic route."

"No. We have to get there fast." Baden could feel the familiar fear returning. "Dad and the others will be there. And, well, I think this is the right thing to do. It's crazy, but something's urging me on, you know?"

Now it was Gail and Owen's turn to stare at him incredulously. Baden figured he was getting a lot of that lately. "You are a vac-head, Hack," Owen said. "Who's gonna help us once we get there?"

"Some new friends." Baden hoped he was right.

"Skipper!" A pirate waved from the back of the cavern. He pulled aside a tarp. It revealed a long, white and tan machine about four meters long and a meter tall. There were boxes piled around it.

Baden and his friends rushed over, with Bell on their heels. "What is it?"

"Like we know, Haczyk," Bell said. "Read it."

Baden leaned in closer to a brass nameplate. "It says, 'Dunn 400 Series Twin-Vault.' And it's—whoa."

"Whoa, what?"

Gail held her hands to her mouth. "Baden, if this is true . . ."

"Yeah." Baden grinned. "We really gotta get this one out of here."

• • •

Nikolaas Ryke was almost beaming. Almost. He considered it unbecoming for a detective chief inspector in Kesek to beam. Or smile kindly.

But blast it all, he was looking forward to this.

He was at his usual haunt behind the command rail on *HMS Interrogator*'s bridge. Captain Sasaki was avoiding him like—well, like a cross-hugger hiding from Kesek.

Ryke chuckled. He was allowed to chuckle, by blazes.

"Coordinates are set, Captain," the navigator said.

The entire bridge crew was strapped into their seats on the hemispherical bridge. The main monitor showed Pryzemsl's star, location of the secret sundoor leading to Alexandria. The Owen lad had told them as much. The tract shift alert lights bathed everything sickly blue. Ryke looked down at his hands. He didn't look good in blue. It reminded him of an ancient image file from Earth he'd dug up—some kind of children's entertainment, little people living in mushroom homes.

"Masts are up. Engineering reports positive hold on the singularity," the navigator continued.

"Stand by for tract shift, on my mark," Sasaki said. He tugged on one of his straps.

Cotes came up from behind Ryke. "I have the men standing by with the assault lander, sir," he said. "They'll be quite ready when we reach this Alexandria."

"Very good, Cotes." Ryke clapped his hands together. He had the satisfaction of seeing Sasaki twitch in his seat. "Well, let's get on with it."

"Are you sure you won't have a seat, Detective Chief Inspector?" Sasaki asked.

I won't bear any weakness before you, incompetent, Ryke thought. "No thank you, Captain."

"Very well. Tract shift . . . mark!"

The navigator grabbed the lever.

Ryke braced for an unpleasant feeling. Tract shifts felt to him as if someone decided he should have his body mashed into a sphere the size of a button while being simultaneously stretched out longer than a starship's hull.

He was still waiting for that feeling when Cotes tapped him on the shoulder. "Excuse me, sir."

Cotes didn't sound happy. That made Ryke irritable. He looked up at the main monitor.

It was still Pryzemsl's star. The sun from which they started. They hadn't gone anywhere.

A low growl arose from deep in Ryke's throat.

"Oh, dear." Sasaki sounded amused. Too amused. "That didn't work, now did it?"

CHAPTER 19

November 2602
Earth Star System

The first thing Simon noticed when *Natalia Zoja* came through the tract shift to Earth was the traffic. It had been a long time since he'd been here. And it had only gotten busier.

"That is a lot of ships," Emi said from the nav console. Colonel Verge, Troop Master Sands, and Alec stood at the back of the bridge, mirroring each other in parade rest.

"No kidding."

"I have at least seventeen contacts in scan range. No—make that eighteen. Six-brace from the Horizon sundoor."

"Well, we better not hang around here." Simon hit the intercom. "Renshu, how's it look?"

"Mains are ready any time, Skipper. Hey—when are you gonna get Owen back? You know how many times I lost the backup coolant modulator?"

Simon winced. He'd laid awake for several nights worried to death about Baden, as well as Owen and Gail. Owen was almost like a brother to Baden—a tremendously annoying brother sometimes. "Hang in there, Renshu, and get the mains up."

"Oh, they're ready. I always treat my girl right. Engineering out."

Sands chuckled. "His girl? He knows you're the skipper, don't he?"

"For the most part." Simon eased forward on the drive controls. "So, fellas, glad to see the old blue ball again?"

"Indeed." Colonel Verge sounded wistful. "It seems like forever since Wyoming, doesn't it, Alec?"

"It does." The teenage cadet smiled at him. "We'll be home before you know it."

"Well, we hope so," Simon said. He had no sooner eased forward on the drive controls when Emi tapped one of her nav screens. "Skipper?"

"Yeah?"

"No one is hailing us."

Simon glanced over at her display. *Natalia Zoja* was moving off from the sun in concert with the three battle corvettes, the carrier, and three transports. "Colonel Verge did have his people rig up our transponder. I think we're running as the *Easy Ben*."

"Ah. So we should expect friends to call."

"I hope not."

"What if we spot them first?" Emi manipulated her controls. Six blips on a right hand screen enlarged. The computer provided holographic images. "Feluccas registered to al-Azhar Mercantile. They're moving off less than a light-second from our position.

Simon scratched his chin. Feluccas. Those were 600-meter merchant vessels, usually modestly armed. Probably not much more firepower than the battle corvettes, but certainly enough to let them tangle with pirate ships and live. "What's the lead ship?"

"*Firuz*."

Simon hit the comm switch, but for audio only. He wanted to make sure before showing his own face. "Hamid! Is that you, friend?"

"Simon! I am so glad to hear from you, my friend. *Salaam* and *merhaba*." A laugh echoed out of the speakers. "Let me see your good face!"

Simon sent the comm signal to the main monitor. A cheery face appeared before him. Abu Zuhayr Hamid ibn Thaqib sat in the command chair on a bridge lit with soft yellow lighting—it was far roomier and well-kept than *Natalia Zoja*'s. The broad smile that festooned his dark face cheered Simon immeasurably. Looking at those warm eyes behind the antique eyeglasses reminded him that real life still existed.

"*Salaam* and *merhaba*. Boy, are you a sight for sore sensors." Simon shook his head. He felt a bit guilty for enjoying this—he was supposed to not reveal them. But Hamid would not betray them. "What in blazes are you doing here?"

"Ah, you must know."

"Know what?"

"Young Baden is part of the reason. Why is he not on the bridge?"

"Oh. Well—" Zepsuty. Where to begin? "He's off on a side trip of his own, Hamid. I'll give you the full download later. What's all this about Baden being part of the reason?"

"I heard him speak the Word," Hamid said. Simon had never seen him so happy. "The Word of God, Simon! It was out on the Reach. You may still be able to find it in some place, perhaps. If not, I was able to pull a partial copy before it was deleted. Oh, there was and is still such joy in my heart! He has done you proud and made this old quiet believer decide to stop hiding."

Simon's jaw hit the console. He knew Baden had been reading that book—but putting a broadcast on the Reach? "Are you . . . serious? You're not pulling a joke on a worn-out guy?"

"Never, Simon! Listen, please." Hamid waved a hand at someone off screen. Simon listened as Baden's voice echoed from Hamid's bridge across the comm: "And Jesus said to him, '"If you can"! All things are possible for one who believes. Immediately the father of the child cried out and said, 'I believe; help my unbelief!'"

Simon heard a soft murmur from the nav station. Emi had her hand pressed to her throat. Simon didn't know what to say. The voice in the recording was Baden's, no question, but there was such determination and devotion in the way he read the words that Simon had to wonder just what his son thought of them.

He was suddenly proud.

"That, however, was secondary." Some of the joy drained from Hamid's face. "My prime motivation was the message sent from the remnant of Congress."

Simon forced himself to focus on the task at hand. "Yeah, we heard that too."

"We were at Eventyr providing aid to a Muhteremi task force. Four ships destroyed, thousands of casualties." Hamid sighed. "There was not much to be done. But as soon as I heard, I gathered these ships and headed for Earth. That, and I gave word to my people on Puerto Guijarro to detain any Kesek personnel."

Simon was impressed. Hamid had never been afraid of Kesek. Of course, some of that came from being unspeakably wealthy.

"But my friend, you have not told me why you are here."

Simon cleared his throat. Emi gave him an appraising look. "Ah . . . we have business on Earth."

Hamid lifted his chin. "So I can see by your companion vessels. They may have tried disguising their drive trails, Simon, but they cannot pull one over on Hamid ibn Thaqib, can they? Those are warships, yes?"

"Sure are." Simon jerked a thumb. "We got ourselves some genuine Lancers to go with 'em."

"Their business is on my behalf, Abu Zuhayr Hamid," Colonel Verge said. He took a few steps forward. "And I would like to include you in that work."

"You are . . . ?"

"Colonel James Patrick Verge, commander of the 21st Lancers Expeditionary Brigade." He said it with such pride Simon couldn't help but feel grudging admiration. "My mission is to restore the king to his throne."

Hamid stared at him. Then he rose from his command chair. "You have my ships and my people, Colonel."

"Thank you. Now, here is what I have in mind."

Simon gave Verge a thumbs-up. The colonel seemed pleased. Maybe calling Hamid wasn't such a bad idea.

• • •

On Earth, Commissioner Gironde was losing patience.

The crowds surrounding the Kesek headquarters campus were becoming intolerable. He doubled robotic sentries along the perimeter and ordered all Kesek personnel to enter through only one heavily guarded entrance when reporting for duty. He had even persuaded a particularly compliant major to deploy his battalion of the Earth Ranger Corps around the campus and in front of the main gate.

None of this seemed to deter the mob. Gironde sneered down at them from the window of his office. It was newly repaired and reinforced after that disastrous showdown. The last scan by Kesek security had put the milling hordes at more than ninety thousand, sprawled around the campus, down side streets and filling parks. The more violent among them busied themselves overturning abandoned groundcars and setting hovercraft ablaze. Many merchants and families had fled the city blocks as these anarchists bashed out windows.

Kesek officers all over had to barricade themselves in their compounds and rely increasingly on their combat robots and Earth Rangers for protection. More protestors were arriving each day. It didn't matter that Kesek had declared a state of emergency in the whole of Europe and had cracked down on all forms of travel in the immediate vicinity of The Hague—people found their way in.

Gironde was sure the escaped members of Congress were involved in this. The pompous announcement by Garrison and Douglas-Verge had started this whole mess. It was not limited to The Hague, or even just to Earth. There had been no way to stop the hacked signal from entering the Reach, though it had eventually been cut off. The experts on his staff were still working to determine its point of origin.

Protests had flared up across the globe, in settlements from Mercury to Sedna, and on worlds across the Realm. Gironde turned to the bank of monitors on one wall of his office, watching the banner-waving, explosive-throwing, window-smashing, chanting fools in a dozen places at once. His Kesek offices on the Five Worlds had sent him regular updates. The Tiaozhanese were cracking down harshly on their protestors, providing a bulwark between Kesek and the demonstrators, for they feared negative impact on their trade. But the Rozsade were doing almost nothing. They severely punished looters, unless those looters happened to target Kesek compounds.

On top of it all, King Andrew had steadfastly refused to sign over his shares of MarkIntech. He still retained control of the corporation and, in doing so, was willingly signing his own death warrant. And that of his family.

Gironde gritted his teeth. This needed to stop.

He punched his intercom. "You get a hold of the Tiu commodore. Get their ships into position in Earth orbit."

The voice on the other end of his intercom sounded concerned. "Yessir. Ah, you do realize it will be at least twelve hours before they can get here . . ."

"Yes, blast it, I do recall elementary astronavigation!" Gironde snapped. "You tell them to get down here and show these rabble who is their ruler. And add that I'm feeling generous. I'm offering the whole of Congress along with the king and his blasted family."

He turned back to the window. If the king wanted to die in Tiu hands, so be it.

One less mess for Gironde to clean up. He was sure he could spin the death to his advantage.

• • •

The crowd was a diverse collection of people from across Europe, with handfuls scattered here and there from around Earth and even some from elsewhere in the solar system. Some stood in silence, unmoving sentinels; others raged at the top of their lungs, jabbing fists in the air and hurling whatever loose objects they could find at the stone-faced guards. The majority waved placards calling for the king's release and condemning Kesek in specific, oppression in general. They writhed under tranquil stands of trees that bore only a handful of their orange-yellow leaves.

Najwa held her own placard emblazoned with "Restore the Crown!" in bold red lettering. It was nothing more than a piece of an old box decorated with sloppy writing. She stood on the fringe of the crowd, close enough to be considered part of the mob but far enough out she could keep an eye on both the protestors and the Kesek men.

"Whisper, this is Home," a voice buzzed in her ear. "Status."

"I'm full of anger and zeal for my king." Najwa gave her sign another rattle. "No activity on the walls—the Rangers are all armed, obviously, but there's no indication of preparations for a push or arrests."

"Understood."

"What's it like at the other positions?"

"Jasper reports similar observations, as do Obsidian and Gamble."

"Lovely." Najwa took a moment to thrust her fist skyward and shout a slogan along with the knot of people beside her. "Sorry, was I interrupting?"

Her handler did not appreciate her humor. "Air traffic?"

"No sign of the shuttles. At least three jetcopter flyovers within the last half hour. That's an increase."

Silence. "Continue regular reports. There's word of Tiu interference possible. Home out."

"Affirmative." Tiu. That would be lovely. They couldn't handle Earth gravity, so if they did show, they would be battle armored. And the Hunsaker Black Bull concealed in her coat would not hurt them much.

Najwa scanned the crowds. She picked out a handful of RG operatives scattered among the groups. Some were dressed as blatantly separatist—observant Jews from Saturn's moons—while others were nondescript individuals who blended perfectly with the protestors. RG had people everywhere this day; it was taking no chances.

And with the weapons and tools secreted throughout the park, they would be ready for whatever Kesek tried.

Najwa stared up at the imposing Kesek towers as the sun flashed around the edges. They had to be ready. Or this would end badly.

Starkweather Lancers and Rozsade fusiliers bustled about the interior of *Natalia Zoja*'s cargo bay. Colonel Verge had called a briefing of all of them. It was no mean feat to get his 72 Lancers and Branko Mazur's 120 soldiers assembled in one place. But they crammed every available space. Some fusiliers perched atop the black, flattened bullet shape of the assault shuttle. Most lined up in the bay. Alec and Benjamin stood at the forefront of the six rows of Lancers.

Alec's chest swelled with pride as his father hopped up onto a pile of ammunition cases secured to the deck. He snapped to attention and saluted.

"Lancers!" Benjamin boomed. "Atten-shun!"

Boots clapped together and arms whipped through the air like birds in flight. Father returned the salute.

Branko stood beside James's perch. "Rozsade! *Attention*!"

His fusiliers bellowed back a battle cry and offered their own salutes to James—Branko too.

Father saluted back. Alec wanted to be a commander of men just like this. But deep inside was the nagging feeling that if it came time, he did not know if he could do what it took.

He did not know if he could kill.

Father held out his hands. "Starkweatherers! Rozsade! You know why we are here. You know why we have spent the past several days packed in here like stinking rations!"

Alec chuckled along with the rest of them.

"We have come back to remove the cancer at the heart of our kingdom!" Father continued. He paced the tiny surface of the ammo case—two steps either way. "We have come back to eliminate the infestation that we have allowed to grow far too strong! Kesek will fall!"

The men roared back their approval. Branko laughed heartily. "So! James, you did not tell me you are part Rozsade, yes? *Na Smierc*!"

"*Na Smierc!*" The fusiliers and the Lancers raised their voices like thunder in the confined space.

"The enemy put their cowardly tactics to effective use on Bethel," Father said solemnly. "Many of our brave brothers died there fighting them and protecting the innocents Kesek and the Tiu chose to endanger. I would ask you all to remember them now."

Dozens of heads bowed in silence. Even Branko looked mournful. Alec closed his eyes and thought of Uncle Jonathan. He could see him gaily playing the guitar or deftly coaxing song from his violin. There was always that joy in him. But now Alec found himself wondering what had become of his uncle. All this talk of God and life thereafter—he was worried and hopeful.

Is there an answer? Let me find it.

Father cleared his throat. Alec and the others looked up. "Our plan is simple but dangerous, gentlemen. This will be no easy landing."

Silence reigned. Alec found himself holding his breath. Even Benjamin looked apprehensive.

"Our ships will skim Earth's atmosphere, and we, along with our fellow Lancers from the transport *Keach*, will make an orbital jump," James said. "This is the moment for which you have been training."

Alec hoped he didn't look as worried as he felt. Only Father and Branko looked self-assured. Of course, Branko always looked self-assured.

"You will not be alone. Our brothers on the transports *HMT Randall Keach* and *Anastazy Cypel* will join us. The carrier *HMCV Crossbow* will bring our comrades of the Gold Beasts Wing to cover us. And Kesek will not see us coming. We have gained allies, you see—six more ships joined our eight nearly as soon as we arrived here, and I have just come from the bridge where I welcomed twelve more captains into our convoy."

"These 26 are proceeding as a merchant convoy. Indeed, that is what our transponders and modified engine performance will tell them." Father pointed sharply at them. "But they will not see *you* until it is too late! And we will take back what is the peoples' right—what both our worlds fight for—the crown and our king!"

The men shouted their approval. Alec lent his own voice. Some raised lances in the air. "Long live the king!" Benjamin yelled.

"*Niech zyje król!*" Branko called in response.

Alec could feel the words reverberating through his body, throughout the hull. Surely Kesek could hear them and tremble.

"Prepare yourselves, brothers. That is all," James said.

"Diiis-missed!" Sands thundered.

The soldiers dispersed to check on their armor and make ready for the assault.

Alec did not see any hurry, as it would take them nearly a day to get there. He pushed his way past a knot of Lancers and fusiliers to where Father clambered down from the ammo cases. "A fine speech, Colonel."

"Thank you." Father grabbed both his arms. "Come, I have something to show you."

Alec followed him to an alcove off to one side of the cargo hold. There stood several suits of slate grey battle armor, their shoulders accented by forest green and the blue ring of eight seven-pointed Starkweather stars. Each one leaned against the bulkhead, completely assembled with the hinged portions open to allow a wearer to don it. James rested his hand on his armor, distinguished by the lieutenant colonel insignia at the shoulder—a gold bar connecting two silver stars. "I added this the other night when I completed my regular check."

Alec realized his father was talking about the rough patch of metal on the suit's waist armor, partially obscured beneath a lowered arm. It was of a lighter grey and blackened around the edges. Alec's heart froze when he realized what it bore at its center—a small gold shield framing a single silver star. The rank insignia of a Starkweather major.

"It is Jonathan's rank bar," Father said softly. "I cut it from his armor and torched it onto my own, so that I would not forget his sacrifice."

Alec reached below the suit's arm and pressed his hand against the emblem. "I will never forget," he said firmly.

"Son . . ." Father choked on the words. "You must promise me—you will survive."

Alec fought back tears. He hugged him fiercely. "I will never leave you, Father."

Night descended on the ever-growing crowds surrounding the Kesek campus at The Hague on Earth. Hundreds erected small tents. Their portable lights made reds, blues, greens, yellows, and many other colors glow like bonfires throughout the parks and avenues. They did not need much illumination, though, as several groundcars were still burning. Firefighters had been allowed through unmolested; a Kesek patrol of three hovercraft had been set upon and demolished. Its occupants were sent running in their undergarments.

Tara Douglas-Verge stood well off to one side at a small park. She could see the glittering Kesek towers less than a half-kilometer away. The sounds of protestors chanting rolled across the night. She pulled her blue coat closer up around her neck. "This is like nothing I would have imagined."

Beside her, Representative Gostislav Baran of Rozsada laughed deeply. "So. There are now more than 150,000 in this city. All of them wish Kesek gone. And yet I worry. Kesek will have a response, yes?"

"Of course. That is why we're standing here in the dark rather than under those illuminating streetlamps."

"True."

Tara watched the Earth Rangers in their blue and black armor patrolling the gates to the Kesek campus. Her stomach twisted at the sight of a squad of maroon-jacketed Kesek men speaking with them. She was glad her daughters Julianna and Bridget were tucked away in an RG safe house—she wouldn't trust anybody other than the Rozsade intelligence group with their well-being.

"There is rumor of starships gathering at the sundoors," Baran said. "Unknown ID. Many are merchantmen from Expatriate shipping concerns."

Tara frowned. "This is not the time of the year for the Magnificent Return to Tiaozhan."

"So. Some say they are here to show support for the king."

"Some say?"

Tara could barely make out the mischief on Baran's mustachioed face. "RG."

"Ah." Tara looked up at the twinkling stars. She had to believe James and Alec, Jonathan and Colleen and Connor were alive somehow and were out there . . . "What is their purpose?"

"I cannot say. But if they do move, RG will be ready to help here."

Tara considered the thousands here and millions on other worlds fomented by her words. "I can only hope we don't let them down."

James, come back to me, she pled to the stars.

• • •

Alec awoke from his nap and clung to the sides of his bunk. His heart thudded mercilessly against his chest. Sweat drenched his shirt.

The tiny cabin's lights were out. They'd tried to catch some rest before they reached Earth. Below Alec, Benjamin was snoring. He sounded like a bear.

But that wasn't what had awakened Alec. He'd dreamed again of the fighting on Bethel, as he'd done every time he'd closed his eyes since that chaotic night. Images assaulted him . . . the flash of the guns, the shouts and screams of men . . . the severed limbs and rent bodies . . . the mangled, oblivious faces of the dead . . .

He shook with sudden cold. It was fear as he'd never known; training had not prepared him for the horror of what he'd seen during the fighting. His body had reacted perfectly in combat, but his mind had revolted.

Now he had to face that fear again, and he felt defenseless.

He rolled over in his bunk. Something rough dug into his side. He'd forgotten the delver was still there; he'd fallen asleep listening to it. It too was "asleep"—he thumbed a wheel in one side to reactivate the audio:

"For if the dead are not raised, not even Christ has been raised. And if Christ has not been raised, your faith is futile and you are still in your sins."

It was Baden Haczyk's voice. Alec was troubled by the words he had spoken on Bethel, especially when he remembered a later description of the second death. He understood precisely what Baden had been saying. Without faith, there was no avoiding the dark end beyond this life.

The prospect of dying and knowing only darkness terrified him. "I don't want to die," Alec whispered.

There was something more, wasn't there? Something about fear. Alec spun through the audio file. He rubbed his forehead as he struggled to remember where it was he'd encountered the message. Then he hit upon it:

"There is no fear in love, but perfect love casts out fear. For fear has to do with punishment, and whoever fears has not been perfected in love."

Alec recalled that this had to do with admitting wrongdoing to God. All people committed wrongdoing, even himself—none but this Christ were guiltless.

He had to know more, so he borrowed what he had seen of the Bethelites. He closed his eyes and bowed his head. "God, please—I sense You are there and I believe this Word of Yours. I don't know what it all means, but I just know that I don't want to be afraid of dying." Alec hesitated. He didn't know what to say or what to do. What were the words he'd read? The promises of forgiveness . . . "Forgive me for the things I've done that displeased You. Show me how to find You and follow You. I seek Your path."

There was no booming voice, no flashing light from his mind. But there was a quiet urging that Alec couldn't put his finger on. Regardless, he knew he wasn't going to get any more sleep.

He eased up in his hammock. Somewhere in his uniform pocket was a pair of earpieces—there. He dug them out and linked the delver to their output. Then he reset the delver to Baden's recordings from Bethel. He had the image scanner copies, but he wanted to hear the Word again.

Alec settled back and listened to Baden preach.

CHAPTER 20

November 2602
Earth Star System

Natalia Zoja and the expanded convoy had to get through two security zones before reaching Earth itself.

The first was a loose net of monitor drones and a half-dozen patrol triremes that ringed Earth in an invisible sphere about eight hundred thousand kilometers across. Even with the heightened security imposed by Kesek, the sentries at this first zone waved through the ships of Hamid ibn Thaqib unmolested and unsearched.

Simon was impressed. They hadn't even needed to bribe anyone.

He watched his instruments carefully as the convoy followed the prescribed approach vector for the moon. Trading vessels destined for Earth were not allowed into Earth orbit except by special permission. With few exceptions, they had to take up lunar orbit or dock at one of several commercial transshipment stations in the area.

"The second security zone will be more difficult," said Colonel Verge. The officer stood behind Simon. Emi rode at the nav station.

"I kind of figured that," Simon said. "Emi?"

"You will not like it." She transferred her nav readouts to the main monitor. A bewildering arrangement of ship tracks appeared.

"*Paskudny*." Simon tensed as the sensors dutifully gave readout after readout on those ships. "Four battle corvettes, three frigates, two cruisers—and is that a man-of-war? I thought the Reach said the Home Fleet got mauled by the Martian pilgrims."

"They did," Colonel Verge said. "Hmm . . . The man-of-war is *HMS Lion*. Admiral Sutar's flagship, one of the few remnants of Earth's fleet to escape the attack, I'd assume. So these are the ships of the second security sphere. They maintain order within the four-hundred-thousand-kilometer region immediately around Earth, as defined by the moon's orbit."

Simon only cared about who they'd shoot at. "You figure they answer to Kesek now?"

"I don't know. We will have to contact them once this gambit plays out."

"Fantastic." Simon groaned. "What else do we have?"

"Nine of the ships come up as 'modified private merchantman, unregistered,'" Emi said. Her eyes narrowed. "Those would be pirates, I believe. Consider their arrangement and maneuvering."

Simon mulled over the ship tracks on the monitor. "Yeah. Looks like it."

Colonel Verge watched both sets of displays. Simon thought the officer looked weary—must be anxious about the coming operation. Simon wasn't exactly thrilled, either. "You sure you want to do this?"

"We have little choice now, Captain. My men are suiting up as we speak. Major Mazur is practically eager to get his assault shuttle into space."

Simon winced at the mention of the name. He rubbed his sore jaw. "I'll bet he is. All right, Emi, get me something nicer to look at."

"Of course, Skipper." Emi removed the nav display from the main monitor. She put in its place the starry space around Earth, complete with tiny sparkles and occasional flare of ship engines. The planet itself sparkled like a tiny sapphire among diamonds.

"Earth is beautiful, even from here," Colonel Verge said.

"It's a planet, all right," Simon said. "Remind you of home?"

"Starkweather is more of a muted blue from this distance. Not as bright. Not as pleasant, either. But it is still my home-world. Earth is home too."

"Well, just remember that I'm flying *my* home into the upper atmosphere of yours, so your plan had better work," Simon chided. "I don't want to be homeless."

Colonel Verge chuckled. "Captain, if our plan fails, you won't be homeless. You'll be dead. And so will I."

Simon shook his head. "*Zepsuty.*"

Commander Colleen Verge ran her fingers across the top of her command console. She watched the holo-display tank at the center of *HMS Herald*'s bridge. They were not far from the boundary of the second security zone.

"We're being hailed by *HMS Lion*, Skipper," said Ensign Jeffrey Belus at the comm.

"Understood." Colleen chewed her lip. Admiral Sutar. He was usually an all right sort to deal with. But he might be less pleasant when realizing four warships and military transports had snuck inside a merchant convoy to within spitting distance of Earth. "Put him on the main screen inset. Keep the nav charts up."

"Aye, Skipper." The rainbow colors of ship tracks and positions took up the entire massive main monitor of *Herald*'s bridge. Belus sent a few commands into the comm system, however, and brought up a distinguished-looking admiral's head and shoulders onto a square about two meters on each side at the center.

Admiral Sutar wore the black and violet of Earth's navy. His rich brown skin contrasted with his snowy, bushy hair and shaggy eyebrows. He stared down his hooked nose. "Greetings, Captain Verge. Well. Imagine my surprise when I saw your ship tracks among the rather sizeable convoy requesting permission to enter Earth's second security zone." His voice was lilting and smooth. "With the estimable Hamid ibn Thaqib at the lead, no less."

Colleen cringed inwardly. She kept a stone face. "Your sensor techs must be very good at their duties."

"Indeed. Whoever altered your main drives to mimic those of a merchant vessel is quite skilled, but not skilled enough." Sutar allowed a tight smile. "Well. Since you are supposed to be dead, and I am supposed to arrest members of the Verge family, where does that leave us?"

Colleen glanced sideways at her first officer. Lucia de Silva stood ramrod straight at attention and made no noticeable response. There was caution in her eyes.

Blazes with caution. Colleen was not willing to negotiate.

"Admiral, let me do you the courtesy of being both blunt and honest," Colleen said. "My brother—Colonel James Verge of the 21st Lancers—and I are the remaining senior officers of the Seventh Royal Task Force and its attached units sent to Bethel in October. Not only did Tiu raiders attack us, but Kesek constables attempted to assassinate our ranking officers, myself included. Coupled with the statements of the missing Congress and the confessions of Kesek men in our custody, we have returned in order to stop Commissioner Gironde's overthrow."

There. She had laid it all bare. Now she offered up a silent prayer to the Bethelites's God that her admission would not be seen as treason, but rather loyalty. She had done much praying in the past few days. As she had heard in Baden's readings, she was seeking in hopes of finding the one whom she believed had warned her in a dream of that attack at Bethel.

Sutar scratched the end of his nose. "Well. I must say . . . I was hoping you would say this."

Colleen's body sagged from the relief. Steady.

"Let us have it this way." Sutar gave her a sly wink. "This conversation did not take place. I will help you elsewise if I can. Good luck and good hunting."

The transmission cut off. "Are you as relieved as I am, Skipper?" De Silva asked.

"Much more." Colleen strode back to her seat. "Chief Lake! Status of *Lion*."

Abraham Lake's voice boomed out from his tactical console. "She's staying clear of our way, Captain."

"Then let's not bother the good admiral anymore." Colleen drummed her console arm in triumph. "Time to Earth orbit?"

"At present speed of 350 kilometers per second, about eighteen minutes, Skipper. And Skipper . . . ?"

"Yes?"

Lake waved a hand at his console. "I'm getting a lot of ships in Earth orbit. You ain't gonna like it. They're Tiu."

Colleen's blood froze. She heard de Silva swear violently. "Tiu? Are you certain?"

"I'd bet the rest of my drones—except we used 'em all at Bethel." Lake sighed. "Oh, yeah, we got at least four *Apophis*-class destroyers."

"That's not too terrible by comparison . . ."

"There's also two dozen 'modified private merchantmen, unregistered.'"

"Oh." Colleen frowned. "Pirates."

"Yeah."

She rubbed her forehead. What were they doing here? Had Kesek hired them, like Captain Bell said they sometimes did?

"Jeffrey! Hail *Firuz* and *Natalia Zoja* simultaneously. Get me Captain Haczyk, Colonel Verge, and Hamid ibn Thaqib."

"Aye, Skipper."

Colleen looked at de Silva. "Let's give them the news.

Admiral Sutar of Earth's remnant fleet kept his word. The convoy of 26 ships including the Starkweather and Rozsade military vessels, Hamid's armed merchantmen and *Natalia Zoja*, proceeded unbothered to Earth. But Kesek intercepted Sutar's communications to Colleen Verge.

The subject matter meant the interception's results were given the highest priority. The contents of the message were delivered to Commissioner Gironde's delver within minutes.

He was alone in his office when he read the message. And he was apoplectic.

"Why can no one kill them?" He threw the delver against his window. "Blast! I want them dead, all of them! Can someone possibly deliver me that satisfaction?"

No one answered.

Outside his window, the protesting masses outside the entrance to the Kesek campus were burning Kesek uniforms in effigy. Where in blazes had they gotten those? Gironde watched the scene in miniature from his perch—Earth Rangers fired scrambler bolts into the crowd while his own men deployed dish-shaped pain amplifiers. Clusters of three, four, and five demonstrators collapsed to the pavement, writhing. Gironde slapped his intercom.

"Get me the *Hastula*!" he snapped. "We have visitors, and I want them destroyed!"

"Are you prepared, Sim— ah, Captain Haczyk?" Commander Verge's beautiful face—Enough, already! Simon chided himself—filled *Natalia Zoja*'s monitor. Her cheeks had probably turned the same color as her hair.

Simon was scared out of his wits. Nobody needed to know that. He was also pining for this lady, this tough starship captain, and was determined not to let her somewhat snobbish brother see that just yet.

Especially as Colonel Verge was standing at Simon's left shoulder. "Just give us the signal, Skipper, and we'll do our part," Simon said. "The colonel and his boys are ready."

"James, please be careful." Such warmth and affection in the way she said it to her brother. Simon fell even harder for her.

"I always am, little sister." Colonel Verge saluted informally. "You have my love."

"And you mine." Commander Verge looked at Simon again. She seemed ready to say something else. Simon didn't know what to expect, but she suddenly blurted, "I hope to see you again when this ends, Captain."

Well, that was something, at least. Simon felt his face catch fire again. But Colonel Verge was still . . . Oh, just forget it! "*Powodzenia*, Colleen," Simon said softly.

Commander Verge blushed furiously. She did smile before the signal cut.

Silence fell on *Natalia Zoja*'s bridge. Simon took a deep breath and turned his chair. Colonel Verge was giving him a strange look. He was either reevaluating the worth of this Expatriate captain or he was figuring out how to have Simon cooked and served to Branko on a platter. Or maybe he didn't know that particular Russian phrase? Simon decided not to ask. He offered his hand instead. "Good luck to you, Colonel."

Verge took his hand without hesitation. Something like a smirk started to curl the corner of his goatee, but he suppressed it. "And you too, Captain Haczyk. In all your endeavors."

He left the bridge. Simon stared after him. It was only after a second that he realized Emi was giggling softly. No wonder he didn't recognize the sound.

"Knock it off, please."

"Sorry, Captain." She stopped. "Skipper? If we do not make it . . . well, how can I say this without sounding trite?"

"Don't say it, then."

"Very well."

"How's about one more haiku, for old time's sake? Maybe Iio Sogi? I always kind of like his."

Emi nodded. A smile flitted across her face. "Of course, Captain." She closed her eyes, and then said, "*Yama kawa mo / kimi ni yoru yo o / itsuks min.*"

Simon wracked his brains for the translation for that one. It took a moment, but he found it. "Shall we ever see / The time your reign brings lasting peace / To all hills and streams?"

"Very good, Captain. I see my lessons were not wasted."

Simon looked down at his console. "Tiu and pirates, eh? Well, it's never boring."

"Not today, anyway," Emi agreed.

Simon watched his console for the signal from Commander Verge's *HMS Herald*. When it came, he put *Natalia Zoja* end over end and decelerated hard along with the rest of the convoy ships. They were aiming for a manageable few kilometers per second so they could skim the upper atmosphere and disgorge their cargo of soldiers without killing anyone.

Aboard *Natalia Zoja* proximity alarms clamored. "What do we got, Emi?"

She leaned over her displays. "It looks like there are four Martian ships coming around Earth into our sensor range. *Apophis*-class."

"Lovely."

"They've not put on much thrust, Skipper, but they're already in missile range. Emi touched her earpiece. "They're hailing *Firuz*."

"Is Hamid replying?"

"Negative."

"Good. Time until we make atmosphere?"

"Six minutes."

In the cargo bay, Branko was herding his fusiliers aboard the shuttle as its engines glowed to life. "Move! Pah, you are lazy! So. My daughters can move faster. Get on! Now!"

"We jump as soon as the shuttle clears the bay," James said to the company assembled before him. His tone was firm and level. "One troop at a time. Our Lancers aboard the transport *Keach* will follow. Questions?"

There were none. James took in the sight of his men, geared in their full armor, and covered with a rough layer of ablative foam. It protected not only their bodies and armor, but also the extra breather packs and folded aerowings in their housings on their armored backs. "Then good luck."

They split up by troops. Hexamblers trundled into position, urged on by their mountkeepers. The robots too, covered with the same foam. Alec stood beside his father. James took him aside. His fatherly love got the better of him in this last moment. He whispered, "Are you up for this? There was barely time to prepare you."

"It's all right. Benjamin has readied me for the worst, and I did remind him that I did well in drop training at the academy."

"For that one session, son. You don't have to go."

"I am ready." Alec met his gaze. "I'm not afraid."

James smiled wryly. "Even I am afraid."

"Death is the defeated enemy, father. My soul is safe with God; who can take that away from me?"

James stared blankly for a moment. That was . . . odd. He knew Alec had shown some interest in the Christian teachings, but this was more than just interest. "You . . . believe this? What the Bethelites told you?"

"I believe what I have heard and read," Alec said. "It is said that is how the Good News is propagated. Christ has my service now . . ."

"We will talk about this later." The subject made James uneasier than the attack before him. "Stick close to Benjamin." He extended his hand. "Good luck, son."

Alec shook it. "God bless, Father."

James watched him go and worried.

The Tiu warships broadcast their warning to the approaching convoy on a continuous loop. They broke orbit and charged out at high acceleration with the hired pirate vessels hot on their heels. Still, the merchantmen continued on course.

Simon watched the changing swirl of course approximations on the nav screen as the computer tracked the mass of ships. He didn't like the looks of it.

Lights flashed on his console.

"A warning shot from one of the pirate vessels," Emi said calmly. Like she was watching a cooking instruction program on the Reach.

"Emi, get our turret up."

"And watch them laugh at us?"

"Just do it. Ready the missiles."

"There is more weapons fire."

Firuz and its three sister feluccas traded energy blasts with the pirate ships. It looked like they had several pulsed neutral particle cannons in hidden mounts. The range between them was too great for accurate targeting, but both sides were reluctant to fire missiles. Simon understood that hesitance—there were strict rules of engagement that levied stiff penalties on anyone whose missiles impacted a planetary surface. Even pirates weren't that nasty.

Simon clenched his hand about the drive controls. Gironde might be, though.

Gironde fumed. He watched a tactical display set up on his monitors. The combat so far was not resolving anything. Incompetent pirates and Tiu. When this was all over, he'd gather more warships for Kesek's specific use.

He gave two commands: engage with missiles and activate automated picket satellites.

Simon watched in horror as the satellites in far Earth orbit erupted in a fury of directed energy blasts. Hamid's ships managed to veer into evasive routes but one was speared mercilessly by a handful of beams. It shattered along its centerline, spewing air, hull pieces, and dead men before exploding in spectacular fashion.

Emi, using *Natalia Zoja*'s lone turret, stabbed back with laser bursts that vaporized two of the satellites.

Then it got worse.

"Missiles out!" Emi shouted. "Multiple dozen tracks from several enemy ships!"

Simon swore and wrenched his ship onto a new vector. "Free fire, Emi! Any targets!"

Emi punched up preset targeting data for *Natalia Zoja* and let the ship's missiles fly. Her laser turret's control screen flashed as it engaged multiple passing warheads.

Simon watched in horror as missiles hit their marks. Two ships exploded. Then two more. He lost track of which one was which.

Colleen staggered as *HMS Herald* bucked under an impact. "Damage report!"

"Grazing hit to starboard!" Lake wiped sweat off his forehead. Red lights flashed around the bridge. "One compartment open to space. Minimal damage otherwise. A few injuries. Got some Bethelite techies movin' in to seal it."

"Good." So far their bravery had been phenomenal for a people who had never seen combat. "And our target?"

"Down for the count," de Silva said grimly.

Colleen searched for the dangerous red blip on her tactical screen and saw it was gone. There were plenty more targets to choose. "Keep those missiles off us, Abe. Helm, break us out of decel and go full evasive!"

Second Lieutenant Isabel Travers didn't even look up from her console. "No prob, Skipper!"

"Target bearing oh-six-seven mark eighty-two!" Lake sang. "She's going for guns!"

"Bring the cannons about!" Colleen grabbed the sides of her chair. "Fire!"

The main displays flickered to show the pulsed particle blasts blazing out at a pirate navastel less than three thousand kilometers away. The pirate's own shots went wild. *Herald*'s did not.

It disappeared in a short-lived ball of fire and light.

"Missiles to port! Sandcasters away!"

Colleen gritted her teeth. No time to breathe.

It was then that she noticed the lone blip on the nav console—one of the Rozsade transports. It was not decelerating for Earth but veered toward the center of the pirates' group. They noticed and directed heavy fire.

They inflicted a few hits before the tiny blip on *Herald*'s tactical hologram exploded—with missiles. Thirty warheads screamed into the midst of the pirates. All detonated in a hellish brew of disablers, nukes, and x-ray blasts. Three pirate ships were destroyed, two all but crippled, and two left fleeing with severe damage. The Rozsade ship blazed through the shattered flotilla and turned to engage more ships.

"You have to give it to the Rozsade," de Silva said in hushed awe. "They have *bravura*."

"I would agree," Colleen said.

"Skipper!" Lake waved. "The transports are hitting the upper atmosphere!"

God, protect James, Alec, Connor, Benjamin . . . and Simon, she thought.

Launch klaxons sounded in pilot country aboard *HMCV Crossbow*. Connor gave his helmet a quick double check as he trotted to the access ramp to Coyote 11's hangar dome. "Hustle, No-Joy, we don't want to miss the party."

Logan caught up with him, and then passed him. "I don't think they'll leave without their squadron commander, Conman."

"That would be in awful bad taste, wouldn't it?" They jogged up the ramp together into the hanger. Coyote 11 sat ready to launch. Donna was disconnecting the fuel umbilical lines.

"About time you two showed up!" She stowed the last of the lines off to one side and tipped back her cap. Sweat beaded along her brow. "C'mon, I got the ladder in place. Mount up."

Logan went first, climbing into the open cockpit. Connor was about to follow when Donna caught his arm. He turned and was about to say something he thought was terribly clever when she planted a kiss square on his lips. Connor swallowed his cleverness and kissed her back.

She pulled away reluctantly. Connor was left with what he was sure was a dazed expression. "What was that for?"

"So you remember to come back in your fighter, not a body bag," Donna said. She patted his cheek. "Good luck, Lieutenant."

"I will come back," Connor said. He clambered up the ladder.

Inside, Logan gave him a curious look but said nothing.

Connor put his helmet on. "I promise."

Donna saluted and scooted from the hangar bay. Coyote 11's cockpit rumbled on its tracks and tucked back into the hull. An armored hatch sealed over the space. It went eerily dark, save for the glow of Connor's instrument panels and display holograms.

"Should I ask?" Logan's voice had a hint of amusement behind it.

"About what?" Connor said with a grin.

"Never mind."

It was time to launch.

HMCV Crossbow rode outside Earth's atmosphere. Her captain put the 1,200-meter ship into a slow roll. All up and down the four sides of her hull, domed hatches split open in pattern. EE-3 Lynx fighters dove from their individual hangars into the atmosphere.

Connor gritted his teeth as his fighter and the Coyote squadron survivors of the Bethel fight dove into the atmosphere, their fuselages trailing fire. Once they were deep enough in, he could deploy the Lynx's stowed wings and recessed cockpit. Right now he was flying on instrumentation and display screens only. "Watch our wing, No-Joy. I don't particularly want to get run over by a transport."

"No chance of that," Logan said from his consoles behind Connor. "We're already ten thousand feet below them and dropping like a rock."

"A very hot rock."

"Yeah. Speaking of that, the integrity readouts are at red line, Conman."

"So don't tell me about it."

"You're the boss."

Simon wasn't worried about heat tolerance as *Natalia Zoja* dipped into the atmosphere. Friction, his ship could handle.

Her hull was already heat-resistant, like all interstellar ships, because she needed to come very close to stars in order to access sundoors.

What bothered him, as his ship bucked and weaved, was that if she got dragged into the gravity well, the impact would destroy a vast swath of land if it hit ground. She'd be a lump of metal no different than a meteor.

The altimeter read 200 kilometers. At the ship's current speed he had bare seconds' reaction time.

Simon punched the intercom. "Go!"

The air blasted into *Natalia Zoja*'s bay as the Rozsade shuttle lurched out. "Move, move!" James bellowed. In twos and fours, proceeding by troops of twelve, the Lancers jumped behind it.

James was the first.

His breath caught at the sight of the thin shell of crystal blue air fading into jet-black studded with diamond-like stars. Far in the distance, the blinding flares the transports *Keach* and *Cypel* showed they were already struggling to leave the fringes of the atmosphere. Below them, tiny glittering specks filled the air—other Lancers making their jumps and the pinpoint glare of Rozsade assault shuttle engines.

James's drogue chute automatically blossomed out of the dive pack affixed to the back of his armor once he reached a certain altitude. It stabilized his fall and kept his body from spinning wildly out of control. The Lancers of his troop were right behind him. His heads-up display showed them following in a wide and loose V-formation. The tiny display also dutifully reported his velocity at 7,000 kilometers per hour.

Flames licked at James's ablative foam as he dove deeper into the mesosphere. The Lancers ahead of him took on the appearance of tiny celestial beings wrapped in shells of golden-orange flickering light. James watched as his internal display's temperature gauge reported a spike from the cold of vacuum to twice the boiling point of water as the suit's computer dutifully showed how much protective foam was being stripped away by the extreme temperatures.

James could hear nothing over his comm but static. They would have no communication until their main chutes opened. He spared another glance at his tracking display. So far the Lancers seemed to be in formation.

He could only hope Alec was all right.

CHAPTER 21

November 2602
Earth Star System

Golden Orchid made the tract shift into a system in uproar.

Baden watched over Captain Bell's shoulder. "Who's attacking what now?"

"Shut it!" Bell waved a hand at him. Then she sneezed, hard. "Go away! We got enough trouble without you buggin' me!"

"There's something about a disguised convoy that fought with Tiu ships and pirates," Dennis said from his station. "It's all confusing . . . and keep in mind this info is eight minutes old."

"Tiu ships at Earth?" Gail stood next to Baden. Owen was peeking at Dennis's controls and offering helpful hints about how to maximize his console's response times. Dennis didn't look amused. "What would they be doing here?"

"Kesek again. As for the pirates . . ." Bell gave Baden a wicked sneer. "Hey, they wouldn't be the first pirates hired by Kesek, right?"

"I guess."

Bell was still watching him. "So you'll probably want to get there, huh?"

"Dad might be there, in the middle of that mess. He said the Starkweather troops were going to Earth. They had some plan to get the king back." It pained Baden to think of it. He had so much he wanted to tell Simon. "I've got to help."

"Yeah, but what about our cargo hold full of priceless valuables of the book variety?"

"Oh." Baden considered this. Probably not wise to go blazing in and face the chance of sudden annihilation.

Bell sneezed. "Pardon me." She sneezed again. "Blast! Hang on a microsec. Dennis, how long to Earth if we burn at max?"

"Ten hours if we do it right."

"There you go, Haczyk. Almost half a day. Might be all over by the time we get there. You still wanna do this?"

Baden prayed for his dad's safety, and that of *Golden Orchid* and everyone aboard. "Yes."

"Alrighty. Helm, go full burn for Earth," Bell said.

Connor Verge's Coyote 11 fighter swooped into a shepherding position several kilometers from the diving soldiers—close enough to cover them but far enough not to buffet them with ramjet exhaust. Then his targeting display buzzed.

"Bogies, Conman." Logan sounded somber. "Looks like Leopards."

"Leopards?" That meant the EE-6G Leopard atmospheric fighters based at Belgrade. "Coming to intercept us?"

"No . . . no they've got a direct trajectory for the troops!"

"Blasted fiends." Connor knew only Kesek would turn Earth-based fighters against Lancers loyal to the king. Kesek, and their foul commissioner. He snapped on his squadron frequency. "Coyotes, this is Conman. You see those inbound bogies. Break off by flights and stand by to engage."

He switched comm frequencies. "Belgrade fighters, this is Lieutenant Connor Verge with Coyote Squadron, Gold Beasts Wing of Starkweather. Be advised, we are on escort with Starkweather and Rozsade forces headed for The Hague. It would be in your best interests to stand down and step aside, over."

No response came. Connor repeated the message.

"Not talking, Lieutenant?"

"They seem shy, No-Joy. Perhaps they have orders to maintain radio silence."

"I've got range and bearing."

"Thanks." Connor took the targeting information that Logan dutifully supplied. He fought back the mounting unease at having to confront fighter pilots loyal to the king, not rebels or Tiu raiders.

"Are we really going to shoot them, Lieutenant?"

"I hope we don't have to, No-Joy. That's up to the good colonel."

James saw the Leopard fighters too. They were slivers of metal moving quickly against the familiar blue sky of Earth. His instruments notified him that he was over the Atlantic Ocean, closing fast on Europe's northwestern coastline. He couldn't help but chuckle—far below the scattered, billowing white clouds, he could see nothing but the deep sea. In the midst of the buffering and sound of air currents, it was a peaceful sight.

His heads-up display flashed more data: he had reached the proper altitude to deploy his aerowing. The device's tiny computer cut loose the drogue chute. The aerowing burst forth from its housing on the back of his armor. The wings unfolded rapidly to their full six-meter span, a pair of directional thrusters popped up over James's shoulders at the same time. The computer turned over control to James, and he used the surfaces of his gloves to manipulate his direction. What had been a rough, noisy plummet became a smooth, steady descent.

Beneath and around him, he could see the obsidian wings bursting into existence as the hundreds of Lancers did the same. It looked like a swarm of cobalt moths he'd seen growing up on Starkweather. Even the hexamblers sprouted their own aerowings and homed in on the signals given by their mountkeeper Lancers.

James broadcast to the Leopard fighters on as many frequencies as he could.

"This is Lieutenant Colonel James Patrick Verge, commander of the 21st Lancers. To the pilots intercepting our force—we ask you to stand down and clear a path for us to The Hague. Our fight is with Kesek. They deceived all the people of the Realm, and we have come to free our king. Stand down, and join us in our cause. We want only to restore the Crown and end Kesek's oppression. Do what is right, and do it now."

There was silence for a moment. "Pretty speech." Branko's voice rasped in his ear. "I would have shot first and demanded surrender."

"Unsurprising, Branko." James watched on his display as the fighters drew nearer. No one was shooting at them. Yet.

Alec was sure his heart would burst through his armor. He squeezed his left hand gently to steer his aerowing and maneuvered into closer formation with Benjamin.

"You still hangin' in there, Cadet Trainee?" The corporal sounded almost gleeful.

Alec felt queasy. "Terrible joke, Benjamin."

"Boy, don't I know it."

Benjamin fell silent. He muttered something that Alec lost in a burst of static over his comm. "What was that?"

"I said, this is about when I'd like all that stuff we read to be right," Benjamin said.

Alec swore he sounded embarrassed. "You mean the teachings?"

"Yeah. I been talking and thinking . . . hope that He meant what He said about forgiveness."

Alec looked out his helmet visor at the continent of Europe sprawling in emerald and ochre beauty far beneath his dangling metal boots. "And you think of that now?"

"When better? Besides, I've been missing Carol. Especially since we jumped."

"Oh."

"I tell you what, kid, there's gotta be something to this . . . what them Bethelites called faith. Well, I'm giving it a shot. Can't hurt."

Alec grinned. "No, it can't."

• • •

To Connor's relief, the Leopards screamed past his squadron and took up escort positions without firing a single shot. He gave a quick salute, admiring the sleek lines of the delta-winged craft with their cantilevered stabilizer fins and flat, jagged profiles. The silver fuselages flashed brilliantly in the sun. "Whew! Nothing like being wrong to cheer you up, eh, No-Joy?"

"Speak for yourself. I don't like surprises."

Connor toggled his comm. "Unidentified wing commander, this Coyote Leader, Gold Beasts Wing. Thanks for not blasting us into crispy atoms. Good move."

"Coyote One, this is Vampire Leader," said a female voice. "We heard your colonel . . . and he was right. We've seen what Kesek does, and we saw Congress's broadcast. Should've known better."

"What changed your mind?"

"After your colonel's transmission, the commissioner ordered us to shoot down your divers."

That figured. He was a cold one, that Gironde. "Again, thanks for not doing so. Welcome to the good guys."

"But we've got bigger problems."

"Do we now?"

In response, Logan's scanner board lit up with contacts. "My stars above, we've got Harpies all over the place!"

"What?" Connor decided then that he didn't like surprises either.

Vampire Leader filled in the blank data. "They arrived the other day, three wings full, and the commissioner's had them parked all around the Baltic Sea. They've been promised immortal homes on Mars if they die in glorious combat. But I didn't think he'd actually let them loose."

"Immortal homes, eh?" Connor's targeting sights were glittering with Tiu fighters. "Let's oblige them."

The Lynx and Leopard fighters swarmed dead on for their Tiu opponents above the Baltic Sea. Connor thumbed his missile control. "No-Joy?"

"Got one painted for you, Connor."

The targeted Harpy flashed red on Connor's display. He switched comm frequencies. "Coyote Squadron, this is Coyote Leader. Stand by for launch on my mark."

The Tiu fighters raced in closer. None fired yet. "They might think the Leopard fighters are with them," Logan said.

"Mark!" Connor shouted. "Fire!"

Twelve missiles shot out from the Lynx fighters of Coyote Squadron. A formation of Tiu planes scattered, but too late—seven were rent into fiery debris. Other Starkweather fighters swooped in for the attack, with Vampire Wing close on their heels. Soon dozens of Earth, Starkweather, and Martian fighters wheeled across the skies as missiles flashed between pursuer and pursued.

Connor banked left as a Tiu jumped on his tail. Its missile streaked by and blew up spectacularly. Connor gritted his teeth and held tight to his controls as the shockwave rattled the plane. "Close one."

"Proximity blast." Logan's seat made a harsh mechanical sound—it swiveled to face him backward. "He's decided to follow us, Conman. Trying for autocannon range."

"Point-defense laser."

"Already on it."

The Harpy's white-hot projectiles chased after Connor's fighter but Logan's rear-facing laser was infinitely faster. It picked off the particles as fast as they came.

"Bozo, I have a persistent one," Connor said into the squadron comm.

"On it, boss."

The Tiu kept up its steady fire. It didn't notice when Bozo's Lynx fighter came shrieking in from behind, ramjet engines sucking air. Its own autocannon tore the Harpy into pieces.

Connor exhaled. "Nicely done."

"No prob, Conman."

"We've got a trio chasing down Vampire Leader," Logan said. "Coordinates on your display."

"Thank you much. Bozo, follow me." Connor spun his fighter hard over and took off toward his new allies.

Far below the spreading dogfight, James steered his aerowing through a thermal. The Lancers and their hexamblers were descending onto the outskirts of The Hague. James was watching his heads-up display for the Wateringen district on the southwest edge of the city. Branko's assault shuttle from *Natalia Zoja*, the landing craft from the Rozsade transport, and a pair of heavy landers from *HMT Keach* were already setting into place. They were tasked with securing the site from any Kesek interference.

"Clear so far," Branko grumbled into the comm. "So. It appears our friends are occupied in the city, yes?"

"I saw that. The protests we heard about on the Reach have grown. There are no doubt thousands of people there."

"Pah. Rabble-rousers and troublemakers."

"They are the reason we're doing this, Branko." James checked his sensors. Alec and Benjamin were descending not far from him. He let himself relax some.

"Yes and . . . Hold. James, there is more. My men tell me there are members of Congress at the protest."

"Who?"

"Chairman Garrison, some representatives . . . and your wife."

James banked his aerowing harder.

Simon wiped sweat from his brow as *Natalia Zoja* shuddered her way back into space. "How's it looking, Renshu?"

"Not good, but nothing's broken down here . . . yet." Renshu sounded distressed over the intercom. "Just get us out of the gravity well. She doesn't like working this hard."

"Yeah, I know."

Simon watched his sensors as the convoy managed to wrench free of Earth's gravity kilometer by kilometer. His ship was not going to be scratch-free on this run.

"Captain! The man-of-war!" Emi said.

Simon saw the same thing on his display. *HMS Lion* and the three Earth frigates from the second security line were bearing down on the formation. "Where's those pirates and Tiu?"

Emi gave her displays a disdainful look. "They are not in a position to do much of anything. Only two of the four Tiu ships are mobile, and they are leaving—swiftly. I count no more than eleven pirate vessels operational."

Hamid. Simon had almost forgotten his friend and mentor in the tension of the orbital drop. "What about the al-Azhar ships? And our other guys?"

"Two of Hamid's ships were destroyed, but *Firuz* is intact. The others . . ." Emi shook her head. "There are so many ships, I'm getting interference in my scans."

"Great. Okay, get me a line to Hamid . . ."

"Ah, that would not be advisable." Emi consulted her earpiece. "He is taking a signal from Admiral Sutar."

"Oh." Simon blinked. "Okay. What's the word?"

"I do not . . . hold on. Hamid is available. Putting you through now."

Emi put the call onto the main monitor. Hamid was beaming. "My friend, good news! Admiral Sutar is bringing his starships in to secure the Tiu and the pirates. He has promised us safe passage. He also informs me that Kesek's observers aboard his ships have been, shall we say, incapacitated for the time being."

"And this admiral just told you all this?"

Hamid waved a hand. "Sutar is an old friend. I knew him as a system patrol lieutenant way back when. An honest man."

"Thank God for your friends." Simon sank back against the chair. He wiped sweat from his face. He was getting too worn out for this.

"I do thank him," Hamid said.

Tara Douglas-Verge stood on the wide firmcrete wall that surrounded the public gardens not far from the Kesek campus. She and the other representatives—Baran, Chairman Garrison, and the others who had gone into hiding—were in plain sight of the burgeoning crowd. There were no guards around her, and Tara relished the feeling. The people before her cheered and applauded as they roared their slogans in support of the king. She waved back to them and wondered fleetingly how many of those people were RG.

Then in the distance came a sound like thunder-sharp cracks and booms, followed by rumbling. Tara felt fear like ice in her chest. She had heard that sound. Every time she and James had watched aerial exhibitions at Connor's home squadron airbase.

Garrison lifted a speech amplifier to his mouth. "You hear now that we tell the truth! Those are fighter planes loyal to the king, battling the Kesek commissioner's allies—the Tiu!"

The crowd's cheers faded to silence as they listened. It was an ugly silence, one of contemplation slowly fading to bitterness. Small groups erupted in jeers and catcalls that spread throughout the masses until one and all were united in angry shouts directed at Kesek. Some were throwing rocks and branches and bottles and anything else they could find at the gates to the Kesek compound. The Earth Rangers and Kesek guards, along with their security robots, patrolled the walls beside the gate.

Tara scowled. Where was Garrison getting this from?

"We demand the release of His Majesty!" Garrison's voice boomed.

Baran had not said a word the entire time. Rather, he had his right hand pressed to an ear and was gazing intently at the delver clutched in his left hand. Eventually he noticed Tara staring. "Tiu shuttles are here," he said.

Garrison looked sidelong at him. "No doubt for their precious cargo."

Tara peered skyward. Sure enough, six oblong shuttles, reddish-brown and with four wings, dropped slowly from behind clouds into the brilliant blue sky. They looked spacious enough to accommodate several dozen passengers, which worried Tara. The king and his family were only a handful.

Someone in the crowd screamed. Those nearest the compound gates pressed back as far as they could go. Tara pressed her hand to her mouth in horror. Hundreds of bloody-armored Martian Tiu leapt from the shuttles as the craft settled toward the landing pads within the boundary of the Kesek campus.

The shuttles weren't there to evacuate anyone. They were there to provide reinforcements for Kesek.

Tara was furious at the sight. She snatched the amplifier from a startled Garrison. "People! Look over there! You can see what Commissioner Gironde and Kesek want the future of the Realm to look like! It will be a future spent under their boot heels, with Martian armor enforcing their reign. What precious little freedoms you have will be lost! Can we stand it anymore? Can we stand having Kesek rifle through our treasured thoughts, our letters to loved ones? Can we stand to have them dictate to us our beliefs?"

The crowd roared in response. It was a deafening rumble that was decidedly in agreement. They churned forward toward the campus entrance. Those at the front screamed obscenities at the guards and shook the charred remains of Kesek uniforms burned in effigy. A handful of Kesek guards fired scramblers into the crowd. A few protestors were hit and collapsed, quivering, to the pavement. But nearby Earth Ranger officers interrupted the assault.

"You're risking an awful lot of lives here," Garrison said.

"I don't think the risk is that great." Tara gestured skyward, where the echoes of the aerial battle drew nearer. "We know help is on the way, in some manner or another. The time is now."

"Hah!" Baran grabbed her arm. His teeth barely showed behind his bushy moustache. "So! The planes are ours! It is the force from Bethel, returned in merchant ships! RG tapped into Home Fleet transmissions. And nearby . . ."

"What, Baran?"

The Rozsade representative looked like he would have danced if he knew how. "They have Lancers."

Tara's heart skipped a beat. "James?" Was it possible? Was he still alive?

She had to know.

Inside the Kesek campus walls, Commissioner Gironde beckoned his guards forward to the Tiu shuttles. The landing craft waited in a wide, empty courtyard of sandstone surrounded by skeletal trees bearing the last few yellow leaves of autumn. A breeze from the sea sent piles of brown leaves skittering across the courtyard. "Move! Get them loaded."

Nervous Kesek men in maroon jackets prodded King Andrew, his wife, Maria, and twin boys Carter and Phillip forward. The Congressional prisoners waited silently and sullenly behind them. The king stared down the guards. He gripped his wife's hand. "Whatever happens, Gironde, this house and our kingdom will be restored," he said.

"I'm sure." Gironde unholstered his gun and held it waist high. "If you're alive."

He looked over his shoulder at the towering Tiu warriors. Their red-splashed armor glinted under the sun. "I'll leave that to them to decide," Gironde said.

A panting Kesek constable came sprinting up to the landing pad. He clutched an assault rifle and was trying to fasten the side clips of his armored vest. "Sir! Commissioner, the situation is getting out of hand. We've used scramblers to keep the more dangerous ones at bay, but the crowd is growing more dangerous. There must be more than a hundred thousand people out there! What are your orders?"

"Disperse them at will. You!" Gironde snapped his fingers at the Tiu commander nearby. "Loose your men on them. Don't kill too many, but just enough to scatter them. My men will clean up the rest."

When the gates opened, Tara had momentary hope that the Earth Rangers inside had joined their cause. But her hope was dashed by the battle cries of the Tiu soldiers. The armored warriors bounded forward in their armor and fired indiscriminately throughout the crowd. They did not use scramblers; instead, they fired heavy machine guns held at hip level.

Bullets ripped through the front lines of the demonstrators. Blood spattered against those behind, sending them screaming. Panic ensued as the protestors pressed away, trying to get to safety. Those without the strength to move were shoved against walls of the buildings surrounding the squares, the low embankments of the gardens, and clusters of trees. When the initial shock was complete, the Tiu resorted to batting people aside with metal fists and claws. They didn't want to waste ammunition.

"I hate to disturb you, Professor, but they are coming this way." Garrison looked pale.

He was right—twenty Kesek men and a half-dozen Tiu were fanning out to their area of the square. The Earth Rangers, Tara noticed, were coming down off the Kesek walls but not intervening. Something was happening . . .

"Come! *Szybko*!" Baran yanked her down from the low wall and into the rush of protestors.

Tara kept hoping for James. She and Baran tried to push by a mass of shouting demonstrators, but they were hemmed in. The Kesek officers reached them first.

"Don't move!" A trio of constables seized Baran. His bellow reminded Tara of a wounded bison. He wrestled free of one man and planted a punch on his nose.

Tara found a gun in her face. The Kesek sergeant looked angry and shaken. "You don't have to do this," Tara said. "Consider it."

He hesitated.

Tara braced herself. If James were no longer alive, she might be joining him.

CHAPTER 22

November 2602
Earth Star System
Earth, Europe, The Hague

Najwa dropped her protestor façade as soon as the Tiu armored troops and Kesek officers swarmed out of their gates. Her orders were clear. Neutralize Kesek forces and Tiu if possible.

Najwa drew her heavy-bore handgun from under her coat. She'd be lucky to get a shot through the Tiu armor. Kesek targets were a better bet. Unless she could grab a machine gun from one of the Tiu. Those odds did not look promising.

She slipped through the gaps in the fleeing crowd and came upon the Kesek sergeant pointing a gun at Professor Douglas-Verge. "Drop it now!" Najwa shouted.

He turned and fired at her. Najwa spun away from the shots and slammed into a tree. Najwa gritted her teeth and fired back. The sergeant crumpled.

Representative Baran socked another Kesek assailant in the face. One lay unconscious at his feet already. Najwa shot the third man through the shoulder.

Two more Kesek men grappled with Douglas-Verge. Najwa wrested one away and disabled him with a knee to the lower abdomen. The second one hit her hard and tried to tackle her. Najwa shook off his grip and elbowed him in the throat. She delivered a pair of punches that left him sprawled and unconscious on the pavement.

"Good to see you again, Professor," Najwa said, breathing heavily. She extended a hand.

"Let's find time to visit later," Douglas-Verge replied.

"Too late," Baran croaked.

Six Tiu warriors loomed over them. One, wearing more red slashes that the rest, barked commands in his native tongue. The aim of their machine guns translated for them.

Najwa stepped into the line of fire. "Now we'll see if RG scrimped on my body armor."

Before either side could react, a shrill volley of railer bursts struck from the air like lightning. Three Tiu were killed instantly and two more were knocked to the ground. Najwa took advantage of the surprise and seized a discarded Tiu machine gun. She fired into the last one standing until he shuddered backward onto the pavement.

Najwa jerked her head against the sky. Had the fighters strafed the area? Remarkable precision.

No, not fighters.

Lancers.

• • •

Tara had tears in her eyes as she watched hundreds of armored Lancers on black wings swoop in high above the rooftops of the buildings around the square. They peeled off in groups of four like dark birds of prey, firing their railers with precision shots that flashed blue white at the Tiu soldiers. Hulking hexambler robots landed first, cracking the pavement with their six massive legs. They trundled forward and exchanged fire with more of the Tiu.

The Martian soldiers withdrew in ragged groups back toward the Kesek compound, some fleeing and some putting up a steady defense.

An entire troop slammed down, feet first, four soldiers at a time, into the pavement not far from Tara. Their hexambler thundered down behind them. The tremor almost made her lose her balance. The first four Lancers to hit the ground immediately bounded forward in pairs as their aerowings folded up against their backs. The two Tiu that had been knocked over propped themselves up and fired their machine guns. Bullets careened off the Lancers, who fired one shot each with their railers. They cut down the Martians.

The Kesek men turned tail and ran off. A few even dropped their guns.

Tara's heart leapt at the sight of a Lancer in worn grey and green battle armor who approached. Even if she hadn't seen the lightning bolt or the rank stars on his arms, she could have named him from the instant he landed. "James! James, you're alive!"

The Lancer got down on one knee and unsealed his helmet's solemn mask. Tara placed her hands on both sides of James's sweating face and kissed him hard. "Tara," he said, "My love. You're all right. Thank the stars. What are you doing here?"

"We are running revolution, Colonel Verge!" Baran patted his armor and grinned beneath his bushy moustache. "So glad we are to see you! Is answer to prayers."

"I would have to say the same," said Chairman Garrison. He looked nowhere near as upbeat as Baran. "Now can we lay low until the shooting ends?"

"Mother!"

Tara cried out as Alec came bounding over somewhat awkwardly in a set of shiny new armor. Benjamin Sands, resplendent in his crimson and green dragon's armor, was at his side.

Tara ran to her son and collided hard with his armored torso. She looked up into his overjoyed face. Tears trickled down the front of his armor.

James put an armored hand gently on her shoulder. "I told you I'd come back," he said hoarsely.

Tara clutched both their hands. "Thank the stars. Thank the universe for my husband, and my son."

"Thank God, Mother," Alec said. "He has saved me."

Tara and James exchanged a look. "Where's Jonathan?" she asked.

James's face fell. Tara followed his eyes to the insignia jutting from his armor. A major's insignia. "I . . . I couldn't save him," James said.

Tara buried her face against him. Tears formed rivulets in the seams of his armor on their way to the ground. Her brother was dead. First joy at seeing her loved ones alive, and now this pain. There was no more wondering or waiting. Kesek had yet another life for which it must answer.

"Sir, you should seal your mask." Benjamin Sands spoke tersely through his dragon's head helmet.

"Thank you for keeping my son safe, Corporal," Tara said.

"Ah, he ain't been much trouble. It's good to see you too, Professor."

Beyond the protective cordon James and his men formed, Tara saw the crowd had thinned considerably. Lancers and six-legged hexambler combat robots had the Tiu and Kesek men on the run. Then Rozsade fusiliers came rushing down the side streets, war cries echoing off the walls and throughout the square. They quickly rounded up the Kesek officers as assault shuttles rumbled over rooftops to provide a deterrent for escape.

Shuttles. Stars, she'd almost forgotten! "James, the Tiu shuttles. They're inside the Kesek compound. We know the king is somewhere in there too."

James sealed his mask. Alec followed suit. Another troop of Lancers in bear's head masks bounded over, shaking trees and the pavement as they came. James beckoned them. "You men! Protect the Congressional representatives and—" James hesitated as he looked Najwa over, standing off to one side in her casual clothing with a Tiu machine gun cradled easily in her arms. "And also their aide. The rest us will storm the compound."

"Yessir!"

"Tara, stay with this troop and wait to hear from me," James said. He brushed an armored hand beneath her chin. "I won't let you down."

James leapt away, with Alec and Benjamin following close. The rest of his troop bounded in threes—two groups hopped forward at close intervals while the third group followed along with the clattering hexambler robot. They headed directly for the gates of the Kesek campus.

• • •

Connor grinned as a Tiu Harpy burst into flame and spiraled into the sea before him. He yanked on the controls and brought his Lynx out of its dive in time to rip spray up from the water's surface.

"We're clear for now, Conman," Logan said from the rear seat. "City's up ahead."

"Roger that." A flashing comm light demanded Connor's attention. He toggled the button. "Coyote Leader."

"Connor, it's James."

"Colonel! Fancy meeting you in the Netherlands. Always thought it was pretty here, even with those ugly black towers . . ."

"It's those towers we need to deal with."

"Would you like me to blast them?"

James's sigh was tinny. "No, interdict. Keep Tiu shuttles on the ground."

"Why certainly. Coyote Leader out." He switched frequencies. "Coyote Leader to Vampire Leader. Think you can clean up the rest of these Tiu for us?"

The grim woman's voice came over sounding confident. "Not a problem."

"Lovely. Coyotes, follow me in. We're grounding some Marty fat birds."

The Earth Rangers at the Kesek gates posed no problem for the Lancers. When confronted by three Lancer troops demanding their surrender, they simply laid down their weapons.

Alec was disgusted by their refusal to fight either way but had little time to ruminate. He followed Benjamin and Father up and over the wall.

They landed in a firefight.

The thirty-some Lancers who'd crossed the wall here were shooting it out with an equal number of Tiu. Except the Tiu had six hexambler robots where the Lancers had only three.

Alec landed heavily. He was instantly knocked aside by Benjamin. Before he could wonder why, a set of Tiu claws slashed by him. Benjamin shouted in fury as he blocked the blow with his lance, "Take a piece, Marty scum!"

The Martian bellowed something in Tiu and slashed again, but Benjamin had pivoted away. He impaled the Tiu on his lance.

The Tiu's dying scream echoed in Alec's ears. Another pair of Tiu charged their way. One of them fired his railer. Benjamin yelled and flew back against the wall. He slammed heavily into it. Yellowing leaves settled softly onto his armor as he slumped to the ground. The blast had nearly taken his left arm off at the shoulder.

"Benjamin! No!" Alec saw his friend—and his brother, possibly?—wounded. He didn't think but reacted with swift reflexes. A single shot from his railer sent a blistering projectile through both attacking Tiu. They actually kept running for a split second before they tumbled over each other in a heap.

Alec scurried to Benjamin's side. He caught a glimpse of Father landing atop a skittering Martian hexambler. His armored body reflected the midday sun as he jabbed downward with his lance. A sharp crackle filtered through Alec's suit speakers as electrical current jumped from James's lance into the robot. It twitched madly before collapsing, inert.

"Benjamin! Can you speak?" Alec ripped open a panel on Benjamin's armor and checked his vital signs. Good. The suit had already clamped down internal barriers to prevent further blood loss. He saw bandaging foam ooze out around the torn flesh and armor.

"Nice shot . . . kid." Benjamin groaned.

"Does it hurt?"

"Your daddy taught you a lot . . . Didn't he teach you not to ask dumb questions?"

Alec grinned.

James slashed his lance at a Tiu. The warrior collapsed screaming, his hand separated from its wrist.

James wheeled about, looking for a Kesek guard. He needed information. One was cowering under a tree. James stomped over to him and, before the man could scurry off, wrapped an armored hand around his neck. He picked him up off his feet and held him dangling, face-to-face with his mask. "Where are they holding the king? Tell me!"

The man choked and sputtered. James was just about to loosen his grip when the guard pointed shakily over James's shoulder.

A keening whine made him turn. The Tiu shuttles were lurching into the air.

The shuttles.

"Disable those shuttlecraft! The king is aboard! They're taking him!" James shouted through his suit speaker and into his comm channel. He raised his railer. "Aim for the hoverjets!"

Eight or so of James's Lancers who were not otherwise occupied fired a volley of railer fire. A hexambler joined them. James fired a shot too. It skewered a wing on the shuttle but only grazed the hoverjet housing. He gritted his teeth and reached for his machine gun. It would take his railer time to recharge.

Several shots hit the shuttles. Sparks erupted from an aft hoverjet on one shuttle. It wobbled and tipped, before slowly sliding toward the ground on its remaining hoverjets. James was reminded of a malfunctioning hexambler he'd once seen crash into a barracks. Fortunately the shuttle was not far off the ground. It slammed onto the pavement, scraping and screeching to a halt.

They can't bring them down. James was losing hope and taking aim with his machine gun at the rising shuttles when blistering autocannon fire sliced across the hoverjets on two more shuttles. Several more streams sliced across the sky until all six shuttles had limped to minor crash landings.

James was stunned. Then he heard the screaming engines in the distance. He shouted into his suit comm, "Connor! That was you?"

"A fine bit of targeting, if I do say so, dear brother!" Connor chortled into his ear. "Eavesdropping on your comm channel turned out to be one of my better ideas."

"I agree." James waved his men forward. Lancers and a handful of hexamblers advanced on the crashed shuttles. Before he could instruct them to search for the king, a Kesek guard staggered out of the hatchway on the shuttle nearest the soldiers. He had a disheveled King Andrew II by the arm and a gun pointed to his captive's head.

"Drop the weapon," James ordered. He raised his machine gun.

"No! Stay back!" The man appeared crazed by fear. His gun hand shook. King Andrew wore a defiant expression on his handsome face. "You put down your guns and let us walk out, or I'll kill him!"

James didn't answer. One of his sergeants' voices came over his suit comm: "We've called up fusiliers into sniper positions. Give us a few seconds."

"Just calm down," James said. "No one will . . ."

CRAAACK. Blood burst from the center of the Kesek man's head. He snapped backward, leaving King Andrew standing stock-still.

James spun to face the gunman. Branko Mazur stomped between a pair of Lancers. He had a squad of dirty fusiliers behind him, an angry expression on his face, and a Brodski 77 heavy-bore pistol in one raised hand. Blood was smeared across the white glove of his gun hand, and his helmet was missing. "So. Negotiations over."

"Branko!" James exhaled. "I see you're not dead, old friend."

"Pah. Not yet." Branko grinned.

Not the way James would have finished things. But it would have to do. He could already see some dazed representatives of Congress and shaken Kesek officers tottering out of the down shuttles. "Get into the rest of the shuttles and secure the area!" James ordered his men. Lancers bounded over.

Branko waved at his squad. "Assist them. Move!"

James unsealed his mask and marched forward to the king. He knelt before him. "Your Highness—"

"Please, James, formality is not necessary." King Andrew grasped his armored shoulders. "I am ever thankful to see you."

He beckoned into the shuttle. Queen Maria and the two princes, Carter and Phillip, came out. Their wide eyes took in the battlefield around them. Phillip shrieked at the sight of the dead Kesek man. Maria covered him in a hug.

Carter, though, walked right up to James. "Is it all over? Are we safe?"

"You are safe." Branko gave a bow. "The Tiu are cornered, James. We may actually have some prisoners, yes?"

A pair of Lynx fighters shrieked by overhead. They wagged their wings in salute. James raised his lance and his men cheered their victory. But the cost was steep. James counted at least fifteen men dead. There would be more.

Alec came bounding over. "Father! Benjamin—Troop Master Sands—he's wounded. He's with the medics!"

"Are you all right, son?"

"I am. God is good." Alec must have abruptly realized who was standing before them, because he gave a stiff bow. "Your Majesty!"

"Is this young Alec?" King Andrew asked.

Alec unsealed his mask. James was relieved to see his son's face unscathed. "At your service, Highness."

"I would be honored if you and your son would escort me to the gates, James." Andrew straightened. "The people must see that I am unhurt."

"Of course, Your Highness. But what about Gironde?"

"He is gone," Queen Maria said with disgust as she led her children away from the shuttle.

King Andrew scowled. "Like a rat to the sewer."

• • •

Nikolaas Ryke decided it was best for *HMS Interrogator* to simply cruise through the midst of the first and second security zones around Earth. After all, they had the clearance, and he was in no mood to observe formalities.

He wanted to break the rail around the command deck in half. Outwardly he maintained a cold mask—inwardly he raged at those fool youths for having deceived him. He considered that his own arrogance might be at fault, but dismissed that idea.

"Sir." Cotes tread carefully around Ryke when he was in these moods. Ryke was glad he was such a cautious fellow. He'd hate to have to shoot such a loyal partner.

"Yes, Cotes?"

"Captain Sasaki is receiving comm updates from Kesek headquarters."

"Very well." Ryke waved a hand at the main monitor. It was a blank screen of space covered with confusing ship tracks. "Has he determined what is the cause of all this mess?"'

"Ah . . . no, sir."

"Unacceptable. Captain! A prompt report, if you please!"

Sasaki gave him a foul look. Let him complain. Ryke had Cotes and Constable DeVoors at his side, and the six other Kesek officers guarding each entrance to the bridge. No interference would be allowed. Plus Ryke had plenty with which to scuttle Sasaki's career once he filed his final report. He reached down and rested a hand against a bulge in the right pocket of his maroon jacket. Well, he hadn't failed entirely.

At least he'd secured the Bible as ordered.

"Communications, put the updates and orders to my console," Sasaki said. He at back in his command chair.

"Aye, sir . . . Skipper!" The comms man's jaw flapped uselessly a few times.

"Yes?"

"You . . . you might want to read these."

"That is my plan." Sasaki gestured again.

"Sorry, Skipper."

Ryke watched him intently as the tiny blue lettering scrolled past on Sasaki's console screen. He couldn't read it from here, but it couldn't have been good news. All the color drained from Sasaki's face.

But then the captain smiled. He stood and straightened his uniform. Ryke saw about him a dangerous confidence. "Bridge crew: Zebra."

Before Ryke could blink, an engineering tech, the nav officer, and the tactical officer had guns trained on the three Kesek men. What in blazes? "This had best be your sad attempt at a joke, Captain."

"Not quite. Comms, get security up here. A troop of marines, please."

"Aye, Skipper."

Since the security substation for this deck was only a compartment away, the marines arrived before Ryke could even fathom what the fool captain was doing. He looked out the bridge hatch as four came in. The men he'd left to guard the hatches were standing with their hands up, pistols on the deck as more marines in shining black and violet armor held them at rifle's end.

Incompetents.

Sasaki walked slowly over to Ryke and Cotes. Ryke tensed. His pistol rode in an open holster on his belt but he didn't chance looking at it. He didn't move when Sasaki reached down and drew it out. "Arrest these two men," Sasaki said.

He sounded much too pleased, Ryke thought. A marine slapped binders on his wrists. "This is outrageous!" Ryke snapped.

"It is that, former Detective Chief Inspector." Sasaki took a deep breath and announced in a louder voice, "By order of His Royal Majesty King Andrew II, all officers of Kesek are hereby placed under arrest by Royal or local authorities until such time as a formal inquiry can be completed. His Majesty has issued a royal decree temporarily banning Kesek as the prime law enforcement agency of the Realm."

Sasaki's face didn't conceal his hate. "Your commissioner tried to ship the king off to the Tiu. The plan was stopped, thankfully, but he has escaped. Civilians were killed for showing their support for the king."

Cotes cleared his throat. "We have only ever been loyal servants of the Realm . . ."

"Shut up." Sasaki turned his back on both of them. "Lock them all up. Strip them of their uniform coats. And do search them thoroughly."

One marine pulled the badges from Ryke's and Cotes's chests.

For perhaps the third time in his life, Ryke was speechless.

Baden walked in silent awe down the main corridor leading to the Congress of Worlds. He squinted in the sunlight coming in through a trio of floor-length windows. The five flags of the Realm hung high overhead. Someone had hastily added the silver-edged black star of the Expatriate Cooperative.

He wasn't alone. Gail walked on his right, holding tightly to his hand, while Owen strode beside him to the left. Captain Bell and Dennis trailed them by a few paces. Baden noticed they were more nervous than awestruck. It could have something to do with the quartet of Lancers in grey-green fatigues marching behind them.

"Hack, this is aced!" Owen was almost whispering. "Man, never thought I'd ever get to see the inside of the royal buildings! You see all those scanners they ran us through? Security systems must beat our encrypts all to blazes."

"Yeah, I didn't really notice, Ozzy." Baden craned his neck at the looming portrait of the first king of the Realm, Justice I. His royal outfit was more elaborate, somewhat archaic, but behind the drooping moustache Baden saw the same handsome features evident in the current king's face.

"Did Commander Verge say where she would meet us?" Gail edged closer.

Baden put his hand at the small of her back. "She said she'd be at the main doors."

Owen pointed. "Those them?"

A pair of massive wooden doors towered ahead, on the far side of a vestibule. The floors were white marble and the walls a polished stone. Purple banners draped the walls. A cluster of people in civilian clothes waited at the door. "Dad!"

He broke into a run and slammed into his dad's arms. Baden squeezed him in a rough hug. He ignored the stares of Renshu, Emi, and Cyril. "Dad! You're okay."

"Yeah, not too shabby." Dad grinned. This was going to take some getting used to. "I'm glad to see you in one piece too."

"Uncle Simon!" Gail joined in the hug. Dad tousled her hair.

Owen sauntered up. "How's about me, Skipper?" He held his arms wide.

Dad rolled his eyes. "No dice, Owen. Nice to see you, though."

Cyril pushed past Renshu and grabbed up Owen in his bear-like arms. Owen yelped. "Ow! Leggo!"

"I missed you," Cyril boomed.

Everyone laughed—except Owen, who was begging to be set down.

Renshu finally pulled Cyril back. He slapped Baden on the back. "You made it, kid! Now we can put you back to work."

"Thanks, Renshu. I missed you too."

Emi smiled thinly. "Even I missed your keen wit, Baden. At one point, I thought you would need a poem read at your funeral, so I have prepared one."

Baden recalled how many times he thought he was going to die. "You and me both."

"This is what I came across: '*Tombo tsuri / kyo wa doko made / itta yara.*' It roughly translates, 'I wonder in what fields today / He chases dragonflies in play / My little boy who ran away.'"

"Aw, that's too sad for Hack's funeral," Owen said. "Mopey."

"Kaga no Chiyo wrote that after the death of her nine-year-old son, nine hundred years ago," Emi said softly.

"How sweet." Baden had forgotten Bell and Dennis were standing behind them.

Dad turned to them. "So, you kept up your end of the deal."

"Yeah. Told you I would." Bell jerked her chin in Baden's direction. "Your kid did good out there, Haczyk. Surprised me."

"Always good to hear." Dad smiled again. "He's full of surprises."

"Speaking of surprises, thanks for sending me that recording from Mom," Baden said. "It meant a lot. And it helped point me in the right direction. I just—"

"Hey, we did this on Bethel." Simon grabbed his arms. "Your mother was the best thing that ever happened to me, and you were the best thing that ever happened to us. I'm sorry I wasted these years making life rough for you."

The pair embraced again. Baden clung fiercely to his dad. All he could think about was when he used to play hide-and-seek in the tight engine spaces of *Natalia Zoja* with Simon. He had a brief flash of memory—Baden seven years old and screaming with delight, Simon grabbing him up in his arms and laughing uproariously. "I love you, Dad."

"I love you too, son." Simon clapped him roughly on the back, and they disengaged. He jerked a thumb toward the entrance to the hall of Congress. "Colleen."

"Colleen?"

"Er, Commander Verge said we should wait out here until she comes to bring us in. Seems she's got some last-minute negotiating to do."

"I thought there's all kinds of civilians here today."

"There are, but nobody else brought pirates."

"Oh. Hey, Bell!" Baden called.

She wrinkled her nose. "What?"

"You leave the Dunn series in the antechamber at the other end of the corridor?"

"Duh." She jerked a thumb over her shoulder. "Give us the signal and I'll go get it. With my hefters, of course."

"Nova."

The massive doors creaked open. Commander Verge stepped through. She made eye contact with Dad. "Hello, Simon."

"Hi, Colleen," Dad said cheerily.

Baden wondered if he'd ever be able to get his jaw up off the vestibule floor. Even Owen lacked a pithy comment.

"You all have been cleared to sit in on this session, thanks in part to testimony from Colonel Verge and his wife."

The colonel stepped up beside her. "Captain Haczyk, good to see you again." The officer shook hands with Dad. He indicated a dark-skinned woman of regal bearing next to him. "May I introduce my wife, Professor Tara Douglas-Verge, alternate representative from Starkweather to the Congress of Worlds."

"Professor." Dad shook her hand. He introduced the crew to the Verges, and then came to Baden. "And this is my son, Baden Haczyk, Professor."

"Ah." Baden found her smooth voice soothing and yet commanding. She held out her hand. "James has told me about your exploits, as has Colleen. It seems we owe you a debt for instigating the proceedings here today."

Baden shook her hand politely and wondered what in blazes she was talking about.

"Now, come, all of you, let me lead you to your seats."

Baden held up a hand. "What about Captain Bell?"

Colonel Verge cast a wary eye in her direction. She waved cheerily. "I think it better she wait down in the first antechamber. With my Lancers."

Baden frowned. "Okay."

They went through the doors. At least Bell would wait in the same room as the Dunn Series machine they'd picked up on Alexandria. Baden wondered if his idea was a mistake.

He'd find out.

CHAPTER 23

November 2602
Earth Star System
Earth, Africa, New Cyrene

The special session of Congress was promising to be far more interesting than the usual. Alcoves and balconies that were typically empty were overflowing with officials, media representatives, soldiers, and members of the public, who were being allowed in as a rare exception. Tara Douglas-Verge watched the murmurs, the craning of necks, and marveled at the new life in the chamber.

Behind the south balcony, which was reserved for the Congressional alternates, the gallery was full of guests—James, with Alec on his left and Julianna and Bridget to his right. Connor chatted eagerly with Colleen—both sat next to the girls. Benjamin Sands was not able to come, as he was undergoing intensive regeneration therapy for the severed tendons and shattered bones in his left shoulder.

The crew of the six-brace *Natalia Zoja* sat in the row, along with Abu Zuhayr Hamid ibn Thaqib of al-Azhar Shipyards and several of his merchant captains. Two towering bodyguards in silver and pearl body armor loomed behind him.

Tara turned her attention back to the twenty-one chairs of the representatives. They were murmuring back and forth. Several looked haggard, no doubt from their recent Kesek incarceration. Despite their incessant discussion, the hall had a peaceful feel to it. Warm sunlight cast everyone in a soft glow.

"All rise!" The bearded sergeant-at-arms, a mountain of a man, rapped his onyx staff against the stone floor three times. His crimson cloak and mother-of-pearl breastplate flashed in the sunlight. "Behold, his royal majesty, King Andrew Justice Markham Douglas, Lord of the Realm of Five!"

Unlike the last time Tara had been before Congress, there was little decorum. The representatives, alternates, and the burgeoning crowd were on their feet and cheering like mad as King Andrew entered the hall with raised arms. He removed his silver crown, holding the thin band bearing five emeralds high for all to see. His purple cape whirled as he turned to face the people. Tara's clapping joined the rolling thunder of applause that filled the hall.

A pair of guards entered the hall behind the king and escorted him up the twenty-one steps to the sienna cushioned chair underneath the white banner of Earth. Tara thought the gold bear at the center of the blue sphere surrounded by black sunrays looked especially proud. She for one was bursting with joy that there was just one chair atop the royal dais. Just a few weeks ago, Kesek Commissioner Gironde's chair had sat beside the king's.

No more.

Chairman Garrison gaveled the assembly to order. He had recovered much of his panache in the past couple of days. "We now bring this session to order," he said somberly. There was restrained joy behind his words, Tara could tell. "I would like to begin by welcoming you all back unharmed from your less than comfortable stay as guests of Kesek."

Laughter echoed throughout the hall. Garrison turned. "And I would also like to say that my heart is overjoyed at the sight of our good king returned to his rightful throne!"

More cheers and applause. King Andrew held up his hands, and silence reigned. "Let me say, to begin this session, that the Hamarkhis people have my full and complete sympathy," he said in his rich baritone. "They were deceived by their Tiu cousins as we were, and their ships of faithful pilgrimage turned into instruments of death and terror. They have suffered cruelty as a result, and I wish it to end as of this moment. Mister Chairman, have it thus recorded."

"Yes, Your Majesty." Garrison motioned to a clerk. "Your proclamation shall be transmitted throughout the Reach at the session's conclusion. And now, our colleague from Rozsada has a matter he would like to address."

Representative Baran rose from his semi-circular desk. He turned his considerable bulk to face his fellow members of Congress and the audience. "You have seen plenty of evidence that the Charter of Religious Tolerance has become anything but tolerant. It was meant as a unifying factor for our Realm by ensuring that all philosophies were treated equally—a credit to your House's foresight, Your Majesty."

King Andrew nodded in recognition of the compliment.

"But look now." Baran thumped his desk. "It is another oppressive tool of Kesek. It gives them license to detain anyone they want, for any reason. Kesek is thought police and faith police. So. That is why I move to repeal the Charter of Religious Tolerance."

Grumbling spread throughout the representatives and the audience. "Now see here, Mister Baran," said Representative Jerome Abernathy from Starkweather. He was one of the representatives who had gone into hiding with Tara. His dark, balding brow was furrowed in irritation. "It's true that we must rid ourselves of Kesek and true they abused this charter for their own purposes. But surely we cannot blame that on the Charter. We must always preserve tolerance to all beliefs. We should add strenuous limitations and safeguards to the Charter so that it may never again be misused. But we cannot throw it all out because of its imprecision."

There was some murmured agreement, but near half the alternates seated with Tara were shaking their heads. Baran scowled at Abernathy. "You preserve oppression, yes?"

"That's uncalled for, Gostislav, especially coming from an Orthodoxy fanatic!" Abernathy snapped.

"Better fanatic than faithless!" Baran said.

Tara hoped Chairman Garrison would have none of that. She was right. He banged on his gavel. "We will have order!" Garrison said. "Take your seats and remain there until you are recognized to comment."

The abashed representatives took their seat. Garrison's restoration of order did not stop the grumbling, however. "Is there a second to Representative Baran's motion so we may continue?"

Representative Carina Sulis of the Expatriate Cooperative stood. Her normally round face seemed more gaunt to Tara, and her well-coiffed silver hair, frazzled. Without her warning,

Tara might have suffered Kesek imprisonment—or worse. "I second his motion."

"Good." Garrison banged his gavel again. "I will now hear comments. Yes, Representative Tze Biyu of Tiaozhan?"

"I find Representative Baran's comments unsurprising, given Founders Orthodoxy's long-established flaunting of the Charter," Tze said. Her weathered face was calm and impassive. "They have come within a hair's breadth of violating the key to the Charter—the claim of exclusivity. It threatens our very stability when any one faith claims it is the true path. That has been proven in years past."

Baran threw up his hands. "Pah! Are your own beliefs so weak that mine threaten yours? We argue about everything else in our society. Why is religious debate disallowed?"

"Because it always becomes an unpleasant matter." Representative Abernathy sat back at his desk and crossed his arms. "Take your pick—the ultra-religious types always make time to kill one another, and innocent bystanders, eventually."

Tara stood and awaited recognition from the chairman. Garrison pounded his gavel. "Let's remember to keep our debate civilized, gentlemen," he said. "One of our alternate representatives wishes to speak, and given the circumstances, I will allow it if the Starkweather delegation agrees."

That meant Tara needed Abernathy's approval. He glanced her way. "My colleagues and I see no objection to letting Professor Douglas-Verge address the floor."

"Proceed, Professor," Garrison said.

"Thank you, Mister Chairman." She stood and moved for one of the microphone pickups embedded in the railing of the alternates' balcony. "The question before us is a simple one—should we revoke the Charter of Religious Tolerance and replace it with a less restrictive law? Or should we simply modify the existing document? I, of course, favor the former.

"It is my belief that any rule that goes so far as to tell people how to think, how to worship, or what to say is a poor one. The Realm suffers most grievously by demanding its citizens submit their personal, private thoughts to government review. As Representative Abernathy points out, there have been many cases of people abusing religion—for power, for murder, for other reasons. But is that not true of every human, regardless of faith?"

Tara gestured at the group seated behind her. "Colonel Verge and his forces have returned from Bethel, a place where religious belief thrived in spite of Kesek, because it was not convenient for Kesek to rigorously enforce the Charter. Kesek—representing our government—terrorized the people of Bethel, and what did my husband receive in return, when the Tiu ambushed his men? Kindness." Her throat tightened. "My brother died because of Kesek's greed, and so have countless others."

"If we remove this rule, we are opening the hatch for every crazed fanatic to seize the chance to tear the Realm apart with strife!" Abernathy sounded distressed. He apparently had not known what arguments Tara was going to make. Pity him for not having paid attention. "Peace will disappear."

"As opposed to the strife Kesek created?" Tara asked harshly. "Peace was replaced with fear."

She continued, addressing the rest of Congress. "The most creative, most resilient, most successful societies have always prided themselves in freedom of thought. That is all I am advocating. But to allow full freedom of thought, we must allow all thoughts—even those we may consider superstitious and full of folly."

A rustling in the seats made her turn. The young Haczyk man, Baden, stood in his spot. He fingered the sleeve of his worn orange shirt.

What did he want?

Baden was terrified. There were so many people in this room. Most of them wouldn't look twice at an Expatriate. But with Gail on his right and Owen on his left, his dad and crew nearby, he didn't feel as alone. He needed to quiet the urging he'd felt ever since this debate started.

"I'd . . ." It came out a croak. He cleared his throat and started over. "I'd like to speak, please."

The elegantly dressed man in charge—Chairman Garrison, from what the other politicians said—frowned at the request. "Congressional protocol does not allow unscheduled civilian speakers, young man."

"Surely we can make an exception." Professor Douglas-Verge looked up at Baden. She seemed like a smart woman, and a nice one. Too bad she'd made that crack about "superstitions." Oh, well. Baden figured it was too late to expect everyone to be on his side.

"I would gladly yield my time," she said.

"The request is denied," Garrison said. "We do not open the floor to outsiders."

"This boy is no outsider." Colonel Verge stood ramrod straight in his crisp Lancer's uniform. "His father and their crew have performed invaluable service to our task force, allowing us to evade Martian forces and return here to liberate our king!"

"It is commendable but not relevant to this discussion," Abernathy called out.

Commander Verge stood too. She winked at Baden. "Perhaps it is more relevant that Baden recorded a Bible and made it available on the Reach."

Abernathy's mouth snapped shut. Representatives either stared at Baden or murmured in huddles. Hisses of "It's him!" or "He's the one?" flittered through the air.

Baden wasn't sure he liked all this attention. But he decided that while they were all still trying to figure this out, he'd plunge onward. "Well, look, I'm an Expatriate and I've been to Bethel. I think that—"

Several representatives rose from their seat and shouted comments at him. He couldn't make most of them out, but there were a few insults about Expatriates in general in there. Representative Sulis was on her feet and shouting right back at them. Garrison whaled away at his gavel. "Enough! Sit down and behave yourselves! There will be no further interruptions."

"Mister Chairman?"

All eyes turned to the king. Baden never thought he'd hear him speak in person. "We would hear the youth speak," the king said sternly. "This is a quite extraordinary circumstance, in our opinion."

Garrison's mouth dropped. As Baden understood it, the king had the prerogative to overrule the chairman, but he had not exercised that power in . . . well, he couldn't remember how long it had been. His history files hadn't said. Garrison simply bowed and sat.

King Andrew raised his hand toward Baden. "Continue, please."

If Baden was nervous before, he was quivering now. In the back of his mind, however, he remembered what he read in the book of Acts. Those believers had asked for help when speaking—why couldn't he?

Holy Spirit, give me wisdom in my words.

Gail reached out and clutched his hand. Owen poked him from the left. He winked up. "Dazzle 'em, Hack."

"Thank you . . . Your Highness." Professor Douglas-Verge directed him down to the alternates' balcony and pointed him toward the microphone. *Sweet nova, this was expensive wood. And this room . . .* He shook away the distraction. "I wanted to say that I, uh, never gave the Charter much thought, except in school when I had to learn it. And then I found a Bible in a wrecked courier ship off Muhterem."

Shouts erupted around the hall. Astonished cries filled the air as Baden pulled the book from his pocket. "This isn't the one," Baden said. "Kesek took the one I found. But we have more."

Audience members tried to push forward but were stopped by guards. Baden saw Simon, Renshu, Emi, and Cyril get up and form a barricade around Baden and his friends. Even Major Mazur charged in to restore order. *Hopefully not with his fists.*

Down on the main floor, Congress was in an uproar. Garrison was bent over an older Earth representative who had, from the looks of things, apparently fainted. The Tiaozhanese were practically in a shouting match with the Rozsade. The Muhteremi looked awestruck. One man was on his knees, with his head bowed to the floor.

Overlapping questions and catcalls assaulted Baden: "Blasphemy! Where did he get it? It's not possible! Can it be true? No one has ever seen such a thing! This is horrible! How can it be? It is the Word!"

Then the king was on his feet. "Silence!" His voice boomed across and around the hall. All activity and speech rumbled to a halt.

"You have . . . more?" he asked, looking at Baden.

Baden swallowed. He turned to Gail. She gave him a slight smile. "If my associate Captain Bell could be allowed to contact her cargo hefters, I can explain," he said. "She's waiting outside in one of the antechambers."

Garrison eyed them suspiciously. "Colonel Verge, have these people cleared this matter with you?"

"They have, Mister Chairman. I do not agree with all his views. But there is no danger."

"Proceed, then."

Baden swept his comm out of his pocket. "Your turn."

The sergeant-at-arms flexed his mother of pearl armor and opened the towering wooden doors to the hall. His red cape swirled as he stepped back a pace.

Captain Charlotte Ruby Bell and her first mate, Dennis, walked through the doors. Four Lancers provided a guard, not just for their cargo but for the pirates themselves. Bell wore her battered old coat and black shipsuit accented by gaudy silver stripes with obvious pride, and offered a cheery wave to the astonished Congress. Dennis looked more furtive, with his artificial eye scanning the room.

Two bulky, bronzed hefter robots trailed them. One walked backward and the other forward. Their massive metal arms held on to the white and tan machine Baden and the others had taken off Alexandria. It was held aloft by a hoverpad.

"Young man, what is this?" the king asked.

"Uh, Your Highness, this is a Dunn 400 Series Twin-Vault. It is, my king, a printing press."

There were more shocked outbursts. Before it got any further, Baden continued, "We found it . . . Well, we found it along with a cavern full of Christian artifacts and writings. And boxes full of Bibles. It's about a hundred years old, but Gail . . . my, uh, friends Gail Salpare and Owen Zinssler here got it working again."

"So. You can . . . print?" Representative Baran asked.

"Yessir. And, see, that's all I'm here to ask for. The freedom to hand this stuff out." Baden held the Bible higher for all to see. "This book and the people who follow its beliefs helped me. I'm only asking for the freedom to follow Christ in the way I want. And if I say that He is the Way and the Truth and the Life, the only path to God, then so what?" He shrugged. "You either agree with me or you don't. So what if I believe I'll be with Him when I die and those who don't believe won't?"

"But you can't stand there and say that!" Abernathy shook off a restraining hand from a fellow Starkweather representative.

"Why not?"

Abernathy gaped. "Because . . . it's hateful, and divisive, and . . ."

"Whoa. Look, I don't hate anybody. The only hate I've seen in all this has come from Kesek. They killed my mom because they didn't like what she believed." Baden's throat tightened as he saw his mother in his mind's eye. Always kind and never wanting to hurt anyone. For you, Mom. "And divisive? Well, maybe it is. But what do you mean by divisive? Are you telling me we can't sit down and talk about this stuff over a drink just because I claim my way's right and yours isn't? Just because we don't agree we have to stand apart and shout at each other?"

Abernathy was glaring openly at him. Some faces held a mix of hostility and contempt. But many others were curious.

Baden turned his attention to the king. "Your Highness, if I can't say that my faith is the true faith, then what good is that faith? If it's no different than any other one, then it's useless—and in my heart, I know that can't be right. People should be allowed to believe with all their hearts, and if I say my beliefs are true and someone else says his are true, well, why can't we talk that over? Why does the Realm have to worry about it?"

King Andrew was tapping his chin with his fingers.

Professor Douglas-Verge spoke up. "I understand the fear of instability. But the Charter goes too far. We should allow freedom of religion, insofar as it does no harm to another person."

Baran stood. "Is reasonable to me. How many people have we needlessly locked away because we do not like what they pray? There will be trouble, yes, but there will also be a better Realm. So. We give them the choice."

Baden was glad to hear at least some people in agreement. That Abernathy guy did not look convinced, but he wasn't yelling, either.

"I suppose you'd have us put your kind on top," Abernathy said. "Enshrine Christians in the law and everyone else be damned, literally."

"Are you kidding?" Baden asked. "I've read my history. No, if God is true, then He can handle everything and He doesn't need the government's help. His followers just need room to believe."

Abernathy had no reply.

"Call for the vote," Sulis said.

"Very well." Garrison cleared his throat. "Debate on this matter is hereby . . ."

"Mister Chairman." King Andrew rose from his throne. Baden watched him, fascinated.

"Yes, Your Highness?"

The king started down the steps to the main floor. His guards scurried to join him.

Everyone at the desks sprang to their feet and bowed in respect. The king waved them off. He stood in the midst of the desks and looked around at the representatives. Then he raised his gaze to the balconies and the gallery beyond. Baden's heart pounded.

"I hereby cancel this vote by royal decree."

Baden didn't know whether the Garrison guy was more surprised than him, but he sure looked it. "Your Majesty, as Chairman of the Congress of Worlds, I must protest . . ."

"I cancel it, Mister Chairman, because it is unnecessary," King Andrew said, tone steely. "Too long have I relied on the wrong advisors. Those on whom I relied convinced me they had the Realm's best interests at heart. You see where that got us. No, I have decided to abolish the Charter myself."

Gasps echoed in the hall. "It is of course your prerogative." Garrison's voice was even but his face betrayed his astonishment. "It was enacted by royal decree . . ."

"And as such can be canceled." King Andrew gestured. "That young man is right—who am I, and who are we, to tell him what to believe? If he harms no one, what is the danger?"

"Would you not, however, prefer a vote of your Congress?"

"I would not." The king smiled. "If they voted to keep the Charter, I would have overruled them and abolished it anyway."

When King Andrew spoke again, it was loudly, to the entire hall. "I hereby abolish the Charter of Religious Tolerance and disband the Convocation on Spiritual Unity, as established by my House, and as such subject to royal decree."

Garrison woke himself from his stupor enough to remember protocol and banged his gavel five times.

Cheering burst forth from the galley.

Baden couldn't believe this was happening. He was watching history unfold before his eyes.

King Andrew raised his hands. "I also decree that all people of the Realm are hereby free to worship whom they choose, as they choose, insofar as they do not directly harm another person."

Someone behind Baden let out a cry. He turned. Hamid had his face turned skyward and had his eyes closed. His face was covered with happiness. "The Lord God reigns!"

Cheers of joy echoed throughout the hall. Baden's heart pounded hard. He shared a smile with a teary-eyed Gail. This was the beginning of something new, something exciting for their generation. For all believers.

"Professor Douglas-Verge will oversee the Standing Committee on Justice and Law in its new role, to craft a new edict on religious freedom."

Baden saw Abernathy come to his feet. "Your Highness, I am currently chair of that committee."

"And so you shall remain." The king stared him down. "For now."

"But I must protest this course of action—"

"That will be quite enough!" the king boomed. Baden almost took a step back. This was not the king he'd seen in Reach vids, numbly nodding his assent to anything Congress and Kesek put on his plate. This was a revitalized king. "I have made my decision, and it will stand."

Abernathy's face went pale. He sat down slowly. "What about that book?" He jabbed a finger at Baden. "That boy should be arrested just for holding it! These people are criminals, after all—we've all seen the charges posted on the Reach. I've half a mind to have them arrested right here. And he says there are more copies. They should be seized at once!"

Baden swallowed. His reflex was to reach for his gun, which he didn't have on him.

"Representative Abernathy, if the charter no longer reigns, then that book is not a text-in-violation, is it?" the king said. "Which reminds me, we must also set to work disemboweling Kesek's glut of laws supposedly drawn from the Charter. But one in particular will do for today: Statute Seventeen, Section Five."

Baden's eyes went wide.

"What's that one?" Owen asked from behind him.

"It bans all printed materials and their manufacture," Gail said.

"Eliminate that ordinance, Mister Chairman, by royal decree," the king said.

"Please, Your Highness!" Abernathy was now holding his hands out. His normally placid expression was fraught with dismay. "Think of the impact on Your Majesty's corporation . . ."

"And the decrease in profit share values you will see if there are other sources of information?" King Andrew cut in. Abernathy went silent. "You see, I'm not the fool you think I am, Representative. MarkIntech can find ways to adapt to the change, I can assure you. Now, repeal the ordinance."

Garrison swallowed. "Yes, Your Highness."

The gavel banged five times again.

King Andrew nodded. "Good. Now, since the ordinance is void, the charges against the crew of . . ." He beckoned to Simon. "Captain?"

"Oh. Uh, the crew of *Natalia Zoja*. Your Highness," Dad blurted.

"Thank you. Those charges are withdrawn. All outstanding Kesek warrants are hereby remanded to the Standing Committee on Justice and Law for review."

Captain Bell cleared her throat. Loudly.

"Who is that woman?" King Andrew asked.

"Captain Charlotte Ruby Bell, Your Highness," she said brashly. "And my first mate, Dennis."

"She helped get this printing press and religious materials out of Kesek's hands, Your Majesty," Baden said.

"Ah. I see."

"She is also a pirate wanted for the murder of a ship's crew at Eventyr!" One of the Muhteremi delegates was on his feet. His white robes rustled softly in contrast to his shouting. "She faces charges of kidnapping and theft, as well!"

"Indeed?"

"Now hold on one microsec," Bell snapped. "If any crimes were committed, they was on Kesek's payroll!"

King Andrew paced. "In that case, I shall extend you and your crew a pardon as well."

Baden couldn't tell if the audience and Congress or Bell was more surprised. Garrison gaveled down shouts of indignation from the Muhteremi and other representatives. "You're not scamming?" Bell asked.

"No, I am not." The king smiled thinly. "Your pardon comes on one condition: that you become licensed privateers in my service, specifically for hunting down other pirates of a more sinister nature."

"Oh." Bell chewed her lip. "If I say no?"

"Then I shall have those fine Lancers escort you to prison to await trial, and I will confiscate your ship for fleet gunnery practice."

Baden whistled low. Some choice. "Lemme think." Dennis started to say something to her, but she wagged a finger at him. "Shut up, Dennis. Okay, King, you got a deal."

"Very good. I will have Admiral Sutar work out the details with you." King Andrew walked back up the steps. He left the hall in near chaos at his back. Baden watched as he settled into his throne. The gold bear emblem shone brilliantly on his cloak. To Baden's surprise, the king smiled across the distance at him. "Young man?"

"Ah . . . yes?"

"Your Highness," Owen muttered into his hand.

"Your Highness." Baden refrained from smacking him.

"When our session is concluded, come see me in my chambers. Alone."

Oh, boy.

An hour later, Baden stood before the king's desk.

The room was a small, circular office accessible by a narrow corridor off the main hall of Congress. Its walls were a faint shade of purple and covered by fifteen portraits of prior kings and queens. The lush, cream carpet under Baden's boots reminded him of walking on the moss at Alexandria. The king sat behind an antique wooden desk, wearing just his plain tan shirt and trousers. And of course, the silver crown.

Behind him was a single window as wide as Baden was tall that offered a great view of the Mediterranean coastline.

"You are a courageous young man," the king said. "Not only for enduring Kesek's excesses but for presenting your plea before Congress."

Baden didn't know what to say to that. "Thank you."

"And I heard that you had preached from this Bible over the Reach?"

"Well, it wasn't quite like that, Your Highness." Baden stopped to think about it. Had he preached? He hadn't even believed what he was reading. At least, so he thought.

The king slid a delver across the polished surface of the desk. "This whole business of printing. I do not oppose it in principle, but there are long entrenched economic and political factors at play. I cannot let printing take place unregulated, at least for the time being."

"I understand." Did this mean he wasn't going to let him keep the Dunn series press?

"Good. To that end I wish to issue you a royal permit to own and operate that printing press."

Baden's feet barely touched the floor. "Yes. Uh, okay. Thank you, Your Highness."

"And when you have another copy of that book printed, make sure that I receive one. I will also require one for my wife."

"Yes, Your Majesty."

"And my sons will each need one. They are not fond of sharing." The king waved his hand. "Perhaps you should just make it a dozen."

Whoa. "You got it."

CHAPTER 24

November 2602
Earth Star System
Mercury, Jagged Ridge Detention Center

Nikolaas Ryke scowled as he considered the bare, pale blue walls of his cell. All he had to look at were three blank surfaces, one locked hatch with an inset audio panel, one corroded metal floor, threadbare mattresses on suspended bunks, toilet and sink in a corner, and a trio of tiny lights overhead. One of those lights flickered.

And he had to wear a hideous yellow jumpsuit.

No badge, no gun, no maroon jacket.

"They're letting people out of Beaudreau's Rock, and I'm stuck in here," he said. He prowled the tight confines. "Stuck underground on a world that's either too blasted hot or too blasted cold. Doesn't that strike you as cosmically unfair?"

George Cotes lay on the bottom bunk. He was reading from a "dumb" delver—it had access to the Reach, but only in the most restricted civilian fashion. It was stripped of all the Kesek databases and secure data he would have had before. Ryke wondered if he missed that access. "Perhaps they think the criminals are no longer criminals," Cotes said.

"Yes, I'm sure that's it!" Ryke snapped. "They have the gall to strip us of our ranks and badges, dump us down this dank pit, and then open the gates for the very people we've spent years putting away! Blazes, doesn't that rile you?"

"It does, sir." Cotes said that with a stony face.

"You don't have to call me 'sir' anymore, Cotes."

"Ah. Sorry . . ." Cotes looked perplexed. He glanced up from his delver. "What should I call you?"

"We shouldn't be in here." Ryke ignored the question. It was ludicrous. "Look at you—entirely unconcerned about our fate."

"Actually, I am reading a commnote from my wife and daughter. It was just delivered."

"After being rifled through by prison censors, no doubt."

Cotes raised an eyebrow at him.

"Yes, I get the irony," Ryke said. "Wait . . . you have a daughter?"

"Of course." Cotes turned the screen so Ryke could see the cherubic face perched beneath the beautiful woman.

"You never told me."

"Actually, I mentioned them several times."

"Hmm." Ryke didn't believe he would have missed such a detail about his own partner. He turned back toward the hatch. "How long do you suppose they'll keep us here before our execution?"

"Do you expect to be executed?"

"Perhaps you don't recall my record. I'm lacking in public relations skills, Cotes."

"Well . . . Nikolaas . . ."

Ryke cringed. "I liked 'sir' better."

" . . . perhaps I am less worried because I did not engage in excessive tactics," Cotes finished coolly.

"Why, you devil . . ." Ryke faced him. "You've held back on our suspects all these years in case something like this happened?"

"No, sir, I held back because it was the right thing to do," Cotes said sternly.

Ryke's eyes widened. In six years of service together, Cotes had never said anything to him sternly. "You've certainly become brave without a badge."

"Not brave. Just truthful." Cotes went back to his reading. "Why did you keep it?"

"Keep what?"

"The Haczyk boy's Bible."

Ryke's blood froze. How could he know it was in his prisoner jumpsuit pocket? The guards had confiscated it upon his arrest aboard *HMS Interrogator*, but returned it a few days later. They'd said the Charter of Religious Tolerance had been repealed. Repealed! Ryke thought he might die right there of shock. Instead Ryke was told he was free to worship as he pleased.

It turned his stomach. Anarchy.

"It is not illegal anymore, you recall," Cotes said.

"Yes, thank you." Ryke lifted his chin. "The only way to know my enemy is to study him thoroughly."

"I see."

Ryke wasn't about to tell him he pined for Hannah Haczyk's recording. There had to be some way to get his personal effects back from the warden. The thought of someone discovering that data stick concealed in his pocketknife's hilt terrified him.

A clang echoed from their door. The audio panel crackled to life. "You two have a visitor," a guard's voice said.

"You must be smoking too much Lander Jet," Ryke said.

"Funny. Stand back from the door."

Ryke complied. A red light above the hatch blinked from red to green, then became a pair of green flashing pulses. The hatch creaked open. Ryke inhaled deeply of the cooler and slightly less stale air.

He broke into a coughing fit when he saw his visitor. Commissioner Gironde smiled broadly. He was flanked by two guards in maroon and violet body armor. "Good day, Detective Chief Inspector and Detective Inspector."

Ryke whipped his hand up in salute. Cotes slipped out his and saluted smoothly, as if he did this every day. "Commissioner! It is an honor to see you in person."

"Enough." Gironde raised a hand. He ordered the guards, "Leave us."

They departed. Ryke watched curiously. "Bribery, Inspector Cotes," Gironde said. "They may have chased me out of my office and out of power, but I took the precaution years ago of secreting funds in blank spaces on the Reach that only I may access."

"We heard you had escaped," Ryke said. "And other rumors that Starkweather soldiers had apprehended you."

"A little too late, it turns out. Several of my recently hired pirate ships were able to slip away."

Cotes stood stiffly at attention. "Why are you here? Sir."

"To remove the chains from you and your comrades. There are no less than two hundred Kesek officers incarcerated here." Gironde waved a hand to indicate his environs. Ryke avoided looking around at the tiny cell. "The fools in

Congress have disbanded Kesek. The king wants to reinstate the Crown Marshals and co-opt some of our own men into his service. Incompetents. I am giving them back their opportunity to serve. If they are still loyal, that is. I want none of the undecided."

Ryke couldn't believe what Gironde was saying. Kesek disbanded. Would the insanity never end? He stepped boldly forward. "I am loyal to Kesek. That will never change."

"Good. You will follow me, then?"

"Yes, Commissioner. Whatever you would have me do."

"I would have you continue Kesek's purpose—to strengthen the Realm, by ridding it of those who would make it weak." He handed over Ryke's badge, delver, and pocketknife. "Your things, according to the warden."

Ryke hid his gratefulness as he put the items into a pocket. The file was safe again. He turned. "Coming, Cotes?"

His partner stood still. "The purpose of Kesek is to preserve the Realm. Not destroy it."

"You think I would do that?" Gironde asked. "I would only build it to its full potential."

"By tearing it apart," Cotes said. "By ridding it of the king."

"That weakling's time will come." Gironde was suddenly cold. His normally suave good looks were marred by hatred. He stared at Cotes with flinty eyes. Even Ryke had to admit the man scared him.

Cotes sat slowly on his bunk. "I cannot join you in that. Whatever my fate is here, I will accept it."

Ryke stared at him. "You're . . . not coming with me? Er, us?"

"I'm sorry, sir. I can't."

"Then you are worthless," Gironde said. "You won't have any part in Kesek."

Cotes considered the image of his family, still glowing on the delver. "There is no longer any Kesek."

Gironde turned and stormed out. His boots echoed on the metal decking.

Ryke didn't budge. He was dealing with a strange sensation. Familiarity? Could it possibly be friendship? "Cotes . . ."

"Good-bye, sir."

That tore it. "Blast it, Inspector! You'll wish to never see me again."

"You won't." Gironde unlimbered a gun from his belt. "I have no use for traitors."

Ryke felt time freeze up on him. Could he let his commissioner shoot his partner? Could he let Cotes die?

Of course not.

Ryke stepped in front of the gun. "Commissioner, sir, he is not worth the bullet." He dumped as much anger as he could into the words. All his best acting, saved for interrogation rooms, went into this moment. "Let him live with his disgrace. A long, natural life ending with death in shame."

Gironde eyed him. Ryke could sense his suspicion. But Gironde lowered the gun and holstered it. "Very well. Come along, Detective Chief Inspector."

Ryke followed Gironde. He didn't look back as the guards slammed the hatch shut.

Good-bye, Cotes.

• • •

Alec followed the squat, rectangular robot into the regeneration wing of the East Cyrene Royal Hospital. It led him into a wide recovery room. Everything was soft white—the walls, the floor, the ceiling, the beds, and cabinets. Stark. Like a picture on a delver that a child had left uncolored. The robot stopped in front of one door and flashed a green signal at the entry. "Thanks," Alec said.

He went inside and found Benjamin Sands sitting up in a bed festooned with all manner of diagnostic displays. It reminded Alec of a gaudy Solstice Day tree.

Benjamin looked more relaxed than Alec could recall seeing him. The troop master waved with his right arm. The left was encased in a curved regeneration unit. A series of blue lights trickled down one peach-colored side. "Hey, Cadet Trainee. Like my new armor?"

"It isn't your color, Corporal, but it seems to fit well." Alec leaned against the bedside. "Are you nearly there?"

Benjamin shrugged. "Eh, doc says I got a few days left. Just got a few tendons left to rebuild."

"Does it hurt?"

"Nope. Docs shut off the nerves to that part. At least, that's what they say." Benjamin leaned back against his pillow. His normally sandy expression looked drawn and pale. "So what did you want here?"

"I wanted to thank you. Again. You saved my life back at The Hague." Alec still had the bruises from where Benjamin had shoved him out of harm's way. "I will never forget it."

"Ah. It was nothing." Benjamin looked oddly bashful. "Hey, you'd've done the same, right? Anyone like us would."

"Like us?"

"Believers, kid." Benjamin reached behind a pillow. He dug out a delver. "Got my recordings right here. Courtesy of the Baden Haczyk show."

Alec was astonished. "So you believe the Word too?"

"Yeah. And that whole bit about laying your life down for another—just like they teach at boot camp. You watch out for your troopers. And they watch for you."

"This is great! I mean, at least I have someone I can pray with."

Benjamin grinned. "All I know is this God ain't bad—you wouldn't believe how different things are now. I've already called Carol to tell her."

Carol. The one whose homeland they overflew. The one whose commnotes Benjamin carried around on his delver. "What did she say?"

"She figured I was some sorta prankster 'cause I didn't get all worked up about stuff like I usually do. You know what it feels like to have somebody who looked down on you all of a sudden show you respect?"

"It must have been quite a change."

Benjamin exhaled. "Hey, I tell ya, it kind of feels like my insides are getting scraped out and new stuff's getting pumped in."

Alec winced at the mental picture.

"No joke, Cadet Trainee." Benjamin thrust out his hand again. Alec shook it hard. "You best get to your daddy the colonel and tell him what's what. He ain't gonna believe me."

"Oh. Ah . . . I might wait a bit before doing that."

"Why?"

Alec wasn't sure he wanted to explain it all to Benjamin. "Because Father might not like what it has led me to do."

• • •

Alec knew what was coming as soon as his delver alerted him.

Not long after leaving Benjamin's bedside, he stood outside the guest quarters set aside for the Verge family. The diplomatic compound was a few kilometers north of the royal palace. The building was low, long, and sported a wide, domed roof. It was sandstone and peach. The courtyard around Alec was a blooming garden of breathtaking beauty, full of flowers and trees, surrounded by tall, thick hedges.

Alec could only stare at the flat, brown door in front of him. It led to the living room.

Father was waiting on the other side of that door. Alec tried to swallow the lump in his throat, but it just wouldn't leave. He reached for the entry key panel and pushed it.

The door swished open. For as warm and inviting as the living room looked bathed in the colors of the setting sun, with its plush couches made of Corazon leather, it seemed to Alec a place of fear and darkness. Father stood stiffly at parade rest as if waiting for inspection. His face was as stony as the courtyard's walk outside.

Alec stepped in. He felt as if someone had turned the gravity up to at least twice normal. His mouth went dry. Unchecked panic raced through him. He didn't know what do to.

Then he remembered from the Bible, "My peace I give you."

Christ was there with him and would not forsake him. The panic subsided. Alec straightened. "You sent for me?"

Father's voice was hollow. "Major Kwen, your advisor at the academy, sent me a commnote."

"I see." Alec braced himself.

"You see?" Father's tone was acidic. "You act as though you expected it."

"I did expect it," Alec said quietly. Now was not the time to confront his anger. "The decision was mine, and I gave Major Kwen permission to tell you if he chose to."

"And when would you have told me?"

Alec didn't have an answer to that one. It had been an agonizing decision to make.

"I raised you to be strong, Alec," Father said. He walked over to a window. The light of dusk bathed him in a crimson hue. "To be an independent man, fit to lead our family. And now your instructor tells me you have withdrawn from the academy for 'religious reasons'?"

Alec let out a shuddering breath. "I thought I was trained for this," he explained. "For war. But I wasn't ready. After Bethel, and the fighting at The Hague . . ."

"You fought brav—"

"Father, please. It wasn't fear, it was more . . . disgust. At myself. At what I'd done. I didn't want to kill anyone."

"But you had to have known that would be required of you as a soldier." Father turned toward him.

"I did. That was before." Alec met his eyes. "Now I find that God has impressed on me not to take this path."

"Your uncle would not be pleased."

The statement stabbed Alec through the heart. He could not believe Father sounded so bitter. "That's not fair."

Father's face was etched in rock. "This is lunacy. You throw away your future with this family for this . . . weakness?"

Alec was struck by the accusation. "Is it weakness to admit that I am a sinful creature in need of a savior? Am I weak for leaning on the promises of an Almighty God who vows to always love me and forgive me for my transgressions, and reward me for faithful service?"

"You need only your own strength. We have always survived by our strength."

"No, our family owes all it has to the one God who ordains all things," Alec said. "Please, Father, understand! We cannot rely on ourselves. If we try to build this House without our Lord—"

"Our *lord* is the king and his royal line!" Father shouted. "We have no other master!"

Alec drew back. His mind raced as he tried to think of the last time his father had yelled at him. He was heartbroken by his father's intransigence and his display of anger.

But it did not change what he believed.

"There is one Lord above all others, who authored this universe and stands beyond time itself," Alec said. "I believe this, Father. I know it in my heart to be true, and I have pledged my life and my soul to the service of Christ."

Father's face went cold. "Does that pledge take precedence over your loyalty to this House? To your family and your people?" He paused. "To me?"

Alec blinked. His mouth was dry—this was not a test he had foreseen. He was being offered a choice.

In that moment he saw it was no choice. Even though it would break his father's heart.

"I am a Verge, and I am a Starkweatherer, and that will never change, Father," Alec said carefully. "This House will have my loyalty, as will the king. But . . . I must serve Christ. You cannot ask me to choose between the two."

"I can and I will demand that you choose!" Father yelled.

Alec looked at his feet. The silence rolled on and on. "Then there is no choice. My God must be first."

James pounded on the windowsill. The evening light framed his body in a hazy aura. "You are throwing away your career and your honor, and for what? For this superstition, this poison. For this Christ!"

"Father—"

"Be quiet!" Father snapped. "You have betrayed me and our family. You refuse to abandon this teaching and bow to my wishes, and so you have no place in your inheritance."

Alec was stunned. This could not be happening. It did not happen to children of noble families.

Father drew his delver from his belt and activated it. "I, Lieutenant Colonel James Patrick Verge, call for Alec Lincoln Douglas-Verge to be cast from House Verge and hereby strip him of his birthright and legal benefits, all rights and privileges therein bestowed. His share of the Verge family holdings on Earth and his portion of the family stake in MarkIntech is hereby revoked. His rights as a citizen of the planets Starkweather and Earth are also hereby revoked. So let it be sworn by the Congress of Worlds and the Freeholders of Starkweather."

He stopped. "Please, Alec. Renounce this foolishness. For me."

Alec did not wipe the tears from the corners of his eyes. He wanted, as he always did, to make his father proud. But turning back was impossible. "I cannot."

Father shut his eyes tight. He continued his recording in cold, hard tones: "Alec Lincoln Douglas Verge is hereby Expatriate, and may no longer carry the name of his House."

The finality hit Alec like a hammer. For a moment he could not breathe. With that unremarkable phrase, his father had taken from him everything Alec had assumed would be his in due time. Now he had nothing. He was cast out, fit only to make his living between worlds, banished from Starkweather and Earth and unwelcome on most other inhabited planets.

James walked away without a word.

Alec was alone.

Deep inside, he knew that was never truly so. He knew God would never leave his side, though all who had once respected him might turn their backs.

Alec went to his small room in the guest quarters and packed his belongings as quickly as possible into a small duffel bag. He knew he did not have long before he was officially and legally considered a trespasser. At least his personal items were his—even the little bit of money he had in his pockets. Realm laws on expulsion were not entirely unforgiving.

He didn't want to cause a scene, so he snuck down the pale corridor toward the small kitchen unit at the back. There was a door from there to the main courtyard of the diplomatic complex.

Raised voices alerted him that he'd chosen the wrong way.

"How dare you!" Mother had never sounded so furious. "You send him away without even consulting me?"

"I have full legal right to brand him an Expatriate," Father said. Alec shivered at the level tone in his voice. "You know as well as I—"

"Of course I know it! Don't patronize me, James. I have no qualms about your position and legal authority. But to not even talk to me about it first . . . Our son, James! You've thrown him out on his own!"

"Alec is fully capable of surviving on his own. It is not as if he has no other contacts or friends."

"Yes, but as an Expatriate he won't be able to seek refuge on any of the Five Worlds, will he? He will have to fend for himself on one of the Freeholding planets or even the colonies."

"What's happened to Alec?" His sister Julianna sounded concerned and irked at the same time. Alec's heart ached. He didn't want his sisters to get mixed up in this dispute.

"Julianna, your brother has chosen to quit the Lancers and to take up with this cult . . ."

"James, they're not a cult," Tara said. "They are a legitimate religion . . ."

"Only because the king changed his own law today!"

Alec couldn't stand hearing his father this incensed. He pressed his head against the corridor wall, unsure which way to go.

"What did you do to Alec?" Julianna's tone was decidedly impatient. "You didn't throw him out, did you?"

"Your father had him made Expatriate, Julianna." Mother sounded consoling.

"You're off your course, Father!" Julianna snapped. "How could you?"

"Don't yell at Father!" Alec's younger sister Bridget must have been in the room the whole time too. She would have listened quietly to the entire conversation.

Alec could stand it no more. He walked purposely into the room.

Everyone went silent. Mother was standing directly in front of Father with her hands clamped to her hips. Bridget looked miserable—she had one hand on Julianna's upper arm and was trying to pull her away from their parents. Julianna was glowering at Father and tugging away from her sister.

"Stop it, all of you!" Alec hoped he wouldn't cry. There was no point embarrassing himself now. "Mother, it is best that I go—I won't dispute Father's decision. My staying here would only tear you all apart."

"It sure as blazes won't do us any good if you run off because of what that vac-head's done!" Julianna threw herself at Alec. He gasped in her crushing embrace. Bridget ran up and nearly bowled them both over.

"Julianna! Watch your tongue!" Mother sounded scandalized. She too came over and hugged Alec. "Son, you don't have to worry. Your father just wants what is best for all of us. You will only be away for a few weeks at most, and then once you renounce this religion you can—"

"No. I will not renounce it, Mother."

"You can't be serious." She smiled at him. "Alec, come now, this is the Bethelites' crutch we are talking about."

Alec pulled from her embrace. "How can you say that? After all you told Congress about our need for freedom."

"Freedom is necessary, but superstition . . ." Mother shook her head. "It is nonsense. Especially for someone with your social responsibilities."

Social responsibilities? He turned to his sisters. "Julianna, Bridget, I am sorry. I must go." Alec kissed Mother gently on the cheek. "Good-bye, Mother."

She stared at him, stunned.

Alec hugged both Bridget and Julianna. His youngest sister sobbed and promised to write him commnotes, but Julianna just held on fiercely. "I'm coming with you."

"What?" Father tried to pull her away, but she wriggled free. "Enough of this lunacy. It's spreading!"

"No, Father! You can't send him out on his own! At least I love him enough to want to stay at his side!"

Father took a step back. "How dare you."

"Julianna." Alec gently but firmly pulled her hands away. "Don't say that. Please. I need you to stay. This is something God has for me."

Father threw up his hands and turned away.

Julianna looked at Alec, then shook her head. "I don't like it."

"I know," Alec said. He smiled. "I'll be fine."

Julianna sighed. "You do what you have to do, I guess. I'll take care of Bridgie here. And keep up your hoop-strike so I can defeat you when you come back."

"I will. Thanks."

Alec turned back to his parents. "I am sorry."

Mother shook her head again. "James, talk him out of this foolishness."

Father looked drawn and pale. He said nothing.

"It's all right. I will come back when he—and you, Mother—are ready to accept my faith." Alec swallowed against the lump in his throat. "Until then, I will always think of you and love you."

He hurried out the back door before they could see his tears.

CHAPTER 25

November 2602
Earth Star System
Moon, Transship Orbital Platform
Sierra Tango

Sierra Tango was an ungainly cluster of spherical habitats and finger-like docking gantries connected by long cargo docks. These cargo spaces were mostly automated, with just a few human supervisors and techs on hand to make sure the robot hefters didn't go haywire. Simon appreciated that efficiency as he watched them carry cargo containers through the open bay doors of *Natalia Zoja*.

The cargo deck was long and wide, with a low ceiling lit by shining beacons. Everything was grey and black and white. The only colorful items were people's clothing and the rainbow assortment of containers. He held his delver up and scrolled through the holographic list hovering before him. It looked like the manifest was nearly complete.

"Yo, Skipper!" Owen sprinted out of the *Natalia Zoja*'s cargo bay. He dodged a hefter. "It's looking like we can leave on time."

"You count all the crates and make sure?"

"Uh . . . no . . ."

"Kidding, Owen."

"Oh, right. Skipper, I ain't used to you having a sense of humor, ya know." Owen scratched at his chin and grinned. "Gimme a week."

"Cute. Quit goofing off and run up to the dockmaster's office. Put up a notice for crew, at least one. Baden and I talked it over. Now that we've got some extra cash from the colonel and his people for this . . . job, run, attack, whatever it is . . . we can afford some extra help."

"Extra cash? That mean I get a raise?"

"If you behave."

"Oh . . ." Owen's tone turned teasing. "Looks like you got a visitor, Skipper. I'll, uh, go get that message on the boards." Then he added, "Hey, Commander. Nice to see you."

Simon was surprised how quickly his palms could start sweating. He about dropped his delver. He turned casually to see Commander Colleen Verge standing amidst the chaos of the loading deck, out of place in her crisp uniform. Her red hair blazed like a nav beacon against the greys, rust-browns, and dirty pastels of her surroundings. "Hey," Simon said. He groaned inwardly. Great. Sound like a hefter out of battery charge.

Her mouth curved in a playful expression. How would Owen or Baden put it? Simon wondered. Sweet nova . . . "I'm glad we could see each other again, Captain."

"Simon." He might as well go for bold.

She paused. "Of course. Simon."

Simon beamed. He hoped he didn't look like an idiot schoolboy. Or Owen. "We, uh, we're loading up." He gestured vaguely behind him. "You want to take a look around . . . Colleen?"

"I do not have the time."

"Oh." That went well.

Colleen stepped closer. She drew her own delver. "*Herald* has been ordered out with a composite task force headed to the Tiu frontier. Several ships from Rozsada and Muhterem have come to Earth in the past few days. It seems the Tiu are harassing Tiaozhanese colonies, and the king wants a decisive action."

More fighting. Simon desperately didn't want her to go anywhere near there. But after seeing her ship in action, he told himself she was more than up to the task. Definitely more so than he.

"Before I go, I wanted to give you something—in person."

Simon blinked. She held her delver toward his, and he got the hint. The two devices exchanged beeps and flashing patterns of light. Then a commnote appeared on his screen with new data.

"It is my personal comm number and security code," Colleen said. "Any message you send there will reach me. No matter where I am."

"Thank you." Simon reached down for her hand. "Maybe during a break in your patrol, there'll be . . . time for just us. To talk, and to spend time together."

Colleen looked him straight in the eye. She squeezed back on his hand. "I would like that. What good is being a captain if you can't use that authority for nonofficial duties?"

Simon chuckled.

Then she leaned in and kissed him on the cheek. Simon closed his eyes, afraid of the inevitable onrush of memories. But he could only see a shadow of Hannah. There was no sense of betrayal, just the comfort of a love that he could never forget. She was at her rest, and Simon could find his.

He grabbed Colleen around the waist and pressed her close. He kissed her passionately, as he'd wanted to do in *Natalia Zoja*'s engine spaces, and was relieved when she returned the kiss with equal vigor.

Suddenly, in that kiss, he felt free to live his life again.

Her eyes stayed shut for a moment after they separated.

"I'll miss you, Colleen," he said. He brushed a hand along her hair.

She kissed his forehead. "And I will pray for you, Simon."

The crowds surging past the job boards up by the dock master's office paid no heed to Alec. It seemed to him that they sized him up immediately as a newcomer. And as such, he was neither despised nor sought after. Simply ignored.

That suited Alec fine for now. He backed away from the boards, which were two meters tall and brilliantly lit in blue on black. A row of six benches made of metal mesh sat against the drab brown corridor wall. There had to be hundreds of people—wealthy traders, down-on-their-luck Expatriates, officers and crew from navies of the Five Worlds—pressing through the thoroughfare. Alec couldn't see past them. He wished he couldn't smell them either. He missed the mingled scents of Earth's breezes already.

He stepped up onto the bench and craned his neck at the job boards. There were many outgoing flights to choose from. A navastel leaving for Tiaozhan and a merchant convoy headed for Townsend both needed short-term hands. One of the three regular ferries on the Earth-Nova Tempus shift was looking for several crewers interested in at least a two-year stint. None hooked his interest.

Then Alec spied a familiar name. He clapped his hands together with delight when he read the destination.

Bethel.

He barked out a laugh. Heads turned his way briefly, but he ignored them.

"I have read that the Lord will provide for my needs," he said, "but I didn't realize how quickly."

Inside *Natalia Zoja's* cargo bay, Baden watched a hefter ease several crates into a secure position. He stood ready to shut the robot down if something went amiss. Footfalls from behind startled him. Gail wrapped her arms around his waist. She kissed her neck.

"I don't think the captain would appreciate us fooling around while on duty," Baden said, pitching his voice low. He gave her a kiss.

"You two seem to be on better terms," Gail said. "I think he'll make an exception."

"You sure?"

"Especially for me." She kissed him again. "What are we going to do when I go back to Puerto Guijarro?"

"I don't know. Why don't you just stay aboard ship with us for a while longer after we make our run to Bethel?"

"Baden, I told you I need to go home."

"Yeah, but—"

"No buts. I prayed long and hard about it, and the more I did, the more it seemed that going home was the right thing to do. For the Lord, and for us."

Baden rubbed his hair. "Yeah. I guess. It's just . . . we just kind of found each other and I don't want to lose that. I thought maybe you'd . . . stay with us."

"If God has a plan for us, it will be," Gail said softly. "But I have a responsibility to Mom and the tavern. She's out of the clinic, but she still needs my help, since she's recovering from those lovely Kesek gunshot wounds. I have to go back."

"What about school?"

"I'm not sure how long I'll stay there."

That didn't sound like Gail. He'd never known her to want to give up.

Her eyes took on an excited light. "Baden, how long do you think it's been since someone preached the gospel on Puerto Guijarro? There may be a Benevolent or two at the Union Synoptic chapel, but that's about as close to the faith as you can get. With the Bibles and other materials we found, the copies of the ancient manuscripts, and the new Bibles you're going to print, there's a great opportunity to teach!"

Baden's heart warmed. There was nobody in the galaxy quite like her. "You really want to teach, don't you?"

"Yes, but not like you think." She smiled up at him. "I want to teach of God's love for us. I want people to know that God's own son gave up his life so that we could live."

"Life everlasting." And a world without end. The words gave Baden chills. The good kind.

"It may never have been offered to them before." Gail looked down. "And . . . if I came with you, I'd have to be near Owen."

"So?"

"He . . . what he did . . ."

"You're holding that against him? Gail, it was all a fake! He was bluffing Kesek!"

Gail flashed him a sullen look. "I know. But it's not as easy for me, knowing that he might want to use me like that, like some brainless robot."

"Oh. Right." Score one more for male insensitivity. Vac-head.

"I need time to deal with it."

"Okay." Baden reached for her again, feeling like a slug for being selfish. He rested his chin on her forehead. Anger at Owen rushed to the front of his mind too. It was his fault she wouldn't stay aboard *Natalia Zoja* for much longer, even if his betrayal had been an act. "Blast it."

"What?"

"Ozzy. He's just . . . It's his fault." Baden gritted his teeth. "Makes me want to pound him."

"No, listen." Gail kissed him. "That's not the only reason. It's mostly Mom. And teaching. Don't you see? And we'll be together for a few weeks before you drop me off at Puerto Guijarro. It isn't good-bye today."

My sheep hear my voice, and I know them, and they follow me. I give them eternal life, and they will never perish, and no one will snatch them out of my hand.

The words echoed softly in the back of his mind. They were remembrances in whispers and a powerful command. They no longer disturbed Baden or made him feel weak.

Comforted, he lifted Gail's chin to face him. "I love you, and I know you'll serve God well. We can still be together, sometime."

Gail smiled and kissed him. "I love you too. And the Lord has work for you to do too."

Baden glanced over his shoulder at the crates. They were full of Bibles, paintings, sculptures, and all manner of relics they'd saved from Alexandria. "I can't believe we're moving it all to Bethel."

"What better place to keep it for believers to access?" Gail said. "And with Hamid footing the bill, it will be very secure."

"Yeah." Baden led her past the crates to a particular alcove. The Dunn printing press sat secured by magnetic clamps to the deck and bulkhead. "And once we get this thing up to full capacity, we'll have more to add to their collection."

"Haczyk Printers, Inc.?" Gail teased.

Baden grinned. "Not a bad idea."

The hefters finished their loading. Baden and Gail secured them in their alcoves. Then they made sure the cargo bay hatches were sealed up tight. "Looks good down here, Dad," Baden said.

"Come on up to the main airlock," his dad said. "I've got someone for you to meet."

"Oh." Baden exchanged a curious glance with Gail. "New crew?"

"Yep."

They bounded up the stairs at the back of the bay and went up to the main deck. It looked like the rest of the ship's interior:

bluish grey, small white lights along deck and ceiling, hatches and access panels and equipment lockers all over. Scratched and worn. Baden ran his fingers along the cool surface. Home.

Owen ambled toward them with Renshu following close behind. "Look, man, I wasn't trying to break nothing!" Owen said. "Just thought if I reprogrammed the secondary coolant monitor . . ."

"You tore it apart!" Renshu waved an unrecognizable tool. Owen dodged it, much to Baden's amusement. "We don't have time for you to mess about with my girl! Go put that console back together, or I'm gonna have Cyril sit on your head until you apologize!"

"Okay, quit! Cool your thrusters!" Owen scurried by. He flashed Baden a grin. "Say a prayer for me, Hack. I might need it."

"You definitely will," Gail said icily.

Owen gave her a look but didn't say anything. Renshu muttered something about unreliable help as he stomped after Owen.

Baden and Gail reached the airlock. Dad stood just inside the outer hatch. Baden could see the long tube stretching beyond to the space station. But he didn't know what to say about the youth talking animatedly with Dad.

"Are you the new crew?" Gail asked.

The young man with pleasant features on his mahogany skin and the close-cropped military haircut reached out his hand. It was that cadet kid they'd met on Bethel . . . Allen?

"Alec V— Lincoln," he said.

Baden shook the proffered hand but wondered at the pause. Then he noticed the boy was wearing a basic midnight blue shipsuit over a yellow shirt. No sign of Starkweather insignia or rank. No "Verge" nameplate in sight. A duffel bag sat crumpled at his feet.

"Alec here's looking for some work," Dad said. "I told him he'd be welcome aboard. He's got some emergency med training, so he can lend a hand with Emi. And he knows his way around some shipboard systems. That, and he's got actual combat experience, weapons training, and can run a suit of powered armor."

"What, is that all?" Baden asked. "So I take it you're out of the Lancer biz."

Alec didn't answer right away. Baden wished he hadn't posed the question once he saw how dejected Alec became.

Dad put a hand on his shoulder. "His family . . . Well, they disowned him."

Gail gasped. Baden had a hard time believing it. He'd seen the way the two of them got along on Bethel.

Baden recalled one of the few times he and Alec had spoken. It wasn't cordial. "What, come here to get an education? In family?"

Alec looked at him. "Perhaps. I said that to you, didn't I?"

"Yeah."

"Look, I'm sorry. I think I was a little—"

"No, you were right. And I got one." Baden grinned at Dad. He sure had learned. An awful lot, in just a few weeks. There wasn't the time to hang on to bitterness. Mom wouldn't have wanted that. He realized that now.

"My expulsion had a lot to do with this." Alec pulled his delver from his pocket and pushed a button. Green holographic words sprang into the air. Baden recognized them instantly from the Bible.

"You believe too?" Gail asked.

"I do. I am glad to be the Lord's servant."

"But your family didn't take it well?"

Alec put the delver away. "It's all right. I don't know how long his decision will last. But for now at least, I am an Expatriate like you."

"That's not all we share." Baden patted his pants pocket. His hand slapped dully against the book inside. "After we get underway, maybe we can compare notes. You, Gail, and me."

"I'd like that. Thank you, Baden—for all that you have done."

Baden ran a hand through his hair, thoroughly embarrassed.

His dad looked amused by that. "Gail, why don't you take Alec up to the bridge and introduce him to Emi? She'll get him acquainted." To Alec, he said, "You can watch her at comm while we head out."

"Thank you, Captain." Alec heaved the bag up over his shoulder. Gail led him into the corridor.

Baden watched them go.

After a moment his dad cleared his throat. "So, what do you think?"

"Seems like a good kid," Baden said. He leaned up against the opposite side of the airlock rim.

Dad smirked at him. "You ain't much past a kid yourself, Baden."

"Yeah, well, can't argue that."

"But I wasn't talking about him." His dad's expression became more mischievous. "I meant Gail."

"Oh." Did he really want to talk to Dad about her now? Probably not. Since they were actually talking, though . . .

"Dad, when did you—er, I mean, how did you know Mom was for you?"

Dad laughed. It was such an odd sound. Baden relished it.

"Man, you would have to ask me that." His dad scratched his chin. "Look. There's no answer in a book for that one. When I met your mother it just . . . was. Okay? She was it for me. And I'll always love her for that. For you too."

Baden's throat tightened. "Thanks, Dad."

"No prob. So . . . I take it it's serious?"

"Oh, I'd say so." Baden stepped by him and grinned. "You should see what I bought her stationside."

Dad reached out and sealed the hatch. "Okay. What?"

Baden dug into his pocket and withdrew a blue satin bag. It bore silvery vines. He opened the drawstring and dumped the contents into his hand.

It was a ring of two silver and gold bands intertwined.

Simon whistled. "So do I make out the invitation list now or at Puerto Guijarro?"

Baden laughed. "Give it time, Dad."

Baden followed his dad onto the bridge. The consoles were glowing and flickering their normal departure data. Alec stood behind Emi, who was seated at the comm station. Gail leaned against the console a pace away.

Emi looked up as father and son approached. "This one catches on quickly, Captain," she said softly.

Dad chuckled as he took the nav console's seat. "You think he'll measure up?"

"Only after I retrain him to my liking."

"Yeah, I'll bet."

"I had to retrain Baden, after all."

Baden waved a hand. "Just remember who's part owner of this boat."

Emi's eyes narrowed.

"Watch it, Baden," Gail teased. "She's got the guns."

"Right." Baden looked at his dad, confused. He was sitting at Baden's seat. "Uh, Dad . . ."

Simon had a funny glint in his eye. "Yeah?"

"You're sitting in my seat."

"Huh. Well, guess you better sit in mine."

Baden took a second to retrieve his jaw from the deck. "Me? But . . . you've never let me . . . Not once."

"Oversight. You do know how she works, right?"

Momentary indignation overruled Baden's caution. "'Course I do."

"Good." His dad reached over and slapped the seat beside him. "Sit down. Take her out."

"You sure, Dad?" Baden slipped hesitantly into the helm chair.

"I'll watch nav. And I've got some reading to do. When you and Gail got time, that is."

"You . . . you want to read the Bible? Really?"

Dad looked almost peaceful. "I think I'm finally ready."

Gail touched the back of Dad's chair. "We'll make the time, Uncle Simon."

"Yeah," Baden said. "When I'm not printing Bibles in the cargo bay on our very own antique press."

"Still can't believe you have a royal commission to do that," his dad said.

"What I want to know," Alec said, "is when Baden will preach again."

Baden thought about it. "You know, I might actually try it. Maybe there's something in the cache that can help me out. We haven't even catalogued everything in it yet."

"There'll be time," Gail said. "I'll help you."

"As will I," Alec said.

The intercom abruptly squawked. "Engine room to bridge. Simon, you ready to haul yet?"

"You bet, Renshu. And Baden's driving this time," Dad said.

"What!" Owen's voice screeched across the intercom. "Oh, stars and novas. Hack! You hear me up there? Don't you get us dumped down a gravity well!"

"Hey, my son won't mess this up." Dad gave Baden a thumbs-up. "He's got a good navigator."

"Thanks, Dad." And thank You, God.

Owen feigned retching. "You guys done with the love fest up there, or am I gonna have to come up and drive?"

Baden laughed at the sounds of a scuffle that followed. A contrite Renshu said, "Sorry, Skipper, I shouldn't have let him near the intercom."

Owen was shouting in the background, "Get off! Lemme go!"

"Cyril's got him," Renshu said.

"Just get the engines ready for our pilot," Simon said.

"Aye-aye, Skipper."

Emi cleared their departure with the dockmaster in her smooth, whispered tones. Baden listened for the clang of umbilicals unhooking and felt the power of the main reactor surging through the ship. As soon as they were clear, he breathed a quick prayer and gently eased forward on the curved handle of the main drive control.

Baden watched on the video feed from station cameras as *Natalia Zoja* soared away from the orbital platform with her ion engines glowing blue. He exhaled. For a moment he was alone with his thoughts, his prayers, and his senses as he pushed the ship—his home—onward.

A little Duke Ellington on the speakers would make it perfect. Baden punched up a quick combination of buttons on the intercom and piped a low-key melody from his favorite file.

Dad gave him a playful punch on the shoulder. "Atta boy, helmsman."

Baden let the memories of Muhterem replay. Just a few weeks ago he'd been sure neither he nor his dad would ever change, and they'd orbit each other in constant combat forever. Then he saw that wrecked ship and dove into its shattered remains. And there was that small box. That insignificant looking box.

The gift inside had changed everything.

Solitude could not be maintained aboard *Natalia Zoja*. And Baden Hacyzk was glad for that.

EPILOGUE

November 2602

Jason's brothers from the Seventy gathered in one dark room.

It had been more than a dozen years since they'd last met face-to-face, but things were different now. Two of their number were dead, and their sanctuary had been emptied.

Most importantly, they were faced with a free Realm that had not existed for decades.

The man named Crescens stood at the head of the long, obsidian table. He looked about at the faces staring expectantly at him. Those nine sets of eyes, noses, and ears were variations on two themes. He pushed aside sadness as his gaze lingered on the seats Timothy and Jason had held.

Jason's and Timothy's faces still haunted him in the expressions of those nine and in his own face reflected in the mirror-finish of the table. He could have been Jason's older brother, with a hint of grey in his chestnut hair and fine wrinkles around his eyes.

They were all brothers, as it were.

"The Word cannot be protected now," said one man. He too looked identical to Jason, except with paler hair and a moustache.

"Perhaps we were foolish to think that was God's will in the matter," said another. He was dark-skinned and the spitting image of two men seated to his right.

"Gentlemen, what matters now is deciding what to do about it." Crescens didn't want to deal with this. Perhaps after seven decades he was finally getting too old to change. "Several things now operate in our favor: Kesek is in shambles, the Charter is dead, and there are glimmers of the Word spreading. There is rumor that the Alexandria cache has been taken to another world."

"But these relics must be protected!" another man insisted.

"I agree. How we go about that, however, may have to change." Crescens manipulated a control on the podium before him. The holographic image of a young man's head and shoulders appeared in the air. "We can start by keeping a very close eye on him. If he is not up to the task, he will have to be . . . replaced."

"Forcibly?"

"Perhaps. Or he may need our assistance. As I said, things have changed."

Crescens considered the image carefully as the young face rotated to face him. "Thanks in large part to Mister Baden Haczyk."

ACKNOWLEDGEMENTS

The Word Unleashed is the second part of the adventure begun in *The Word Reclaimed*, but originally both were part of the same manuscript, entitled *Commissioned.* So forgive me if my acknowledgments are somewhat redundant—the same people lent me considerable assistance on the entire project.

So without further ado, thanks go out to: Jeff Gerke of Marcher Lord Press; MLP author and publicity guru Jill Williamson; my wife, Carrie, my boys, and my family both on the East Coast and in the Rocky Mountain states; Jeff Scott, Elizabeth Leight and her husband, Tim Joseph, and David Grima; Linda and Harold Dunn at Clear Creek Printers in Buffalo, Wyoming; the ladies of the Johnson County Library in Buffalo, Wyoming, especially my proofreader and critic, Deb Stoetzel; and my fellow MLP third list authors Kerry Nietz and Kirk Outerbridge.

Thanks also to my new fans—that's so strange to think about, let alone say—who have gotten as much enjoyment out of reading *The Word Reclaimed* as I did out of writing it.

Breinigsville, PA USA
13 April 2010
236032BV00001B/4/P